THE STRENGTH OF A MAN

"You do not care, do you?" she asked, jerking away in direct defiance of his orders. "You do not care for anything or anyone. It must be terrible not to care, not to love. I pity you, Captain Morgan."

Kade jerked her to her feet, the brush she held falling unnoticed to the floor. He plunged his fingers into the silk of her hair, forcing her head back. He brought his mouth down on hers in a fierce, demanding kiss.

Kathleen fought his embrace and he pressed her closer, molding the softness of her body against his hard strength. He moved his lips to her neck. She drew a desperate, ragged breath as he tore open her shirt.

Kade seared her flesh with burning kisses, igniting her soul with passion. He would make her his mistress, a partner to his illicit desires, desires she shared. She would exchange her innocence for the ecstasy of being held by this man, of being kissed by him and having him make love to her.

And though it was wrong, terribly, horribly wrong, Kathleen could no more stop what was happening than she could prevent the sun from rising tomorrow . . .

DEFIANT CAPTIVE

KATHY JONES

ZEBRA BOOKS
KENSINGTON PUBLISHING CORP.

ZEBRA BOOKS

are published by

Kensington Publishing Corp.
475 Park Avenue South
New York, NY 10016

First printing: November 1987

Printed in the United States of America

This book is dedicated to the memory of Errol Flynn.

I would like to thank Wendy McCurdy, my editor at Zebra; Pat Teal, my literary agent; and Ernie, my husband. To the talented, loyal and gracious people who comprise the Pacific Palisades Writers' Workshop, I owe not only my thanks but also my deepest gratitude. As a result of your support and help, I learned to believe in myself almost as much as I believe in each of you.

Chapter 1

Hate. It blazed clear and bright in the torrid blue-green of the girl's eyes as she stood among the human flotsam littering the raised platform of the slave auction. Though her dirty clothes and body marked her as one of the unfortunates to be sold, she was not the same as the others. While they slouched in despair and defeat, she stood with back erect and head held high, surveying the crowd in the marketplace as though judging them to discover their worth.

The hate in her eyes went unnoticed by everyone except Kade Morgan. From across the square he watched the girl, captivated by the passionate emotion that raged within her. He tried to shake off the feelings that surged through him, but it was too late. A fire had ignited in his soul, destroying forever the indifference that had become a way of life for him.

Beside the girl was a short, overweight man, his stringy hair shiny with sweat and grease. He held a chain that was attached to an iron collar fastened around the girl's slender neck. He spoke with her; then an ugly snarl sliced across his face and he backhanded her violently. The small, proud head snapped back from the blow. The girl turned to face her attacker and gave him a smile so cold a chill went down Kade's back. Her swollen lips twitched, causing the smile to change into a contemptuous sneer.

The fat man hit her again, knocking her down. She broke her fall with her hands, drawing Kade's attention to the shackles on her bloodied wrists. His fists clenched and his black eyes narrowed.

The violence excited the crowd. People shopping in nearby food stalls hurried across the square to the slave platform, eager to witness the humiliation of a white woman. They pushed and shoved to get closer. Kade was repulsed by their attraction to the girl's pitiful plight.

Her ragged dress fell off one shoulder, and her long hair lay in a tangled pool beside her. While her owner talked to the black auctioneer, she turned her contempt to the crowd. The blazing heat of her hatred was like an aura surrounding her. It scorched the air, causing several people to mutter prayers against the devil in their midst.

The girl's eyes moved across the crowd until they met Kade's. Reality wavered, then faded. Kade was aware of the beating of his heart. He saw through the girl's fear and pain, discovering within her a pride as solid and substantial as the iron that bound her flesh. He knew that to destroy that pride would be to destroy the girl herself.

The moment passed, and reality rushed back in a wave of hard facts and unpleasant surroundings, bringing with it the cold skepticism through which Kade viewed the world. The girl will think I am interested in her, he thought. She will start flirting and try to convince me to buy her.

He was wrong. A muscle in her cheek twitched, and then with a flash of blue-green eyes she lifted her chin and spat in Kade's direction. It was unbelievable. He threw back his head and laughed.

A wiry old man came up beside Kade. He was

shaking his head and scratching his neatly trimmed crop of red hair. "I be lookin' all o'er this African 'ell'ole for ye, lad, and 'ere ye be in the very midst of these 'eathens, makin' noise like a jackass. 'Twas it not business ye came 'ere to discuss wi' that Cathcart fella?"

Kade did not appear to notice the old man, much less hear his question. He stood in the middle of the street with booted feet spread apart, as though on the deck of a ship, his midnight black eyes glowing with respect for the girl's spunk. A breeze pushed aside the fine linen of his white shirt to reveal a broad chest covered with crisp black hair, and his muscular thighs pushed tight against the fine black cloth of his pants. His hands were large, and they rested on the leather belt that rode lightly on his slender hips. A sheathed sword and a brace of expensive pistols were thrust into that belt; in the top of his right boot was a jewel-handled dagger. Powerful weapons for a powerful man.

Across the square was a bar called Lil's Place. It specialized in strong whiskey and easy women, many of whom were standing in the doorway watching the crowd near the slave platform. A big brunette caught Jake's attention and waved.

"What be so entertainin' up on that stage that yer willin' to stand 'ere in this filthy street, Kade? It's a drink ye promised me at Lil's, and it's a drink I be 'oldin' ye to!"

"Just what do you think your wife would say about your eagerness to see the inside of a brothel, Jake McBradden?" Kade said. "Stop complaining and look at that girl on the slave block, that one over on the side. Have you ever seen such hate?"

"What Mattie McBradden don't know won't be 'urtin' me," Jake muttered. He stretched up onto his toes and tried to see over the crowd that blocked his view of the stage.

11

At that moment, the girl was dragged to her feet by the fat man and forced into the center of the platform. Her incredible eyes began to flash and burn. She tossed back her hair, spread her feet and lifted her chin to defiantly face her impending fate.

"Aye, lad, I've seen 'ate like that, every time I look at ye." Jake turned to leave.

Kade grabbed the Scotsman's arm. "What are you mumbling about?"

Jake shook himself free. "What be so interestin' about a slave wi' a nasty disposition?" Kade's set expression caused Jake to shrug his shoulders in defeat. "Fine. Stand 'ere all day while an old man dies of thirst."

"It is not Lil's whiskey you thirst after, Jake. Pipe down or Mattie will hear all about your 'drinking habits' when you are away from Mistral."

The fat man shoved the girl to her knees on the platform and kicked her in the stomach. Her already pale face went white as death. Kade could almost feel the quiver that shook her small shoulders.

The auctioneer proclaimed the offered piece of merchandise a virgin, then had to shout for bids over the jeers that greeted his announcement. Female slaves sold along the waterfronts in northern Africa were those raped by the pirates capturing them; virgins went into the harems of rich merchants. The offer of such a prize to this crowd was so unbelievable that proof was being demanded. Kade pushed through the closely-packed bodies that stood between him and the stage, shouldering aside anyone who did not move out of his way fast enough.

"You, how much for the girl?" he called out, his deep voice drawing everyone's attention. A hush fell over the crowd. Kade fixed his gaze on the girl's owner, who leisurely scratched his bulging stomach before answering the question.

"You'll have to bid like everyone else . . ."

The whining voice faded as Rat Anders took in the stature of the man facing him. Kade's arrogant self-confidence and impressive array of weapons were enough to frighten even the bravest of men, and Rat Anders was far from being a brave man.

"Name a price, fat man. I do not bid against scum, and I am not accustomed to asking twice." Kade's eyes bored into Rat like hot irons.

What Rat lacked in courage, he made up for in greed. There was a sale to be made here, and shaking like a sick dog was not getting him any closer to making it. His head rolled sideways as he took in the obvious signs of Kade's wealth. He ran a thick tongue over equally thick lips and wound his fingers over the rusty chain as though it were a silk ribbon.

"One hundred pounds is the price for this pretty young lass."

With her head lowered, the girl's appearance was the same as the other slaves, possibly worse. She was extremely dirty and small enough to blow away in a light breeze.

"Pretty?" he asked sarcastically.

Instantly her head lifted, her eyes opening as she looked directly at him. The swirls of blue and green seemed to surround Kade, pulling him into their liquid depths. His pulse quickened; his breathing became shallow and uncertain.

"I will give you ten pounds," he said and stepped onto the stage to stand beside the girl. Involuntarily his hand moved to touch her. He grabbed the hilt of his sword instead, allowing his fingers to trail over the intricate engravings. Though the gesture was not meant to be threatening, it caused a fresh flood of sweat to break from the fat man's brow.

Rat could not stop staring at those fingers as they curled around the sword's handle. He was afraid, very afraid. This bitch has been causing me trouble ever since Quint sent me to get her off that filthy pirate ship, he thought. I should've got rid of her a long time ago, just done away with her. If Quint finds out I sold her, he'll be real mad. But ten pounds. I could use ten pounds. He hauled the girl to her feet.

"Ten pounds wouldn't even pay me back for what the girl's cost me." He waited breathlessly, beady eyes watering in the bright sun. They almost seemed to be drooling.

He held the chain so tightly that its pressure on the iron collar cut open the girl's neck. A single drop of scarlet blood fell onto her half-exposed breast. A shadow of desperation flickered in the depths of her eyes, and for a moment Kade felt the metal slicing into his own flesh. Then the girl dropped her head, taking back her heavy burden. Kade gripped the handle of his sword so tightly his fingers ached.

"I will give you fifty pounds, gold. Take those chains off her immediately." He raked his eyes across the crowd, daring anyone to oppose him. "Pay the snake, Jake." He stepped off the platform and bullied his way through a group of disgruntled bidders.

Jake followed him. "Have ye lost what little sense ye 'ave, lad? That girl will be trouble, just look at 'er."

Kade glanced back at the platform. The girl was staring at him, a grimace of disgust twisting across her bruised face as she transferred her hate for the fat man to her new owner. Kade suppressed a grin.

"Aye, Jake, she is a stubborn one. Still, she deserves better than what she would get from the rabble in this town. Besides, she is only a child, how much trouble can she be?" He stalked off, calling back over his shoulder, "Take her to the *Black Eagle,* we sail with

14

the tide."

"I never thought Kade Morgan would turn into a bloody humanitarian," Jake muttered.

Kade did not notice the path that opened before him; his mind was on the girl. Jake is right, she is going to be trouble, he thought. I should give her some money and turn her loose. No, she would only end up back on that stage chained to someone else.

He walked into Lil's Place, determined to finish his business as quickly as possible. There was a lot to do before the *Eagle* sailed. The heavy smell of cheap cologne that pervaded the brothel was as repulsive to him as the rank odors of the marketplace. Why a man with Cathcart's wealth frequented such a place Kade could not understand. He made his way through the lounging women to the stairs at the back of the room. Taking the steps two at a time, he quickly reached the landing. He walked past the guard outside the room at the end of the hall, shoved open the door and greeted Quint Cathcart.

Kathleen O'Connor tasted the salty sting of blood in her mouth and felt the shackles cutting her wrists as she fell onto the stage. It was foolish to taunt Rat Anders, especially in front of this crowd. She could not help herself, though; it had become a habit.

She was too weak to stand, so she knelt on the platform, her ragged dress bunched around her knees as they pressed against the dirty wood. Rat was talking to the slave auctioneer and pointing at her.

I am to be sold next. Me, a slave. This must be a nightmare. I will wake up and be back home where the air is cool and the rain soft. Father will be waiting for me by the stables and Niall will tease me about oversleeping.

The humid air of the marketplace clung to Kathleen, and the sun beat down on her, proof that this nightmare was real, too real. Emerald Hills and Ireland were far away; it had been months since she had last walked free among the green fields and smelled the blooming rosemary.

Jarrett O'Connor, Kathleen's father, had taken a routine trip to England to deliver two horses, both prize hunters, to an estate outside London. He was gone less than a week when pirates swarmed over the peaceful fields of County Kerry, slaying Kathleen's mother and brother, capturing her and setting fire to the house and stables. They had locked her in a small cell in the hold of their ship and at infrequent intervals shoved food and water through a slot in the door. There had been no facilities for waste, no light, no fresh air. After what seemed like an eternity, the door to Kathleen's cell opened. A lamp was held close to her face. Blinded, she recoiled from it like the loathsome creatures that shared her cell. In that moment, she had felt like one of them.

"She's alive, and for that you'd better thank Allah, you bunch of heathen thieves," the bearer of the light had said before dragging her onto the deck of the ship. When Kathleen could see again, it was Rat Anders' greasy face that confronted her. That had been two months ago. And instead of being ransomed or rescued, she was to be sold as a slave. Her fortunes were not improving.

Kathleen knew the fate that lay in store for her. The men gathered in the marketplace of this Moroccan port were there to buy women to work in the local whorehouses. It was a harsh fate and she recoiled from it.

If only I had not been captured, or if only I had died. She sighed heavily. I might as well wish for the sky to

16

turn green and the grass blue. Wishing will not remove these chains, nor will it make me any less afraid. I must face what is happening, overcome it and go home again. If only my stomach were not so empty, and if only I could stop shaking.

No matter how hard she tried, Kathleen could not summon enough pretty pastel paint from her dreams and wishes to hide the reality that surrounded her. The air was hot, the smells rank. Her chains were heavy, her strength exhausted. The only thing she had to sustain her was pride. It was enough. She squared her shoulders, reined in her crippling fear and defiantly glared straight ahead.

The crowd pushed closer to the stage. They pointed and stared, laughed and jeered. I should not feel sorry for myself, Kathleen thought; they deserve my pity more, these people who deal in human flesh the way Emerald Hills deals in horses.

At the back of the crowd something caught her attention, and Kathleen's eyes met those of the most incredibly handsome man she had ever seen. He towered head and shoulders above everyone in the square, his features rugged and strong. His hair was as dark as Kathleen's own, and his black eyes promised things both evil and wonderful. She fell into those bottomless black pools, willingly drowning in the danger that waited there.

The man saw through her mask of bravery, going deep into her soul until there was nothing between them except her pride. As he probed its depths, Kathleen pulled back. There was no way she was going to allow this stranger to threaten the only thing she had left in the world. She lifted her chin and spat at him. He started in surprise, then threw back his head and laughed. Kathleen turned away, horrified to discover tears burning in her eyes.

17

Behind the slave platform, the women sold earlier pleaded for mercy as their buyers came to take possession. The aristocratic voice of an Englishwoman could be heard over harsher accents. Kathleen was disgusted by their weakness. I will never grovel or beg, no matter what my fate. It is Irish that I am, and it is the Irish spirit I will show this bunch of heathens.

She stumbled to her feet as Rat pulled on her chain, forcing her to the center of the stage. Terror crept over her like the icy fingers of a cold fog. Her strength gone, she almost collapsed. Then she remembered the stranger's laughter. Anger filled her, pouring strong and fresh into every part of her body. I will not be laughed at again; not now, not ever. With a toss of her head, she scornfully confronted the crowd and her future.

The collar bit into her neck and Kathleen fell to her knees, gasping for breath. Before she could recover, a booted foot rammed into her left side and the world went black. She sank her teeth into her lower lip to stop the cries that rose in her throat. Dear God, give me strength to withstand this pain, do not let me die!

It was some time before Kathleen was again aware of her surroundings. She heard someone say virgin. The word lingered in the air, echoing in her mind along with the memory of Rat confirming the status of her maidenhood that morning. She remembered the smell of his breath, fouled by cheap whiskey and rotten teeth. Her stomach heaved.

The crowd fell silent. Kathleen tried to concentrate on what was happening. Someone was refuting Rat's statement that she was pretty. Her hazel eyes snapped open. She was instantly captured by the intense gaze of the tall stranger. He was only inches away. Kathleen was suddenly aware of the stench of her unwashed body as the clean smell of his cologne reached her nose,

18

stamping itself on her memory like a brand.

The black eyes held hers possessively. Kathleen's head began to spin. Then they turned away, breaking their hold on her. She went limp. What is wrong with me? I feel as though the marsh fairies were dancing in my stomach, weaving webs of magic fire in my soul.

"I will give you ten pounds," the stranger announced and stepped onto the platform to tower above Rat, who was laughing at the offer.

The impressive array of weapons slung through the stranger's belt drew Kathleen's attention. The sword was being slowly caressed by his strong, sure fingers. She wondered what it would feel like to have them touching her face or stroking her hair. I must be mad, she thought and glanced up at the man's face. There was a hard glint in his eyes, a firm set to his jaw.

Rat stopped laughing. He was nervous, jumpy. He pulled Kathleen to her feet, causing her collar to cut open her neck. The pain was terrible. She threw back her head to stop a rush of tears and forced an unconcerned look onto her face. The stranger was watching her, and her bravery faded beneath his scrutiny. Despair and fear overcame her. A flicker of light in the black eyes showed he recognized her panic. Kathleen instantly dropped her head. How could I be so weak, have I no shame?

"I will give you fifty pounds, gold." The stranger's voice was soft, almost gentle. Then he barked a command that contained the most beautiful words Kathleen had ever heard.

"Take those chains off her immediately."

Gratitude flooded into her. She lifted her head to thank him but he was gone, pushing through the crowd with an old man close behind him. She swallowed hard. Why should I be grateful? Now I am more than just a captive, I am also a slave. The word tasted bitter. She

19

held onto that taste, her lips curling into a sneer as she stared after her new master.

A key scraped in the lock of her collar, bringing her attention back to the wonderful thing the stranger had ordered. When her wrists were freed she involuntarily touched the lacerated skin, unable to ignore the painful throbbing. The old man stopped chasing her new owner, kicked at the dust and returned to the platform. While he counted out the money to pay Rat, Kathleen kept her eyes straight ahead, refusing to acknowledge the transaction.

The old man led her off the platform and through the marketplace, down one narrow street and into another. Finally they reached the noisy waterfront. Weak from hunger, Kathleen forced herself to put one foot in front of the other. Do not think about water or food, she told herself, think about home.

The foreign faces surrounding her and the strange language that vibrated through the town disappeared as Kathleen found herself back on the rolling meadows of Emerald Hills. Her father's eyes, as green as the land he loved, smiled at her, and Niall's laughter rang above the surf as the ocean crashed on the beach near their home. Kathleen's mother, a whimsical creature who lived in a fantasy world of magic and myth, was leaning out the kitchen window and trying to catch a ray of sunlight in her outstretched hand.

"Look out below!"

The cry pulled Kathleen back to the present just as she was shoved sideways. A barrel crashed onto the spot where she had been standing. She ignored it completely. Her attention was on the beautiful ship that loomed above her, its rigging silhouetted against the azure sky. The hull was painted as black as the eyes of Kathleen's new owner, and mounted on the bow was an eagle glaring out to sea.

"Is this his ship?" she asked.

"Aye, miss," the old man answered, squinting into the sun. "This be the *Black Eagle,* finest ship afloat. She be captained by Kade Morgan, the meanest, most dangerous demon I e'er want to meet. His 'eart be as cold as ice and 'is soul as black as this ship, and aye, 'twas Kade what just bought ye."

"I am sure Captain Morgan's soul is no blacker than my hate for him," Kathleen said, her voice cold and hard. "Who are you, sir?"

The old man hustled her up the gangplank. "Jake McBradden is me name and I 'ail from the 'ighland moors of Scotland. Step lively now, miss, for if I don't get ye on board, the Cap'n will send me back there wi' me 'ead in me scabag."

Every step Kathleen took up the rough plank drew her further into an unfamiliar darkness that blocked the bright morning sun. Her ears began to ring, and her head was so light it felt detached from her body. When she stepped onto the level deck of the ship, she gave in to the void that called to her and fainted in front of the surprised eyes of Jake and the entire *Black Eagle* crew.

21

Chapter 2

The sounds surrounding Kathleen began to take shape, forming into something more than random noises. She knew she was on a ship for she could hear the slap of the sea against wood and the muffled voices of men scrubbing the deck above her. Canvas sails cracked in the wind, and ropes creaked, as did the ship's hull.

Nearby someone was talking, a relaxed blending of words and sound. Kathleen tried to remember where she had heard that voice before. It belonged to someone accustomed to giving orders and to having those orders obeyed. It was a rich voice, deep and compelling.

Who is that, she wondered. The name Kade Morgan leapt into her mind, the tall stranger who had bought her at the auction. So it had not been a dream, it had really happened. She touched her neck to assure herself the iron collar was really gone. The talking stopped and Kathleen's stomach knotted up.

"You can open your eyes now, I know you are awake," Kade said with an edge of irritability in his voice.

Kathleen's apprehension at meeting the captain of the *Black Eagle* vanished beneath a flash of temper. I have done nothing to earn his anger, she thought. Then he remembered that although she was free of Rat Anders, she was now a slave. Her pride ached but she did as her master ordered.

She was in a bed positioned along one wall of a large room—cabin to be exact, she reminded herself. A window curved outward along the back wall; beneath it was a leather chair, immense and inviting. On the wall opposite the bed were a table with several chairs, a desk and bookshelves. In front of the desk was Kade Morgan, his head almost touching the ceiling. Kathleen glared coldly at him.

His jaw tightened visibly at the ice in her eyes. "Who was it that sold you to me?"

"Rat Anders."

"Not much of a name." He pulled the dagger from his boot and turned to drop it on the desk behind him.

Kathleen shrugged. "Rat was not much of a person. A bloated tick would be a better description."

Her soft, gravelly voice, graced with a lilting Irish accent that made it sound like music, filled the cabin with sensuous vibrations. Kade whirled to face her, his eyes narrowed to slits. Kathleen misinterpreted his reaction, and her temper flared again.

"Am I not allowed to speak, *master?*" she snapped. The husky voice flowed like thick silk, giving the impression she was calm, pensive. It was her eyes that told how she truly felt, for they were full of fire.

The delicate fingers of her voice trailed a thousand sparks along Kade's flesh. He had thought her a child, but that was no child's voice. It was a woman's voice, promising everything and denying even more. He wanted to drag her into his arms and crush her lips against his, drinking deeply of the music that filled her.

"What is your name?" he asked.

Kathleen considered the question for a moment, fearing that if she told him her name it would give him the key to imprisoning her soul forever. The corners of her mouth twitched. What a silly idea, she thought even Mother would have laughed at such nonsense.

"I am Kathleen O'Connor from Emerald Hills in County Kerry, Ireland," she said. A movement near the foot of the bed caught her attention, and she realized Jake McBradden was standing near the cabin door. He watched her closely, as though expecting her to murder his precious captain and make a mad dash for freedom.

"Take off your clothes," Kade said to her. "Jake, I want you to burn those rags she is wearing while she bathes."

Kathleen noticed a copper bathtub beside the desk. It was full of water and bubbles. She had not been allowed to wash since being taken off the pirate ship. To feel the touch of hot water again would be to experience heaven. Curling wisps of steam rose into the warm air, an enticing sight.

"I told you to take off your clothes!" Kade shouted, causing her to jump.

"Not with you in here," she said and pointedly looked from Kade to Jake. I will not undress in front of these men, even if it means never bathing again.

Such deliberate defiance of his orders made Kade's temper erupt. "I am not going anywhere, you miserable excuse for a female! This is my ship, this is my cabin and your filthy body is in my bed, on my sheets. And if that is not enough to inspire you to obey, I will remind you that you are my slave, to do with as I please. Get up, take off those rags and get in this bath *now!*"

His voice had started as a low rumble. It changed into a loud roar as he advanced on the bed. Kathleen felt the masculine power of him wash over her like a thundering river swollen with spring runoff. Her body went limp as he towered over the bed.

Drawing a ragged breath, she tried to ignore the

effect he was having on her nerves. "No," she finally managed to say.

"I'd best get out of 'ere," Jake said as he slipped out the door, closing it behind him.

With one swift move of his powerful arm, Kade grabbed Kathleen's shoulder. His fingers dug painfully into her flesh as he dragged her to her feet. Then he stripped the tattered dress to shreds. Rage blinded her and she lunged at him. The world went dark, and she collapsed at her master's feet.

He shook his head in disgust. In the marketplace this girl had shown extreme courage. Now she was acting like a spineless jellyfish, fainting just because he ripped that horrible dress off her. If she did not want to wash, he would do it for her.

He bent over and lifted Kathleen from the floor. It was like holding an armful of wind. He took a closer look at his small slave. The fascinating eyes were closed, the tiny face covered with old and new bruises. A cascade of dark hair tumbled over his arm as her head rolled against his chest. An ugly bruise covered her left side from beneath her breast down to her stomach.

"I am surprised she can even breathe, much less spit like a wildcat backed into a corner." He lowered her gently into the tub as he called for Jake. The door opened and the old man stuck his head into the room.

"Cap'n?"

"She fainted again, probably from hunger. It looks like she has been starved. Better not give her anything too heavy to eat, bring some soup and dry bread. I could use something also; make it more substantial than soup, though."

"The lass be fakin', Kade. I told ye she'd be trouble."

Kade studied the small face. "She is too weak to cause much trouble."

"Whate'er ye say." Jake picked up the towel Kade

25

had knocked off the table and tossed it over the back of a chair before leaving.

Kathleen regained consciousness just as Kade mentioned food. Her mouth watered. It had been days since Rat last fed her, claiming it was a waste of food. A waste of hog slop, she had thought.

Before the wonderful delight of being allowed to eat totally captivated her, Kathleen realized someone was washing the caked dirt from her itchy body. She dismissed all other thoughts to devote her entire attention to this wonderful sensation, wondering just what she had done to have so many of her prayers answered at once. The only problem with her current situation was her arrogant master, who was kneeling so close beside Kathleen she could almost reach out and touch him.

There was something about Kade Morgan that attracted Kathleen even as it frightened her. On top of whatever that elusive something was, he was handsome to the point of making her nervous, with his hair rakishly hanging over his forehead and dropping carelessly below his collar. Kathleen longed to tangle her hands in that thick mane. His skin was bronzed by hours spent in the wind and sun, which added to his virile looks. The strong shoulders, muscular legs, and slim hips made her body ache with a need she had never known before. His eyes were black, full of danger and intrigue. They effortlessly drained Kathleen's will until she was helpless as a newborn foal.

She could not understand her reaction to this man. Kade Morgan was obviously some type of pirate, a blackguard, an evil rogue. He had bought her at a slave auction, treated her like a common whore by demanding she remove her clothes in front of him, and even now was washing her in his bathtub in his cabin.

Kathleen's eyes flew open. "Stop!" she cried and

26

jerked as far out of his reach as the tub allowed.

Kade watched as Kathleen's shock turned to fury and hate. He was so surprised that he did exactly as she ordered. That surprised him even more.

"How dare you touch me, and how dare you be present in this room when I am unclothed!"

Kade instantly forgot his surprise. He rose to his full six-foot, four-inch height and glared down at this impudent female with undisguised fury in his eyes.

"This is my ship, and this is . . ."

"Yes, I know. This is your cabin, your bathtub and I am your dirty slave." The lilting voice was almost submissive in tone as it purred seductively up to Kade. The blue-green eyes told another story. The girl would not give an inch. Ever. Kade experienced a strange thrill of excitement at that thought, and a great deal of anger.

"You *are* my slave, bought and paid for in gold," he roared, fists clenched tightly at his sides. "If you do not start washing this instant, I will do it for you!" He almost felt sorry for this poor girl who had dared to bring his wrath down upon herself.

He quickly discovered his pity was unfounded when Kathleen O'Connor stood to her full five-foot, two-inch height. Her voice filled the cabin as she gave vent to her anger.

"I will wash when you leave this room! I may be your slave, and though you think I am a miserable excuse for a female, it is a female I am and I deserve privacy!" She braced herself in the slippery tub by spreading her feet apart. Shoulders squared, clenched fists on her hips, she was totally unconcerned that she was naked.

Kade did not miss that fact. They were standing extremely close, and he took a step backwards to fully appreciate the sight before him. She was full of soft curves that invited intimate exploration. Her skin glowed like ivory in the soft light of the room, highlighted by the myriad of soap bubbles that clung to her in several delightful places. One small rainbow-hued bubble slid suggestively over her right breast. Kade longed to let his fingers follow its slippery trail, touching the wetness and feeling the softness. He moistened his lips, then dropped his gaze over the entire length of her body, his pulse racing.

Kathleen remained standing as the bubbles slid slowly down her body. She was not about to back down from this man, not after daring to confront him in all her naked glory. That thought, along with the strange glow in the black depths of Kade's eyes, made Kathleen blush from the tips of her toes to the top of her head. It was the first time in her life she had ever blushed. It was also the first time in her life anyone had ever looked at her like that.

As a delightful flush caused Kathleen's wet skin to glow with warm color, Kade realized his defiant slave was more than pretty, she was beautiful. She had delicate cheekbones and a small nose that was closer to being perfect than anything he had ever seen. Her hair hung past her waist, the tangled ends wrapping provocatively around her hips. As black as his own, it absorbed the light and sent out slivers of reflections like sparks. Feathery eyebrows curved artfully across her smooth forehead like the wings of a graceful seabird.

Her eyes held Kade captive. They were like brilliant opals, opals that were even now glaring at him as though he, Kade Morgan, was the lowest form of life on the planet. He allowed his eyes to travel once more down the exquisite form before him, then locked them with those incredible jewels.

"I am not leaving and you will wash," he stated flatly.

Kathleen was so acutely aware of Kade's lips that she found it extremely difficult to remember just what they

28

were arguing about. "I would continue to discuss the point with you, Captain, only in doing so, this lovely water would become cold. Winning a fight is not worth causing such a tragedy." She lowered herself into the tub, gratefully sinking beneath the fragrant, bubbled surface.

"You think you could have won? A most interesting theory."

In Kade's eyes Kathleen saw a hungry, smoldering desire, which instantly disappeared. Within her something stirred, something primitive and uncontrollable. Regardless of the risk, she had to see that look in those black eyes again.

Aware that he watched her every move, Kathleen soaped her hair. She rinsed it by sinking deep into the tub, causing the water to splash over the sides. When she sat back up and ran a hand over the mass of ebony, it was squeaky clean. She let it fall outside the tub, the ends floating in the spilled water. Kade stared intently at that puddle of water filled with black curls. Kathleen smiled secretly. This was fun.

Next she lifted a shapely leg above the water. Her hand trailed sensuously through the bubbles as the soap slid across her pink-flushed skin. Kade's eyes narrowed suddenly, and Kathleen had to struggle not to shiver. I am handling this rogue quite easily, she told herself, completely ignoring her own reaction to her master's hot eyes.

When she tried to wash her back, it soon became evident she needed help. She lifted imploring eyes to Kade, and he responded immediately by taking the soap from her bubble-covered hand. The tips of his fingers lingered against hers. Kathleen was very conscious of his touch. Then he knelt and began to run the soap across her back.

"It was a good thing you stayed after all," she said

and was shocked to realize her voice was scarcely more than a whisper. Embarrassed, she lowered her lashes slightly. Something was wrong. This game was supposed to affect him, not her.

Kade's hand moved in ever-widening circles as she spoke. Her voice curled around him, pulling him to her. The voice of a devil it was, making his senses burn and freeze all at once. With her lashes veiling the beauty of her eyes, he leaned close to her damp skin and blew gently onto her slender back.

The delightful sensations his fingers were creating made Kathleen steam with anger. When his breath caressed her tingling skin she almost jumped from the tub. This is not fair, she fumed. She grabbed the soap from him, noticing as she did that he was looking into the bathwater.

The concealing layer of bubbles had disappeared so that her body was completely exposed to those dangerous black eyes hovering only inches from her shoulder. Kade trailed his hand across her ivory skin to gently touch a rosebud-colored nipple.

Waves of wonder washed over Kathleen. She was aware of nothing except the feel of Kade's flesh against hers. He rubbed her nipple between his fingers, drowning her in a sea of pleasure. The heel of his hand brushed lightly along the curve of her breast. Her back arched as her body sought for more contact. A low moan reached Kathleen's ears, her moan, and she shivered.

"I—I think this water's too cold," she breathed, almost overcome by his touch.

Kade's breath was warm and moist, seeping slowly inside her ear as he said, "You think it is the water, do you? You certainly are full of interesting theories."

He stood up abruptly, holding the towel just out of her reach. Kathleen had no choice except to stand without benefit of cover. Kade watched the drops of water cascade across her breasts and down her slender legs. He wrapped the towel around her, and the feel of those arms, so strong and possessive, melted Kathleen's will. A fire raged in her body, and it centered alarmingly between her legs when Kade leaned over, his lips almost touching hers.

At that moment, Jake McBradden kicked open the door. He was carrying a tray from which the enticing smell of food wafted. "Better let it cool, Cap'n," he said. "We need ye on the bridge."

The *Black Eagle* tacked into the wind, momentarily stalling the ship's forward movement. Kathleen was standing in the pool of water beside the tub, and she lost her balance, falling into the warm expanse of Kade's open arms.

He held her tightly, a savage light in his eyes. The hard muscles of his chest pressed against her breasts for a brief, wonderful moment. Then he set her firmly away from him.

"Do not eat my steak, Kate," he said, grabbing his spyglass from the desk and slamming the cabin door behind him.

Kathleen reached for the edge of the desk to steady herself. The heat trapped within her cooled, and her heart slowed its erratic rhythm.

"I am a fool," she said, "a small piece of kindling playing with the fire that will decide my fate." As she sampled the soup Jake had brought, Kathleen resolved to control herself in the future when faced with the piercing black eyes of Captain Kade Morgan.

Chapter 3

Kade returned to his cabin several hours later, wet from the storm the *Black Eagle* was sailing through and as hungry as the devil himself. He threw open the door, walked confidently into the dark cabin and tripped over the bathtub. Kathleen was asleep on his bed, wrapped in the folds of a white sheet. All the dishes on the table were empty. She had finished every bite of her food and completely devoured his. Damn the wench!

He lit a lamp and dragged the tub into the passageway before going to the galley to order another meal. Kathleen was awake when he stalked back into the cabin. She stretched like a cat, rubbing her eyes and curling her toes. Long, silky masses of black hair lay strewn over his pillow, framing her face. Kade tensed when her sheet slipped to reveal a soft breast.

Unaware of her state of undress, she stretched again. "I am sorry about eating your meal, Captain Morgan. I had not been fed for days and could not resist." A flash of a smile crossed her face. "Your steak was excellent," she added as her hand wrapped in the heavy weight of her hair.

Her husky voice washed over Kade's frayed nerves, soothing and exciting him. His breathing grew shallow and his pulse raced as he leaned over the bed, her lips a magnet to his smoldering desire. She was his to command, and Kade had only one request.

They both started in surprise when a young boy kicked open the cabin door, a tray of food clutched in his hands. "Dinner, Cap'n," he announced, then his eyes widened at the sight of Kathleen stretched out on the bunk. He nearly dropped the entire meal in surprise.

Kade pulled the sheet up over Kathleen and spun around just in time to grab the tilting tray. Clutching the sheet under her chin, Kathleen gave a quick prayer of thanks for the boy's interruption. It was disconcerting to know that even in the face of her resolve to shield herself from Kade's captivating effect on her, she had still fallen under his spell the moment he approached her.

She had been frozen by the power of the man, the same thing that attracted her to him. The palms of her hands were damp, and she was grateful she was not standing; it was doubtful her legs could have held her. She felt like a tree buffeted by a violent storm.

"Does anyone know how to knock around here?" Kade grumbled as he pushed the lad out with one hand and kicked the door shut. She grinned at him.

Kade was transfixed by her eyes; they looked like the sun skimming along the top of a translucent wave. He swallowed to dispel the scratchy feeling deep in his throat.

"What do you find so funny?" he asked. She laughed, the full, throaty sound filling the cabin with sweet music. Kade's throat started to ache.

"You, shouting at that poor child. He obviously did not think I was the same dirty waif Mr. McBradden brought on board earlier." She sat up in the bed and wrapped the sheet around her chest, tucking it in tightly. Kade set the tray on the table, and Kathleen found it difficult to prevent her eyes from following his

33

every move. Even when she looked elsewhere she was aware of him. Very aware.

"I am having trouble believing it myself," he said, his voice deeper than normal. He forced a frown onto his face and crossed his arms over his chest. "I thought you might be pretty once we got you cleaned up."

The remark hurt Kathleen, though why she did not know. She concerned herself with smoothing the wrinkles in the sheet.

"Tell me what an Irish girl is doing in Morocco chained to a bloated tick like Rat Anders." Kade unbuttoned his shirt as he talked. Kathleen tried to ignore him and found it impossible not to notice the sculpted muscles displayed before her. Every inch of his body was perfection, and she discovered her eyes following the tapering line of his waist into the top of the snug-fitting pants. When he dropped those pants, she was horrified.

He pulled a maroon robe from the armoire and shrugged into it while she tried desperately to look anywhere except at him. She did not succeed. It seemed as though there was nothing else in the room except those massive shoulders, firm stomach muscles and— Kathleen bit her lip and thought about Ireland.

"I asked how you got mixed up with Anders. You do have an explanation, I suppose. You are not the type normally sold at those auctions."

Kathleen remembered the women begging for mercy and offered a quick prayer of thanks that she had not succumbed to such degrading actions. "Of course I am not," she snapped, misunderstanding the reason for Kade's comment.

She fixed her gaze on the shelf of books over the desk. It was difficult to erase the memory of Kade's virile body from her mind, especially when there was only a robe and a few feet of space between her and it.

After a moment she allowed her eyes to slide back to his face, firmly refusing to look any lower.

"As I told you before, my home is in County Kerry on the western shore of Ireland. We were attacked by pirates and I was taken prisoner. I think I was on their ship for a month. There was no light in my cell and I lost track of time. Rat took me off the ship, said I was in Morocco in the port of Tangier. He locked me up and after two months sold me to you."

Kade's lips parted slightly, and Kathleen found she could not pull her eyes away from them. "On the western shore? That is a bit out of the way for pirates, most unusual."

"Since I am here it obviously is not that unusual."

"Tell me what happened."

There was a moment of silence, filled only by the sea washing against the hull. Kathleen focused her eyes past Kade, past the walls of the ship, past the heartache.

"It was morning, just after dawn. It had rained the night before, a soft rain that sparkled like diamonds on the grass. The air smelled of the sea and burning turf, sweating horses, and rosemary. I could hear the ocean crashing on the beach and exploding on a rocky outcrop of land just south of Emerald Hills.

"I had fed the pigs and milked the cows. Taran was waiting—he is my stallion—and we went for our morning ride. It was wonderful; a mist came up and blanketed the bogs so I felt like we were flying through the clouds. We broke out of it just as we reached the field behind the house. Niall had finished feeding the mares in the stable and was in the corral preparing to exercise the yearlings.

"I heard them just before they swarmed over the rise sloping up from the beach. Hideous creatures they were, coming at us from everywhere at once. I heard

35

guns. Niall was hit. Mother ran out of the house. A sword came down on her head, splitting it open."

She told the story as though it had happened to someone else. No emotion, no feelings. Yet Kade saw the blood pooling in the damp earth of the corral, watched it flow down the limestone steps beneath her mother's crumpled body, heard it drip onto the flowers that he imagined lined the front of the house. All country houses had flowers, just as they had mothers. In Ireland, all the houses also had blood on the front steps. Even if it had been shed a hundred years ago, to the Irish it was always fresh, always red.

"I ran to Niall. He had been hit in the chest, a terrible hole open all the way to the bone. He told me to run, to escape. Blood trickled from between his lips. I knew he was dying and I wanted to die, too. Instead I mounted Taran. We whirled around to run. One of the pirates grabbed Taran's bridle. He reared, jerking himself free, and I fell. That was the first time in my life I had ever fallen from a horse." A frown creased her forehead, and she appeared to be more upset by the fall than the attack.

"Before I could get back on my feet, the beast captured me. He slung me over his shoulder and headed for the beach. I watched as my home burst into flames behind me. I saw Niall crawling across the yard to where Mother lay; then he collapsed. The barn was on fire and there were horses trapped inside. Their screams tore through the air. Taran charged past the pirates to the beach and I lost sight of him."

Kade was surprised by how cold and uncaring Kathleen sounded compared to the way her eyes seethed like a boiling cauldron of hatred. There her pain took on a life of its own as she relived the terror of the attack, the horror of the deaths, the senseless destruction.

"Who was Niall?"

Kathleen's chest ached unbearably. "My brother."

"What about your father? Where was he?"

"Away on business, delivering some horses to England." She pushed her hair back from her face. "We raise horses, the best in Ireland, England or anywhere else. We also train hunters and jumpers. Everyone has a horse from Emerald Hills, that is why I do not understand."

Kade reached over the table and pulled a decanter and glass from the shelf there, knocking the bottom of the glass against the small railing that kept the shelf's contents immobile. He removed the stopper from the decanter and poured himself a drink. The smell of whiskey was heavy in the room. He replaced the stopper and decanter, then seated himself on the edge of the desk. Kathleen had swung her legs to the floor, and he watched her dig her toes into the carpet.

"That is not Irish," she said. He looked into his glass, then at her.

"How can you tell?"

"Smell."

It was top-quality whiskey, the same kind he always drank. He took a sip and had to force himself to swallow. It most definitely was not Irish. Their whiskey was like Kathleen's voice; smooth and rough, wild and mellow, warm and wonderful. He had never liked Irish whiskey, yet now he found himself longing for a taste.

"What did you mean about not understanding?" he asked.

"The ransom, it was not paid. As soon as I arrived in Tangier, Rat took my locket, the one Mother and Father gave me last year for my birthday, and made me write to Father as proof I was alive. Last week he came into the room where he had me chained. I thought he was going to beat me. I leaned against the wall and

37

waited. Then he laughed, snickered actually, and said since Father had not paid the ransom he was going to sell me at the next slave auction."

The memory of that moment was bitter, and Kathleen had to struggle to suppress a shudder of horror. It had been her good fortune that Kade Morgan had purchased her. He seemed a reasonable man, one who had no need for a slave with no skills other than training horses. It should be easy to convince him to send her home.

She stood up and adjusted her sheet. "I will write a letter to my father instructing him to pay whatever ransom you request, Captain Morgan. Do you have paper and pen available?"

She was so pale beneath the bruises, so trusting. The light in the cabin fell on the silken skin of her shoulders and slid down the length of her raven hair.

"I have no intention of ransoming you."

Kathleen narrowed her eyes. "What do you plan to do with me then?"

Kade set his glass on the desk. Just what did he plan on doing with her?

"That is my concern," he answered.

The blue-green eyes flashed. "I have a right to know!"

"You have no rights except those I give you. There will be no more talk of ransom, or of your father. Since he did not respond to Rat's request, what makes you think he even wants you back?"

"Of course he wants me back! Something must have gone wrong with Rat's letter, Papa would have paid if he received it. Maybe he sent Rat the money and that slimy rodent decided not to send me back. Or maybe the ship sank or was delayed!"

"Or maybe your father did receive the ransom demand and decided you were most likely already dead

38

and decided to save himself a bundle by not replying."

Kathleen flew at Kade's face, hands clenched in rage. He grabbed her to prevent her from reaching her target and held her. She vented her fury on his chest with blows that hardly affected him. Quickly drained of what little strength she had, her attack slowed. He captured her hands in his, crushing her against him and circling her waist in an iron grip.

When Kathleen was first taken captive, she had believed that at any moment her nightmare would end and she would go home. After a time she began to wonder if she would be imprisoned forever, chained in total darkness and constantly subjected to abuse and starvation. To preserve her sanity, she had thought about home. During the long days and nights of inactivity and fear, she wove a golden dream that someday she would return to Ireland and everything would be the same as it had always been.

Mother and Niall would be alive; Father would be laughing at either Lord Silas Pennington's latest offer to buy Emerald Hills or his demand that Kathleen marry him. Taran would be shaking the seaweed from his mane, and gulls would be circling overhead. Flocks of gannets would be fishing off the coast, and the white-headed geese would be arriving for the winter. Niall would be weaving his way through the ancient stone ruins near the shore as he headed for his favorite fishing spot. Kathleen would mount Taran, and they would ride into the lonely mists she loved so much.

Faced with Kade's refusal to ransom her, Kathleen's golden dream died. She forced herself to stand stiff and erect in Kade's arms, even though her heart was breaking. She had to face reality, a reality that was holding her so very close, so very intimately.

Kade brushed a lock of hair from her face, and the gesture was so gentle, something she did not expect from this brute of a man, that her resolve began to melt away like an ocean mist at sunrise. He touched her face with one finger, tracing the place Rat had punched her. The depths of his eyes were shadowed by something Kathleen did not recognize, something that made her heart ache. She forced herself to turn away from him, to hide the feelings on her face and in her heart.

Before she turned, taking with her the agony of her private pain, Kade saw tears shining on her lashes. The tough front she showed the world dissolved at the first crystal drop of liquid, revealing the vulnerable side that Kade had glimpsed for a moment on the slave platform. After all the abuse she had endured during the auction without complaint, the touch of his hand had reduced her to tears.

Her slender body trembled as silent sobs tore through her. His embrace became tender as he held her against him. Laying his head on top of hers, he breathed deeply of the fresh scent of her hair and skin. He knew she would prefer to die than cry in his arms, yet he could no more release her at that moment than he could have left her on that slave platform. And so he held her close and ignored the erratic beat of his heart.

By crying, Kathleen had revealed to Kade more of her inner self than she had allowed anyone to see. She expected him to laugh at her. But he did not laugh, nor did he offer sympathy. All he did was hold her. The cold, uncaring scoundrel had changed into a man who understood her pain and acknowledged her despair. Wrapped in his arms, comforted by his presence, Kathleen silently swore she would never allow this man to witness her in so weak a position again.

Her oath was going to be hard to fulfill because at that very moment Kade's intimate embrace was threatening to undo her completely, especially when his robe began to fall open. She tried to pull away,

40

struggling desperately against his strong arms and warm body. It was useless. He only held her tighter until she stopped, then cupped her chin and tilted her face so she was forced to look at him.

If he was planning to dry her tears, Kathleen gave him no opportunity. She pulled together the remnants of her pride and threw away the shattered fragments of her dream. No one came to rescue her from Rat Anders, no one would rescue her from Kade Morgan. She was a slave with nothing except her pride to keep her strong and her wits to save her. That would be enough. It had to be.

She lifted the tangle of lashes that veiled her eyes and met Kade's piercing gaze, revealing to him the full extent of her hatred for him. Coming so fast after the flood of tears that had dampened his robe, the strength in her gaze took Kade by surprise. Instead of a heartbroken child, he was holding a vengeful woman. She pulled one hand free from his grasp and slapped her master full across his handsome face.

His tenderness disappeared instantly. "Never try that again or I will break you in half, Kathleen. Do you understand?" He shook her roughly.

"Only if you never say again that my father would not want me back. Whatever the circumstances that put me in your path, it was not of my father's doing. He loves me."

Kade held Kathleen's arms, watching the colors of her eyes churn as she fought against the turbulent emotions that held her captive as surely as he did.

"Aye, Kate, I am sure he does."

Her father had abandoned her, not even caring enough to pay whatever ransom Anders had demanded. Yet, when faced with that fact, Kathleen still believed passionately in the man. What would it be like to turn that passion to more delightful pursuits, Kade

41

wondered. A rush of desire spread through his body.

He leaned close to the lush promise of her waiting lips. Her eyes froze to glacial coldness. The need to melt the ice princess in his arms burned hot inside Kade, a need he was determined to satisfy. The closer he came, the more she resisted his embrace. And the more her lips parted to accept his coming kiss.

Chapter 4

Kade leaned over Kathleen, his intention clearly reflected in his eyes. She froze. There was no way to avoid what was about to happen. The terrible thing was that she did not want to avoid it. She longed to feel his lips on hers, to experience his kiss, to sample what had been exciting her since the first moment she saw him. Danger, desire, passion. They all called to her from inside the circle of his arms.

Closer he came, his warm breath touching her face. Her lips trembled and a shudder shook her body, bringing her abruptly to her senses.

"Let me go," she said firmly. Neither of them moved; then he released her.

"Are you hungry?" he asked, waving a hand at the tray on the table.

The question took Kathleen by surprise. While her body fought to dispel the effect of his touch, he was thinking about food. She clenched her fists. I have no more sense than a newborn filly. Naturally he has forgotten, I mean nothing to him. His knees are not shaking, his heart is not racing. Only mine. If he had really wanted me, nothing could stop him.

Kade ran his hand across the back of a chair and fought down the surge of emotions caused by holding Kathleen. The feel of her body pressed against his, the

43

smell of her skin, even the sweetness of her breath had greatly affected him. Why had he let her go? What was it in those strange eyes that made him want her to respond willingly to his touch?

Kathleen shook her hair behind her shoulders before seating herself at the table. She sniffed appreciatively at the delicious smells coming from the covered dishes. Food always made her forget her troubles, no matter how serious. Kade filled their bowls with stew, then sliced the loaf of bread with his knife.

Kathleen concentrated on eating, glancing up only when he offered her more coffee. She nodded yes and held out her mug. He held her hand steady while pouring the steaming liquid, the touch of his fingers making her skin tingle. When her cup was full, she pulled away from him and spilled the coffee on the table.

"I guess I am not used to the ship's motion."

"You have not sailed before?" He wiped up the mess and refilled her cup.

Kathleen wrapped her hands around the heavy mug and stared into the dark liquid as though it held the answer to all her problems. "We owned a curragh for fishing near the offshore islands. I rarely went out in it. The pirate ship was my first real experience of being at sea."

Kade sat back in his chair. "Did you get sick after your capture?"

"I was much too angry to be sick, in addition to being hungry, hot and uncomfortable."

"You must be a born sailor, Kate."

"What do you mean?"

"You sailed under terrible conditions without becoming ill and show no signs of being sick now, even though we are sailing through a storm and the *Eagle* is being tossed about by heavy seas and a strong wind.

44

Instead of feeling queasy, you have nearly eaten me out of house and home."

Kathleen laughed. "My mother used to say that. She said if I kept eating so much I would never find a husband." For the first time since the tragedy of her mother's death, it did not hurt to remember the whimsical smile and magical laugh that accompanied all Kathleen's memories of Mary O'Connor.

"Were you looking?" Kade asked.

Kathleen placed her mug on the table and pulled her feet up into the chair. With her arms wrapped around her knees, she returned his steady gaze. "Absolutely not. Emerald Hills is all I want."

"Why is that?" He lit a cigar, and aromatic puffs of smoke drifted throughout the cabin. Kathleen inhaled deeply, enjoying the smell.

A dreamy feeling came over her, and she could almost taste the wonderful air of home. "Emerald Hills is the most beautiful, most peaceful, most wonderful place on earth. The sea and shore, the sun and grass, the wind and sky. It is a place of flowers and leprechauns, magic and dreams. What more does one need?"

Kade tapped his ashes into his empty mug. "Food, shelter, money."

"Food can be grown, shelter can be built, money can be earned, but only if there are hills and mountains, fields and valleys. Land for horses to graze on, run over, conquer beneath thundering hooves. It is the land that really matters."

Kade shook his head in disbelief. "Strange theories you have, girl."

"Not so strange. I love Emerald Hills and have no desire to live anywhere except there, plus no one has asked to marry me except Silas Pennington."

"That name is no more Irish than my whiskey. Who

is this heartsick swain?"

"A most titled Englishman, Lord Silas Pennington. And he is neither heartsick nor a swain, more of an old lecher. The king graciously took away some land belonging to an Irishman and gave it to Pennington. It borders on Emerald Hills. It is his lordship's belief he should have our land also. Lord Pennington is constantly after my father to sell and me to marry."

"Cradle robber," Kade said distastefully. The thought of that old man lusting after Kathleen made him ill.

"Not quite," she said, "though at seventeen I am a bit young for the likes of him."

And for me, Kade thought until the curve of the sheet over her breasts caught and held his attention. Age did not seem important when he was faced with such deliberate evidence of how far removed Kathleen was from a cradle.

"So before the pirate attack your plans were to live forever in the same house, growing old alone."

Kathleen grimaced. "You make it sound so distasteful. Besides, I was not alone. I had my parents and Niall, though someday he would have left home to marry and have children."

"You did not want the same? I thought women only lived for that."

"Not all, at least not me. My life was horses. I lived with them, dreamed of them, assumed my future was with them. There was no time to think of anything else, no reason to. I was happy." Kathleen sighed and pushed aside thoughts of home. "What about you, Captain Morgan? What do you care for? Your ship, your crew? There must be something."

"My ship serves a purpose, my crew hires on for a percentage of the profits from each voyage." He laid his cigar on the edge of the table and went to the armoire.

46

He pulled out clean clothes and began to get dressed.

Kathleen looked at her feet. Why did his cold, casual attitude toward life bother her? No, she decided, it was not casual, it was an emptiness, as though nothing mattered to him. He did not seem to care for anything, not even himself.

What does it matter if he hates the entire world, it is escaping that I need to occupy my mind with, not Kade Morgan's lack of a soul. Yet, how can I possibly escape from a ship in the middle of the ocean sailing God only knows where?

She glanced up. Kade was dressed now, wearing light brown pants, brown suede boots and a loose white shirt that rippled when he moved. He picked up his cigar before sitting at the desk to record the details of his meeting with Quint Cathcart in his log.

"Captain, may I ask where we are headed?"

"I fail to see what concern it is of yours."

She propped her chin on her knees. When Kade was not jumbling her emotions by being arrogant or overwhelmingly masculine, she had enjoyed talking to him. Why did he have to ruin her first pleasant moment since her capture by blatantly reminding her of her position as a slave whose feelings and thoughts did not matter?

She pushed her chair back from the table, stacked the empty dishes on the tray and went to the bookshelf, intending to find something to read. There were a number of volumes dealing with navigation, some novels and plays, and several books of poetry. On the top shelf was a book with strange characters on its binding. Kathleen squinted up at them, trying to decipher their meaning.

Once a missionary traveling across Ireland had stopped at Emerald Hills for the night. In exchange for a meal and a place to sleep, he had talked about his

47

travels. There were tales of Europe, Africa, even China. Fascinated, Kathleen had listened to every word, dreaming of the far-off lands this man brought to life in his stories. At her request, he had drawn a map to show where China was in relation to Ireland. In the corner of the paper he had written several symbols that were examples of Chinese writing, symbols that bore a striking resemblance to the strange characters on these books.

As Kathleen remembered more of what that missionary had told her of the Orient, the decorations in Kade's cabin began to take on an exotic look. The rug was woven of rich wool, decorated with red and black designs similar to the Chinese writing. From the dark wood on the walls to the unusual starkness of the stained-glass window, the cabin had a sinister strangeness that was frightening. An object on the desk pushed her imagination over the limit.

"Surely we are not going all the way to . . ." She picked up a small jade dragon from the desk and waved it at Kade. He glanced at it, nodded, went back to his work.

"Oh my goodness, no!" Kathleen cried. China was a world away from Ireland, a lifetime away. Would her nightmare ever end?

Kade put his quill pen in the top drawer of the desk, closed the ink bottle and shoved his log aside. "No is right, we are not going to China. I am not sure I could tolerate being on board with you all that way, Kate. I was trying to irritate you since you were doing the same to me while I was trying to work. In respect to the decor of the cabin, I did some business in the Orient a number of years ago, right after I had the *Black Eagle* built. Some of these things came from there, including that expensive piece of jade you are fondling."

Kathleen dropped the dragon like it was a hot

potato, not liking the way he said fondling. "Where are we going?"

"Mistral."

She cocked her head to one side, not sure she had heard him correctly. "I thought that was a wind."

Kade ran his hand through his shaggy hair. "Mistral is also an island, my island. Why are you so curious? Planning an escape?"

She was astounded. How did he know? The look on her face gave her away, and Kade smiled, a slow, contemptuous movement of his lips that irritated Kathleen beyond reason, as did the fact he owned an entire island. Whoever heard of such a thing?

"No need to worry, kitten, it will be our secret. Jake would be devastated to think you did not enjoy our hospitality on the *Black Eagle.*"

"You are insufferable!" Kathleen whirled around, intending to put as much distance between them as possible. A hand on her arm stopped her. The touch of his fingers on her bare flesh made her think of the way he had caressed his sword at the auction. She had wondered then how it would feel for him to caress her like that. Now she knew. It felt wonderful.

Kade turned her to face him and pulled her between his open legs. He wrapped his hands in her hair, pulling it aside to allow his lips to travel up her arching neck. The world was spinning; her senses centered on where he touched her. Her body was melting, her soul was burning. His tongue slipped into her ear, and a moan tore from her lips.

"Please stop, let me go." She pushed against his shoulders and wriggled backwards. The hands that held her waist and tangled among the ends of her ebony curls refused to release her.

"You called me insufferable. I wanted to see if I could indeed make you suffer." He ran his lips across

49

the tops of her breasts. Kathleen tightened her grip on his shoulders as her legs threatened to give way beneath her.

"You succeeded, Captain. Please let me go now."

"I think not, love, for if I did then I would be the one to suffer."

His left hand moved up her back, slipping into the top of her sheet and pulling it down. Then his fingers moved along the underside of her exposed breast. Kathleen's head fell forward, sending a shower of silken hair over Kade's arms as his thumb lightly brushed her nipple. His lips closed over the rigid peak. She gasped and threw her head back, lost in the turmoil of sensations erupting inside her. His teeth grazed her nipple, his tongue flicked it, his lips caressed it. She was trembling, she was dying. And still he took her higher.

His lips moved to her neck. He cupped her chin, drew her lips to his. Kathleen tried to fight what was happening to her. It was like fighting to stop a raging storm. Lightning exploded inside her head, thunder shook her slender form.

The sheet fell in a whisper of softness down her hips and legs, the linen sighing as it pooled at her feet. Kade worshiped her nudity with his hands, touching the glowing skin with a tenderness and reverence he had never felt before.

Her small hands began to touch him with hesitant innocence, drawing him closer to her. The music of her voice as she cried out with need and the sweet brush of her lips as she touched her mouth to his drove him mad. His kiss was a sacrifice he offered on the altar of her body.

He was a man of the world, had held in his arms beautiful, experienced women. With them he had felt carnal pleasure, nothing more. Now, holding in his arms this young girl, Kade knew for the first time the true joy of being human, of being male. He wanted more, needed more.

Kathleen drifted helpless in the turbulent sea of sensations and emotions aroused by Kade. Her soul spun in one direction, her body another, the room yet another. The only thing not spinning was Kade. He was a constant, steady, powerful anchor, and she clung to him desperately.

Kade crushed Kathleen against him, enfolding her within his embrace. His kiss tore aside the obstruction of her fear and the hesitation of her innocence. Her hands circled his neck as she pushed her tongue against his and turned her head to drink deeply of his kiss.

He lifted Kathleen and crossed the cabin to his bed. Unwilling to release her for even a moment, he held her in his arms and kissed her. He silently willed her to open her eyes, to reveal to him the beauty of those shimmering jewels. Her lashes cast trembling shadows on her smooth cheeks as the delicate lids lifted. The blue-and-green prisms looked at him, moist and hesitant in their surrender. Kade lost himself in their magical softness, and he again sacrificed himself on her swollen lips.

Reality ceased to exist for Kathleen. There was nothing in the universe except the man holding her, touching her, consuming her soul with his kisses. Inside she burned, she froze, she erupted in a turmoil of quivering sensations that threatened to destroy her if she could not find a way to stop this madness.

Kade drew back to gaze at her with passion-swollen eyes, his lips heavy and wet with her kiss. From somewhere within Kathleen came a voice she did not recognize. It was cold and sharp, a stark contrast to the hot, melted being she had become.

"I assume you will rape me now," the voice said.

She gasped and covered her mouth with her hand.

51

When she had been Rat's prisoner she had been frightened by his cruel beatings. To control her fear, she had forced herself to provoke him into hitting her. Her disregard for his abuse had caused him to be frightened of her so that he often left her alone after only a few slaps and punches. Provocation had been an effective weapon against a weakling like Rat. It was not the way to deal with a man like Kade Morgan.

He stiffened, his desire immediately masked by anger. He threw her on the bed. One hand spread her legs; the other ripped open his pants to expose the throbbing shaft of his need. Now it represented revenge. Kade buried himself deep inside her, tearing brutally through the shield of her maidenhood.

"Bitch," he growled as his powerful body drove into her again. Kathleen accepted the terrible pain, accepted the torment and torture, using it to punish herself for wanting this man.

His body attacked her, hurt her, crushed her. Slowly the primitive thing in Kathleen began to come to life. She could not subdue it, it possessed her even as Kade did. When next he surged into her, she welcomed him. When he stabbed into her, she raised her hips to receive the knife of his anger. When he slammed into her, she closed her legs around him and drew him deeper within her. He gave her pain, she gave him passion.

She ripped open his shirt, tearing it from his shoulders so her breasts could press against the expanse of his chest. Her lips touched his bronzed neck, tasting the salt of his sweat. Her tongue searched his flesh, finding and enveloping a hard nipple. There was a hesitation in his movement, a stop to the destructive rhythm. Kathleen's body responded with a moist flow that flooded the part of him within her.

He hovered above her, lost in the hot wetness

surrounding him. His arms were braced on the sides of her head, his hands tangling in her silken hair. To steady himself, he pulled his right leg up and placed his knee beside Kathleen's hip. His boot rubbed against her naked flesh, and a quiver claimed her fragile features. Her head thrashed from side to side, a moan escaping from her parted lips. Kade stroked the rough suede down the length of her leg, then pulled it back up to her hip. She shuddered and arched against him, her teeth sinking into his arm as her body stretched and strained in wanton ecstasy.

"Witch," he breathed. He lowered his lips to her face. He hated her for turning his desire into anger, hated her for taking from him that anger and giving him back the desire. His hate was lost in their kiss, lost in the touch of their bodies. Lost in his need.

He ran his fingers across her stomach, the flesh flushing beneath his touch. Lifting her hips, he showed her how to position herself. She responded by wrapping a leg over his boot, thrusting her hips upward and taking him completely into the velvet wetness that soon brought him to fulfillment.

His body shuddered, flooding her with his essence, filling her with a bloodless sacrifice. When it was over, he laid his forehead against her cheek.

"You called me a bitch."

He raised his head. "Yes. It was deserved."

"Aye, that it was," she said and closed her eyes to the hard muscles of his arms, the broad strength of his shoulders, the wet hair on his chest. "You also called me witch."

The smell of their sex was musky, entrancing. She turned slightly and the rough boot brought another wave of desire.

"You tremble," he said softly and slid his boot along

53

her leg. She clutched his arm as her body responded to the erotic sensations caused by the suede.

"Yes, I tremble. And I burn." Kade's lips brushed her temple. "Maybe I am a witch," she whispered.

He lowered himself onto her, held her against him as he turned onto his side. "Nay lass, I think not. Yet, if it were so, I would sell my soul to the devil to taste again the sweetness of your lips."

Kathleen touched her hand to his chest, feeling his heart beating steady and sure beneath her fingertips. "Why do I feel empty inside, as though something that was almost mine had slipped through my fingers?"

Kade smiled into her hair. "When people make love they seek to reach an emotional release that fills that emptiness, a climax of the feelings you experienced. It was your first time; to climax then is difficult for a woman."

There was a tug at Kathleen's heart, and she was afraid. "Was it love we made?"

He started to answer, then hesitated. He ran a finger across the lips so close to his own. "Some of what happened was love, kitten."

Kathleen pulled away from him. "I do not love you."

"Nor I you."

"Then how . . ."

"People can make love without being in love, just as those who are in love can be angry without hating."

It was all too much for Kathleen. She needed time to understand. She rolled over and covered herself with the blanket. "Go away."

The curving line of her back beneath the wool intrigued Kade. He reached for her, wanting to fill her emptiness. A knock on the door stopped him. He mumbled an oath as he rose from the bed, fastened his pants and jerked open the door.

"What do you want?" he asked, his voice so calm a chill went over Kathleen. Apparently it had the same effect on their visitor. The cabin boy, Michael, was standing in the passageway, eyes bulging up at his captain as he swallowed convulsively.

"Jake sent me." His voice broke, and he gasped out the message in a rush. "Ship followin', sir, comin' fast! She's ridin' high, no flag on her mast. Jake alerted our gunners, wants you to come quick!" The last word was scarcely out of his mouth before he broke and ran, his footsteps pounding down the passageway as though the hounds of hell were pursuing him.

"Fool boy," Kade said. He dragged his shirt onto his shoulders. The buttons were missing. He left it hanging open, tossed a final look at the small mound under his blanket and left.

Kathleen's hand closed around the buttons she had torn from Kade's shirt. They were small and hard, cutting into the palm of her hand. She threw them against the wall. They struck the dark wood, clattering loudly in the silence of the cabin before tumbling to the floor.

Some fell on the carpet; others rolled across the bare floor, under the desk and between the legs of the table and chairs. Kathleen watched the last one disappear before pushing aside the blanket and getting up. There was no time to think about what had happened or why. If she did not hurry, it would happen again.

A ship was following the *Black Eagle,* bearing quickly down on them. "This might be my only chance," she told the scattered buttons. Using the discarded sheet as a towel, she dried the moist reminder of her shame from between her legs, leaving a red streak on the white linen.

In the armoire Kathleen discovered Kade's sword

and pistols along with shirts, sweaters and breeches. There was also a complete set of evening clothes, from ruffled shirt to satin cape. Running her hand briefly along the slippery satin, she pushed it aside and took out a pair of breeches. She pulled them up over her bare thighs, then groaned. Both her legs could fit into one leg of Kade's pants.

She put the breeches back, took out a black shirt and pulled it on. The sleeves dangled past her fingers and the hem brushed her knees. It was absolutely huge, like wearing a market-day tent. She slipped it off and searched the cabin for scissors. The jewel-handled dagger flashed from among the desk's clutter. Perfect.

She deftly sliced off the end of each sleeve, then with a few more cuts fashioned a belt out of the remnants of silk. She dropped the shirt back over her head and tied the belt around her waist. The shirt gaped open in the front, exposing a major portion of her breasts.

"There is no time to search for anything to hold it together. I will have to live with it like it is."

She opened the cabin door. The passageway was empty. Down the corridor to her left was a small hatch that had been opened to allow fresh air below deck now that the storm was over. At the end of the passageway were steps leading onto the deck above.

"If I use those I might be seen, but no one will be watching a hatch."

It took several jumps before she caught hold of the framed edge of the opening. A terrible pain shot through her chest, and she froze. She dangled in midair, refusing to let go. Sweat beaded her brow, and her arms ached.

"I am wasting time, it is now or never."

With a tremendous surge of determination, she overcame the crippling agony in her chest and heaved herself up through the hatch. Near the stern, less than twenty feet from where she crouched on the wet deck, stood Kade Morgan. His spyglass was against his eye, his attention fixed behind the *Eagle*. His boots were firmly planted on the wooden deck, and Kathleen shivered at the sight of them. The memory of that leather touching her naked flesh was almost as immobilizing as the pain had been.

She turned slowly. The crew were either concentrating on their jobs or looking in the same direction as Kade. No one had noticed her. She ran over to the starboard railing, then moved along it to the bow, taking cover behind a keg lashed to the rail. By pushing her head between the keg and the rail, she was able to see her objective. A ship trailed in the wake of the *Black Eagle,* its sails completely unfurled in pursuit of its quarry.

Kade lowered the spyglass. "Change course by two degrees to port, Mr. Grimstead, to take full advantage of the wind. Raise more canvas on those masts, Mr. McBradden. We are not at capacity."

The ship plunged into a trough between swells, and Kathleen cast a furtive glance around to insure she had not been spotted; then she threw herself over the rail. The wind caught her shirt and hair, plastering them against her as it pushed her beyond the water churned aside by the ship's hull.

She heard someone shout, and then she slammed onto the surface beneath a cresting wave. The rock-hard impact knocked the air from her lungs just as the wave avalanched down upon her. Kathleen had not known water could be so cold, had not known anything could be so relentless in its grasp as she was dragged down into the vast expanse of blue, wrapped in the frigid embrace of the sea.

The outer edges of her vision began to recede. The ocean changed from blue to black until there was only a pinpoint of light remaining on the surface above her. A sudden burst of white ripped through that light, descending and growing larger. Then it disappeared as everything went black, leaving Kathleen alone with the cold that crushed her chest and immobilized her body.

Chapter 5

A heavy cloud had settled over Kathleen, weighing her down, smothering her. She struggled out from beneath the crushing weight, awaking from a sleep so deep it was frightening. Water surged over her, filling her mouth with salty coldness. After an eternity it drained away. There was light on her face. Her eyes would not focus. The world was a kaleidoscope of colors that taunted her with blurred images.

Something took possession of her chest, wrapping itself around her until she wanted to scream. Just when she thought it was as bad as it could possibly be, it intensified. She squinted against the bright world surrounding her. The haze of colors sharpened, and Kathleen focused on a pair of furious black eyes.

"What the hell were you doing?" Kade bellowed in her ear.

She tried to answer him, but there was no air in her lungs. She inhaled, causing splinters of fire to shoot through her chest. "Escaping," she gasped. "Could you not tell?"

"It looked more like you were trying to kill yourself." Kade pulled her tighter against him, and they began to rise above the clinging grasp of the ocean that swirled around their legs.

Kathleen was surprised to discover that while Kade

held her with one hand, the other held onto a rope being hauled up the side of the *Black Eagle*. When level with the deck, he swung his leg over the rail. The rope had been tied around his waist, and Jake cut it off. Kade threw Kathleen over his shoulder like a sack of potatoes and headed for his cabin. She had no strength to complain about her embarrassing position; she was too busy coughing up the water she had swallowed.

Kade kicked open the door to his cabin, flung his wet burden into the leather chair and left. There was a ship pursuing the *Eagle*. Because of Kathleen, it was almost on top of them. It would take a miracle to prevent a fight now. Kade intended to produce that miracle. He had encountered Barbary corsairs before, and though he had never lost a skirmish, the damage the heathens caused was always extensive. There would be time to deal with his wayward slave later.

The *Black Eagle* had been designed for speed and maneuverability during Kade's years of pirating. There was not a ship that could outrun her nor a captain that could outmaneuver Kade Morgan. His crew was well trained, and they eagerly responded to his commands, pulling from their ship every bit of speed possible. The distance between the two ships lengthened, and then the *Eagle*'s pursuers disappeared over the horizon. The men gave a rousing cheer at having avoided what would have been a bloody fight.

Kade gave orders for an extra ration of grog after that night's meal, bringing another cheer from the men hanging in the rigging. Satisfied that he had rewarded them for a job done well, he turned the helm over to Jake and went below to confront Kathleen. His muscles tensed as he approached his cabin. Her foolishness had endangered her life and his, in addition to placing the safety of his ship in jeopardy. He threw open the cabin door. Kathleen had not moved since he dumped her in the chair. Her clothes and hair were wet, her face flushed.

"Just because I foiled your attempt to escape is no reason to catch a fever. Put something dry on. I will pour us both a brandy."

Kathleen took a shallow breath. The terrible pain on her left side erupted again. She fingered her neck, trying to wipe away the stinging irritation of the seawater in the largest of the cuts caused by her iron collar.

"Stop rubbing it," Kade ordered. He swore softly under his breath as he pulled Kathleen's chin up to look at the sores. A small trickle of blood wound its way into the hollow at the base of her throat, and his anger was forgotten. He wet a towel in the washbowl at the foot of the bed.

Gathering Kathleen into his arms, he dropped into the chair with her on his lap. He cleaned her face, neck and arms of the crusted salt, tossed the towel aside and produced a small jar of ointment from a trunk beside the chair. He dipped a finger into the cream and rubbed it on her right wrist.

"It hurts!" Kathleen complained as she tried to pull away.

"You take a punch better than most men I know and hardly flinched when Rat kicked you in the stomach, then you whine when a little salve stings."

"I was not whining, I was stating a fact." Kathleen lifted her chin to allow him access to her neck.

"Whatever, just sit still." He rubbed cream into the area that had been bleeding.

"Stop!" she cried and sprang off his lap.

"I told you to sit still! Come back here and let me finish treating those cuts before they get infected."

Kathleen touched her neck gingerly. "I do not need any medicine."

61

"I said get back over here!" Kade grabbed her arm, forcing her back onto his lap.

"I would rather my neck fall off than have that stuff on me."

Kade deliberately put another dab on her largest cut. "I do not particularly care what you would rather have happen."

"Just as you do not care that I want to go home."

He put the lid back on the salve and set it aside. One arm was locked around her waist, preventing her from moving. "I bought you and I intend to keep you."

"I will try again."

"Warning your enemy of an impending attempt to escape is not very smart. Your chances would be better if I did not know."

"Consider the warning my way of thanking you for saving me from drowning." She tried to break free of Kade's grasp. It was useless. He simply held her tighter. I should know better by now, she thought. Whenever I try to get away, he pulls me closer.

"I accept your warning in the spirit it is offered," Kade said, "and offer you one in return: Forget about trying to escape again. You belong to me, kitten, and I keep what is mine." He thought of her lying beneath him, the rapture of her passion shining like a beautiful beacon from those aqua eyes. Another session in bed and she would forget all about leaving.

"It is my bet you will soon beg me to never let you go," he said, a gloating smirk on his face.

Kathleen gaped at him, impotent fury turning her eyes into a tumultuous whirlpool of color. Kade ignored her anger, concentrating instead on the drops of water that glistened like tiny diamonds on her lush lashes. The black silk shirt clung to her body, provoking him to finish what had been interrupted earlier.

62

The sudden gleam of lust that sparked the depths of his eyes went unheeded by Kathleen. She leaned closer to him until they were eye to eye.

"You filthy bastard!" she yelled. "If you think I would ever be begging you for anything, much less the opportunity to stay with your slimy self for one moment longer than it takes a flea to—"

Kade did not want to know what the flea was going to do, so he covered Kathleen's mouth with his in a savage kiss. Instantly he was consumed by the fiery need only this stubborn, willful girl had ever aroused in him.

Kathleen's anger evaporated like steam in the overheated cabin. All the burning passion she had experienced during their lovemaking came back in a blinding rush. She began to shake uncontrollably, a sobbing moan rising from deep within her as she struggled to free herself.

"What the hell?" Kade asked as he released her.

She bolted from his arms in an effort to put as much distance as possible between his lips and hers. She never made it past the first step. The air in her lungs was expelled by an explosion of pain, and she collapsed at Kade's feet, a wet heap of black hair and silk.

Blinded by lust and not realizing what had happened, Kade dragged her off the floor and into his arms. She was completely limp, a groan escaping from between tight blue lips as her head rolled against his chest. It was a frightening difference from the spitting wildcat that had faced him only a moment before.

"Jake, get down here *now!*" Kade thundered, his voice carrying through every part of the ship.

He put Kathleen on the bed, and picking up the dagger from his desk, sliced the wet silk from her. The bruise on her side was larger, and an ugly swelling rose from the center of the purple discoloration.

"Broken ribs," he said just as Jake appeared at his elbow. The Scotsman laid his hand on Kathleen's forehead.

"I'm not surprised she collapsed, 'er 'ead's on fire. Get 'er dry, I'll fetch me things."

Kade dried Kathleen as best he could and squeezed the seawater from her hair. He was bundling her in blankets when Jake returned with the few medicinal supplies they carried on the *Black Eagle*.

"We can bind 'er ribs an' tie 'er to the bunk to protect 'er from hurtin' herself, but that fever will kill 'er, Kade. She 'as no strength for fightin' this."

For a week they fought Kathleen's fever, constantly bathing her in cool water and feeding her rich broths in the hopes of maintaining what little strength she had. When not in the cabin with Kathleen, Kade paced the deck finding fault with everyone and everything. He inspected the coiling of ropes, the mending of sails, even the preparation of the crew's meals. The men slaved to perform every task perfectly, moving around the *Eagle* on silent feet to prevent attracting their captain's attention and temper.

One morning Kade cornered Skinner, his chief gunner and oldest crewman, in the powder magazine. He ordered Skinner to shave off the scraggly beard the old man claimed to have been born with. Skinner immediately borrowed a razor and scraped his face clean. Kade Morgan in a rage was a man to be obeyed.

Not once did Kathleen recognize Kade or Jake as they attended her. Most people rant incoherently while in the grip of a fever. Kathleen endured hers in silence, staring blankly out of eyes drained of color and life. Kade knew if she lost the will to live there was no hope. He talked to her constantly, saying anything he thought might provoke her enough to break through that eerie silence. He criticized Ireland, the Irish, her father and herself. He asked her about horses, about her family. Sometimes he read to her, using the poetry of Robert Burns to soothe his own anxieties while keeping up the constant barrage of sound.

Then one day the fever soared to new heights. Kathleen moaned for the first time, turning aside when Kade tried to coax her to drink some water. He moved away from her, unable to watch her suffer. A few minutes later he heard a sigh behind him. He rushed to Kathleen's side in time to see her lick her lips and wrinkle her nose as though it itched. Then she fell into a natural sleep.

Kade touched her forehead. It was damp. Beneath that film of moisture, her skin was cool. He sat beside her for a time listening to her steady breathing, then pulled the leather chair beside the bed and sank into its comfortable embrace. The sun set in a burst of red and orange glory, evening passed into night, and still Kade kept watch on his small slave.

It was after midnight when he fell asleep. He woke less than four hours later, stretching his legs and trying to work the cramps from his knotted shoulders. Though the leather chair was big and comfortable, it did not make an adequate bed for someone of Kade's size. Kathleen had curled herself into the blankets and had one arm hanging off the side of the bed.

"How is she?" The cabin door swung open and Jake entered, carrying two mugs of coffee that steamed in the predawn air.

"Still sleeping. It has been almost twelve hours." Kade lifted Kathleen's arm and tucked it under the covers before taking the mug Jake offered him.

"I still don't ken 'ow she made it," Jake said as he sat on the edge of the table. "She was so 'ot we could've fried eggs on 'er forehead."

Kade took a long drink, wincing at the bitter taste of the brew. He could not wait until they reached Mistral. Mattie McBradden made the best coffee in the world. He wanted a cup of that heavenly brew and a plate of her grilled swordfish or baked ham or—no use thinking about it, that would only make the wait longer. The *Eagle* had picked up a stiff wind that was carrying them in a southwesterly direction at a good clip. They should be home in a little over a week.

Kathleen dropped her arm back over the side of the side. Kade smiled. If that was the way she wanted to sleep, let her.

"She did make it, though," he said. "She is a tough one."

"Aye, the lassie's game enough. What do ye plan on doin' with 'er?"

Kade was silent. He had plans for Kathleen, ones that Jake would not like. When he did not answer, Jake took up the subject again.

"Ye don't 'old with slavery, lad, or be ye forgettin'? Even if ye was plannin' to work 'er, she'd not be much use in the cane fields. Too small to even carry water to the workers. Maybe there's somethin' else ye 'ave in mind for the lass, somethin' ye'd not be wantin' to tell me."

"This is none of your business, Jake. She belongs to me."

"She's too young, Kade."

Kade remembered Kathleen's husky voice and entrancing eyes as she stood in the bathtub covered with blushes and bubbles. He saw her in his arms, writhing beneath his sweating body in the throes of passion. Nay, she was not too young.

"Send the lass 'ome, lad, like she asked ye. Ye might own 'er but she will never really be yours if ye don't set 'er free."

Kade looked at Jake, looked at the pattern of lines on the aging face, at the wisdom in those faded blue eyes. When at eighteen Kade had run blindly into a world he was not ready for, Jake had gone with him. They signed onto a ship and headed out onto a sea neither of them knew anything about. Years later when they sailed back to Scotland, Kade was master of that same ship.

In the busy shipyards of Oban on the Firth of Lorn, Kade supervised the building of the *Black Eagle* while Jake collected his wife, Mattie, from the highlands. When Kade set sail for the West Indies and a new life, the McBraddens went with him.

Kade had taken to the seas as a pirate, and Jake had sailed with him. After he tired of the blood and death, Kade lowered the black-and-silver flag he had made famous and built his own shipping line. Jake had stayed by his side, helping to run the business. Not once had the Scotsman complained, nor had he offered advice. Until now.

Kathleen turned over, drawing Kade's attention to the bed. Her face was as pale as the white pillow that cradled her head. The need inside him suddenly became so tangible that he shivered.

Someday, just as I promised her, she will beg me to never send her home. Only then will I be able to purge this witch from my mind and do as Jake says, only then will I set her free.

·

Chapter 6

The wind slipped through the grass, fingering the flowering tops and making them sway like clouds before a storm. Kathleen leaned forward, becoming part of Taran as the stallion stretched his legs in great strides, racing mile after mile across the empty expanse of the Irish bogs. Rain gurgled around Taran's hooves, and the air smelled like coffee.

Kathleen's forehead wrinkled as she tried to concentrate. *I feel the sun on my face, not rain. And I am lying down, not riding.* She opened her eyes, leaving behind the pleasant dream of home. The room she was in was large, one side curving outward with a window that was thrown open, flooding the bed with sunshine.

The room moved, swaying from side to side, and the living scent of seawater filled the air. Through the ceiling came the muted sounds of men talking, canvas cracking, wood creaking. *A ship,* she thought, *why am I on a ship?* Somehow she had escaped from Rat Anders, from the beatings, chains and darkness. Eager to discover if the ship was headed for Ireland and if her father was aboard, she sat up.

"Gracious heaven, I have been killed," she gasped and clutched her left side. It was extremely sore to the touch and painful when she breathed. She lifted the covers to investigate and discovered she was wearing a cotton shirt so big it resembled a sheet. Beneath its billowing folds, her chest was wrapped in great lengths of bandages.

"Broken ribs," she said. The soreness was worse than the pain. She pushed back the tumble of her long hair and scooted off the edge of the bed. The floor was covered with a carpet marked with strange designs, and her feet sank into a patch of red wool.

She took a hesitant step. Her knees cracked and she winced. She kept walking and her knees kept complaining until she reached the center of the cabin. Heavy footsteps were approaching the cabin. She stood still and nervously clutched the shirt tighter against her.

The door opened and the largest man Kathleen had ever seen confidently shouldered his way into the room, a tray balanced lightly in his hands. When he turned to face her, she frowned. His black hair and black eyes were familiar. Too familiar. And the way he regarded her so possessively, the arrogant tilt of his head, the sarcastic lift of those full lips; she had seen these things before and realized they had bothered her then as much as they bothered her now.

Recognition came to her in such a rush she became dizzy. Reaching out for support, her fingers closed on air. She was a slave, this man's slave. And he was Kade Morgan, captain of the vessel *Black Eagle*. Emerald Hills was so far away that for a moment Kathleen doubted it had ever existed.

"What are you doing out of bed?"

"Are you not even going to wish me a good morning, Captain Morgan?" Kathleen locked her knees as the ship surged up over a swell, pitching the floor sideways. If I could time my unsteadiness to blend with the ship's unstableness, I could stand up, she thought as the ship plunged downward and she weaved backwards

69

to compensate.

"Good morning, now get back in bed." He set the tray on the table and came toward her. Kathleen watched him. *He has no trouble moving, I should be able to do that.*

"I am extremely hungry, is that for me?" Her stomach gave a grumbling growl as she squared her shoulders like Kade's and deliberately took another step closer to the table just as the ship surged upward again. Her head started spinning; her knees shook, cracked, then buckled beneath her. Before she hit the floor Kade was beside her, lifting her into his arms.

"I told you to get back in bed, Kate."

He was so strong, so steady as he carried her over to the bed. She leaned back onto the pillow, missing the security of his embrace. Kade pulled the covers up over her exposed legs and sat beside her. His face was so close. The world tilted, hesitated.

"Maybe you wanted me to carry you," he said, his hand touching her face.

The ship plunged into another trough and the world righted itself. Kathleen shoved his hand away and yanked the covers over her chin. "I did not want nor need your help, Captain Morgan."

"Are you hungry?" He was already back at the table, uncovering a steaming bowl of oatmeal.

She swallowed and lowered the blanket slightly. "Yes, desperately. It feels like I have not eaten for weeks."

Kade moved the tray onto Kathleen's lap and sank into the armchair. "It has been exactly nine days since you last ate, excluding the broth that was forced down you."

There was a pitcher of honey on the tray, golden and thick. Kathleen poured it over the oatmeal and into the coffee. Both were delicious.

"What happened to me?" She indicated her side with her spoon, noticing as she did how tired Kade looked.

He got up to pour brandy into his coffee. "You tried to escape."

Kathleen tapped the biscuit on the tray. It was hard, most likely from the ship's stores, so she dipped it in the coffee to soften it a bit. "It is obvious I was not successful."

"There was a ship following us, and you jumped overboard. Instead of swimming to our pursuers, you sank. After we hauled you back on board the *Eagle* you informed me that you would escape at a later date and promptly fainted."

"Rather dramatic. Then what?" Kathleen diligently scraped the bottom of the bowl for the last bite of oatmeal. He took her spoon and dropped it on the tray. There was some oatmeal stuck to the sides of the bowl. Kathleen reached for the spoon just as Kade moved the tray to the table.

"Jake declared you were going to die. I disagreed."

A knock on the door interrupted them. Jake McBradden stuck his head into the cabin. "Is the lass awake, Kade? I'll be needin' to look at those bandages."

"I will send Michael for the tray," Kade said. He sat his empty cup down and left.

Kathleen regarded Jake critically. "You thought I was going to die. Why am I still alive?"

He sat on the edge of the bed, his red hair gleaming brightly in the sunlight. "Just ye lie still, lass, an' this'll not take long." He probed gently on her ribs. Kathleen caught her tongue between her teeth to keep from crying out in pain.

"You did not answer me, Mr. McBradden. Why am I not dead? It would be preferable to being a slave."

"Why, ye ask? Partly because me and Kade did all we could to make sure ye did not die, but mostly because

71

the Irish be too 'ard'eaded to do what anyone expects."

Kathleen wrinkled her nose at the mention of Kade's efforts to save her. "Did not want to lose his investment, I suppose."

"Can't rightly say what did come o'er the lad, surprised me more than a loch monster."

"A *what?*"

"Loch monster, beasties that live in the lakes in Scotland. Always poppin' up when ye least expect 'em, then breathin' fishy breath all over ye and disappearin' wi' a splash big enough to sink even this brig."

Kathleen was fascinated. She had never met anyone who had actually seen a monster. "At home I often saw fairy lights on the marsh and leprechaun trails across the bogs. A loch monster sounds wonderful! When can I get up, Mr. McBradden?" she asked, changing the subject so fast that Jake blinked in confusion.

He peered into her eyes, felt her throat and fingered the newly healed scars on her wrists. From the dour expression on his face, he obviously thought she was going to collapse at any moment.

"Week or two, dependin' on 'ow fast yer ribs mend. Ye need rest, lass. Get some sleep. That's what I've got in mind for meself, 'aving spent most of last night standin' watch." He opened the cabin door, and Michael almost fell into the room.

"Sorry Jake, I wus gonna knock. Cap'n sent me for the tray."

"Watch where ye're goin', lad, one patient at a time is all I care to be lookin' after."

After Jake left, Michael seemed at a complete loss. He just stood there, not moving, until Kathleen smiled at him. Then he blushed and ducked his head, the sunlight touching on his blond hair.

"Ya feelin' better, miss?"

Kathleen guessed he was about ten years old, big for

his age and clumsy with his size. "Yes, I am," she answered. "Do you think you could find some clothes I could borrow? You are not much smaller than I, maybe something of yours would fit."

Michael's eyes grew so big they almost took up his whole face. "I'd not have nothin' fit for you, miss, just some things the crew gave me when the Cap'n hired me on in New York last year. That stuff wus purty near worn out then an' it ain't no better now."

Kathleen lifted her knees and wrapped her arms around them, causing the sheet to pucker beneath her fingers. "I grew up in my brother's old clothes and I doubt whether anything could be worse than his things, they usually smelled of fish. Could you check for me please?"

"I gotta take this tray to the galley first, then I'll see what I can find."

The cabin door closed behind Michael, and Kathleen slid out of the bed, one hand held tightly against her chest. Though the food had restored some of her strength, she was still weak. Escaping Kade would be difficult, if not impossible, in this condition. *If only my knees would stop shaking, and if only I could get a full breath without it hurting so much.*

"Exercise is what I need, that and somewhere to wash. I wonder if there is any water around here, besides what we are floating on."

A screen at the foot of the bed, which Kathleen did not remember being there before, concealed a chamber pot and a pitcher of fresh water. She made use of both. Being clean made her feel better. True, she was a slave, the worst possible thing she could imagine being, yet there were no chains, no beatings. She had been fed, allowed water to wash with, and at that moment was standing in front of an open window in the sun, something she had not seen while Rat's prisoner. Even something she had always taken for granted before the pirate attack now seemed a great luxury: the porcelain chamber pot.

She attacked her tangled mess of curls with Kade's hairbrush. Order was restored just as Michael knocked on the door.

"Are ya decent, miss?"

Kathleen held the front of her shirt together and let him in. "Did you find anything that might fit?" she asked. The boy was carrying an armful of clothes, which he dumped on the bed.

"Cap'n said Skinner was about yer size so I brung some of his stuff."

"Who is Skinner?"

"Chief gunner on the *Black Eagle,* we's real good friends. Skinner knows more stories than anybody alive, though right now he's too mad to tell any of 'em. There's also some female things from a chest down in the hold an' some sewin' stuff if ya wanna make changes. I got duties waitin' so I'll be goin' now."

Kathleen thanked him before he left. She tossed the needle and thread on Kade's desk. She had taken a few stitches to close small cuts on their horses at Emerald Hills and once had sewn a rip in the ear of her mother's favorite pig after it ran into a nail. Those jobs had been difficult enough; sewing clothes would be impossible.

Bundled among the clothes was a dress made of black velvet, yards of it that fell in a soft puddle on the floor as Kathleen held it against her. It was too large. She rubbed her hand across the material. It felt like Taran's nose. She remembered that after one of the pirates grabbed her, the rest had started chasing Taran, driving him into the sea in an effort to corner him.

What fools, she thought with a smile. She buried her face in the thick velvet. She rarely wore dresses at home and had never owned one this fancy. It was covered

74

with lace and ribbons, had ruffled sleeves and enough buttons to fluster a saint. She laid it aside, along with a frothy handful of petticoats.

Among the clothes remaining was a pair of breeches, the rear shiny from wear and the fabric an ugly shade of gray from repeated washing in salt water. Kathleen pulled them on and fastened the buttons in the front. They were loose and baggy, with wide legs that ended at her ankles. There was also a cotton shirt on the bed. It was almost as gray as the pants. She put it on and rolled up the sleeves.

The pants were causing her problems. They kept sliding down her hips, threatening to fall completely off. Tangled in the petticoats on the chair was a bit of faded red that Kathleen pulled free. It was a long scarf with tasseled ends. She hitched the breeches up and tied them securely with the scarf. Michael had also supplied a pair of boots. Since it was so warm, she decided to go barefoot.

She looked in the mirror over the washbowl and scarcely recognized herself. Her face was pale, the skin almost transparent. White scars traced a circle around her neck, a lingering reminder of the iron collar. Her hair was limp, her lips as faded as the scarf around her waist. Only the eyes were alive, sparkling and snapping with color.

"It is hard to believe I feel so good, considering how terrible I look. A little sun, a lot of food and a chance to escape will set me to rights again."

She rolled one sleeve up higher and jerked open the cabin door with her left hand. Pain shot through her chest, down her arm and up into her back. *Maybe Jake was right, maybe I should stay in bed.*

"Ye'll not be actin' like a weaklin' just because ye feel a wee bit of pain. Remember that ye 'ave O'Connor blood runnin' in ye," she told herself firmly in her father's Irish brogue, repeating what Jarrett O'Connor had said to her brother every time Niall was crushed against the stable wall by some feisty yearling he was trying to saddle. Niall would grumble beneath his breath, rub his bruised ribs and cast a despairing glance at Kathleen before approaching the horse again. Though Niall liked horses even less than they liked him, he never stopped trying.

Memories of home were as painful to Kathleen as the throbbing discomfort in her chest. She ignored both and walked briskly out of the cabin, passing beneath the hatch where she had made her aborted escape attempt. Kade's voice boomed out above her, giving orders and reprimanding mistakes.

She climbed the steps to the deck, stopping at the top until her eyes adjusted to the brightness. Then she stepped into the yellow warmth and looked around the *Black Eagle*. The billowing sails cast shadows across the deck as they cracked sharply against their confining ropes. The *Eagle* swayed in the embrace of the sea, cutting through the ocean beneath white clouds that moved across a sky so intense it was almost purple. Beyond the railing, past the foaming wake and beneath the silver wings of flying fish was the bluest water on the face of the earth. The swells were crested by a frothing of white foam that spilled like fine lace over the shining surface.

An awareness came over Kathleen that someone was standing nearby. She turned and squinted up at Kade.

"Is there some particular reason you came up here, such as another try at escaping? I will not have my crew endangering themselves to pull your skinny carcass out of the sea again, although this water is somewhat warmer than what you jumped into last time."

Kathleen had an urge to laugh. Kade looked so

fearsome, towering over her and twisting his face into a scowl that creased his forehead and made wrinkles around his eyes. Biting her lip to stop her smile, she scanned the horizon. It was empty.

"Since there seems to be nowhere to escape to at the moment, Captain Morgan, you need not worry. I am not a fool."

"Did Jake give you permission to come on deck?"

"He did not object to my wanting some fresh air and sun, Captain."

There was something disturbingly personal in the way he looked at her, his eyes lingering in some very private places. A memory moved along the outskirts of Kathleen's mind, disappearing before she could fully grasp the disturbing images.

Kade had sent Michael to the hold to find something for Kathleen to wear besides the things the boy had scavenged from Skinner. When the boy came up from the hold, he had been carrying a black dress. Kade had been thinking about what she would look like with it on. He had also been wondering what she would look like with it slipping off her in the flickering light of a single candle.

"Why are you not wearing the dress Michael brought up from the hold?"

"It was much too large, Captain. I would not be able to keep it on."

Kade's throat ached. He nodded curtly and swung sharply on his heel. He climbed the three steps to the stern, where the helm was located. After checking the compass mounted beside the wheel, he made an adjustment in the helmsman's steering. Kathleen was standing on the deck just below him. Her hair was blowing in the wind and her eyes, once again swirls of brilliant color, were taking in every detail of the ship. The *Eagle* heeled to starboard and Kade shouted instructions to the men in the rigging to adjust the sails accordingly.

Kathleen was glad Kade had left her alone. There was so much to see she did not want to be distracted. The ship was like a new world to her. The deck was different from the merchant vessels she had helped her father load horses onto for shipment to buyers. Those were vessels whose holds were designed to be filled with every type of merchandise imaginable. The *Black Eagle* made them look like fat old ladies waddling through thick grass on the way to church. This was a ship built for speed and beauty, as Kathleen had observed when she first saw the black hull and magnificent figurehead on the bow.

The *Eagle*'s lines were sleek and sensuous. The deck was almost completely flat, only rising slightly near the stern, where the duties involved in steering and navigating the ship were carried out. The helm consisted of the wheel used for steering, a boxed compass with an eagle emblazoned on the side, and a post mounted on the deck behind the wheel. The post was used during storms by the helmsman, who would lash himself to it to prevent being washed overboard.

Kathleen noted the beautiful carved railing she had jumped over to escape, and the taut ropes that secured the mast as they stretched down the side of the ship to where they were attached to the deadeyes, round pieces of wood with three holes near the center. The deadeyes were mounted just above the waterline on the hull. They maintained an even pressure on the ropes to keep the masts erect and steady. It was the deadeyes that Kathleen had heard creaking and groaning when she woke up.

The stern and bow each had an anchor tied against the railing. The double-hooked pieces of iron were as large as Kade. It would take a great deal of strength to drag them up from the sea, and Kathleen could not imagine that the *Eagle* had enough men on board. She looked around. The deck, rigging and yards were full of men, more than enough to handle the anchors. They were everywhere; adjusting lines, fixing torn sails, repairing pieces of the masts and rail, scrubbing the deck and idling away the time by putting endless numbers of intricate knots in various lengths of hemp rope.

She wandered about, ducking beneath the horizontal yards attached to the masts. Near the center of the ship was a small enclosure that housed four half-grown pigs, a goat with a bell tied around its neck, and two crates of chickens. There was a bale of hay secured beside the pen. Kathleen pulled out a handful to feed to the goat. It accepted the offering with dignity, extending its upper lip slightly to take the hay from her fingers.

The ship and the sea were beautiful, doing for Kathleen's mind what a breath of fresh air does for the lungs. It was so wonderful to be alive, to feel the breeze and taste the glory of being free. But that thought destroyed her happiness, for she was not free.

Involuntarily her eyes searched out the tall form of her master on the stern of the ship. He was leaning against the railing, rubbing the back of his neck while talking to Michael. The boy nodded and hurried below. Kade glanced at the sun, then threw his head back and shouted at the sky.

Kathleen was startled. What had possessed him? She looked up. On the top of the mainmast, a man appeared from behind a rail that appeared to be as fragile as a spiderweb. He descended a ladderlike set of ropes, eventually dropping onto the deck. Another sailor sprang lightly onto the swaying ladder and climbed upward, eventually disappearing behind the spiderweb rail.

"What a perfect place to sight other ships, ships that could take me home," Kathleen told the goat. "When I am able, that is where I will be spending my time."

She walked to the bow, burning her feet on the hot deck. As she moved into the shadow of a sail, she tripped over a coil of rope and was forced to grab the foremast to keep from falling. Kathleen refused to give in to her body's weakened condition. She concentrated on being more careful. It did not help. Before she had gone another twenty feet, she had bumped into a keg, stubbed her toe on a hatch covering and hit her head on a piece of lumber a man was carrying.

"Captain Morgan does not have to worry about me jumping overboard; at the rate I am going I would bruise myself to death before I reached the railing."

Kathleen noticed that most of the crew were staring at her. Several purposely spat over the side of the rail before turning away; others curled their lips into sneers as they scowled at her. Michael was feeding the pigs. Kathleen went to see if he knew why everyone was glaring at her.

"You should ask the Cap'n, miss," he said, pausing to glance at Kade on the stern.

"I am asking you, not Captain Morgan."

Michael nervously cracked his knuckles. "It's 'cause yer a girl. Men don't hold with havin' a female aboard, supposed to be bad luck."

Kathleen rolled her eyes to heaven and shook her head. She was thinking about the ignorance of believing in superstitions until she remembered her own belief in the little people of Ireland and the marsh fairies. And then there was Jake's loch monster to consider.

She sat on the bale of hay and sighed. "They are right, Michael, being here is about the worst luck I have

80

ever had."

Michael grinned, displaying the lack of several teeth. He stopped cracking his knuckles, grabbed Kathleen by the arm and dragged her behind him. Dodging between masts, ropes and men, he headed for a pile of folded sails stacked in front of the helm. There was an old man sitting there, his knobby fingers picking apart a tattered rope and piling the debris beside him.

"What is he doing?"

"Pickin' oakum, it's for stuffin' 'tween loose boards. That's Skinner. He don't care what kinda luck ya are long as yer willin' to listen to his stories. Skinner, this here's . . ." Michael stopped.

"Kathleen O'Connor," she supplied for him.

"She's that girl what fainted when Jake brung her on board back in Morocco."

Skinner's hair had once been black; now it was sprinkled liberally with gray and seemed to be sticking out in all directions at once. Though most of his face was as brown as tree bark from long exposure to the sun, his chin and neck were newly burned. It looked as though he had recently shaved off a beard worn many years. Kathleen thanked him for allowing her to borrow some of his clothes.

He cackled gleefully when she turned around to show her outfit to him. He turned the oakum picking over to Michael so he could take Kathleen on a tour of the *Black Eagle*. Not strong enough to go up and down the numerous ladders used to descend to the hold, she insisted on staying on deck. Skinner explained to her what the sailors were doing as they went about their various tasks and answered every question she asked without hesitation.

When he went to check the progress of some work being done in the powder magazine, Kathleen climbed into one of the four longboats tied along the rail. It

81

contained items necessary for survival in case of an emergency: a keg of water, a barrel of hard crackers and salted fish, a set of oars and a compass. With the aid of a knife and a bit of luck, one person could maneuver the longboat over the side of the *Eagle* and down to the sea.

When her wanderings led her back to the bow of the ship, she leaned back on the bowsprit and peered up at the lookout perched on the mainmast. It would be a great day when she could climb the rigging to stand there among the clouds, because on that day she would be strong enough to escape.

Michael joined her, shrugging into the wind and salt spray. "Cap'n wants ya immediately, Miss Kathleen. He's down in his cabin."

"Thank you, Michael."

As she approached the door to Kade's cabin, Kathleen felt the effects of her strenuous morning. Her shoulders and neck were stiff, and her legs felt like she had ridden for hours at a hard gallop. Her entire body was twisting into one massive cramp. She knocked on the door, heard Kade's command to enter and stepped confidently into the cabin. Her eyes went directly to her master, drawn as though to a magnet.

He was seated with his back to his desk, his legs stretched out into the center of the room. There was something familiar about his pose, something that made her palms sweat. Jake sat at the table, a disapproving frown on his face. Kathleen knew she was in trouble.

"You sent for me, Captain?" she asked, trying not to notice the way Kade's gaze lingered on her breasts. His eyes had the effect of a physical touch, and a tingling sensation spread across her nipples. Much to her horror, they stiffened and pushed boldly against the thin fabric of her shirt. The hazy memory that had eluded her earlier moved across the edge of her mind again, and her palms grew wetter. She wiped them on the sides of her pants.

Kade had a difficult time restraining himself when confronted with Kathleen's arousal. She was extremely desirable, standing so defiantly in the open door with her raven hair tossed into such attractive disarray. Her face was painted delicately with color from the morning's sun, and those incredible eyes sparkled like the sea itself. The baggy clothes she wore made her look so vulnerable that his throat started to ache.

"I told ye to stay in bed," Jake said to Kathleen, "then find out ye were on deck all morning. Ye need yer rest, lass."

"I was unconscious for a week, you cannot get more rest than that. It is exercise that I need now so I will be capable of performing whatever task Captain Morgan assigns to me, no matter how disgusting it might be."

Kade almost laughed. The little minx had deliberately disobeyed Jake's orders then effectively turned the blame on him. He raked a hand through his hair.

"You can leave us now, Jake."

The Scotsman grunted something beneath his breath as he closed the door behind him. Kade winked at Kathleen and allowed his grin to surface.

She was taken totally by surprise. His smiles had always been sarcastic before. This was something completely different. His handsome face became devastating, his captivating charm became deadly.

Kathleen could not help but notice the way his hair had been tossed by the wind, the rough shadow of his beard. She saw how tight his pants were and the way they bulged in the front. The elusive memory she had been chasing all morning suddenly plunged into the center of her mind and stayed there, causing more than just her palms to sweat. Could it be real, could that possibly have happened? The black eyes were watching her, sparkling with amusement at her assessment of his body. She knew then her memory was real.

"You effectively made it look like my fault that you disobeyed Jake," Kade said. "I am impressed."

"Thank you," she managed to say in a voice so weak it scarcely carried over the sound of the ocean. Unable to stand any longer, she collapsed into the leather chair.

"Jake worked hard to keep you alive and his orders are intended to keep you that way. Though it is obvious you are not as weak as he thought, you are also far from being completely well."

"I am fine!"

"Then why did you spend the entire morning stumbling around the deck, wincing every time you drew breath and holding onto everything you could for support?"

Kathleen grimaced. He was right. He was always right. "Can we compromise?" she asked, hoping to keep at least a small piece of her freedom.

He considered for a moment, then nodded. "The remainder of today will be spent in bed. Starting tomorrow you will spend mornings in the cabin; after lunch you will have deck privileges until dinner and again be confined to quarters for the night. Jake will continue to monitor your progress. If you find his doctoring excessive, talk to me."

It was better than what Kathleen had expected, and she smiled her acceptance of his terms. "Do you have a cabin for me, Captain?"

"You will sleep here."

Without thinking, she asked, "With you?" and instantly wanted to die.

"This is my cabin, Kate. Where else would I sleep?"

Panic chilled her, then exploded in flames as she remembered the feel of Kade's arms around her, the power of his body as it possessed her. She tried to pretend that the matter was of no consequence, changing the subject back to their discussion of her recovery.

"I would like to take a walk after dinner, would that be possible?"

"Do you promise not to spend every afternoon searching through my longboats to see if they are properly equipped for an escape?"

Kathleen felt like a little girl caught doing something naughty. "How did you—yes, I promise." Obviously she could not hide anything from this man; he saw through her like clear water. Escaping was going to be difficult.

"Then the walks are approved based on your condition each day. Anything else?"

"I would like to learn something about sailing."

"An excellent idea! That way when your strength returns there will be no need to worry about your sinking one of my longboats before I can apprehend you." The light in Kade's eyes almost danced with amusement. He dismissed her with a devilish wink, spun his chair around and began making entries in the ship's log.

Kathleen knew she should be angry with his assumption he would catch her, and that he knew what she had been doing that morning. Instead she laughed.

Kade glanced over his shoulder and gave her one of those devastating smiles. Her laughter became a bit breathless. He turned back to his work, dipping his goose-quill pen in the bottle of ink secured in a slot near the back of the desk. Kathleen noticed a pile of parchment rolls stuck behind the ink bottle. They were similar to the charts her father used to mark all the places in Europe and England where the horses they trained had been sold. If they were maps, and if she could learn where the *Black Eagle* was headed, she could figure out how far it was to Ireland and if it was possible to get there in a longboat.

"Captain Morgan, where are we headed? You told me before I became ill and I cannot remember."

"Mistral, and it is not on these charts."

"What charts are you talking about?" she asked innocently, trying to ignore how irritating he could be.

"The charts you are trying not to notice." He shuffled them with one hand. "These are for the coast of Europe. I will have Jake bring you the ones of the West Indies he has in his cabin, and after dinner tonight I will give you a lesson in navigation."

It was one thing to have Kade know her escape plans and quite another to have him help her with them. She started to tell him what he could do with his lesson. It is a long way from the West Indies to Ireland, she told herself. Pride will not be getting me there. I will take his help, and his boat, then use both to escape from beneath his nose!

Tired of pushing the hair off her face, Kathleen went in search of the brush. She pulled a piece of string from a hook beside the mirror to use in braiding her hair.

"It is my bet that you will like Mistral, Kate. You might forget about Ireland entirely."

Kathleen almost threw the brush at him. "Nothing could *ever* make me forget about Ireland! It is the most beautiful place on earth, like a green jewel in the midst of an emerald sea."

"A jewel no one wants except the Irish and the English, though why the British should want it I cannot figure."

Kade tossed the log on top the jumble of charts. He made a mental note to have Michael set up the tub so

Kathleen could bathe that night. The memory of her standing before him covered in bubbles and pride almost made him forget his decision to wait until she was completely recovered before making her his mistress.

"What does a pirate like you know of politics?" She curled up in the chair and began to braid her hair. "Ireland is a rich source of income for the English and it gives them the opportunity to dominate people, something they love more than money."

Kade frowned. "Pirate? Is that what you think I am? Certainly I do not fit the description you gave of the men that captured you."

He was right. Kade did not resemble the hideous creatures who had destroyed her home, but neither did he look like the reputable sea captains she had met in the harbors of Shannon and Dublin. They usually commanded lumbering cargo vessels and had salt-encrusted whiskers and wrinkled faces. Kade reminded Kathleen of the stories she had heard about pirates who used to raid Spanish ships sailing from the New World with cargoes of gold and silver. Those pirates had been men of courage and daring who lived life by their own rules. She could envision Kade swinging on board an enemy vessel, brandishing his bloody sword and slicing his way through heaps of dying sailors.

"While it is true you are not like the low-life scum who kidnapped me, Captain Morgan, you must be involved in some thievery. The *Black Eagle* alone is enough to convict you of pirating. She was obviously built for speed, and her black hull would make her almost invisible at night, except for the sails. There are probably replacements in the hold, either black or dark gray silk."

Kade was surprised. "Very good, kitten. How did you know they were silk?"

"Common sense. Canvas makes a racket when set, silk sounds like the wind itself. What do you steal?"

He stretched, causing his shirt to pull tightly across his shoulders. "Nothing anymore, though I do still carry the black sails. I made my fortune relieving prominent merchants of their best goods, then retired. Those men are now my competitors."

"Competitors?"

"Shipping. I have a fleet of seven including the *Eagle*. The other ships carry regular cargo. They were built wide in the beam and ride low in the water. The *Eagle* handles specialty items, rush shipments and perishable items. Aside from Morgan Shipping, I also raise sugarcane on Mistral."

"You, a farmer?"

"A plantation owner, not a farmer." There was a trace of arrogance in his manner.

"Pray tell me what the difference might be 'tween the two?" Kathleen snapped so quickly she sounded more Irish than usual. Jarrett O'Connor had insisted that his children speak the King's English with as little brogue as possible, since most of Emerald Hills' business came from that country. Kathleen and Niall had obediently suppressed almost everything Irish from their speech except the accent itself, yet when Kathleen was angry or frustrated she always sounded exactly like her father.

Kade raised an eyebrow, surprised by the sudden spurt of back-country Irish. He grinned and crossed his arms over his chest.

"Plantation owners hire farmers to take care of trivial details."

Every chore on Emerald Hills, no matter how trivial, had fascinated Kathleen. It would have been impossible for her to allow someone else to take care of the horses, to train them and sell them. Maybe growing sugar was so boring no one wanted to know what was happening.

"How do you know your foreman is doing his job properly and that he is not stealing from you?" she asked. "Does someone run Morgan Shipping for you or do you handle everything?"

Kade did not want to think about sugarcane, shipping or anything else that did not involve touching Kathleen. He stood up and walked over to her, cupping her chin and tilting her head back so he could see her eyes. She turned away and he grasped her face firmly, his fingers crushing the soft flesh.

"Never pull away from me, Kate."

The tone of his voice demanded obedience. Kathleen stopped struggling. Kade relaxed his grip and lightly traced the line of her jaw, noticing with displeasure the red marks he had caused. He would have to be more gentle; she bruised easily.

Ripples of pleasure spread through Kathleen at the tender touch of Kade's hand. She hated herself for reacting to him but did not want to stop the warm stroke of his hand or the caressing movement of his fingers. That all changed when she saw his expression. It was cold and uncaring. While her body responded to his caress with desire, he felt nothing. Toying with her was only a way to pass the time.

"You do not care, do you?" she asked, jerking away in direct defiance of his orders. "You do not care for anything or anyone. It must be terrible not to care, not to love. You are not living life, you are tolerating it. I pity you, Captain Morgan."

Kade jerked her to her feet, the brush she held falling unnoticed to the floor. He unraveled her braid and plunged his fingers into the silk of her hair, forcing her head back. He brought his mouth down on hers in a fierce, demanding kiss.

Kathleen fought his embrace and he pressed her closer, molding the softness of her body against his hard strength. He moved his lips to her neck and breasts. She drew a desperate, ragged breath as he tore open her shirt and claimed a throbbing nipple as his. She stopped fighting him then, clutching his hair to pull him closer. The bruising assault eased. He touched her lips in a gentle kiss. Her fingers glided over his face and shoulders, delighting in the strong curve of his jaw and the sensuous ripple of muscles beneath the fine cloth of his shirt.

Not even when he had thrown her on the bed and destroyed her virginity had Kathleen felt as totally, completely helpless as she felt now. For the first time in her life, Kathleen knew the supreme pleasure of being a woman. And for the first time she knew a woman's ultimate thrill, to be held so possessively by such a powerful man.

Kade seared her flesh with burning kisses, igniting her soul and smothering her in the heated reality of their future. He would make her his mistress, a partner to his illicit desires, desires she shared. She would exchange her moral beliefs and religious convictions for the ecstasy of being held by this man, of being kissed by him and having him make love to her. And though it was wrong, terribly, horribly wrong, Kathleen could no more stop what was happening than she could prevent the sun from rising tomorrow.

There was no way to imagine herself out of this situation, no way to pretend it was all a dream. This was truth, this was reality. It was painful, crippling. This man had taken her strength and reduced it to need, he had taken her beliefs and changed them to desires, he had taken her will and replaced it with dependence. Kathleen had nothing left except pride. And for the first time in her life that was not enough.

Without warning Kade released her. Unable to stand, she wilted into the chair behind her and began a slow descent from the towering passion that had engulfed her.

"I have no need to care," he said in a rough voice. "I take what I want and I want you. When you are well, you will be mine."

"No, never," Kathleen managed to say, desperate to deny what they both knew.

He cupped her chin and tilted her head back. She suffered the thrill of his touch without moving. "You have learned your first lesson well, kitten."

He slowly removed his hand. The cabin door opened and closed. She was alone. Her skin tingled where his fingers had rested, and tears pooled in her eyes. It was some time before they disappeared, unshed and unnoticed, trivial things to someone whose world had just been shattered.

Chapter 7

The air in the room was heavy, thick with the smell of old sweat and perfume. Cobwebs clung to the ceiling, and dust clung to the cobwebs. Quint Cathcart stood at his office window staring toward the harbor. He could not see the ocean, nor smell the fresh salt air. He was glad. Quint did not like the sea.

He ran a pampered hand over his beard. On the street below him people moved in uneven rhythms, making the city appear to be in a state of confusion. Quint longed for the quiet splendor of his house outside town, the thick walls draped with silk hangings and the floors piled high with cushions. It was a grand house, opening onto a large park that his slaves kept well watered against the dry heat of the African sun.

Quint liked nice things, liked the best of everything. He also liked horses. The grace of their muscles as they moved, the line of their bodies as they awaited his next command. He liked the Arabians best with their dish-shaped noses and fluid speed. He had a stable of Arabian broodmares, the best in Africa. What he needed now was a stallion worthy of his beauties. A stallion that could sire magnificent foals, the best anywhere.

His desire for that perfect stallion was the reason Quint was waiting for Rat Anders. He leaned out the window, looked around and frowned. Anders was nowhere to be seen. Quint pulled a scented handkerchief from his pocket and waved it under his nose to disguise the fetid stench in the room, a stench caused by the type of customers Lil's Place attracted. Lil's was a filthy place to do business, one far beneath Quint's station in life. Still, it served its purpose.

Because his office was on the top floor of a low-class brothel, the men who visited him on business thought him a stupid, unimportant man. They were careless in their talk, careless and vain. Quint listened to their talk, listened to their conceit. Then he took them for everything he could, stripping away their shiny veneer of wealth and adding it to his own.

He began to pace the room with quick, jerky steps while rubbing his hands together. He stopped beside his desk and picked up the letter lying there. His blood ran hot just as it had done when he received it that morning.

During a trip to Ireland earlier that year, Quint had found the stallion of his dreams, the most magnificent beast imaginable: Taran. The stallion was the pride of Emerald Hills, an extremely reputable breeding farm. Taran was at least eighteen hands tall, with a wide forehead and a chest like a barrel. His legs were almost dainty compared to the rest of his body, yet strong and tireless. Quint had experienced an incomparable thrill when he first saw Taran. He had known immediately that he had to have that stallion.

Although he had offered Jarrett O'Connor an incredible amount of money for Taran, the old man had repeatedly refused to sell the stallion. Frustrated and angry, Quint had returned to Africa and immediately hired corsair pirates to attack Emerald Hills and take the horse. When the stallion had eluded the pirates, they had captured Kathleen O'Connor for use as a hostage to be exchanged for the stallion. That had been four months ago.

Quint traced the embossed crest on the expensive stationery and smiled as he licked his lips. There was a knock on the office door. He carefully laid the letter back on his desk and gave permission for entrance. Rat Anders crept into the room.

"Anders!" Quint put a surprised expression on his face. "What can I do for you?"

Confusion clouded Rat's face. "You sent for me, Mr. Cathcart."

"I sent for you? Oh yes, I remember now." Quint smiled. He liked to keep people unbalanced. "It has been such a busy day that I had forgotten. I wanted to talk to you about the O'Connor girl."

"I was gonna come today and tell you about her, Mr. Cathcart." Rat's eyes darted around, not resting on anything and never looking directly at Quint.

"Tell me what, Anders?"

"The girl took sick, real bad. I did everything I could but she died last night."

"Died? You let her die?" Impotent rage nearly choked Quint. He poured some brandy into a snifter and tossed it down in a single swallow.

"I didn't let her, Mr. Cathcart, she just did. She weren't real strong, that's why I kept askin' for more money to feed her good."

"You're lying, I know you are! After three months it is hard to believe she would die now. You killed her, admit it!"

"I ain't lyin', Mr. Cathcart. She was sick, I swear!"

Normally Rat was dressed in sagging breeches and a fouled shirt. Today he wore new boots, his clothes were clean and almost fashionable, his belt had a gold buckle. There was only one explanation for Rat's wealth. The brandy began to spread its soothing warmth through Quint, and he refilled his glass.

"You sold her," he said.

"I didn't! She died like I said."

"How much did you get, Anders? It must have been a lot, just look at your boots and that belt. Maybe Ahmad can convince you to tell me the truth." Quint reached behind him and pulled on a bell rope. The girl had to be found, and quickly.

Rat's eyes were wide with terror at the mention of the Moslem giant who on previous occasions had effectively convinced Rat to do anything Quint wanted. The office door opened, and the hulking figure of Ahmad appeared.

"Fifty pounds," Rat mumbled. "I got fifty pounds for her." His face flushed as his body visibly shrank away from Ahmad.

Quint swirled the brandy in his glass. "Who bought her and when?"

"It was a month ago. I don't know who he was, never saw him before."

"Was he from here, from Tangier?"

"No, he had the girl taken to a ship."

"Describe him."

"Big man, black hair and eyes. Real mean lookin', carried pistols and had a fancy sword that he kept fingering. He had his own ship in the harbor where an old Scotsman that was with him took the girl."

Quint's stomach knotted up. "Did he pay in gold?"

"How did you know?"

"Because the man you described is Kade Morgan and he always pays in gold." Quint gritted his teeth. It was bad enough that Kathleen had been sold. That she had been purchased by Kade Morgan, whom Quint hated with such a passion it almost made him ill, was a nightmare.

He finished his drink and set his snifter on the

95

cabinet. He wiped his mouth with the back of his hand, wiped his hand with his handkerchief and went behind his desk.

"Why did you sell her, Anders?"

"I couldn't stand it no more, her starin' at me with those eyes, like a demon darin' me to hit her." Rat was crying now, the tears mingling with the sweat on his face.

"Do you see this, Anders?" Quint picked up the letter. "This arrived today from Ireland. They have agreed to exchange the stallion for the girl, only I no longer have her."

Rat watched the paper as it moved ever so slightly in Quint's fingers. The rolls of fat under his chin began to quiver. "I'll go get her, Mr. Cathcart, I'll bring her back."

"Do you think I would trust you again? I will go after her myself."

He nodded to Ahmad, who stepped into the hall and closed the door behind him. Quint reached into the top drawer of his desk, his hand closing over something small and hard. He liked the feel of its ivory grip and slippery steel.

"You betrayed me, Anders, betrayed my trust in you. I cannot allow that."

Quint lifted the pistol and leveled it across the desk at Rat's chest. The drooling eyes widened, the sweating face blanched, the pudgy hands extended in protection of the body. It was too late. A red stain appeared on the front of his shirt. It spread across the left side of his chest, ran across his stomach and dripped onto the floor. Rat's fingers spread open, then went limp as his body collapsed.

The gun was warm; it felt good clutched in Quint's fingers. He thought about his new mistress, Sarita Ridley, thought of her lush body and harlot ways. She

96

had once been involved with Morgan and claimed that he loved her. That was why Quint wanted her, she was something Morgan wanted. He would take Sarita with him, flaunt her in front of Morgan while stealing the Irish girl from beneath the bastard's nose.

He put the pistol back in the drawer and walked around the desk, past the bleeding body. He opened the door and motioned to Ahmad.

"After you clean up this mess, send for Ivan Flesher, captain of the vessel *Christabel* anchored in the harbor. I want to book passage with him to the West Indies. If anyone asks about Anders, it seems he beat up one of the girls downstairs then came up here and attacked me. I'm going down now to make sure one of Lil's whores has some bruises to support my story."

Quint smiled as he walked past the silent Ahmad. He would enjoy this. The sound of a female screaming always relaxed him when he was excited. And Quint Cathcart was very excited.

Jarrett O'Connor walked up to the blackened ruin that had once been his home and laid a weathered hand on the wet limestone. The roof was completely gone; the back and side walls had caved inward. Only the front wall remained, a reminder of what had once been a place of happiness.

Everything was gone now; even the barn that had once stabled the finest horses in Ireland lay in a crumbled heap that covered the charred bones of the mares who died in the fire. Even the rich green of the land had turned to a gray waste that gave insult to the name Emerald Hills. It was so hard to believe it was over, his dream destroyed. There was nothing left except the deed to the land.

The rain stopped, and from behind the gray clouds a

golden stream of sunshine drifted to earth, its slanting rays falling on Jarrett. Suddenly the hills were green again, sparkling beneath the diamond caress of the rain. Jarrett lifted his head. All was not lost; the land was still there.

He straightened his shoulders and stepped down from the stoop of the ruined house. There he hesitated, looking at the stain of blood on that stoop, Mary's blood. It had been a risk to raise horses in County Kerry, a risk Jarrett had taken once Mary gave him her love and support. As newlyweds they came to Emerald Hills on the night the *daoine sidhe,* the fairy people, danced there in the fairy ring.

Jarrett had built his barn on that enchanted place, hoping the magic would seep into the bellies of his breeding mares. Mary had given birth to Niall, and then four years later Kathleen had been born. When Kathleen was twelve, Jarrett realized the fairy magic that had not appeared in the Emerald Hills foals had taken root in his daughter.

Mary had told Kathleen a story about the *each uisce,* the legendary water stallion that answered to the call of none save the fairy folk. Kathleen had immediately gone down to the sea and stood in the foaming surf, raising her hands to call forth the magical beast. Jarrett had laughed at his daughter until the sea around her began to churn as though it were angry. From that frightening fury had galloped a great gray stallion, the *each uisce.* Kathleen had thrown herself on the beast's back. The stallion had reared, screaming and slashing the air with mighty hooves. When it settled back onto the beach, the stallion had been tame, responding to Kathleen's commands and answering to the name of Taran.

Black-headed gulls screamed overhead as Jarrett walked across the front lawn to the corral. He kicked at the black dirt crusted with Niall's blood and un-willingly glanced across the wide green sea. On the horizon were islands that appeared to be little more than shadows against the sky. He lifted his fist and waved it at those shadows.

"I'll not be lettin' ye destroy me dream! Aye, as long as there's breath in me lungs, I'll wait. Ye'll come home, I know ye will."

"Do not wave your fists at the empty sea, Father, I stand behind you."

Jarrett whirled around, and a smile spread across his face. "Niall! I knew ye'd come home!" Tears filled his eyes as he clasped his son's arm. A nightingale trilled and Jarrett raised his head to listen to it.

"That be the *rosin-ceol,* singin' just as it did when first I came to live 'ere alongside the fairy circle. We'll rebuild, Niall me lad, and when I'm gone Emerald Hills will belong to ye." The sun sank into the sea in a quiet blush of pale rose color; then the rain clouds closed in again.

Niall turned to look out over the ocean to the darkening horizon. "I don't want it, Father. I never wanted it, and that you would know if you had ever listened to anyone except yourself. It's time for me to live my own life, time for me to start breeding sons, not horses."

Jarrett stood up as straight as his bandy legs could make him and glowered at his son. "Horses be yer life like they be mine!"

"Nay, Father. I never wanted to raise horses, that was your dream. I am a fisherman, like Mother's folk before me. My life's out on those islands now with my wife."

"This be yer 'ome, son, yers and Alice's."

"There is no home here, only a lonely grave and an emptiness that cannot be filled."

"The land still be 'ere, son, the land is ours, 'twill always be 'ere. We'll rebuild the house, rebuild the barn. I can't be lettin' me dream of Emerald Hills die like Mary, I won't lose it like me Katie is lost."

Niall put his arm around his father. "We have no money, Father, no way to buy mares, no way to find a stallion to sire foals."

"The *each uisce* still comes. He made our foals great before, 'e will do it again."

"Nay, Father. Taran comes looking for Kathleen, not for his lost mares."

"The legend says the *each uisce* will come while 'is 'uman master lives."

"Aye, that it does," Niall said, "and though Kathleen is my sister I wish her dead, for while she is a captive of those heathens it is not living she does, only existing."

Across the darkness of the sea a light appeared, a flickering welcome to those not yet home. Niall watched it for a moment, then withdrew his arm from around his father and started toward the beach.

"Yer goin'?" Jarrett asked.

"Aye, Father, 'tis late and someone waits for me. Come with me, you should not be sleeping here."

Jarrett glanced back at the ruined house, at the stain on the stoop. It had been four months since Mary's blood was spilled, four months since Kathleen had disappeared into the emptiness of the sea with the murdering pirates, and nary a word had been received from the thieves asking ransom. The *rosin-ceol* broke the silence with its sad and melancholy song, echoing the loneliness in Jarrett O'Connor's heart.

Chapter 8

Kathleen was caught in a terrible dilemma. Kade had promised to wait until she regained her health before making her his mistress. To delay that fate, she needed to remain ill. To escape, she had to get well.

She longed to be alone to be able to think, to sort out the feelings Kade aroused in her, to come to terms with the fact she had made love to her handsome, arrogant master. Never before had Kathleen so desperately needed the isolation of the gray mists, the silence of the moist air and the touch of the rain on her face. She was tired of the constant press of people on board the *Black Eagle*. She was never alone, there was always someone nearby. And usually that person was the tall, powerful captain of the *Black Eagle*.

After dinner each night, Kade schooled her in the basics of navigation. He joined her on her nightly walks, pointing out stars and constellations. Her afternoons on deck were crowded with lessons on sailing as he sought to insure that she learned everything necessary to accomplish her goal of escaping him.

To her surprise, Kathleen enjoyed the lessons. She had never considered herself undereducated, yet there was so much she did not know. She looked forward to the time every night when she and Kade leaned over the table in his cabin, plotting distances and directions on

101

the bundles of maps and charts strewn over everything except the bed.

Forced to spend mornings in the cabin, Kathleen took advantage of Kade's bookcase. The volumes of poetry appealed to the whimsical part of her nature, which she kept hidden from the world. She wondered why a man like Kade kept such books, but soon forgot the question in the verse of Robert Burns.

On the afternoons when Kade was too busy to attend her, Kathleen sat with Skinner beneath the shade of the sails and listened to stories from the old man's vast repertoire. His tales of killer storms, deadly calms and giant waves gave her a delicious fright, as did the accounts of hideous monsters that lurked in the depths of the sea waiting for a chance to attack becalmed ships.

Kathleen loved sitting on the *Black Eagle*'s bowsprit, riding it as she had once ridden Taran and taking great delight in the pods of dolphin that sported beneath the *Black Eagle*'s masthead. Once, while watching a spotted dolphin and her tiny gray calf swimming off the starboard bow, she leaned over so far she almost fell. Kade grabbed her by the seat of her baggy breeches and hauled her back onto the desk. Though he gave her a stern lecture about being so careless, his eyes sparkled with what Kathleen thought looked suspiciously like laughter.

Jake taught her the names of the seabirds and how to sight schools of fish feeding at the surface. Once he pointed out a shark, its stiff dorsal fin cutting through the water fifty yards off the port beam of the *Eagle*. Kathleen shivered with delight as she watched the sensuous movements of the beast, its sleek body a dark shadow beneath the waves.

Even though she thought the sea a placid, unexciting creature, she had fallen in love with it, thrilling at the touch of its salty breeze and its wonderful smell. She loved the smooth swells and cresting waves, loved the feel of it beneath the ship.

One morning the sea changed its placid image for another of its many faces when a squall unexpectedly struck the ship. Confined in the cabin, Kathleen heard the bullet-hard rain striking against the deck above her. She was thrown against the cabin wall as the *Eagle* heeled over beneath the onslaught of the storm. The ship plowed through the sea with her starboard side almost completely under the surface; then she valiantly righted herself.

Unable to stay inside while all the excitement was outside, Kathleen ran out of the cabin the moment the *Eagle* regained her poise. By the time she reached the deck, the squall was already moving away from the ship, a dark shadow against the brilliant blue sky. The air smelled even fresher and cleaner, the sea was even bluer. The wet sails filled anew with wind and drove the *Eagle* south at such a speed it was almost as exciting as the storm.

Kade saw Kathleen run out onto the deck, hair tossed by the wind and face glowing with excitement. Though she had disobeyed his orders to remain in the cabin, he pretended not to notice her as she explored the deck, touching the wet ropes and railing as though a miracle had been performed.

So the days passed. From dawn until well after sunset Kathleen soaked up rest and strength, sun and knowledge, loving every moment of her days on the *Black Eagle.* It was only the nights she did not love, and those she dreaded with such a passion it almost made her ill again.

When Kathleen had first come on board the *Eagle,* she had thought the bed in the captain's cabin the largest she had ever seen. Now, forced to share that massive sleeping couch with Kade, its true size was revealed as she realized how incredibly small the bed was. No matter how far away from her master she lay, she could feel his body heat, smell his clean skin and hear his steady breathing.

Because of the horror of her ordeal with the pirates and Rat Anders, Kathleen was plagued by nightmares. Once when the dream became more terrifying than usual, she woke to find herself curled tightly against Kade, her hands clutching him desperately as she sought rescue from her mind's terror. His arms were around her, his lips against her forehead as he tried to soothe her fears. She immediately jerked away from him to huddle against the far side of the bed, pushing so close to the wall the texture of the wood could be felt through her nightshirt. Soon afterwards Kade rose from bed, dressed and left the cabin. Kathleen did not sleep any more that night, and all the next day she fought against the memory of Kade's flesh touching hers, his lips pressed into her hair, his breath warm on her face. It was an extremely long day.

One afternoon the sails on the *Black Eagle* were reefed, and some of the sailors climbed into the rigging to search for safe passage among the coral reefs the ship was moving through. Kathleen scrambled up from her seat amidships and went in search of Jake.

"Are we there, is this Mistral?" she asked as a small piece of land rose from the sea less than a mile ahead of the ship.

"Nay, lass. This spit of sand ain't big enough to even call an island, much less compare with Mistral."

He was too busy giving orders and hustling around the deck to talk, so Kathleen went to the animal enclosure. There were only the goat and two pigs left now; the other pigs and all the chickens had been slaughtered for fresh meat.

"What do *you* think is happening?" Kathleen asked the bearded goat, who responded by trying to eat the sleeve of her shirt. She pulled the gray cloth free and went to the starboard rail, peering down over the side of the ship. The *Eagle* appeared to be floating on air. The water had changed from blue to completely clear.

"Cap'n wants ya, Miss Kathleen!" Michael shouted to her from his position halfway up the rope ladder, called a ratline, that stretched to the crow's nest. The boy pointed at the stern of the *Eagle* where Kade was manning the helm. Kathleen cast a final look at the land they were approaching before joining her master.

"You sent for me?" she asked.

"Aye, Katie. I want you to go to the cabin and stay there until I come for you."

Jake was standing at the bow. He shouted something to Kade, who responded by giving orders to lower the stern anchor. He let go of the wheel with one hand, grabbed Kathleen's shoulder and pulled her against him in time to keep her from being trampled by the men who ran to carry out his commands. A chain rattled, squeaked. A man cursed as the anchor line was cut, freeing the heavy iron hook so it splashed into the sea where it grappled for purchase on the seabed.

"You are in the way, go below before you get hurt," Kade told Kathleen.

"I was not in the way until you ordered me to come back here." She pulled away from him. He grabbed her again as the ship lurched in the grasp of the anchor. If not for the support of his arm around her waist, she would have been thrown to the deck.

"Secure the bow!" Kade called out to Jake. The bow anchor was immediately released. Within minutes, the

Black Eagle was bobbing in the gentle backwash of the waves that curled onto the shimmering white sands of the island that rose from the midst of the reef, her twin anchors preventing the hull from tearing open on the sharp coral of the reef. Birds soared over the *Eagle,* and fish nibbled at the marine growth on the bottom of the hull.

Kathleen pulled free again. "Let me stay on deck and I will give you my word I will not try to escape," she said as Kade released the wheel.

"Your word?" He looked at her from beneath lowered brows. The sun sparkled on her hair, and her eyes kept straying to the spit of land off the *Eagle*'s port side.

"As a loyal daughter of Ireland," she said to reinforce her promise.

Kade considered the situation. There was absolutely nowhere she could escape to; plus, he had her word. She would probably enjoy being on solid land again.

"You may stay on deck, and I also give you permission to join the landing party tonight."

"I can go ashore?" she asked in disbelief.

"Yes, after dinner." His decision was rewarded with the most beautiful smile he had ever seen. Kade whistled softly to himself as he went below to check the condition of the cargo in the hold.

Kathleen spent the rest of the afternoon helping Michael with the fishing lines the boy had dropped over the stern of the *Eagle*. A wide variety of striped fish were caught, which the cook tossed into a boiling pot of stew in the galley.

The crew dove for oysters, cracking open the shells and eating the slimy contents raw. Kathleen tried one and got sick. It was definitely an acquired taste, she decided, and went back to her fishing lines until the sun sank over the horizon, staining the western sky the color of crushed rose petals. Kathleen waved to Michael as the boy joined the crewmen who were rowing to the beach. She went below, where Kade was working on his log.

"Crew ashore?" he asked.

"Yes, Captain. Michael said they would eat when we get back."

"How do you feel?"

"I can breathe without pain. My ribs are still very sore, though."

He nodded and put aside his log just as the cook delivered their dinner. After they ate, Kade had a glass of brandy. Then he ushered Kathleen on deck, told her to wait for him and went below to fetch a sweater for her. He pulled it down over her head, and her arms became tangled in the massive folds of wool. She almost suffocated before he was able to work the neck down over her head. She collapsed backwards onto the deck, her face red and eyes watering.

"I thought you had decided to do away with me," she gasped, looking up at him accusingly as she freed her hair from under the sweater. "Is this thing really necessary?"

When she tried to get up, the sweater twisted around her legs and tripped her. To keep from falling, she grabbed for Kade's waist. The laughter he had been battling to subdue vanished instantly as he caught the warm bundle of silky curls and scratchy wool in his arms.

"Yes," he said quickly and set her away from him. The lights hanging in the rigging cast a soft glow onto Kathleen's uplifted face. Kade could think of nothing except kissing those moist lips and making love to that luscious body.

Jake stuck his head over the railing. "Are ye comin'

or not? I can't be 'anging 'ere on the side of this ship all night!"

"She is tangled in this sweater. We will be right there."

Kathleen righted the sweater on her shoulders, shoved her arms into the sleeves and rolled them up to her wrists. "Ready, Captain," she said, then squealed as Kade lifted her into his arms. "What are you doing?"

"Carrying you to the boat below. If you fall in the water with that sweater on, you will be heavier than the anchor." He had climbed over the side of the ship and down the rope ladder and was standing in the longboat beside Jake before he finished talking.

"You certainly move fast," Kathleen said as Kade sat her in the boat's bow.

Jake pushed off from the *Eagle* and Kade rowed them to shore. Two of the crew walked into the surf to drag the boat onto the sand. Kade lifted Kathleen out, carried her above the reach of the waves and stood her on the sand. The wind stirred in her hair, the starlight reflected in the ocean of her eyes.

"Stay with Jake," he said and stalked off into the darkness.

Kathleen watched him leave, feeling suddenly alone and unsure of herself. "What do we do now, Jake?"

"Sit and wait."

Kathleen flopped into the sand and Jake squatted beside her. The only light on the island was the soft wash of moonlight on the white sand. The men huddled in small groups along the shore, talking in soft whispers. When Jake finished the tedious routine of cleaning the bowl of his pipe, refilling it from the bag he kept tucked inside his shirt, lighting the fresh tobacco and inhaling the first puff of pungent smoke, Kathleen leaned closer to him.

"What are we waiting for?"

Jake inhaled again. "Turtles."

Kade's boots scrunched in the sand behind Kathleen as he paced the length of the island. She pulled the neck of her sweater higher and tried not to think about how eerie the *Black Eagle* looked hovering offshore, her rigging lights reflecting on the dark sea. It felt strange to be on solid land, no swaying, no creaking of ropes or wood. She dug her hands into the sand, uncovering a few seashells. She laid them on the sleeve of her sweater and rolled them up in the cuff.

The men suddenly stopped talking, and Kade stopped pacing. Kathleen looked to where Jake was pointing with the stem of his pipe. Looming like a rock from the foaming waves was a huge creature. Its flippered feet ponderously pulled it higher on the beach, right past some of the crew. The shell on the creature's back was as wide as the table in Kade's cabin, and the beast was so big it had to weigh several hundred pounds.

"Turtle?" Kathleen asked.

"A small one, but she be the first."

Jake resumed smoking, and Kathleen got up to follow the turtle. When it reached a stretch of sand above the last mark left by the tide, it scooped out a hole in the sand with its front flippers. Then it turned and positioned its tail above the deep hole.

Kathleen peered into the hole, aided by the slanting light of the moon. After a few minutes, the turtle began laying eggs. First a few, then more until at least a hundred of the round, wet eggs covered the bottom of the hole.

Michael crouched down beside Kathleen and reached under the turtle, eggs falling onto his hand. He extracted four of the eggs, placed them gently in a sack he carried, then reached back for more.

"Are they good?" Kathleen asked.

"Almost as good as the turtles." Michael cleaned out the last of the eggs as the turtle turned and began to cover the empty hole.

"You eat them, too?"

"Sure. These are green turtles, they make great soup."

The turtle laboriously made her way down the beach to the ocean. Before it could reach the safety of the water, two men flipped it upside down and tied its flippers.

A lump formed in Kathleen's stomach, then moved into her throat. There were turtles everywhere now, dropping their eggs in the holes they dug. The men were taking the eggs, then the turtle as she tried to return to the sea.

The glow of Jake's pipe caught Kathleen's eye from near the southern tip of the island. He was standing beside a particularly large turtle that was just beginning to dig a hole. She went to join him. Kade was there also. He took an egg from Michael's sack, split it open and swallowed the contents.

"You eat them raw?" Kathleen asked, unable to keep the revulsion from her voice.

Kade handed her an egg. "Try it before you complain."

She took the warm, leathery egg, and using her fingernail, pierced the shell. She dumped the slippery contents into her mouth. It slid across her tongue, then down her throat. Almost like eating oysters except the egg tasted better. She tossed the shell into the darkness behind her and wiped her hands on her pants.

"Want some more?" Michael asked, pushing his sack at her.

Kathleen swallowed two more, then declined when the sack came her way again. The big turtle was dropping her eggs now, the blunt head swinging at the end of her thick neck, not in the least disturbed by the presence of the people beside her. Jake scooped the eggs into Michael's sack. Kathleen waited until there were only about a dozen left, then put her hand on Jake's.

"Leave the rest," she said.

Kade pulled her away from the hole. "These are worth a fortune in Nassau. The turtles will just lay more."

"How? You are taking them also." Kathleen noticed the turtle had almost finished filling in her hole, covering the remaining eggs before Jake could get them. At least a few had a chance for survival.

"Turtle meat is worth almost as much as the eggs. There are plenty of turtles in the world, Kathleen."

"There are now, but for how long? If you take all the eggs and females, someday you will come here and there will not be any turtles. Please, leave just a few in each nest."

It would be easy to say no, to send her back to the ship. Then Kade noticed Michael looking forlornly into his sack of eggs and saw that Jake was allowing the big turtle to slip quietly into the surf. Maybe Kathleen was right. Turtles used to come onto the beaches of Mistral. The islanders had gathered all the eggs and slaughtered the turtles for soup. Now it was rare to see a turtle anywhere near the island.

There was a pleading look on Kathleen's face as she placed her hand on his left arm. "Please," she said softly, *"please."*

She would never ask anything for herself, yet for these silent giants she was willing to beg. "Michael, tell the men to leave half the eggs in each nest and only take the medium-sized turtles," Kade ordered. "You decide which ones, Jake. Let the biggest and smallest go."

Kathleen's hand stayed on his arm for a moment longer, her luminous eyes holding his. "Thank you,

Captain," she whispered, the husky voice washing over Kade like warm honey. His throat began to ache. She left him and went to help Jake untie the first turtle that had come ashore that night.

One of the crew finished packing his sack of eggs in a box of sand, then tossed it into one of the longboats. Kade grabbed him by the collar. "Treat them like gold, Mr. Johnson, or you will not be sharing the profits of this run." He shoved Johnson away from him and stalked off to make sure the men were following his order about the eggs. There was a spring to his step and a certain place on his left arm tingled just a little.

At ten o'clock the next morning, Kade went to his cabin for a chart he had left on his desk. He kicked open the cabin door, expecting to see Kathleen in the leather chair reading. It was empty. The entire cabin was empty. Where did she get to this time, he wondered. We passed several islands right after dawn this morning; she must have slipped overboard.

He stormed up onto the deck, stopping dead at the top of the steps. There she was, leaning over the rail beside Michael. The boy was hauling a rope up the side of the *Eagle*. Kade felt like strangling both of them. He quietly went up beside them and looked down.

A bucket of water dangled at the end of the rope. Michael dragged it alongside the deck, and Kathleen untied the bucket. She spun around to set it behind her, bumping directly into Kade. She could not move. The black eyes drove spikes through her, nailing her to the deck.

"If you are well enough to carry that bucket, I have another task for you, Miss O'Connor, one we have discussed before." His voice cut through her like a hot knife through butter. She could feel her face turning

112

red and prayed for the deck to open and swallow her.

"I'm supposed to carry it for her, Cap'n," Michael said. "She's just settin' it down while I coil the rope." He took the bucket from Kathleen's clenched hand. She scarcely noticed it was gone.

"Jake said he could help me," she said defensively.

Kade kept his eyes locked on hers. "Help you what?"

"Wet the turtles."

Any other explanation in the world could not have surprised him more. "Wet the *what?*" He spoke so loud everyone on deck turned to stare. He grabbed Kathleen's arm and dragged her after Michael's retreating back. "Show me."

They went down the ladder leading to where the *Black Eagle*'s thirty cannons waited behind their closed gunports, down another ladder and into the passageway where the storage room with the turtles was located. The door was open and Kathleen pushed inside ahead of Kade. There were the turtles, positioned on their backs to keep them immobilized. Michael was carefully pouring the contents of his bucket on the head of one of the beasts.

"Is there some reason you are wasting the time of my cabin boy to pour water on a bunch of turtles?"

Kathleen touched the head of a turtle that had not been doused, pointing to the stream of mucus coming from its eyes. "See? Tears, or what I thought were tears. This morning I asked Jake to show me where they were. When I saw them crying . . ." She stopped suddenly and turned her head to the side.

"Wait outside," Kade told Michael. He took the boy's bucket and closed the door behind him. He laid his hand on Kathleen's arm. She did not look at him.

"You what?" he asked gently.

"I know what it is like to be locked up, to be alone and afraid." She swallowed before continuing. "Jake

113

said these were not tears, he said they did it to keep their eyes wet. But it looks like tears."

"And you did not want them to cry?"

She finally looked at him. The colors of her eyes were quiet, like silent pools of water. "I wanted them to go free."

Kade lifted the bucket and slowly poured water over the head of the turtle Kathleen had been stroking. It opened its mouth and pushed its head closer to the bucket. When the pail was empty, he opened the door and stepped outside, shutting it behind him. He handed the bucket to Michael.

"Get some more water and have Jake assign someone to help you. Wet them every four hours." Michael grinned before dashing up the ladder with the bucket banging against his ankle.

Kade went back into the storage room and leaned against the doorjamb. Kathleen was running her toes through the spilled water under the turtle's head.

"Do you ever wear shoes?" he asked.

She moved away from the water. "I have to help Michael."

"The boy does not need your help. Answer my question."

She ducked her head. "I am sorry that I disobeyed your order to stay in the cabin. I had to see them, I had to know that they were not hurt or . . ."

"Or chained to the wall?"

Kathleen did not answer. What could she say? Kade would never understand that she had wanted to let the turtles know they were not alone, that somebody cared.

"Come here." He pulled her into his arms. She stiffened against him, her hands on his chest to prevent closer contact. She stared straight ahead, eyes not fully focused and lips drawn into a tight line.

"You did not want them to be alone, right?"

She nodded.

"Turtles are not like people, Kate."

"But they are uncomfortable, their eyes need water. I cannot let them suffer." She glanced up at him, then back down. Kade saw a glimmer of tears in her eyes.

"I have ordered that the turtles be doused every four hours until they reach Nassau. This room is below the surface of the sea, they will not overheat."

"What about food?"

Kade looked at the shining hair that fell past her shoulders and over his hands, caressing his skin like a soft breeze. It felt so good to hold her. "They can go months on the fat stored beneath their shells. Satisfied?"

He put a finger beneath her chin and tilted her head so he could see her face. She had not mentioned her ordeal with the pirates or with Anders since her first day on the *Black Eagle,* yet he knew she often thought of that time. Just as he knew she was thinking about it now.

"You pretend your own problems are nothing, then worry about a bunch of turtles. I do not think you are even half as tough as you want the world to believe."

A clatter of footsteps sounded on the ladder. Kade released Kathleen just as Michael appeared at the bottom of the ladder, followed in turn by Jake, Skinner, and Alan Thorpe. They all carried buckets with them and went into the storage room where they poured seawater over the heads of the tearful turtles.

Kathleen watched for a second, then looked at Kade. A smile twinkled in her blue-green eyes. "Maybe not, Captain Morgan, but neither are you."

Chapter 9

The next day the *Black Eagle* changed course, the sleek hull and defiant masthead slicing through the blue waters as the ship closed in on Mistral. Kade told Kathleen they would arrive around noon and she could come on deck early if she wanted. She was so excited she almost hugged him. The islands they had passed during the last week had been places of intense color and tropical appeal. She looked forward to living on Mistral for a time, thinking the Caribbean would be a pleasant place to escape from.

She fastened the top button on her shirt, ran a brush through her hair, and smiled at her reflection in the mirror before bolting out the cabin door. After skipping up the steps to the deck, she stopped to blink at the sudden blast of white sunlight. When she stepped out onto the bustling deck, Kathleen got her first glimpse of Mistral.

It shimmered on the horizon, rising from a sapphire sea to stand like a beautiful sentinel against the azure sky. Mounds of clouds clung to the top of the twin mountains that reigned over the island while a scattering of smaller clouds sailed across the sky like swans on a crystal lake. There were at least a dozen different shades of green on the island, and it appeared as a living, breathing thing. It was a place of dreams come true, of peace and softness, of warmth and serenity.

"It is beautiful!" she called to Kade, flashing him a smile so brilliant the sun dimmed in comparison. She ran to the bow of the *Eagle,* eager to be as close to the island as possible.

Kade could not take his eyes off her small form. She was so alive, so free. She practically danced across the deck, the wind catching her silky curls and lifting them in airy fingers to float in the warm breeze. The gray pants and shirt clung to her in the embrace of the wind, bringing back to Kade the memory of the beautiful body he had taken in anger and worshiped in desire. He longed to hold it now, to feel again the softness of Kathleen's lips, the firm push of her breasts against his chest.

He had made a mistake ordering her to sleep in his bed when he could not make love to her. Every night had been torture. He had wanted to pull her against him, to drink deeply of her kisses and hear that husky voice call his name at the climax of their passion. Instead he had listened to the soft sighs that occasionally broke the steady rhythm of her breathing.

Several times she had curled into his arms while fighting the terrors of a nightmare. He had held her close, unable to breathe or think with her snuggled against his bare skin. Eventually her fear would subside and she would sleep peacefully in his arms until he could not stand the sweet agony another moment. He would then release his hold on her, rolling out of bed to go on deck and pull deep breaths of cool air into his aching lungs. Once she had awakened in his arms, her eyes growing wide as she felt the touch of his lips against her forehead. She had immediately pulled away from him, leaving him feeling empty and alone.

Now as he watched her press against the railing of

the *Black Eagle,* he felt his need for her growing inside him, just as it had been growing ever since the first moment he had seen her in Morocco. He could not wait any longer to quench his thirst for her kisses; tonight she would be his.

Kathleen leaned over the bow, tasting the salty spray of the sea. As they drew closer to Mistral, she saw a number of smaller islands just off the northwestern shore. They were pieces of the original volcano that had formed Mistral, worn to jagged edges and steep cliffs by the restless sea. Flocks of seabirds spiraled around them, landing and taking off, fishing the sapphire waters and soaring on the warm breezes.

Mistral towered over these volcanic guardians, its intense tropical beauty radiating out like a beacon. The air smelled of living things, rich soil and the perfume of a thousand flowers. The tops of the mountains changed from vivid green to musky blue as wispy fingers of gray clouds embraced the heights, pouring torrents of rain onto the forest canopy. A waterfall exploded from the top of a sheer cliff and cascaded into the foaming sea below. The blue ocean turned aqua, then green as it surged onto a narrow strip of sand beneath the cliffs, exploding into shards of sapphire crystals against broken piles of pitted limestone.

They approached the reef enclosing the windward side of the island, and the *Eagle* leaped through a break in the coral. The blue water parted beneath the eager bow, disrupting a school of yellow parrot fish beneath the surface. Gulls and a lone albatross flew above the masts.

It was all too much. Kathleen was drained by her effort to see everything at once. She walked back to the stern, climbing the three steps to where Kade grasped the spokes of the wheel, towering over everyone and everything. The sleeves of his white shirt were rolled up over browned arms; his black hair rippled in the wind. Kathleen caught a glimpse of his teeth between parted lips that were full and sensuous. A day's growth of heavy beard made him look even more dangerous, and even more desirable.

He spun the wheel, guiding the ship into a harbor shaped like a horseshoe. One side was an immense stretch of beach lined with palm trees and disappearing out of sight to Kathleen's left. The other side of the harbor marked the edge of Mistral's tallest mountain where another waterfall fell into the sea. The volcanic rock ended abruptly behind a small village perched between the brooding cliff and the shore. The palm-thatched houses were built in a neat row and shaded by flowering trees. Three warehouses huddled on the edge of the jungle. A pier jutted into the lagoon, its surface almost completely covered with crates and barrels.

There was a crowd of people on the beach near the pier, all dressed in clothes as vivid and exciting as the colors of the island. Reds, yellows, blues and greens flashed in the sun along with sparkling white smiles. Hands were raised in greeting to the cheering crew of the *Black Eagle*. A number of the people were black, a reminder of the slave trade that was such a big business in this part of the world.

Those black faces reminded Kathleen that she was one of them, a slave. Her stomach lurched sickeningly as the anchor rumbled over the side of the ship. It dragged the *Eagle* to a halt as it caught on a mass of coral. I will not allow him to see how afraid I am, she swore silently as Kade took her hand and led her to the rail where they would board the first boat for shore.

She is so beautiful, Kade thought as the ever-present wind on Mistral carelessly tossed Kathleen's hair around her hips. He wanted to pull her against him, to feel her heart beating and to taste the sweetness of her lips. She was looking at his island with wide, excited eyes, and Kade turned to look at what she saw.

Mistral had been purchased to serve a particular purpose when he was running the *Eagle* under the black pirate flag marked with a silver skull and bloodied sword. The island had numerous caves for hiding stolen goods, in addition to coves and harbors for hiding the ship when necessary. Now the island served as a base of operations for Morgan Shipping and a place where the families of his crew lived. The plantation on the other side of the island was a bonus, not a reason for ownership.

Now Kade looked at Mistral through Kathleen's eyes. Everything was new to him, from the clean sweep of beaches to the towering majesty of the ancient volcanos. The rich green of the jungle and the aqua water surrounding the island were like a balm to tired eyes, a salve to a restless soul. There was peace here, peace he had never stopped running long enough to notice. He turned back to Kathleen, drinking in her beauty as he had that of Mistral.

A slow smile lifted the corners of her lips. "Your island is beautiful. I had not imagined a place could be so perfect."

"More perfect than Ireland?"

"Not more perfect, different perfect. Ireland is a land of rain and mist, a magical place of fairies and leprechauns. Mistral is solid, substantial. It is so beautiful, Kade, that I cannot find the words to describe what it is."

A warm light filled his black eyes. Kathleen's knees went spongy beneath her. Kade's hand captured her waist, and her heart threatened to leap into her throat.

"Do you realize that is the first time you have said my name? I like it," he said as he leaned closer to her ear.

I must resist him, Kathleen told herself. This man is

my master, my enemy. And, God help me, I want him so much it hurts inside. Her hand lifted to Kade's chest, the tips of her fingers brushing aside his shirt and exposing crisp curls of hair that glistened in the sun.

"I like that, too, kitten."

He tucked a finger under her chin and lifted her face. The sun sparkled in her eyes, it played along the soft skin of her face. Kathleen's heart froze as his lips descended on hers. His breath moved over her tongue. The world began to disappear.

"Cap'n!" a harsh voice barked behind them.

Kade released Kathleen as he turned. She offered a quick prayer of thanks for the interruption and struggled to compose herself, to rebuild her defenses against the magic of Kade's charm.

"The boat's ready, Cap'n. Will ya be leavin' for shore now, or later?"

There was a smirk on the sailor's face as he looked at Kathleen. She struggled to remember his name. Johnson, Pete Johnson.

"Watch your tongue, mister," Kade ordered sharply. "I will not tolerate insolence." He pushed the man aside and started down the rope ladder hanging over the side of the ship, dragging Kathleen with him. He stepped into the longboat and lifted her down from the ladder, depositing her beside him.

Kathleen knew Pete Johnson was watching them, as was most of the crew. She stared at her knees and tried not to imagine the lusty jokes and crude humor her relationship with her master would create among not only the *Black Eagle* crew, but also the people she had yet to meet.

The longboat drew alongside the pier, and Kade stepped out to offer Kathleen his hand. She hesitated, fear clutching at her. I have to be strong or these people will laugh at me. She exhaled a shaky breath and gave him her hand.

Kade was unaware of the emotions that battled inside Kathleen as he led her through the piles of crates that surrounded them, her small fingers locked in his big hand. A short, round shape extricated itself from the crowd on the beach and ran toward him. He left Kathleen on the edge of the pier and lifted the laughing woman off the ground, swinging her in dizzying circles.

"Mattie!" he exclaimed as he set the old woman down and planted a big kiss on her flushed cheek.

"Gracious, Kade, ye almost killed me!" Mattie McBradden cried, her broad face beaming. "We didn't think ye were e'er comin' 'ome. Where 'ave ye been hidin' that ugly face of yers?" Her smile faded as she spotted Kathleen standing in the shadow of a pile of crates.

Kathleen's stomach turned upside down as Kade pulled her into the sunlight. She forced herself to stand unwavering in the face of Mattie's inspection. When she tried to pull free from his grip, he tightened it until all feeling in her fingers disappeared. That she also accepted without complaint, staring straight ahead and feeling the same hatred for these people she had felt for the crowd in Morocco.

Mattie was astonished by the girl Kade so arrogantly displayed like a prize. Her hair was as black as sin, and her strange eyes were full of so much anger Mattie was sure she had to be face to face with Kade's bastard offspring. Who else could be capable of fathering such a raging temper as the girl was obviously cursed with?

She looked up at Kade for an explanation and discovered he was watching the girl with an odd expression on his face. Possessive, dominating, yet tender and warm. She had never seen him look at anyone like that.

"Who's the child, Kade, one of yer spawn?" she asked.

What a fool, Kathleen thought as she disdainfully smirked at the old woman. These people are rude, staring at me like a horse displayed at a show. If Kade does not put me through my paces, I will show them off myself. Her jaw set in a fierce line of determination.

"Where do you get such ideas, Mattie? The girl's naught of mine." Kade looked at the people around him. "This is Kathleen O'Connor," he said as he pulled her in front of him, one hand tangling in the long curls that tumbled down her back. He held her arm tightly with his other hand.

Too tight, Kathleen thought. She did not try to pull away; she was too busy trying to maintain her arrogant glare, a difficult feat in the bright sun.

"Miss O'Connor is my . . ."

"Slave," Kathleen finished for him. She said it proudly, proclaiming to these strangers that it was not her choice to be here; then she turned to face Kade. He released her reluctantly, an apprehensive frown on his face. Now is the time to go into my act, she decided and fell into a graceful curtsy.

Her face was almost touching Kade's boots, which were polished to such a high gloss she could see her reflection. A hush settled over the crowd, and Kathleen could almost hear herself sweating. A gasp was heard, most probably from Mattie because immediately afterwards the old woman pulled Kathleen upright.

"Land's sake, child, nobody's a slave on this island. These all be free folk. Whate'er made ye say such a thing?" The girl must be demented, Mattie thought. She tried to haul Kathleen away from Kade, whose temper looked ready to explode. His face was red and his eyes narrowed to slits.

123

Kathleen planted her bare feet in the warm sand and refused to budge. The show was not over yet. She shook off Mattie's clinging fingers and watched the small muscle in her master's jaw twitch as he clenched his teeth.

When she had first bowed to him, Kade had wanted to throttle her. Now he wanted to laugh. She had effectively gained the sympathy of the village, and Mattie, by her impudent curtsy. As she recognized his change of temperament, her eyes sparkled with amusement.

He had intended to present her as his guest. Maybe it was better this way. No one would dare help her escape if they knew she was his slave. He nodded to her with an almost imperceptible movement of his head, saluting her nerve at chancing his anger.

"You are wrong, Mattie," he said. "Miss O'Connor is my slave. I bought her at an auction in Morocco and have refused her petition for release. Take her to the house and get her into some decent clothes, what she is wearing is a disgrace. She is to attend me at dinner tonight."

He dismissed Mattie and Kathleen with a wave of his hand, as arrogant as a king reigning over his subjects, and directed his attention to the unloading of the *Eagle*'s cargo.

Kathleen had no intention of allowing Kade to have the last word. "My lord?" she said, her voice like the liquid notes of a piece of beautiful music. It drew everyone's attention immediately.

Kade had moved several steps away, his back to her. The broad shoulders tensed, straightened. He pivoted on his heel and the people on the beach moved back from him.

"I wanted to thank you for your kindness, Captain Morgan, and to inform you that I will do nothing to bring further disgrace on the honorable reputation of my lord and master." Her voice was so weak it almost whined. She dropped into another deep curtsy, then lifted her eyes to his. All pretense of humbleness was gone.

"I may slit your throat while you sleep, but I will not disgrace you." With an arrogant flourish she stood, spun around and marched away in her best imitation of a man being led to the gallows.

The people on the beach waited for Kade's reaction. At best, they expected him to kill her on the spot. They were astonished to discover he was smiling.

Chapter 10

Kathleen followed Mattie up the path as it went beneath a tree fern on the edge of the jungle. They rounded a slight turn and entered a large clearing. In front of them rose the northern mountain, its slopes shrouded with trees and clouds. At its base, nestled among a riot of flowers and fruit, was the house, an elegant two-story building painted a dazzling white. It had huge windows and a wing on each side that together extended toward Kathleen like the welcoming arms of a comfortable chair.

Trellises covered with flowering vines, rose bushes and exotic plants scented the air. Directly in front of the house was a paved court where a fountain spewed water in a graceful arc over layered tiers of colorful tiles. The crystal drops fell into a shallow pool that invited one to dip hot, tired feet in its blue wetness.

The tension of arriving at Mistral began to take its toll as what little strength Kathleen had regained drained away. Though there were benches along the path, tucked among the intimate greenery of the garden, she ignored them. To stop and rest would show weakness. She had to be strong.

The house was an impressive structure, solid and strong. There were four doors opening onto the paved terrace, all made of panes of beveled glass fitted into

126

frames that looked like windows. The beauty of the garden flooded into the house like warm sunshine.

The walls of the house were over a foot thick, preventing the heat from entering, and keeping the interior as cool as a cellar in summertime. The main room was long, stretching casually in front of the glass doors. Above it was a vaulted ceiling that arched to the top of the house in a rugged display of wooden beams that crested in the center and tapered outward to the plaster walls.

"I've got business to tend, so make yerself comfortable, lass," Mattie said. "As soon as I check on what Effie's doing in the kitchen, I'll come back and we'll find ye something else to wear."

Kathleen waited until Mattie had gone before sagging against the wall to allow her breathing to return to normal. On the left side of the living room a staircase led to the second floor, opening onto a landing that stretched across the room just above the entrance. At the top of the steps was a set of double doors, which she assumed was the entrance to her master's private domain. There was another door nearby, and on the other side of the landing, over the right wing, were two more doors. In the center of the landing sunlight poured through an open window, slanting across the arched ceiling and chasing away the dark shadows between the beams.

Under the staircase a door opened into another room. Kathleen looked in. It was a study and library. There was a window seat piled high with cushions on the front wall. Two leather armchairs and a small table sat in the center of the room on a braided rug. The walls were lined with shelves full of heavy books and sculptures. Near the back of the room were an oak desk and padded chair, the top of the desk piled high with dusty papers and a lamp with a green glass shade.

Kathleen went back into the living room. A massive fireplace dominated the long wall opposite the entry. In front of the hearth, two sofas faced each other over a low table. She trailed her hand over the red brocade upholstery and admired the crystal vase of exotic white flowers in the center of the table. They scented the room with a perfume reminiscent of the garden, and she glanced out at the blue-tiled fountain glistening in the sun.

To the right of the entrance was an armchair that looked uncomfortable, the fabric stiff and dark, the legs carved like grotesque animal claws. Beside it was a large cabinet with leaded-glass doors. Inside were two shelves that held decanters and wineglasses. In the opposite corner was a piano, its bench covered by an intricate piece of needlepoint that looked like an old tapestry. On the piano were sheets of music and a gold candelabra with thirteen white candles.

Between the piano and the liquor cabinet was an arched opening. Kathleen moved toward it, avoiding the Oriental rugs scattered around the living room because she liked the cool touch of the terra-cotta tiles beneath her bare feet. Through the arched doorway was the dining room. Another, smaller door opened on the right wall of that room, leading into a hall connected to the kitchen.

The dining room was a place of wonder and delight. A chandelier was suspended from the low ceiling, and the light from the window struck its crystal prisms, exploding into thousands of tiny rainbows. Dozens of candles sat among the prisms. At night, when those candles were lit, the room would still be full of rainbows.

Beneath the sparkling chandelier was an oblong table surrounded by high-backed chairs with curving arms and padded seats. A white carpet covered the floor in this room, and inset into the thick wall was a china cabinet full of crystal bowls and glasses that gave off minute shards of broken rainbows as the sun struck their angled surfaces.

Kathleen touched the chandelier with one finger, causing it to swing slightly. Rainbows danced around the room, and a delightful tinkling noise accompanied the movement. It sounded like fairies dancing on the hills at midnight. The music and rainbows enveloped her as she whirled and dipped in the steps of an ancient Celtic dance.

She stopped and leaned against the back of one of the chairs, breathless and in pain. Though she had stopped spinning, the room continued to whirl around her in a kaleidoscope of color that made her dizzy. She felt herself falling, tumbling helplessly through the profusion of color and sound.

Suddenly someone grabbed her from behind. Kathleen stiffened, remembering the horror of the pirate attack on Emerald Hills. There was no air in her lungs, and the scream that swelled in her throat choked her. Terrified, she struggled against her powerful captor.

Kade turned her to face him, and she stopped fighting. "I thought . . ."

"I know what you thought. It was my fault for coming up behind you, but you were about to fall."

Kathleen knew she should resist his embrace, yet her body and mind craved the comfort of his touch, the safety of his arms. Would it be wrong to give in to her need to be held for just a few minutes? She laid her cheek against Kade's chest. He was so strong. She moved closer to him, closer to the security he offered, closer to surrendering to the need that was growing inside her.

A noise drew her attention, and she lifted her head. Mattie was standing in the small doorway, watching them. Kathleen's face flamed. What would the old woman think? She started to pull away, then stopped.

Kade will take what he wants no matter what Mattie McBradden or anyone else thinks. If only he did not want me. If only I had not been kidnapped. If only— Kathleen stopped herself. Wishing would not help her. Common sense would. However, with Kade holding her, it was difficult to concentrate on such an illusive thing as common sense.

"You will have to excuse us, Mattie. Kathleen has not been well, she needs to rest. I will put her in the room next to mine. You can do something about her clothes later."

Kade lifted her into his arms so quickly her dizziness returned. He carried her through the living room and was starting up the steps to the landing before her senses stabilized.

"I am perfectly able to walk, Captain." Kathleen placed her hands firmly on his chest and pushed. It did no good whatsoever.

"You are right. In fact, I like the way you walk. Right now, though, you do not have enough strength to walk two inches, much less climb these steps. Now hold still or I will throw you over the rail."

He passed the entrance to his own chambers and kicked open the next door. There was a canopied bed against the far wall. He crossed to it and stood Kathleen beside him. She was forced to clutch at his arm to keep from falling.

He pulled back the covers and motioned her into the bed. Too exhausted to argue, she collapsed onto the clean sheets. Instantly she was jerked out of bed and dumped on the floor in front of Kade again.

She glared up at him angrily. "Now what? You tell me to go to bed and when I obey, pull me right back out."

"Take off your clothes," he ordered, pulling at the collar of her shirt.

A shudder of fear gripped Kathleen, and her exhaustion disappeared in its wake. There was a door to her left. She made a mad dash for it, wrenching it open and fleeing into Kade's bedroom.

She had time only to note that the bed was absolutely enormous before she heard Kade behind her. She dashed around the bed to put it between them until she could decide her next move. There was not one. She was trapped; both entrances to the room were on the same side of the bed as Kade. He was leaning against the wall between them, his arms crossed and a snide smile on his handsome face. Kathleen reached behind her, grasped something hard and threw it at him.

It was a candlestick. He ducked beneath it and moved closer to her. She threw a book next, which he sidestepped. The only object left on the table was a glass lamp. It made a resounding crash as it hit the door, shattering into a thousand pieces. Kade continued to advance on her.

Kathleen bolted to her right, jumped on the bed and flung herself in the direction of the door that led back into the other bedroom. Her feet became tangled in the blankets, and she fell face down. She rolled over just as Kade threw himself full length on top of her.

She was completely exhausted and lay panting beneath his heavy weight. He waited until her breathing slowed, then lifted up onto his elbows to look down at her, that same snide smile pulling at the corners of his mouth.

"If I had realized how eager you were to share my bed, kitten, I would have brought you directly in here."

"Eager? You think I am eager?" she shrieked. "I would as soon share the bed of a pig! How dare you—"
He placed his mouth on hers, effectively stopping

her tirade.

"That is better. Now, about what happened in the other room, I was merely telling you to get undressed before getting in bed. I had not planned to join you, but since you have stormed into my bedroom and dragged me on top of you, maybe I will change my mind."

Kathleen forgot how to breathe as Kade pulled her right earlobe between his teeth. Her body began to float in a shimmering mist of desire. Involuntarily her back arched, pressing her breasts against his chest. She shivered as he brushed his lips across hers. Her mouth opened to take his tongue into her, and they kissed.

A moan rose within her as a swirling tide of ecstasy drowned all her reasons to resist. There was no reality except the touch of Kade's lips, the beat of his heart and her own throbbing need. He ripped open her shirt, exposing the taut peaks of her nipples and pulling one into his mouth. He raked his teeth across her tender flesh, causing her to cry aloud her pleasure. What he was doing to her was torture. It was maddening. It was wonderful.

Then he stopped, moving off her to reach for the waist of her breeches. Kathleen plunged off the bed and into the other bedroom. She slammed the door behind her, threw the bolt and collapsed onto the bed, burying her face in the pillow. She felt faint as her body struggled against the intense need Kade had created. She lifted her head and knew that she was not alone.

She turned. Kade was standing in the open doorway to the landing. The smile that twisted across his face was cruel and cold. Kathleen hated him, hated what he made her feel, the primitive emotions and urges. She was afraid of them, afraid of herself. The only way she knew to handle fear was to face the cause of it, acknowledge it and provoke it. Only by fully exposing her vulnerability could she find her strength.

She rose from the bed and shrugged off her shirt. Then she dropped her pants to stand before her master totally nude, her breasts swollen from his attentions.

"Shall we finish it now or did you want to degrade me further?"

He did not move. She lay on the bed and pulled the blanket slowly up over her legs, then her hips and waist. Her breasts she left exposed to the almost physical touch of those black eyes.

Kade walked into the room and placed his hand on her right shoulder, then dropped it to her breast. He ran his fingers lightly over the curving softness, around the hard peak of her nipple, down into the shadowed cleft between her breasts and onto the left one. Kathleen did not fight the shiver his touch caused, nor did she pull away.

His fingers moved up her neck, across her chin and through the edge of her hair. He stopped there, removing his hand and hooking it in his belt. Kathleen swallowed and moistened her lips.

"If lesson number two is over," she said, "I would like to sleep now."

"And if it is not?" The words were spoken almost as a challenge in a voice so harsh it sliced through Kathleen like a knife.

"Then I await your next order, master. Tell me how wide to spread my legs and I shall obey."

He spun on his heel and stalked out of the room, slamming the door behind him. Kathleen got up, threw the bolt and climbed back in bed. She had won for the moment. How much would that victory cost her?

Kade clenched his fists as he heard Kathleen slide home the bolt on the door. He had seen the hate in her eyes, yet she had intentionally provoked him into

133

touching her just as she had provoked him into raping her.

What was it she had said? "Shall we finish it now or did you want to degrade me further?" He slowly unclenched his fists. Now he understood. She was telling him that her inability to resist his lovemaking was not a disgrace to her, only to him because of his exploitation of her vulnerability.

"If you think that what I have done so far has been exploitation, dear child," he murmured into the silence of the landing, "you are badly mistaken. Soon I shall teach you the true meaning of the word. I will not be the one begging for relief, it will be you. And begging is a disgrace that belongs to none but the beggar."

Chapter 11

Rain fell outside the window of Lord Silas Pennington's study on his Irish estate. The cavernous house was
quiet except for the rain. A fire burned steadily in the
soot-blackened grate, and a spermaceti candle flickered on the desk, creating skulking shadows on the
paneled walls between the portraits of monarchs and
over English landscapes painted in dark oils and
mounted in heavy gilt frames.

Lord Pennington picked up a gold locket lying on his
desk, holding it near the candle and watching the light
play across the fine engravings. He thought of its
owner, and a smile creased his wrinkled face. He wet
his drawn, pale lips with a tongue as thin and gray as
the hair that straggled down across his forehead and
over the velvet collar of his smoking jacket. He laid the
locket on his desk beside the letters that had
accompanied it and smiled again.

The ransom demand was a strange one. The Emerald
Hills stallion, that unusual beast Silas had so often seen
Kathleen O'Connor riding, was the only thing the
kidnapper wanted. What type of a fool would go to the
trouble of attacking a farm and capturing someone just
to ask for a mere horse?

Silas ran a hand over his face and wet his lips again.
The local peasants claimed the stallion was the *each*

uisce, a legendary beast of the deep sea that answered to the call of none save the fairy folk. They also claimed that the girl had been able to ride the stallion because of magic; she was blessed or some such rot.

He had scoffed at the story until one night he had actually seen the horse appear from beneath the waves. It had shaken the seaweed from its mane before galloping around the ruins of the O'Connor house. Then, as quickly as it had come, it left, going back into the sea and disappearing beneath the surface.

Silas glanced out the window of his study. He could just make out the outline of the hills to the west against the rain-soaked sky. He wanted that land, wanted all of Emerald Hills. If he could add Jarrett O'Connor's land to Pennington Estates, Silas would be master of the biggest holding in Ireland.

Emerald Hills was not all Silas wanted. There was also the O'Connor girl. He had wanted her ever since the first time he had seen her lithe, young body mounted on that stallion. She had set his blood running hot as he thought about what it would feel like for her to be mounted on him like that and what it would be like to watch her ivory flesh turn red as he whipped her like the child she was.

His pulse began to race as he imagined her crying as he forced her to beg him for his touch, beg him to run his hands over her firm breasts and rounded behind, beg him to bite and bruise her flesh while she lay tied to Silas's bed. Her young, tight body was just the tonic he needed to make him young again, just the thing he needed to feast upon on nights like this when the damned Irish weather made his bones hurt.

Yes, Silas thought, I want her as much as I want Emerald Hills.

He remembered all the times he had done her the honor of offering to marry her, remembered Kathleen's reaction to that honor, her strange eyes flashing with laughter each time she turned him down. She was a peasant, a simple Irish peasant. What right did she have to refuse his proposal? She should have considered herself privileged that a titled Englishman had even noticed her, much less made an offer of marriage.

Silas fingered the scar on his neck. This kidnapping was just the chance he needed to acquire both Emerald Hills and Kathleen O'Connor. He should have thought of something like this himself. What a great opportunity this was to pay back that O'Connor peasant for refusing to sell his land, and to make Kathleen pay for refusing Silas's generous offer of marriage. Oh, how he would make her pay for that!

It had been a stroke of luck that the packet containing the ransom demand along with the girl's locket and personal letter verifying she was alive had been delivered to Pennington Estates when the messenger could not find anyone at the ruins of the house on the shore of Emerald Hills.

"Such a stroke of bloody good luck," Silas said, watching the shadows on the walls stir and shift as his wheezing breath disturbed the candle's flame. He had already sent word to the kidnapper agreeing to the exchange of the stallion for Kathleen, not that he had any intention of fulfilling his part of the agreement. He planned to wait until the girl was delivered to Dublin as he had stipulated in his letter; then Silas would have the king's troops that were stationed in Ireland arrest the stupid fools responsible for her capture.

And now it was time to set into motion the second part of Silas's plan. Just that day he had seen Jarrett O'Connor walking across his land, and he had again offered to buy Emerald Hills. The Irishman had barely responded to the generous offer Silas made, simply shaking his head no and walking away. When Silas

137

called after him, asking about Kathleen, Jarrett had hesitated in midstride, his shoulders suddenly drooping with defeat and desolation. Then he had moved off across the wet, lonely fields where rosemary scented the air and the ocean's chill frosted his breath. The rain clouds had closed over the sun, pouring their gray contents onto the land while Silas watched the Irishman fade from sight.

The fire in the grate was almost out. Silas lifted his pen and dipped the sharpened point in the bottle of ink on his desk. He pulled open his stationery drawer and chose a piece that did not have his family crest embossed on the top. He moved the locket away from the center of his desk and laid the paper down. He thought for a moment, then began to write the words he had composed, words that would make Emerald Hills his.

Chapter 12

Kathleen came awake instantly, sitting bolt upright in bed. Her eyes hurt. She rubbed them, discovering they were wet. "I have been crying!" she exclaimed in surprise. Then she remembered the confrontation with Kade. "It is not crying I should be doing, it is murder! The man wants to force me to bend to his will. He has obviously never dealt with the Irish before; we do not bend easily."

Though firm in her belief that she could mentally withstand Kade's torture, she was less sure of her body's ability to ignore the exquisite pleasure of her master's burning touch. The blanket brushed against her sensitive nipples, causing her to shiver. She slid out of bed and forced her mind onto other matters.

The room she was in was no less than spectacular. The wall behind the bed had two tall windows, both open to allow the sweet smell of flowers and ocean into the room. Palm trees swayed in the trade winds, and beyond them the *Black Eagle* could be seen in the harbor. The last light of day faded, and the sea turned dark blue, then black. She never failed to be surprised by the quick change from day to night, and night to day, that happened in the Caribbean.

She struck a light and held it to the small lamp on the table beside the bed. Behind her the curtains billowed in the night breeze, the fabric so filmy it reminded Kathleen of fairy wings. The bedspread, now lying in a heap on the floor, and the lace-trimmed canopy over the bed were made of the same material. Mosquito netting hung from a rod over the head of the bed. There was a dressing table in the corner to the right of the bed, its surface covered with an assortment of jars and bottles. A round mirror with beveled edges hung on the wall over the table, catching and reflecting the lamplight.

Kathleen lifted one of the little jars. It was decorated with a pink cupid. Pretty but overdone, she thought. She opened it and sniffed at the scented cream, wondering what it was. She rubbed some on the back of her hand. It was smooth and slippery, making her skin soft. Nice, she decided and rubbed it on her other hand.

Beside the dresser was an armoire whose doors were carved with vines and flowers, hummingbirds and butterflies. A green rug stretched across the floor, the pile so deep Kathleen's feet sank into the wonderful lushness with every step, her toes curling with delight.

A large trunk bound with leather straps sat just inside the door that led to Kade's room. It had not been there before or else she would have tripped over it when she ran away from him. She looked at the latch. Not only had it been opened, it was completely missing.

Did I really think he would allow me to lock him out? No doubt he could rip the entire door off the hinges if he really wanted in. Kathleen sat in the rocking chair in the center of the room. With her arms wrapped around her uplifted legs, she propped her chin on her knees and stared at the unlocked door.

"This was not here before either!" she cried, jumping up to stare suspiciously at the rocker. It was padded with thick cushions, and a lace shawl was draped across

140

the back. "What else has he done?"

She threw open the doors to the armoire and raised one hand to her throat in surprise. It was the most incredible display Kathleen had ever seen. There were petticoats, chemises, dozens of dresses and bunches of frilly petticoats. Some of the things were so strange she did not have the slightest idea what they might be.

Kathleen riffled through the clothes. "All this and not one pair of breeches."

She scavenged a blue velvet robe from the back of the armoire and slipped it on. It was so large it dragged on the floor around her. Kathleen pushed her hands into the pockets and snuggled her nose into the wonderful softness. She glanced at the mirror, then turned to face Kade, who was lounging against the door.

He was dressed in black evening clothes, wearing the classical style with casual diffidence. His vest was quilted satin, his breeches and waistcoat silk. The white shirt had no lace or ruffles, the starkness accenting his masculinity. He had shaved the rough shadow of beard from his face, and his hair had been trimmed. He looked dangerous, unpredictable. And incredibly attractive.

He smiled that devastating smile, and Kathleen could not help smiling back. The total effect of his dress and manner was so different from when last she saw him. Then he had been playing the part of arrogant slave owner. Now he was the charming host. She lifted the hem of her robe and glided across the floor to him.

"Shall we go down to dinner now, Captain Morgan? My appetite is most hardy this evening."

"Although you are most beautiful in that lovely robe, my dear, I think our guest is expecting us to appear in something less casual. We always dress for dinner on Mistral, a most uncomfortable habit that helps preserve the illusion we are civilized."

"I can understand your dilemma, Captain, for even in that elegant attire you look most savage."

He flashed that deadly smile, and Kathleen melted all the way down to her toes. "Your tongue is as sharp as it is sweet, dear Kate. As much as I would love to fence with that delightful weapon all night, we have someone waiting to dine with us. You must dress quickly. I will wait downstairs."

His statement threw Kathleen into a quandary. Never in a thousand years would she be able to figure out how any of those dresses should be worn, or even what might be appropriate for dinner.

"Kade, wait!" she called out when he turned to leave.

He stopped, startled by her husky, sensuous voice. No matter how often he heard her speak, it was always a shock to his system. And the sound of his name coming from between those inviting lips had an almost catastrophic effect.

"At your service," he said, slowly turning to face her. He wanted to sweep her into his arms at that moment. That blue robe did wonderful things for her eyes, and its huge size made her appear so soft, so vulnerable. Kade deliberately put his hands behind his back and clenched them tightly together.

"I do not know how to wear these things," Kathleen said, pointing at the array of dresses spilling into the room.

Kade felt a stab of guilt. The girl had been raised in the wilds of Ireland, growing up in breeches on horseback. How could she possibly know about silks and satins, corsets and garters? He went to her, putting his hands on her shoulders and looking into those trusting blue-green eyes.

"Mother tried to teach me about the right way to wear dresses and fancy petticoats. I refused to listen to her because it seemed so unnecessary. Now I realize there is more to the world than just Emerald Hills and I am stuck in the middle of it, not knowing anything except how to train horses and muck out stalls."

Kade wanted to enfold her in his arms. He swallowed against the ache in the back of his throat and considered the problem at hand. The clothes in the armoire had been made for his ex-mistress, Sarita Ridley. Though he had always considered Sarita a small woman, her robe was practically falling off Kathleen. Kade rummaged through the closet and selected a gown of deep blue silk.

He held the dress in front of Kathleen and critically appraised the fit. "This appears to be smaller than the other dresses and is most appropriate for dinner. You wash up"—he nodded at the screen in the far corner that concealed the chamber pot and washstand—"and I will send Mattie to help you dress."

Kathleen ran her hand over the blue silk. "Do you really intend to dress your slave in such a lavish fashion?"

The lines around his eyes softened. "Aye, my lady, I do indeed." He tossed the dress on the bed and touched her cheek. "I shall expect you downstairs in twenty minutes."

After he left, Kathleen washed quickly, then lifted the dress from the bed and held it against her while she stood in front of the mirror. There was a knock on the door, and Mattie McBradden came bustling into the room.

"Kade sent me up sayin' I was to 'elp ye dress, lass, though why I wouldn't be knowin'. I'm no lady's maid."

"It is help I need, not a maid. I have never worn anything like this and have not the slightest idea how to go about even getting it on, much less what to

143

wear underneath."

Mattie took the dress from Kathleen. "Did Kade pick this out?"

"Yes. He thought it might fit. Whose clothes are these?"

"A widow what 'ad 'er cap set for the lad. She came sailin' in 'ere like a queen, determined to replace 'er name with 'is." Mattie began pulling items from drawers beneath the armoire, tossing them on the bed and pulling out more.

"What happened?" Kathleen asked.

"He 'andled 'er like 'e 'andles most of 'is problems, went off to sea and didn't come back. After two months of poutin' and cryin', 'er ladyship packed 'er trunks and 'eaded back to England. The next day the *Black Eagle* sailed into the 'arbor and dropped anchor. Kade 'ad been waitin' offshore for that female to give up. Less than a week later, 'e discovered 'er ladyship 'ad charged these clothes to 'is accounts in London. He took off after 'er, laid some shots across the bow of 'er ship and stole every stitch she 'ad."

Kathleen tried to picture Kade boarding his mistress's ship, his expression cold and heartless while she begged him to leave her the blue gown as a reminder of the love they had once shared.

"If he had to pay for the clothes, it was not stealing," she said in defense of his action.

Mattie snorted. "Ye sound like the lad 'imself. That's what 'e told me when 'e stacked 'er ladyship's trunks in me storeroom." She began to sort through the undergarments stacked on the bed. "Now we 'ave to figure out in what order it all goes on."

Kathleen stared in astonishment at the pile of ruffles, lace, and ribbons. "Do you mean I have to wear all this just to eat? I would rather starve!"

"Looks to me like ye been doin' a bit of that already,

lass. Yer nothin' 'cept skin and bones now."

"This is fat compared to how I looked when Jake led me off that auction stage in Morocco."

"Did Kade really buy ye like 'e said?"

Kathleen sat on the bed and pushed the mound of clothes aside. "Aye, that he did, Mrs. McBradden. Paid fifty pounds for me, gave orders that I was to be unchained and told Jake to take me to the *Black Eagle*. I fainted from hunger twice before anyone thought to feed me."

"Why did ye not ask for something to eat, lass? 'Tis no shame to say what ye be needin'."

"It is when you are a slave. I have no rights. If my master wants to starve me to death or beat me to pulp, that is his privilege." A hard edge came into her voice and she dropped the piece of lace she was fingering.

"Kade's not treated ye like that."

"That is true. I would be dead if not for Captain Morgan."

"Then why did ye talk to 'im like ye did on the beach, lass? He's a 'ard man and won't stand for such."

"How should I talk to him, with humble words of gratitude? I am his slave. Even if he were the kindest man on earth, I would hate him. I know that he is a hard man but it matters not, for I am hard, too."

Mattie sighed. "I'll not be agreein' with what ye say, lass, nor do I 'old with what the lad be doin'. It be 'tween the two of ye an' none of my concern. Right now all I want to worry 'bout is gettin' ye dressed and downstairs or he'll 'ave me 'ead. Up on yer feet, girl, so we can figure out 'ow these fancies goes on ye."

Kathleen shook her head decisively. "Not everything, Mrs. McBradden; I would suffocate. Pick out the basics. Everything else we shall ignore."

Mattie chose several items from the bed, and Kathleen removed her robe. After donning a chemise, stockings and garters, she was handed a corset.

"Is this necessary?"

"No lady would be caught wi'out one."

Kathleen wrapped it around her and tugged on the laces. It was stiff, clumsy and made her ribs hurt. She tossed it back on the bed.

"And I will not be caught with one. How could I possibly breathe in such a thing, much less eat? Tie those petticoats on me and let us finish with this masquerade." Her nerves were becoming frayed. All this just to eat, it was unbelievable. Why did women put up with such foolishness?

Mattie dropped the dress over Kathleen's head. It slipped over her shoulders and floated down her body. The silk moved like water out over the lacy petticoats and made a delightful rippling sound as it settled onto the floor. At her wrists was an edging of ivory lace that tickled the back of her hands as she adjusted the plunging neckline of the gown. More of the lace decorated the front of the dress, shadowing the cleft between her breasts and flaring outward at her waist, accenting the slender curves.

"Too long," Kathleen said as she lifted the trailing hem from around her feet.

"No matter, lass, 'old it up when ye walk so ye won't be trippin'. Sit so I can do yer hair."

Kathleen sat quietly for a time, then said, "Captain Morgan said he had a guest for dinner."

"Aye, Bog Daniels. He 'elps Kade with the shipping business," Mattie said as she finished fussing with Kathleen's hair and stepped back.

A stranger looked back at Kathleen from the mirror. The wild Irish lass had been transformed into a lady wearing a silk gown and an ivory hair comb. She hesitantly touched a curl that dangled just above the lace at her breast, wondering what her father would think if he could see her.

She could almost hear that familiar brogue saying, "Ye may look like a lady, Katie me child, but it be takin' more than just a dress and a fancy comb to make ye one, just as it takes more than a saddle and a four-legged creature to make a 'orse."

Mattie handed Kathleen a pair of slippers. "Put these on, lass. They match the dress," she said.

Kathleen slipped her stocking feet into the butter-soft leather. Like the gown, they were a little large.

"Now off wi' ye, lass, afore Kade comes stormin' after ye. He's not a patient man."

Kathleen put her hand on the doorknob. "Thank you for helping me, Mrs. McBradden," she said before pulling open the door and walking onto the dimly lit landing. She looked over the railing at the room below. Kade was there, his back turned to her as he stabbed the logs in the fireplace with a brass poker. She gathered her skirts and started down the steps.

Bog Daniels took a sip of wine and nodded his approval of the dry taste. He started to ask Kade about his meeting with Quint Cathcart. His question died unspoken. At the top of the stairs in the shadows of the landing, a vision had materialized. With a rustle of silk, the girl lifted her skirts and floated down the stairs. Bog held his breath, afraid the slightest noise would make the angel approaching him disappear.

Kade placed the poker in the wall bracket and turned around just in time to see Kathleen step into the golden light of the fire. It caressed her smooth skin and glistened on the black curls that brushed her bare skin just above the plunging neckline of her gown. Every inch of her was perfection, every curve and line of her body an invitation that a man could not resist.

She smiled up at him, and Kade's breath caught in his throat as he remembered the passionate kisses he had received from those moist lips. The wineglass he held dropped onto the stone hearth, sending a tinkle of sound into the silent room. He did not even notice.

Bog stood and reached for Kathleen's hand. "My lady," he murmured as he bowed to kiss the tiny fingers, allowing his lips to linger for a moment.

"Sir!" Kathleen jerked free from his grasp. "We have not been introduced!" She turned her shoulder to him and faced Kade. The fingers of his right hand were curled as though still holding a glass.

"Master," she whispered, seeing her reflection in his eyes. Taking her small hand in his big one, he bowed and kissed her fingers.

"Miss O'Connor," he said as he stepped closer to her, keeping her hand imprisoned in his and sliding his other hand around her waist. "Allow me to present Bog Daniels, captain of the *Gypsy Lady,* one of Morgan Shipping's vessels that handles cargo shipments between the islands and the newly formed American states. He also handles a great deal of the business for Morgan Shipping. Bog, I would like you to meet Miss Kathleen O'Connor from Ireland."

Kade trailed one finger across Kathleen's palm. Shivers raced up her arm, then over her entire body. She tried to pull free. He tightened his grip until she ceased to struggle, then resumed the secret caress.

Clenching the fingers of her other hand until her nails cut painfully into her palms, Kathleen fought to maintain her poise. It was difficult to act properly when such improper things were being done to her, especially improper things that made her bones melt and pulse race.

"Captain Daniels, it is a pleasure to meet you." Her

voice was huskier than usual, betraying Kade's effect on her senses. "Please forgive me if I was rude before. I prefer to meet someone before having my hand devoured." The smile she gave him belied her words. It was several seconds before Bog recognized the reproach. His face flamed red.

"Kade, do we have enough time for a glass of wine before dinner?" Kathleen asked.

Kade led her to the sofa and released her hand as she sat down. He crossed to the liquor cabinet and poured the wine. The glass he handed her sparkled in the firelight. Kathleen admired the beauty of the crystal as she twirled it in her fingertips.

She took a small sip of wine, rolling the wonderful flavor over her tongue. Bog seated himself across from her and crossed his legs, drawing Kathleen's attention to his boots. They were brown. Brown suede. Kathleen stared at them, her face burning.

Kade was standing beside her, leaning against the mantel over the fireplace. She could not stop herself from looking up at him. She knew immediately that he, too, was thinking about the brown suede boots he had worn on board the *Black Eagle*. His smile draped itself over her, enclosing her in its intimate warmth while his eyes devoured her. Kathleen forced herself to turn away from him. She tried to remember how much she hated this man, her master. All she could think of was how very tall he was.

Dinner was announced. Bog stood and offered her his arm. "I would be honored if you would allow me to accompany you to the dining room, Miss O'Connor." His accent was decidedly English, aristocratic and pure. She laid her hand on his arm.

"How kind of you, Captain Daniels. I would not want to get lost between here and there, it is such a short distance."

149

He caught the barbed remark instantly and laughed heartily as he handed her into the chair Kade indicated next to the head of the table. Kade sat beside Kathleen, reclining easily in the master's chair. Bog moved to the seat opposite his host. Kathleen looked at the display of silver and china spread before them. It seemed as though the table was prepared for thirty people, not three. She had never seen so many forks, spoons and plates in her life.

Bog was watching her, his eyes following her every move. At first it made Kathleen nervous; then another thought occurred to her. He might help me escape!

"Kathleen," Kade said. "I know what you are thinking. Forget it."

She ground her teeth together. This is unfair, she thought. Can I not have privacy within my own mind? She took a big drink of wine and promptly choked.

"Katie wants you to help her escape from Mistral, Bog," Kade said in answer to the question on Bog's face. "If you do, I will kill you."

Kathleen stared in disbelief at him. Did he mean it? Would he kill anyone that helped her?

"What do you mean, escape?" Bog asked.

"I am not a guest on this island as Kade implied earlier, Captain Daniels," Kathleen said with a defiant lift of her chin. "I am his slave, held with no hope of ever obtaining my freedom." His shocked expression pleased her.

"That is not the complete truth. I have taught Kate quite a bit about sailing and navigation. Once she is fully recovered from an accident she had on the *Black Eagle,* she plans to steal a boat and escape."

Kathleen nodded confirmation, then had to suppress a laugh at the incredulous look on Bog Daniels' face. A servant entered the dining room and placed a silver platter in front of Kade. It contained the largest rib roast Kathleen had ever seen, surrounded by a veritable mountain of vegetables.

Bog lifted his wineglass. "I propose a toast. To Kade Morgan and his most attractive slave, Kate O'Connor!"

The words had scarcely left his mouth before Kathleen's eyes flared wide and wild. "English scum!" she screamed as she leapt to her feet and grabbed the carving knife from Kade. An instant later she was holding it against Bog's throat. "I'll be a slittin' yer throat like a Christmas goose if'n ye e'er dare to call me Kate again!"

Even with the knife pressed so close that he could feel the sting of its sharp blade, Bog could think of nothing except the burning heat of Kathleen's anger. What would it be like to feel that anger turn to passion?

From the first moment he had seen her descending the stairs, he had wanted her. She was so exquisitely beautiful with that perfect face and thick hair that was blacker than sin itself. And those strange eyes, that husky voice. Bog wanted to kiss her lips, her face, her neck. He wanted to explore the curves spilling over the ivory lace on her bodice, to lift the rustling silk that brushed against his leg and discover the secrets it concealed.

He swallowed to dispel the desire that was so strong it was almost choking him. "I am sorry that I offended you, Miss O'Connor. It was a mistake that will not be repeated."

"Kathleen, sit down," Kade ordered sharply.

She looked at him, his eyes holding hers. She lowered the knife and returned to her place at the table, shaken and more miserable than she had thought possible as she realized that Kade had been calling her Kate ever since that first day on the *Black Eagle*. Only her father called her that. It was a special name, something she would not allow anyone else to use. Why did it not bother her that her master called her Kate? Or Katie, or even kitten?

Kathleen's outburst against Bog had surprised Kade. He knew she had a temper but had not realized it might be violent. On the beach she had threatened to cut his throat. There was no time like the present to see if she was serious.

"Kate, hand me the knife."

Something glimmered in the depths of her eyes, something that made the skin on the back of Kade's neck crawl. Seconds stretched into minutes. Finally she turned the knife around and put the handle into his outstretched hand.

Kathleen drew a shaky breath. She could have killed him, could have run the knife through his throat or into his chest. But she had not, could not. Instead she had obeyed him. Without question, without anger. Just as she would eventually obey him when he ordered her to share his bed. The room closed in around her, as did her fate.

Chapter 13

The rest of the dinner went quietly. Kathleen handled everything with ease, including the second glass of wine Kade poured for her. A warm glow spread over her, and the tension she had felt earlier eased, then disappeared. During the meal, Kade and Bog Daniels talked about Morgan Shipping. The only time the plantation was discussed was when Kade asked about his foreman, Harry Timpson. Bog immediately directed his full attention to the meal, saying only that Timpson had been working on the construction of a building to be used in making rum.

Kade asked several more questions about the plantation. When he received answers that contained only words, not information, he turned the conversation back to a subject Bog had briefly mentioned earlier. It was a problem that involved Ivan Flesher, the captain of the *Christabel*, Morgan Shipping's newest cargo ship.

Bog had received complaints from several regular customers, men who shipped sugar and rum to England from their plantations in the Caribbean. They reported that some of their cargo had been left sitting on the docks in Barbados and Martinique, though payment had been made for the shipments. Bog suspected that Flesher was using cargo space reserved for those customers to ship unscheduled merchandise for his own profit.

White lines of anger ran out from the corners of Kade's eyes. The muscles in his jaw and neck were tight, and he clenched the delicate stem of his wineglass so firmly Kathleen was surprised it did not break. When next Ivan Flesher brought the *Christabel* to Mistral, his reception on Mistral would not be a pleasant one.

After dinner they went into the living room, the men smoking cigars and sipping brandy as they relaxed on the sofas across from each other. Kade motioned for Kathleen to sit beside him. She thrilled at the warmth in his eyes as he watched her cross the room, then intentionally sat on the end of the sofa farthest from him, smiling innocently at him and watching as the room seemed to mist over slightly.

"Tell me about yourself, Kathleen," Bog said as he flicked his ashes into a dish on the table between them.

"There is not much to tell, Captain Daniels. I am from Ireland, I am Kade's slave, and I am going back to Ireland."

Kade lifted his cigar to his lips, puffed and watched the smoke curl up to the ceiling. "I like a blunt woman," he said. "Don't you, Bog?"

Kathleen took a sip of wine and hiccuped. "How strange," she said, holding one hand to her mouth as she hiccuped again.

Someone laughed. She looked accusingly at Kade. He was concentrating intently on the glowing tip of his cigar. Bog was busy tracing the design on the cushion beside him. I am positive someone laughed at me, she thought. Another hiccup broke the silence.

"Perhaps I should have some more wine," she said, handing her empty glass to Kade.

"Perhaps you should not," he told her, saving the delicate glass from an uncertain fate as it slipped from her fingers.

For some reason, Kathleen's eyes seemed to be glued to Kade's face. The movement of his lips and the slight flare of his nostrils as he breathed were wholly fascinating to her. I should not be staring, she told herself. Her face was so hot it burned when she touched it.

I must have a fever. That must be why I feel so strange, like the room is spinning and my arms and legs are so light. The air was so thick she was having trouble breathing. Her lips were dry. She wet them with the tip of her tongue, remembering the feel and taste of Kade kissing her.

His right arm rested along the back of the sofa between them, his fingers brown and strong against the delicate material. Only a few hours ago those fingers had touched her flesh, moving tenderly across her breasts and down her stomach. Chill bumps rose on Kathleen's arms and she shivered.

"Are you cold?" Kade asked.

"Yes," she said, her lips taking forever to form the word as her eyes locked with his. Kade pulled her over beside him and wrapped his arms around her.

"It is much warmer in here," she said, and he held her a little closer.

"I cannot imagine why," Bog said. Kathleen had forgotten he was in the room. His face was red and he was loosening his collar.

"I guess you have never been in here," she said. A rumble sounded from inside Kade's chest, and his face was almost as red as Bog's. Why was everyone hot except her?

"No," Bog said, sounding a little choked. "I cannot say that I have."

"Kathleen," Kade said as he cupped her chin with his hand. "Was tonight the first time you have ever had wine?"

"You are quite perceptive, Captain," she said, stumbling a little over "perceptive." "It is also the first time I have ever worn stockings like these." She pulled the hem of the blue gown up past her knee to reveal a shapely leg encased in a silk stocking. Her foot was bare. She lifted her other foot. It was also bare.

"It appears that I have lost my shoes. They were too big, just like this dress. I assume I will be losing it next."

Bog let out a guffaw of laughter, dropped his cigar and began to frantically search for it among the cushions on the sofa. What a clumsy man, Kathleen thought as she listened to Kade's chest rumble again. It sounded like he was laughing inside but not outside.

She pulled open his satin vest. "What is going on in here?" she asked and began to work on the buttons of his shirt.

"I think it would be best if you went to bed, Kate."

"What a wonderful idea, master," she whispered up at him as she pushed her hand into his shirt, fascinated by the broad expanse of his chest.

Kade heard Bog's quick intake of breath at the intimacy in Kathleen's husky voice. He purposely leaned forward to press a lingering kiss to her forehead. Then he stood, lifting her in his arms. The skirt of her gown spilled across his hands in a froth of blue silk and ivory petticoats.

"I do not want to be a bad host, Bog, but apparently Kathleen has had too much to drink. I must take her to bed," he said and watched Bog's face flush a deeper shade of red.

As Kade started up the steps, Kathleen's lips touched his neck in a tentative kiss, and then her tongue ran across his burning flesh. Her hands moved across his chest and shoulders, exploring and exciting him. At the landing outside his room, Kade stopped to look down at the woman in his arms. Her lips drifted into a smile, her eyes lifted to his beneath the shadow of her thick lashes. Kade gave a low growl before claiming Kathleen's open lips in a scorching kiss, not releasing her mouth until he had kicked open his bedroom door and walked into the dimly lit room.

In the dying light of the fire, Bog Daniels watched the scene on the landing above him. When the door closed behind Kade, he began to swear softly. The brandy that remained in his glass was swallowed in one burning gulp. The memory of Kathleen's petite form crushed in Kade's powerful embrace was more than Bog could stand. He tossed the stub of his cigar into the fireplace and grabbed a bottle of whiskey from the liquor cabinet. It was going to be a long night, one he did not want to remember.

Kade put Kathleen down on his bed and tore his jacket and vest off, freeing himself from the tight bonds of fabric. She lay on the burgundy bedspread, curling her hands into her hair, dislodging the comb that held the masses of raven silk captive.

He sat beside her and ran his fingers through the tangled curls, then leaned down to touch his lips to hers. She returned his kiss, her tongue slipping into his mouth as her fingers held tightly to his shoulders. He circled her waist with one arm to draw her closer to him, the kiss becoming deeper, desperate.

"Why is the room moving?" she asked when he released her lips and moved his head to take her earlobe between his teeth.

"It is not, kitten. You have had too much to drink."

She tried to sit up. "Do you mean that I am drunk?"

He began to undo the buttons on the back of her dress. "Not drunk, just a little tipsy. Hold still while I

157

finish these." Kathleen rested her head on his shoulder, and he impatiently ripped the last two buttons off the blue silk.

"Then I am not a fairy?" she asked as he laid her back on the bed. He pulled the dress down over her breasts. The sheer fabric of her chemise moved entrancingly as she breathed. Kade ran his fingers lightly over the ivory surface that imprisoned her.

"A fairy? Nay, 'tis no fairy I touch."

He kissed her again, exploring the warm sweetness of her mouth as she opened herself to him like a rose blooming in the spring sunshine. She touched his face hesitantly, then let her fingertips drift across his skin as she moved them down to the open neck of his shirt. Kade trailed his hand across the curving softness hidden by the chemise, and Kathleen moaned an impassioned response while he kissed her throat, his tongue touching the sensitive hollow lightly.

"But I feel so strange," she breathed against his neck, "like I am floating. And my body tingles where you touch me." Her hands moved into his hair, and she pulled his head up so she could see his face. "How do you know I am not a fairy?"

There was such innocence and trust in her eyes. Kade did not want to see this side of Kathleen, he wanted to see the woman who had trembled at the touch of his suede boots, the woman who had given him pleasure and passion such as he had never known. The little-girl image did not disappear, though. It hiccupped, then giggled.

"Because fairies do not hiccup or threaten people with carving knives." He pulled the bodice of her gown up over the tempting peaks of her breasts, even though his throat ached and his loins demanded satisfaction for their throbbing need.

Kathleen nodded seriously, as though he had

clarified an important issue. He gathered her into his arms, carrying her into her room. He sat her on the edge of her bed to remove her dress and petticoats, then knelt before her and slipped the silk stockings from the slim length of her legs. The only thing left was the chemise. Kade hesitated. Though it was only a thin barrier between them, once it was gone he would not be able to resist what she so innocently offered.

Kade had known many women. None of them had meant anything to him; not even Sarita Ridley, though she had been closer to him than any of the others. He had met Sarita in England after her elderly husband's death. She had been looking for a lover to satisfy her without imposing demands upon her socially or financially. Kade had been attracted to her cool, elegant beauty, and they had established a satisfying relationship that lasted until Sarita spent the fortune her husband had left her and decided to make her rich, handsome lover into a husband.

Sarita had always been in perfect control of her emotions, never raising her voice or losing her temper until the last time Kade had seen her, which was when he confiscated all the clothes and personal items she had charged to his London accounts. Kade's memories of her serene gray eyes, ivory complexion and pale golden hair that caught and held light like a frosted window were not unpleasant ones.

Kathleen's lashes cast fragile shadows on her sculpted cheeks. She was as unpredictable and as volatile as an active volcano. She bullied her way through life without trying to affect grace or charm, yet exuding both with such careless abandon she had taken Kade's heart by storm.

Ever since her capture by the pirates, Kathleen had lived through more hells than most women ever experienced. Somehow she had come through it with her innocent, trusting nature intact. The enigmas of her personality were traits of the Irish, Jake had said. If so, Kade thought, then the Irish were strange people; hardheaded, unpredictable, provocative. Very provocative.

From the first moment he had seen Kathleen on the auction stage in Morocco, bravely confronting a world that had turned against her, Kade had experienced something he rarely felt: sympathy. He had bought her with the intent of discovering where she belonged and returning her there. At least that had been his plan until her voice, pride and body got in the way of his reason. Then his charitable intentions had vanished in a heated wave of desire.

Kathleen rolled onto her side, her arm falling off the edge of the bed. Kade tucked it back up beside her and pulled the blanket over her, kneeling to kiss her soft lips. She returned the pressure of his kiss, surprising him. He drew a finger along her jaw as she opened sleepy blue-green eyes.

"Kade," she whispered, smiling gently and touching his hand. Her eyes closed and she was asleep again.

"Good night, kitten," he whispered, pushing aside a curl that had fallen across her cheek. She made a little sound like a sigh as he kissed her temple. The sweet smell of her filled Kade's senses, flowing through him like a powerful tonic that set his blood racing and his mind reeling. He quickly left the room without looking back.

The darkness over Mistral was giving way to dawn as Kade finished dressing and began to pack his seabag. He thought he heard something and stood quietly beside his dresser, a handkerchief in his hand. A moment later he heard it again, a frightened cry that dissolved into a sob. He threw open the door that led to Kathleen's room. She was frantically thrashing about in a tangle of quilts.

As he approached the bed, she sat up and screamed, "No! Stop touching me!" Her voice became pleading and desperate, "Please, *please* stop."

Kade sat on the edge of the bed and pulled her into his arms. She beat against his chest with clenched fists, trying to free herself. His superior strength won out, and she stopped fighting, lying limp and forsaken in his tender embrace.

"Wake up, Kathleen," he said as he stroked her hair lightly.

Her lashes, wet and glistening in the pale dawn light, lifted. She started in fear when she saw Kade. He held her tightly, whispering comforting words until recognition sparked in the beautiful aqua eyes.

"I was dreaming," she said, making no move to escape his embrace. Her hands clutched his arm.

"What about, kitten?"

The lashes lowered, the soft lips trembled. "About Rat Anders. He was trying to—to touch me."

Kade pushed her head down onto his chest, holding her so close he could feel her heart beating. "Did he ever touch you, Kate?"

She nodded and sniffed. "When he took me off the pirate ship he let me wash and gave me that dress I was wearing when you bought me, the one you ripped." He felt her smile against his neck.

"Before I could put it on, he came into the room. I was already chained to the wall so there was no way to get away from him. He pushed me into the corner and started touching me, it was horrible." She looked up at Kade, the trust and innocence he had recoiled from last night once again shining in her eyes. "Not like when you touch me. I like that."

161

For her to make such an admission meant she was still partially drunk or partially asleep. Possibly both. She laid her head on his shoulder and he pressed a kiss against her hair.

"Then Rat knelt down and put his mouth on my . . . my . . ." A sob tore from the depths of her soul.

"On this?" Kade asked, running his hand up her leg and under her chemise, cupping it over the hidden treasure of curls between her legs.

"Yes, there." She sighed contentedly as he began to stroke her gently with his thumb.

"What happened, then?" He eased her back onto the bed.

"It made me sick, it was so awful what he was doing. I wanted to die, he was making disgusting noises and I could not push him away. Then he stood up and slapped me, saying that I was not any good, that he could not even get hard." Kade dried her tears with his handkerchief. She took it from him and blew her nose.

"Have you had nightmares about this before, Kathleen?" He slipped his hand back under the chemise, touching her ever so lightly.

"Yes," she said. "I had them on the ship sometimes."

Kade continued to rub the tight nest of curls between her legs while running his lips over the rigid peaks of her nipples so hauntingly concealed by the chemise. Suddenly Kathleen took a deep breath, and her legs parted to allow him greater access. He pushed one finger into the moist folds, delighting in the wet wonder of her.

"You must forget about Rat, Kate. What he did to you was wrong."

"You are touching me there. Is that wrong?"

"I touch you to give you pleasure. If you do not enjoy it, I will stop." He moved his hand away, laying it on her thigh.

Kathleen placed her fingers on his hand, moving it back between her legs, back into the wetness. She does not know what she is doing, he told himself. Wine is fogging her senses, sleep is clouding her reason. His fingers touched her, moving through the moisture, over the swollen need. Her breasts rose and fell under the ivory silk. Her lips parted, her tongue caught between her teeth. Kade knew he was taking advantage of her condition, knew what he was doing was wrong, knew he should leave.

He lowered his head. His mouth pressed against the wetness. Exquisite sensations coursed up Kathleen's stomach, across her breasts, into her mind and soul. She strained closer to him, wanting more of his touch, more of his intimate kisses.

Kade lifted his hands to her breasts, ripping the fragile chemise to free the softness it concealed. He took her nipples between his fingers, skillfully manipulating the tender flesh and adding to her pleasure. And to his.

She writhed against the sheets, moaned into the stillness. Her fingers clasped Kade's head, wound into his hair, pulled him tighter against her. A darkness came over her. It throbbed and pulsed, a living thing that expanded and enlarged as his tongue pushed into her.

He moved his lips onto her stomach, the touch of his unshaven face feeling like rough suede against inflamed flesh. She wanted more, needed more. His hand slid between her legs while he sucked on her nipple. She could not stop the cries of pleasure that came from inside her, and the sound of them excited her, taking her deeper and higher so that the darkness intensified, changing shape as it went out of control. The change

163

frightened her, her loss of control frightened her, and she pushed Kade away.

"Do not fight me, love, you are almost there."

The rich, confident voice soothed her, reassured her. Kade held her hips steady and lowered his head again. His tongue stroked her, licked her, possessed her. It sent Kathleen spiraling into a realm of ecstasy she had sampled once before but not fully explored. Now it lay before her, a world without end, a universe without bonds. The darkness within her exploded and she was plummeted into a sea of pleasure, deep wonderful wet pleasure that surged over her, into her, through her.

Kade continued to kiss her secret places until the last quiver of joy passed; then he trailed his tongue up over her stomach and breasts before pulling her into the haven of his arms. Ever so slowly the darkness in her mind began to clear.

Kade kissed her, his lips moving so gently she wanted to cry. "Did you enjoy it, kitten?"

She pulled his mouth down and they kissed again, a deep searching kiss that gave Kade the answer to his question. Her head fell back against his arm, and she touched his lips with a tentative finger.

"Was I good?"

He laughed. "Aye, sweet Kate, you were *very* good." He placed her hand on the bulge in his pants. "And I am very hard."

She bent her head and kissed the bulge, then cuddled back into his suddenly stiff embrace. "I am glad," she murmured. Seconds later she was asleep.

It was some time before Kade was able to overcome the effect of the light brush of Kathleen's lips on the front of his pants. When his head stopped pounding and his heart slowed enough to allow him to breathe again, he laid the sleeping girl aside and covered her with a blanket.

He went back to get his seabag, then dashed out of his room like the demons of the netherworld were after him. He went into the kitchen and was startled to discover Mattie was already awake and cooking.

"What are ye lookin' at me like that for, lad?" She shoved a mug of coffee into his hands and pushed him into a chair. "I'll not be lettin' neither ye nor that 'usband of mine sail off into the unknown wi'out a 'ot breakfast." She set a plate of food in front of him.

"I am not hungry, Mattie."

"An' it's me bet that I'd be knowin' why," she said. "That ragamuffin ye fetched 'ome 'as got to ye, lad."

Kade snorted. "Will you ever stop trying to get me to settle down? That ragamuffin, as you call her, has not gotten to me." He shook his head to rid himself of the memory of Kathleen's lips brushing against his pants. "Do not try to play matchmaker, Mattie, you will hurt everyone concerned except me." He picked up his fork and attacked the eggs on his plate.

"Why did ye buy the lass, Kade? Surely 'twas not to be workin' on the plantation."

"You sound like Jake." He finished his coffee in one swallow and glanced out the window. The golden morning light was moving across the flowers in the garden, bringing them to life one at a time. Mistral had to be the most beautiful place on earth.

He looked around him. On the table were a dozen loaves of freshly baked bread. They smelled of ripe wheat and melted butter. Who got up so early to make that bread, who ate it when he was at sea? This was his home, yet he knew so little about what went on outside his office.

Mattie stood beside the counter, her arms crossed over sagging bosoms, and her salt-and-pepper hair tightly braided and wrapped several times around her head. Had she always been this old? Wrinkles traced over her face, and her dark gray eyes had faded to silver. She was like Jake, always there, always patiently serving Kade without question or complaint. Why had he not noticed them before, really noticed them? A warm rush of emotion for these two people who had been with him all his life filled Kade, and he smiled at the unfamiliar feelings.

"Jake and I will not be gone long this time, Mattie. Take care of Katie for me."

"Does she know that ye be goin'?"

"No, she was in no shape last night to discuss anything."

Mattie busied herself with cleaning up Kade's dishes. "What about this mornin'?" she asked. "I was thinkin' I heard some noise upstairs afore ye came down."

Kade's face burned. "She had a bad dream," he said shortly, cutting off any further comments. "Have that doctor Bog Daniels convinced to move to Mistral come up from the village today and look her over, she has been ill. She can go out into the garden, no further than that. If she does anything more strenuous than climb those steps in there . . ." He tried to think of something that would make her obey. "Disobedience will result in the stables being permanently off-limits when she is well." That should get her attention, he thought with a grin.

"An' that is supposed to make 'er behave?" Mattie wrapped two loaves of bread in brown paper and stuffed them in Kade's seabag.

"Katie used to raise horses; depriving her of riding would kill her. Do we have someone who can sew around here?"

Mattie laughed. "A few."

"Good. I will bring some material back from Nassau, meanwhile see what we have here and have some dresses made for her. Sarita's are much too large. She will also need a maid, otherwise she will never be able to get dressed properly. Is there anyone on the island?"

"Nay, lad, none 'ere would do for that."

Kade tried to imagine Kathleen surrendering to the ministrations of a lady's maid, remembering instead the way she had taken a knife to Bog Daniels. "Maybe a maid is not a good idea. Last night Katie put a knife against Bog's throat and threatened to carve him up like a Christmas goose. Damn near scared the life out of him. I would hate to think what she might do to a maid." He ran his hand through his hair and picked up his seabag.

Mattie shook with laughter. She had never seen Kade in such a state. Worrying about lady's maids, fancy clothes and the like. And all over a slave he claimed not to care a whit about.

"What is so funny?" he asked.

"Nary a thing ye would be understandin'. Any other orders?"

"Never, *ever,* call her Kate."

He left then, swinging his seabag over his shoulder. The bread was warm against his back. The sun sparkled on the fountain in front of the house, and the garden smelled of fresh air and flowers. Kade walked down to the harbor, the breeze ruffling the open neck of his shirt. After this trip he would spend some time on Mistral, learn who made that bread and who ate it.

On board the *Eagle* Kade ordered the anchor to be weighed, the sails unfurled and hoisted. He sent a lookout aloft, checked the direction of the wind and

167

steered his ship past the volcanic cliffs and through the reef opening. Then he handed the wheel over to the helmsman and stood at the stern of the ship, watching as Mistral faded into the hazy blue horizon. When he came back, Kathleen would be waiting for him. She would surrender her pride and come to him. Yes, when he came back, she would be completely, totally his.

Chapter 14

Sunlight poured through the windows in the bedroom, filling the air with golden light and waking Kathleen from a pleasant dream. She felt wonderful, relaxed and somehow different. The covers on the bed fell to the floor as she stretched. Her body tingled all over, and she was so hungry she could eat a horse. She jumped out of bed, eager to dress and go down for breakfast. Her head almost fell off her shoulders. She lifted her hand to her pounding temple and noticed that clutched in her fingers was a handkerchief with the initials KM in one corner.

Where did this come from, she wondered. The piece of linen brought back memories that made Kathleen gasp. She sat down so quickly she missed the bed and landed on the floor. It could not be true. She had been dreaming, that was all. Or had she? There was more evidence than just the handkerchief. Her chemise was torn, hanging open to her waist and completely exposing her breasts.

"It was a dream!" she cried, wincing at the sound of her voice. The thought of dark eyes and powerful muscles made her shiver. She had to know the truth, had to know it was just a dream. The blue robe was hanging on the edge of the wooden screen. Kathleen slipped it on and went into the shadowed interior of

Kade's bedroom.

It was an extremely large room, the floor covered with a carpet marked with Oriental designs like the one on board the *Black Eagle,* the walls were paneled in dark wood. The drapes were made of the same burgundy material as the spread covering the bed. There were books stacked on the tables flanking the bed, and a beautiful lamp made of red glass was on one table. The other table was conspicuously empty, its lamp a victim of Kathleen's temper the previous day.

She leaned against the wall. This room was like Kade, dark and mysterious. And so very masculine. Life used to be so easy, she thought; now there are strange emotions, strange handkerchiefs and torn chemises to deal with. Yet those things did not bother her as much as the strange dream that she knew was not a dream.

Kathleen went back into her room. There was a pitcher of fresh water behind the screen. She did a brief toilet, then began sorting through the clothes in the closet. After pushing aside more than a dozen dresses and twice as many petticoats, she gave up and threw herself into the rocking chair.

"Why be ye so sad, child?" Mattie asked as she bustled into the room.

"Nothing to wear," Kathleen said dejectedly.

The old woman stared at the open closet, at the profusion of silks and satins spilling out onto the carpet. "Land's sake, what more would ye be wantin' to wear? Them gowns be fit for a queen!"

"I am a slave, not a queen. Wearing one of those things for dinner was bad enough, during the day is out of the question. If Captain Morgan wants them worn, he can wear them." Kathleen scowled at the closet as though she could make the dresses disappear by sheer willpower.

Mattie burst into such a fit of laughter she collapsed against the bed, her breasts heaving and double chins bouncing. "I can just see him, gussied up in some frilly yellow thing with puffy sleeves!" She wiped her streaming eyes with the corner of her apron and opened the trunk sitting against the wall, pulling forth a white skirt and blue blouse, both made of soft cotton. "This should be more to yer taste, lass."

"No breeches?" Kathleen asked as she lifted the skirt.

Mattie ignored the question. "Get dressed and come down to the kitchen. Breakfast be ready and waitin'," she said as she left the room.

Kathleen threw off her robe and dressed. "Comfortable," she decided, "but not as good as breeches."

It took a few minutes to return the room to an orderly state; then she headed for the kitchen. The smell of bacon greeted her as she walked through the dining room and down the hall that led to the kitchen.

In the center of the massive room was a table with benches pushed underneath. Wide counters lined the walls and there was an oven large enough to cook an entire horse. The sink was almost as big as the oven. A pump handle, painted bright red, poured a stream of water into the sink's cavernous depths beneath the determined efforts of a little black girl sitting on the counter.

There were at least six other people in the kitchen performing a variety of tasks. A black girl about Kathleen's age scooped a heap of bacon from the pan she held and dropped the sizzling meat onto a plate already filled with eggs and biscuits. She put it on the table and added a bowl of oatmeal and a cup of coffee.

"Your breakfast is ready, miss," she said shyly to Kathleen, then lifted the little girl, who was still working the pump handle, down from the sink. Together they ran out the back door. Mattie came out of the pantry carrying two dead chickens.

"Sit down, Kathleen, and eat afore e'erthin' gets cold. Effie ain't much good at reheatin' eggs."

Kathleen pulled out a bench and seated herself at the table. "Is all this food for me?"

"No one but," a man's voice said. She looked around, seeing Bog Daniels come in from the dining room. He dropped onto the bench opposite Kathleen and filched one of her biscuits. His eyes were bloodshot, and there were definite signs that he had a hangover; Kathleen had seen the symptoms before on her brother Niall.

And on myself this morning, she realized as her head began to throb again. She took a big drink of coffee, feeling its healing effect almost instantly.

"Kade wanted the doctor to call round and check on ye today," Mattie told Kathleen. "He said ye'd been ill." She set a jar of honey on the table and went back into the pantry.

"I do not need a doctor."

Bog liberally smeared his biscuit with butter and honey. "The boss wants you to see one anyway."

"Where is the boss?" she asked, taking the last biscuit just as Bog reached for it.

"Gone, sailed away into the dawn to deliver turtles and sugar to Nassau."

"Gone? Kade is gone?" she asked, looking at Bog instead of her biscuit and pouring honey on her eggs.

"No need to look so disappointed, he will return."

Fingering the edge of her knife, Kathleen fixed him with a level stare. Bog looked from her to the sharp blade. He put up a hand to signal his surrender. Kathleen laid the knife down and finished her breakfast while thinking about the wonderful opportunities Kade's absence presented.

She placed her dirty dishes in the sink and pumped

some water onto them. To that she added some that was boiling on the stove. Just as she finished washing them, Mattie came into the kitchen carrying two more chickens.

"What be ye doin', child? Kade will 'ave my 'ead. He gave orders ye were to do naught more strenuous than climbin' steps and 'ere ye be, washin' dishes."

Kathleen dried her hands. "Kade is not here and I fully intend to do a lot more than just climb steps." Like explore this island and find a way to escape. "How long before he gets back?"

"Two weeks," Bog said. "He will transfer the sugar onto the *Jamaican Queen* to be sent to the Carolinas. The turtles he wants to sell in Nassau, something about not sending them too far or else they might get dry. I have no idea what he meant."

Kathleen folded the towel she was holding and placed it gently on the counter. He had not forgotten. She smiled at the wall.

A bell sounded in the front of the house, and Mattie motioned to Kathleen. "That'll be Dr. Benjamin Williams come to see ye."

"I'll let him in, Mattie," Bog said, wincing and rubbing his head as the bell sounded again. "Do you want him to wait in the living room, Kathleen?"

"Tell him to go home." She headed for the back door.

"But Kade said . . ."

"I do not care in the slightest what Kade did or did not say."

"Maybe ye should," Mattie said, "for if ye don't do as 'e ordered 'e'll not allow ye use the stables when 'e returns."

Kathleen whirled to face Mattie. She had assumed somewhere on Mistral there would be horses—tired, overworked beasts with sagging backs. She had not

173

considered the fact there might be horses for riding, sleek graceful creatures of speed and beauty. Her throat ached at the thought of being astride a horse again.

"Where is the stable?"

"No matter, ye'll not be goin' there before Kade comes 'ome, and only then if ye do as 'e said. An' that was to see the doctor an' to go no further than the garden. Ye must get well before ye go any further than that. Until then ye're under my supervision, child. An' don't ye be thinkin' for a minute I'll not tell the lad if ye take it into yer 'ead to ignore 'is orders."

It had been so long, a lifetime, since Kathleen had ridden Taran. She could think of nothing except the need to touch a horse again, to smell the earthy scent of flesh and hay inside a barn, to feel beneath her the surging power of a horse flinging himself into the wind as he stretched his muscles to the limit.

Kade's threat took all the fight out of Kathleen. Because he used her own weaknesses as weapons against her, she had no defense against him. It was a most unfair strategy, and a most effective one.

"Kade Morgan is a black-hearted, irritating bastard, and I damn him to hell and back a thousand times," she said calmly, causing Mattie to blush and Bog to grin.

"You don't need to worry about me disobeying Kade's orders, Mrs. McBradden," she said. "I'll let the doctor examine me, I'll do nothing more strenuous than climbing stairs, and I'll sit in the garden like an invalid, waiting for the return of that demon who owns me. And someday I will make Kade Morgan pay for pulling this trick on me."

Dr. Benjamin Williams, an English physician only recently transplanted from the crowded streets of

London to the beautiful serenity of the West Indies, pronounced Kathleen overly fit for someone with broken ribs, then ordered her to do nothing more strenuous than climb stairs and recommended she spend time in the garden while recuperating. Kathleen ground her teeth together and thought about throwing the good doctor out the window of her room. He closed his medical bag with a snap and left her alone.

Kathleen sat on the edge of her bed and dug her toes into the rug. She had to find a way of getting some exercise. It would be impossible to escape in her present condition. And before she could escape, she needed to know where she was. There had been a basket of charts in Kade's study; one of them might show Mistral. She jumped up from the bed and searched through the drawer in the dressing table, finding an assortment of hair ribbons. She chose three of various colors.

She dashed out the door and ran down the steps. At the bottom she stopped to catch her breath, her legs aching and her head spinning. Kade had specifically said she was allowed to do nothing more strenuous than climb steps, an activity that became extremely strenuous when performed at a dead run.

"I shall climb these steps until I wear them out," she announced to the empty room. "At the end of two weeks I will be fit as a fiddle and twice as curvy."

Her brother had often said that when describing a girl he liked, which was every girl he saw. Kathleen laughed, thinking of those buxom Irish maids who had made poor Niall's life miserable with their teasing and flirting ways.

Bog Daniels was walking through the garden outside the house when he heard Kathleen's laughter. The memory of her in Kade's arms the previous night was strong within him, and he stopped to listen, unable to ignore the tightness in his loins or the emptiness in his heart.

There was no doubt in his mind what Kade intended doing with Kathleen. He would use her up, then toss her out with no more thought than he would give an old shirt. She deserved better than that, just as a plantation like Mistral deserved better care than Kade Morgan gave it. He neglected everything, leaving Harry Timpson in complete charge.

The foreman knew almost as little about growing cane as Kade himself. He drove the workers to do more than humanly possible, threatening them with torture and death if they dared report the cruel punishments to Kade. Not that it would do any good if they did; Kade would demand evidence to support the complaint, and it was almost impossible to prove how recently whip marks had been inflicted once they healed.

Several months ago an island whose fields had just been hacked out of the sweating depths of the jungle had been brought to Bog's attention. Someday, under the right owner, it could be every bit as productive and beautiful as Mistral. All it took was someone who cared.

Bog cared. He wanted to buy that island, make it and the plantation his. He knew the type of house he would build, one with an iron portcullis enclosing the balconies and gardens, one with elegant lines and graceful arches surrounded by rich crops of sugar and tobacco, bananas and coffee, crops like those grown on Mistral. And there would be a woman in that house, a woman with soft skin and shining eyes who loved to smile and whose laughter filled his heart with sunshine and his body with longing.

He fingered the crimson petal of a hibiscus flower,

thinking about Kathleen O'Connor walking through the rooms of his imaginary house as he watched her come through the open doors of Kade's house. She shaded her eyes against the bright sunlight, smiling as she saw him in the garden. His throat tightened. No matter how much he wanted her, he would have to restrain himself. There was something unusual in Kade's attitude toward Kathleen. And since it was unusual it had to be considered deadly.

"I would like to send word to my father so he will know I am alive. Will you help me?"

"Absolutely not," he said, noticing the way the light came through the thin cotton of her skirt, outlining the slim length of her legs.

She removed her hand from her brow, and her sleeve caught on a bush. Her blouse fell off her shoulder, revealing the top of a breast that curved seductively under the dark blue cotton. Bog crushed the petals of the flower he was holding and watched dry-mouthed as she freed herself and straightened the blouse.

"Why not?" she asked. "Kade threatened to kill you only if you helped me escape."

"You will soon learn, Kathleen, that Kade Morgan does not threaten, he states facts. If you try to contact your father, Kade will regard it as an escape attempt. So the answer is no, unconditionally and without hope of negotiation."

Kathleen had not expected success, so she was not unduly disappointed, just annoyed. She glanced around her. "I assume this is the garden where I am to be held prisoner until my master returns. How far does it reach?"

Bog pointed out the boundaries. "Does it meet your approval?"

"Would it matter if it did not?" she snapped, her annoyance changing into anger as his eyes strayed yet again to the front of her blouse. She spun around and went back into the house.

She wiped a film of perspiration from her face. "How can it be so hot so early in the day?" The sun streamed in through the doors, soaking into the terra-cotta tiles. She closed the glass doors, pulled the drapes together and went into the study.

This room fascinated Kathleen. In addition to those on the crowded shelves, the entire floor was covered with mounds of books, stacks of books, crates of books. There seemed to be not enough space in the entire house to hold such an assortment of printed matter. There had been little opportunity for reading at Emerald Hills. Books were hard to come by in Ireland, and there had always been work to do. Now that she had time to read, it was a delight to find herself surrounded by a lifetime supply of books.

Here, as in his bedroom, she could feel Kade's presence. The chairs and desk were oversized, the air had a lingering aroma of expensive tobacco, and the leather chair behind the desk smelled of Kade's cologne. Quill pens lay in an unusual leather dish beside a small decanter of ink; ledger books were stacked on a shelf nearby.

Kathleen could imagine Kade sitting there, sorting through the paperwork piled haphazardly across the top of the desk. The lamp would cast its intimate, warm glow across his face, touching the edges of his shaggy hair as he dipped his pen in the ink to answer a request for a shipping estimate. He would do most of his work at night, as he had done on the *Eagle,* his dark eyes glancing up now and again at the window.

Her fingers touched the leather chair while her mind touched Kade's face, brushing aside the hair that fell across his forehead as he leaned over her, his lips curving into that smile that never failed to set her blood

178

racing. Her body leaned forward, seeking his warmth, wanting the security of his embrace.

Her shoulder bumped against the chair, bringing her abruptly back to the empty study. *What is wrong with me? I cannot stand the man, I detest him, I hate him. And I want him.* She sank into the large chair and tucked her feet under her. *In two weeks he will be back here, surrounding me with that charm and smile. I must build up my defenses against him and be ready to escape at the first opportunity.*

She leaned her head back and inhaled the cologne that clung to the chair. Her lips curved into a smile, and she turned her face closer to the smell. Realizing what she was doing, she jumped up.

"I hope the first opportunity comes quickly," she said and forced herself back to the task of discovering Mistral's location.

A large basket sat against the wall behind the desk, filled to overflowing with charts. Kathleen deposited them, and herself, in the center of the floor. Some of the maps were quite old, the edges of the parchment crumbling at the slightest touch. She unfurled each chart carefully, sorting them into three stacks: West Indies, Ireland and England, everywhere else. The last stack contained most of the charts.

"Surely he has not traveled to all these places," she said as she picked up the last stack of charts and put them back in the basket. Still, each held notations in a hand she recognized as the bold style of her master. She tied together all the charts of the region around Ireland and England with a red ribbon from her pocket and slipped them back in the basket also. Now she would concentrate on the ones of the West Indies.

One by one she opened the charts, checking the location of islands marked on them against her memory of those on the charts that had been in Kade's cabin on the *Black Eagle*. There were two that contained similar island groupings, plus quite a few additional islands. Kathleen looked at the names printed beside the tiny dots of land. Mistral was not among them. It was either one of the unmarked islands or was not there at all.

"I do not even know the shape of this place. How can I figure out which one I am on?"

The answer to her question was to explore the island. Unfortunately, that was impossible. Even if Kade had not given orders for her to remain in the garden, she was much too weak for any extensive exploration. It would take a climb to the top of one of the mountains to see Mistral's outline.

"I will study these charts until every island is committed to memory. Then, when I am able to climb that mountain, I will know immediately if Mistral is on one of these charts."

Kathleen carefully rolled the two maps together and tied a green ribbon around them before replacing them in the basket. She carefully searched the room for any other items that might be useful. There was an old brass sextant and a boxed compass. She placed them on a shelf over the basket of charts. She had one ribbon left in her pocket and used it to tie back her straying curls.

Since it was well past noon, Kathleen headed for the kitchen, walking into the center of a mass of activity. There were mounds of peeled potatoes and carrots, cabbages and beans on the counters. The chickens Mattie had brought from the storeroom that morning had been stuffed and were baking in the large oven. Effie was basting them with melted butter.

"Smells good," Kathleen said.

"They is good. Miss Mattie makes the best stuffin' ya ever did taste."

"What are they for?"

"For supper, child," Mattie said from across the room. "I cook 'em early afore the 'eat gets too bad in 'ere, then steam 'em to heat 'em up before supper."

"I am a little hungry, Mrs. McBradden, do you mind if I cut a couple of slices of bread and take it to the garden?"

"Land's sake, I forgot all 'bout making somethin' for ye. What would ye like?"

"Just the bread, and maybe some jam or honey. Back home I never ate much at midday."

"Marge will fetch ye some butter and jam. Marge! Don't be moonin' around, get in the pantry and bring some jam out 'ere!" Mattie picked up a knife and began to slice the bread while one of the servants scurried to the pantry.

Kathleen followed her. "I will get it, Marge, just show me where you keep the jam." She stopped and stared around her in amazement. The pantry was almost as big as her home in Ireland and contained more food than she had ever seen in one place. There was also a trap door in the floor that probably led to even more storage in a cellar below the house.

"Da jam over dere," Marge said, pointing to a row of jars lining the far wall, "and da butter is beside it."

Kathleen selected a jar of peach jam and a small dish of the fresh butter. With the objective of her search firmly in her grasp, she looked over the shelves of stored food, thinking about what supplies she would need when she escaped.

Crocks of honey and kegs of flour and cornmeal lined one wall beneath a row of smoked hams, sausages and bacon hanging from the ceiling along with dried bunches of onions, garlic and peppers. The opposite wall was covered from floor to ceiling with shelves on which rested thickly iced cakes and crispy meat pies, baskets of dried fruit and vegetables, crocks of pickles and olives, tins of biscuits and crackers. There were stacks of soap and candles, bottles of oil and vinegar, bowls of herbs and an assortment of hard candies.

Mattie stuck her head in the door. "I thought ye were lost, lass. Ye should 'ave let Marge get that," she said as she took the jam and butter from Kathleen, who followed Mattie back into the kitchen.

"I have never seen such a place before, Mrs. McBradden. All that food, you could feed an army."

"This be naught compared to the kitchen that feeds the plantation workers. Sometimes we 'ave enough food cookin' there to feed all of Scotland and 'alf of England."

Mattie placed the buttered bread on a plate, smeared a liberal amount of peach jam on each slice and handed Kathleen a glass of milk. "There ye be, child. If ye want more, let me know."

"Thank you, Mrs. McBradden."

"Call me Mattie. Even after all these years of bein' married to Jake, I still think of Mrs. McBradden as 'is old ma."

"That would not be proper. I have no status in this house."

"Ye 'ave as much status as anyone."

"I am Kade's slave."

Mattie leaned against the counter and wiped her hands on her apron. "Aye, that ye do seem to be. I don't know what 'as got into the lad but don't let it be gettin' ye down. He 'as no intention of puttin' ye to work."

Kathleen could feel her face redden. "He has already decided what my duties shall be."

"He 'as?"

"I will be his whore."

The room instantly fell silent. Mattie looked as though her eyes would bulge right out of her head, and Kathleen knew everyone was staring at her. Why did I say that, she thought in horror and prayed desperately to disappear into the floor. There was no heavenly response to her plea so she squared her shoulders, lifted her chin and smiled at Mattie.

"Thanks for the bread," she said airily and casually strolled out the door into the garden.

Chapter 15

The next two weeks passed quietly, except for when Mattie discovered Kathleen was spending several hours every day climbing up and down the staircase. The old woman hysterically ordered Kathleen to stop, an order she ignored.

"You said Kade gave orders I was to do nothing more strenuous than climb steps. Since he left no instructions regarding how frequently I was allowed that activity, I am not in violation of his orders," she said, causing Mattie to throw up her arms as though pleading to a higher source for support. She then hurried out of the room, leaving Kathleen to continue her exercise.

Kathleen was apprehensive about Kade's return, knowing what it would mean to their relationship. Still, she could not deny the fact that she missed him. She was alone in the midst of a sea of strangers and longed for the one face that was familiar, the one face that could make her smile, the one face that could set her heart racing. Kade Morgan had become more than Kathleen's master, he was her friend. And he was more than the man who wanted her as a mistress; he was the man whose mistress she wanted to be.

The day Bog told Kathleen to expect the return of the *Black Eagle* was the longest day of her life. When sunset began to color the sky crimson and lavender, an unusually spectacular display even here where every sunset was incredible, Kathleen scarcely noticed. Her attention was directed to the east as she searched the horizon for a set of sails unfurled in the wind, a black hull cutting through a wave, a wooden eagle glaring at the world.

After dinner she went into the garden to look at the stars above Mistral, a scattering of silver light that looked like fairies' dust flung across the sky. Though Kathleen loved to stand in the darkness and inhale the moist smells of the island, on this night she found it impossible to appreciate Mistral's beauty.

Her thoughts were so full of Kade that every sight and sound reminded her of him. The wind in the coconut palms reminded her of the way his hair moved in the breeze, the moonlight reminded her of his breathtaking smile, the stars twinkled in the dark sky like a flash of laughter in the black eyes that haunted her day and night.

She returned to the house. Bog was at the piano, leafing through sheets of music he had written. As Kathleen started up the steps to her room, he chose a piece, and his skillful fingers moved over the ivory keys, coaxing from them a haunting melody. All the longing and love in the world was in that music. Kathleen stopped at the top of the steps, leaning over the rail to listen, letting the liquid loneliness surround her. The song ended, the final note fading into silence the way heartbreak fades into bittersweet memory.

"Did you like it?" Bog asked. His brown eyes lifted to her, filled with a need for her understanding.

I know he cares for me, Kathleen thought as she looked down at him. The way his eyes follow me, the way he hesitates before smiling, the way his words stumble when I laugh. Her appreciation for the beautiful music disappeared in a flash of temper. If he really cared he would help me escape, not write music.

"Aye, 'tis a bonny piece, though it does need some polish."

The plaintive look on his face was replaced by one of pain. Kathleen immediately regretted her words, hating herself for being so cruel. Regardless of the reason he had written the piece, it had been exquisite, expressing all the terrible emptiness inside her, all the aching need she could not suppress.

"I am sorry, Bog. The music was lovely, really lovely. This waiting had made me tense. I should not have taken it out on you." She turned away from the rail and went into her room. It was going to be another long night.

The next day dawned clear and bright, the sun glistening on the sea and the warm trade winds touching the island with the tender caress of a lover. Kade climbed from the longboat onto the pier at Mistral, stretching his legs in massive strides as he headed to the house. The last two weeks had been the longest of his life. The beauty and quiet of the sea, normally a soothing potion to his soul, had irritated him beyond reason. Every wave had reminded him of a pair of blue-green eyes, every black night had reminded him of silky curls tangled between his fingers. The sooner he could ease his desires on Kathleen's exquisite body, the sooner he could forget her and get on with his life.

As Kade approached the house he saw Kathleen curled in a white wicker chair, her head bent over a book she was reading. Her long hair was pulled back from her face and the sun washed over her delicate features gently. Her feet were tucked under her, and only her toes could be seen from beneath the green skirt of her dress.

She had gained weight; the ravaged lines of hunger that had marred her beauty were gone, replaced by a light glow of color so she looked radiant with health. Kade stood in the shadow of a tree fern, drinking in every detail of the vision before him. She closed her eyes and leaned her head against the back of the chair. A sigh filled the air around her. Her lips moved slightly as she spoke one word.

Kade. She had said his name. He felt as though someone had just given him the most precious gift in the world. Confidently striding up to Kathleen, Kade waited for her to acknowledge him. When she did not move, he bent and kissed the top of her head, his lips lightly touching the silk of her ebony hair. Her lips parted, her lashes lifted to reveal those incredible eyes.

Kathleen blinked. Her mind had been full of Kade Morgan's face. The bottomless eyes, the strong chin and thick mane of unruly hair. She had felt his warmth, smelled his rich cologne on a wave of ocean breeze. The light touch of his lips on her hair had been a part of her dream. To discover him standing so close to her that his leg brushed her foot was a shock. It was almost as though she had conjured him from her imagination.

"Captain Morgan," she said, her heart racing. Kathleen wanted to throw herself into his arms and know again the thrill of his touch, the ecstasy of his kiss.

"Kathleen."

His voice caressed the word, surrounding it with warmth and richness, letting it float in the air between them. She resisted the urge to open her arms to it, to hold it against her and cherish it like the most treasured of gifts.

"How are you?" he asked. His hands moved almost

imperceptively, the palms turning toward her, open and waiting. Something inside her sounded a warning bell as she realized he expected her to come to him. Her spine stiffened, her chin came up.

"You have nothing to fear in respect to my health, Captain. Mattie informed me of your orders and I have obeyed." Her voice was cold and hard, bitterness dripping from the words "orders" and "obeyed."

He did not react as she expected. The black eyes did not narrow, squint or even glare. They became softer, caressing her like gentle summer rain. She felt foolish. It was disconcerting to show someone anger and have that anger ignored.

"Thank you for your concern," she said somewhat lamely. Not sure what to do, she dropped her head and stared at her lap, fingering the edge of the book of poetry she had been reading. The wind rustled through the rosebush beside her, and a bird spun its magic song into the air nearby. A bee droned; the sounds of the sea came up from the cove.

When she looked up, Kade was gone. On the arm of her chair lay a perfect red rose, its petals softer than a whisper. All the thorns had been carefully cut from the green stem. She picked it up, her heart aching a little as she touched the flower to her face. The lines of the Shakespeare poem she had been reading came back to her, and she crushed the stem of the flower as the ache in her heart turned to despair.

Being your slave, what should I do but tend
Upon the hours and times of your desire? . . .
So true a fool is love that in your will,
Though you do anything, he thinks no ill.

Kathleen dropped the rose beside her chair. I will not be a fool in love, or in whatever it is I feel for him, she told herself firmly. She rose from the chair to run into the house and up the stairs to her room.

Kade did not knock before entering Kathleen's room. He simply pushed open the door and walked in. She was in the rocking chair, her legs drawn up and chin resting on her knees. The light from the window fell on her, encasing her in a golden glow. She did not move except to lift her eyes to him; then she exhaled slowly and dropped her feet onto the floor.

"I assume you are here to continue my lessons," she said, referring to Kade's lessons forcing her to tolerate his touch. The words of the poem burned within her, preventing her from again falling victim to his presence.

Kade leaned against the bedpost and crossed his arms over his chest. "If you like. I came here, however, to ask if you would like to go riding with me." It was as though all the burdens of the world had suddenly been lifted from her shoulders.

"I would love to!" she cried and catapulted from the rocker. She was almost out the door before he could stop her.

"Hold on, Kate. Get back in here."

"What is wrong?"

"You are not dressed for riding. Were you planning to wear that?" he asked, pointing at the dress that swirled around Kathleen's legs as she stood poised and ready to leave.

"I have no breeches."

He went to the armoire and extracted a gray riding habit. The thick velvet flowed across his arm as he presented it to her. "Put this on and I will show you my island." Kathleen took the heavy fabric from his hands and frowned at it.

"Now what?" he asked, matching her frown with one of his own. "Certainly this is good enough for you. It was the latest fashion a year ago and even if out of style now, you will not be riding with the London ton, only me."

"I have not the slightest notion of what is or is not in style, nor what the London ton might be. The problem with this thing," she indicated the velvet, "is twofold. First, I have never worn such an item before and have no idea what ruffles and billows have to do with riding. Secondly, this might prove a little warm for riding around in that heat outside."

She dumped the riding habit on the bed. There was no doubt the outfit was beautiful, but wearing such a thing was ridiculous. It would require a sidesaddle, which Kathleen hated, and boots, which she did not have, and a great deal of patience, which she had never possessed.

Kade inspected the contents of the closet again. He pulled out a skirt and blouse of vivid blue, both made of thin, flowing cotton that would be cool and comfortable.

"Put these on and meet me downstairs in five minutes," he said and walked into his room, shutting the door behind him.

Kathleen took off her dress and petticoats, putting on the clothes Kade had selected. The skirt flowed out from her tiny waist, falling in ripples of blue to her ankles. The blouse came off the shoulders slightly, gathering into a froth of fabric that dipped down over the top of her breasts. The sleeves were full and ended in a small ruffle just below her elbows. Kathleen was trying to pull the neck of the blouse higher when she heard Kade downstairs.

"Do you want to ride or not, Kate? Get down here this instant!"

190

"Coming!" she called and dashed down the steps.

"Comfortable now?" Kade asked as she almost bumped into his pacing figure.

"Yes, master," she said, unable to keep the smile of excitement from her face. "Which way?"

He pointed at the widest path in the garden, the one that led behind the house and through the tiny kitchen garden where Mattie grew herbs. Kathleen practically danced along in front of Kade. The blouse clung to her seductively, exciting his imagination. When she came running down the steps, he had been able to detect the outline of her nipples through the thin fabric. The skirt whirled around her ankles, occasionally exposing a flash of leg as she walked. Pleased that he had not insisted on her wearing the confining riding habit, Kade threw the sack he was carrying across his shoulder and followed her through the garden and into the jungle that lay between the house and the stables.

He picked a white orchid from a plant clinging to a gum tree and turned Kathleen to face him as he laid his sack beside him. She stood quietly while he placed the beautiful flower behind her left ear. Then he reached around and untied her hair ribbon, spreading the ebony waves over her shoulders.

"That is how the native girls wear their hair," he told her. "Loose and free, full of flowers and sunlight." He ran his fingers through the silken mass.

Kathleen's legs were having a lot of trouble supporting her while Kade touched her hair and caressed her face with his gaze. When his fingers reached the ends of her hair, he cupped his hand over the curving softness under her skirt and pulled her against him.

Though her mind told her to resist, her body refused to listen to reason as it moved against the hard length of his. His hands explored the hollows of her back, and

191

she watched breathlessly as his head lowered until his lips touched hers. The kiss was soft, gentle as the brush of the wings of a butterfly.

Kade ran one hand up Kathleen's back; the other stayed firmly around her waist. Her red lips were moist and inviting, her neck curving backwards with the graceful elegance of a swan as she looked up at him. He could feel himself drowning in the blue-green depths of her eyes and never wanted to be rescued.

"What color are they?" he asked, the words scarcely more than a whisper of breeze between them as he brushed a finger over her lashes. "Sometimes they are green, as brilliant as the trees on Mistral after a rain, then suddenly they turn blue and I feel as though all the glory of the sky were before me. Your eyes remind me of looking into the sea on a clear summer day, peaceful and wonderful. And when you storm and thunder at me, they swirl with such incredible light I want to hold you and feel all that fury change to passion."

Kade leaned back against a tree, pulling Kathleen with him. She buried her face against his throat. He felt her lips move but could not hear what she said.

"Say it again, kitten." He put a finger beneath her chin and tilted her head back so he could hear her.

"Ha—hazel." Her voice was choked and hesitant. "My mother had the same color eyes, only hers were pale." Tears filled her eyes. Kade lowered her head to his shoulder and kissed her hair. She clung to him, needing to feel his arms around her.

"Do not cry, love," he said.

Something in her snapped upon hearing those words. *This is wrong. I have never needed anyone in my life, least of all Kade Morgan.* She jerked away from him, her fists clenched tightly at her sides as she blinked away the tears.

"Why should I not cry? I have reasons, plenty of

them. My mother and brother are dead; Father probably believes I am dead, too. I spent a lifetime locked in the filthy hold of a pirate ship, living in total darkness with roaches and rats. I was chained to a wall and forced to endure the pawings of Rat Anders. After two months of starvation and beatings, I was dragged in front of a horde of beasts and offered for sale like a common swine. You bought me and hold me as your slave. And worst of all, the closest thing to a friend I have ever had in my life is my master!"

Kathleen fled into the jungle, stumbling through the tangled branches and ignoring the sharp leaves that caught at her hair and skirt. It was imperative that she run as far as possible from the arms she longed to run to, to be held by, to belong to.

Kade tore through the underbrush, forcing his way through the thick growth of trees as he fought to catch up to her. He made a desperate grab for her, his fingers closing over her left arm. He jerked her into his arms.

"You little fool!" he bellowed at her. "This island is full of dangers for stupid people who do not look where they are going." He pulled a branch from the tree in front of them. The branch changed into a slender, writhing animal. It had no legs, a pointed head and scaly skin.

"What is it?" Kathleen cried as the creature's yellow eyes turned in her direction. She clawed at Kade, trying to escape both him and the thing he held.

"Try not to act so stupid. It is a snake."

The snake projected a forked tongue from its mouth, which flickered from side to side. Its whiplike body curled around Kade's arm, and Kathleen shuddered.

"I am not stupid, I just have never seen a snake before. St. Patrick chased them all out of Ireland centuries ago."

Kade laughed. "I had forgotten that old folktale.

193

Since that is the case, let me introduce you to your first snake, Miss O'Connor." He was enjoying the feel of Kathleen snuggling closer to him to avoid contact with the reptile. When she buried her face against his chest, he dropped the snake onto the ground. It quickly disappeared into the shadows.

"That one was harmless. The next time you might not be so lucky." He carried her back to the path and set her back on her feet. "Some snakes on this island are deadly, Kate. Even that one could have made you ill if he had bitten you. There are also poisonous spiders and beetles on Mistral. It is best to always stay on the path, paying close attention to where you step and everything you touch."

"I will be most cautious in the future, Captain Morgan, sir," Kathleen said meekly. The snake had been a rude awakening to the dangers the jungles of Mistral concealed. Ireland was a much safer place to live.

"Another thing, my name is neither captain nor sir."

Kathleen ducked her head. "I will be most cautious in the future, Kade," she said.

He smiled and ran a hand over her hair. "We better get moving or it will be too late to do much riding." He retrieved his sack and headed down the path with Kathleen following close behind. She checked the path for spiders and beetles before every step. Intent upon her task, she walked directly into Kade when he stopped.

"Watch where you are going," he said, grabbing her before she fell. "Stay here and try to keep out of trouble, if you think you can manage it. I will get Sam to saddle the horses."

"I would prefer not to use a saddle," Kathleen said, realizing for the first time they were in a large clearing with a stable and barn.

"You want a blanket?"

She nodded yes and Kade went into the stable. Kathleen breathed deeply, loving the wonderful earthy smells of warm flesh, clean hay and fresh manure that pervaded the clearing. There was a corral beside the barn, and Kathleen went to investigate.

She caught her breath as a gigantic black stallion ran to the fence for a closer look at his visitor. He stamped his enormous feet in the dust and tossed his sculpted head with an impatient jerk of his neck. His nostrils flared aggressively as he exhaled with a loud snort, spinning on his hind legs and racing around the paddock, feet lifted high and tail streaming behind him.

The stallion reared, his powerful muscles rippling beneath his glistening coat. He slammed his hooves back on the ground and rolled wild eyes in Kathleen's direction. She climbed onto the top rail of the corral for a better look. The stallion pawed the ground, whirling and dashing to the opposite side of the enclosed area.

"No need to worry, I would not hurt you for the world," she told him, and his ears cocked in her direction. "You are almost as magnificent as Taran, though a lot more earthly. Come over here, fellow," she coaxed.

The stallion snorted and tossed his head. He quieted as Kathleen maintained a steady flow of soft words. She slid off the fence into the corral and began to move closer to him. He shied a little to one side, never taking his eyes off her.

Kade came out of the stable leading two horses, only to find that Kathleen had disappeared. He walked around the side of the barn, his face blanching when he saw her.

"If that beast does not kill her, I will." He dropped the reins of the horses and moved slowly over to the railing of the corral. Keeping his voice low, he called instructions to her. "Just walk backwards, Kate, and keep your eyes on him." She continued to walk closer to the wild-eyed horse.

"Damn!" he bellowed in irritation, startling the stallion, who reared and bolted.

"Damn yourself, Kade Morgan!" Kathleen shouted, stomping past the raging horse as though he did not exist.

"I am going to wring your neck!" Kade swung her over the fence. "That horse is a killer. Just look at him."

The stallion tore around the corral, hooves grinding the soil into a billowing cloud of dust. The whites of his eyes flashed as he tossed his head and screamed.

"I was in no danger until you frightened him. He is no more a killer than that ancient gray mare over there." She pointed at one of the horses Kade had led out of the stable.

"That stallion is off-limits to you and everyone else, Kathleen. He almost sank the ship he was on, killing two men and crippling another."

"A creature like that cannot be handled with force, Kade, he must trust his handler. Only in friendship can fear and mistrust disappear, and only in friendship can love take root. Watch."

A hush fell over the clearing, then over the entire island. Kathleen's eyes took on a strange, almost unearthly light. A peaceful calm settled over everything, like a mist blanketing the sea. The stallion stopped his mad dash around the corral. He stood quietly switching his tail, his eyes on Kathleen. She slipped through the fence and into the corral.

Though he wanted to stop her, Kade's arms refused to obey his commands. They hung limp at his sides. The serenity that covered Mistral made him think of Scotland. He heard the mournful wind on the open moors, smelled the moist black earth and blooming heather. He almost expected to hear his mother's voice calling to him across the dark waters of the loch. Never had Kade missed home more than at that moment.

Kathleen approached the stallion confidently, reaching out a hand to touch his nose. The velvet softness pushed against her fingers. The teeth that only moments before had been bared in anger now nibbled at the sleeve of her blouse. She pulled the stallion's head down to her level and whispered something in his ear. He stepped sideways and Kathleen grasped his mane to swing herself onto his back. The black skin quivered, the nostrils flared, the eyes showed a rim of white. Kathleen ran a small hand down the strained muscles of the horse's neck. He relaxed and flicked his ears in her direction.

Jake McBradden came up beside Kade and leaned on the top rail of the corral. "I've 'eard of the like, but never believed it," he said.

"Heard of what?"

"There be tales 'bout those blessed in their dealings with animals, especially 'orses. 'Tis said certain people can whisper in the ear of a ragin' beast and it quiets instantly, doin' whatever its master wants."

Kathleen tugged lightly on the stallion's mane and it nickered in response. It took a small step, then another.

"That horse is responding to more than just words, there seems to be a spell in the air around us. I feel as though we were standing on an empty moor. You can smell the peat and hear the wind blowing through the heather, yet the air over Mistral is still."

Jake nodded. "Aye, an' that alone be enough to make me cry magic, for this island be the windiest place I 'ave ever seen. Yon lassie be one of the blessed."

It was evident the giant stallion was aware of his tiny rider as he trotted across the corral to where Kade and

Jake stood. The horse carefully turned so that the top rail of the fence brushed Kathleen's foot. She whispered something in his ear. The great head tossed and Kathleen slid off his back onto the rail. She ran her hand one last time across his arched neck before jumping onto the ground beside Kade.

Instantly the horse changed back into a savage creature. He galloped furiously around the corral and snorted his anger at the world. If anyone other than Kathleen were to set foot in the corral, the stallion would not hesitate to attack. Maybe Jake was right, Kade thought, maybe she is blessed. That does not excuse her from disobeying my orders, however.

"Well?" she said, her head cocked over to one side as her eyes captured Kade's for a brief instant.

He drew his brows together and regarded her smug attitude coldly. "That was the most foolhardy trick I have ever seen, to purposely approach a beast that is a known killer and place yourself at risk. If you ever go near that stallion again, I will turn you over my knee and give you the spanking you deserve!"

"How dare you threaten me like I was a child, Kade Morgan! I will not tolerate anyone laying a hand on me in that fashion; not man, woman, beast, or brute!" Kathleen stamped her foot in the dust.

"I will threaten you any way I like!" The muscles in Kade's face were set in such hard lines that a vein on the side of his head pulsed as though ready to explode.

Kathleen was not in the least intimidated by his display. "That horse is no killer, you saw me in there. Let me work with him. You can sell him and that would repay you for buying me and sending me home!"

"I never want to hear you mention going home again, nor will I tolerate any more talk about that horse. This is my island, that is my horse, you are my slave and you will do as I say!"

198

His face was so red, his manner so arrogant as he stood there with his legs braced apart while bellowing like an angry bull and reciting one of his many lists of ridiculous reasons. Kathleen began to smile, and then she broke into peals of laughter.

"Oh yes, master, anything you say!" she bubbled into the face of his rage. With a running jump, she vaulted onto the back of the gray mare. There was also a beautiful chestnut gelding Kade had brought from the barn, obviously his mount.

"I assume you intended this poor thing for me," she said. A muscle in Kade's cheek twitched spasmodically. Kathleen started laughing again.

"I still think I should wring your neck," Kade muttered, finding it difficult to maintain his anger with the music of her laughter surrounding him. He picked up the chestnut gelding's reins and stepped into his saddle. "You think you are so hot, hellcat, try to keep up." He kicked the gelding's sides and the horse took off at a gallop, heading down a trail that led into the jungle.

Kathleen looked down at her mount, then jumped down and ran into the stable. A black mare with a white blaze tossed her head and whinnied. She opened the mare's stall and slipped a bridle on her, pulled a blanket off the wall and threw it across the horse. An old black man came out of the next stall carrying a pitchfork. His eyes were big as saucers as he watched Kathleen mount the black mare.

"You should ride dat dare little gray, missy," he said.

"That horse should be retired to pasture, not ridden. What is this lady's name?"

"Glory, but she ain't no fit horse for a little thing like you. Boss ain't gonna like you ridin' dat horse."

"I do not care what the boss likes or does not like." She rode Glory into the clearing. Jake was holding the

199

reins of the abandoned gray. "Which trail did Kade take?" she asked him.

He pointed the stem of his pipe to a path that led into the jungle between the two mountains. Kathleen hesitated, thinking of all the snakes and spiders waiting for her in that moist darkness. She gave a piercing cry to bolster her courage and kicked Glory into action. Together they tore off into the underbrush.

"No sir, da boss ain't gonna like dis one bit," Sam muttered to Jake.

Their last look at Kathleen showed that her skirt was bunched up to reveal strong legs gripping Glory's sides as the pair sped from the clearing. Jake laughed.

"I would like to be there to see the lad's face when 'e gets a look at what 'e'll not be liking."

Chapter 16

Glory's mane tangled with Kathleen's hair as she leaned close to the mare's neck to avoid low branches. It felt so good to be riding again. For the first time since the pirates had attacked Emerald Hills, she was happy. Really happy. The stretch of the mare's muscles beneath her was easy, not strained or difficult. Kathleen wondered what type of foal Glory would produce if mated to the black stallion.

They came out of the jungle onto an open stretch of pasture. A few cows grazed among the thick grass, along with several horses. Kade was just ahead where the trail merged with a road. Kathleen placed a hand on the mare's neck and laughed.

"We are almost there, girl! Give me just a little more."

She applied light pressure to Glory's sides. The mare responded immediately. Moments later they were alongside Kade, and Kathleen saw anger spark in his eyes as he looked at her mount.

"I like this horse better," she said. She was glad he did not answer. She did not want to argue, she wanted to enjoy the ride, the island and the day.

The two horses walked together along the road, avoiding the ruts caused by carts. The space between Mistral's two mountains widened, the rain forests retreating further up the slope as fields and orchards began to dominate the land. Kade found his gaze constantly straying to Kathleen, her presence and beauty soothing his frayed nerves and exciting his senses.

Her wild ride through the jungle had blown her hair into glorious disarray, the orchid falling down over her cheek. The blue skirt rippled back over Glory's flanks, exposing a goodly portion of Kathleen's shapely legs. Her blouse had dropped off one shoulder, exposing even more of her curving charms. He wanted to turn the horses back to the house and take her straight to bed.

"What is his name?" Kathleen asked.

"Who?"

"The stallion." Kathleen leaned over and ran her hand over the chestnut's flanks. "And this gentleman, too."

Kade caught a brief glimpse of her full breast as she stroked his horse. "This is Deprived," he said, thinking the name described him better than the horse. The astonished look on Kathleen's face made him laugh. "Mattie felt sorry for him when she discovered he was a gelding and named him Deprived. He is getting a bit old but is still a good horse."

A flock of green birds flew overhead, screeching and screaming. "Parakeets," Kade said as he watched them go into the jungle along the rim of the mountain on their left.

"What about the stallion?" Kathleen reminded Kade. A butterfly glided past Glory's nose, and the little mare tossed her head indignantly.

"He does not have a name, nor does he deserve one." Kade pressed Deprived to pick up speed.

Along the road on the right were the plantation orchards: acres of oranges and apples and mangos, forbidden fruit and lemons, limes and pears. On the left were vegetable gardens: acres of peppers, carrots, yams, potatoes, beans, peas and plantains.

The road crested the center of the island and began to slope down to the western side of the island. The sea sparkled so brightly Kathleen had to shade her eyes. Below her was the main village on Mistral, a veritable beehive of activity and civilization. There were boats anchored in the harbor, which was twice as big as the one on the other side of the island, and other boats could be seen out on the ocean. Warehouses were positioned along the harbor near a pier; to the right of them were two more large buildings, one still under construction.

Houses lined the curve of the harbor, stretching all along the left shore. They looked exactly like those on the other side of the island, with whitewashed walls and thatched roofs, flowering trees and vines shading the yards. Since it was Saturday, there was no plantation work being done, only personal work by the islanders. On Sundays no work was done at all.

There were children everywhere, running up and down the road that went past the houses, playing in the edge of the sea, climbing trees and chasing dogs. A group of women were washing clothes in the stream that cut through the center of the village. Behind the village were vast fields of plants with tasseled tops, their tall stalks and narrow leaves bending before the warm trade winds.

"What is that? There must be miles of it," Kathleen said as she reined Glory to a halt.

Kade turned in his saddle and waved an expansive hand at the rows of plants. "Sugarcane. It covers almost all the flat land on the island, about three hundred acres. There are a few acres planted in tobacco, bananas, coffee and pineapples. All told, we

203

have three hundred and fifty acres cultivated for crops, about twenty for gardens and orchards, another fifty in pasture for livestock."

"I thought you did not bother yourself about the plantation," Kathleen said. "It sounds like you know quite a bit."

"When I first bought the island, I converted the plantation from tobacco to sugar, hoping it would at least pay for itself. That gave me a basic idea of acreage. After I hired Harry Timpson I turned the operation over to him. Since then I have not been involved. On my trip to Nassau, however, I went over the plantation books, so the figures are familiar."

"And does it pay for itself?"

"Yes and no. It does not cost me anything, yet it does not earn anything either. From what I learned in Nassau by talking to other plantation owners, we should be pulling in quite a large profit. That is something I plan to investigate."

Kade pointed at the building under construction. "Over there Timpson is putting in a place to process some of our sugar into rum. The sugar is milled in that other building. Mistral is one of the few plantations that produces clayed, or white, sugar. Most produce muscavado, a wet brown sugar which is not worth as much. That is why Mistral should be showing more of a profit, our product is in greater demand and commands a higher price."

They rode into the village, the horses weaving among the children. Kathleen noticed the women all wore bandannas on their heads, piled half a foot high. They had scarves wrapped around their shoulders and tucked into the waists of their skirts. The men wore only trousers that came to just below the knee. The children were mostly naked, their brown bodies flashing in the sun as they laughed and shouted.

Among the village were whites, blacks and natives. It sounded like a dozen different languages were being spoken, a dozen different accents and speech patterns within each language.

All along the beach, poles had been erected in the sand to support the fishing nets stretched out for drying, the great lengths of them glowing golden in the sunlight. There were four men standing waist-deep in the sea, their net filled with fish they had caught. The trapped fish made the surface of the green water erupt in white foam as they thrashed and panicked.

The fishermen were dragging the net into shore when three of them stopped to stare at Kade and Kathleen. The fourth, whose back was to the road, continued to pull by himself. He fell over backwards, disappearing beneath net, water and escaping fish. He finally surfaced, water streaming from his hair and face as he shouted obscenities. Then he noticed the two riders and joined his companions in staring at the visitors.

Kathleen looked around and realized the whole village was staring at them, mouths open and eyes wide. "You do not come over here often, do you?" she asked Kade.

"Hardly ever. Only once in the last year. Morgan Shipping keeps me too busy. Besides, Timpson is responsible for running the plantation. Wait here, I want to talk to someone for a few minutes." He stopped Deprived and dismounted. After handing the reins to Kathleen, he walked up to the last house in the village.

Sitting in the shade of an orange tree was an old man. His brown skin was covered in a spiderweb tracing of fine lines. Gnarled fingers lay quietly on the arms of his rocking chair, the silver in his thinning hair catching the sunlight.

"How are you, Sampson?" Kade asked.

The eyes of the old man looked past Kade to the road

where Kathleen sat on Glory, watching the men with the net try to recapture their escaping fish.

"I done heard yo got yoself a slave. Dat her?"

"Aye. What do you think?"

Sampson ran a pink tongue over his big lips. "Don't women like yo none, boy? Yo gotta buy 'em now?"

"It is not like that, Sampson. She was in trouble. The only way to save her was to buy her."

"So yo done her a favor by makin' her a slave. It wus yo what done freed me from slavery, like yo done the rest of us on dis island when you done bought it from dat fool Englishman what wus growin' 'bacco even though da leaves weren't sellin' and da land wus givin' out. Bad luck to start up with terrible things like dat again."

Kade picked an orange and peeled it, tossing the peeling onto a heap of trash beside Sampson's house. "I told you to get someone to clean up this mess. It is not good to have garbage lying around like this."

"I'm old, I forget."

Kade gave the orange to Sampson and picked another one for himself. "Timpson should send someone around to gather trash in the village. Have you talked to him?"

The old man concentrated on the orange, pulling the sections apart and slipping them into his toothless mouth. "Nobody talks to da foreman 'cept dose want trouble."

"Timpson is here to take care of the people, not cause trouble. Talk to him, he will listen." Kade watched Kathleen scratch between Glory's ears. "How is that old widow you were chasing after?"

"Maybelle died last Christmas, boy."

Kade dipped a cup into the bucket of water outside the door of Sampson's house and brought it to the old man. "I am sorry, Sampson. I did not know."

"If yo gave attention to what wus happenin', yo might learn more than just who ain't alive."

"What are you talking about?"

Sampson sipped the water and handed the cup back to Kade. "What yo gonna do with dat girl?"

Kade tossed the cup back into the bucket. He pulled off a section of his orange and slipped it in his mouth. "What do you think I am going to do with her?"

The old, rheumy eyes fixed on Kade. "I know what yo gonna do with her, and I know what yo already done. Rape ain't nice, boy."

"How do you always know everything, Sampson? And it was not completely rape."

"I know because that mask of hate yo wear over yo head ain't thick enough to fool an old Eboe like me. The drums tell what yo do, where yo go. The stars tell what yo run from."

Kade laughed. "You have always known more about me than anyone else, Sampson. Maybe that is why I let you call me 'boy.' If anyone else ever tried that, he never would again."

"I done call yo boy 'cause that what yo be. Yo act like a man, I call yo dat."

"Tell me what I should do with Kathleen."

"Send her home. She don't belong to yo, she ain't no sheep or cow, ain't no piece of land. No matter how yo treat her, no matter how much yo make her need yo or love yo, she still go home."

"I will talk to Timpson about this garbage. If I see it here again, I will have you put on a daily ration of nothing except bananas."

"Not dem things!" Sampson cried. "I don't like dem things, ain't natural food for man or beast."

"I have been called both and I like bananas. It would do your old bones good to eat a few, take away those aches and pains that bother you in the morning."

"How ya know 'bout dem, boy?"

"The drums, Sampson. They may tell you what mortal sins I have committed, but they tell me you have not been seeing the doctor about the pain in your joints."

"Won't do no good, he can't do nothin'."

"See him anyway."

"You'll think about da girl?"

Kade put another piece of orange into his mouth and winked at the old man. "She is all I have been thinking about."

Sampson's crackling laughter followed Kade all the way back to the road. Kathleen tossed him Deprived's reins and he gave her half his orange before mounting. They rode out of town side by side. The road turned to their left along the edge of thousands of rows of cane.

"Who was that?" she asked when the village was no longer in sight.

"Sampson. He was head slave when I bought Mistral."

Kathleen finished her orange and wiped her hands on her skirt. "Anywhere around here to get a drink of water?"

"The livestock barn is just ahead."

Kade pointed out the fields of sugarcane that were of different ages. "It takes fifteen months for the cane to become completely mature. The crops are staggered so some are always ready for harvest. That keeps the mill in constant operation." He pulled a knife from his boot and nudged his horse up against one of the plants. He sliced through the stalk, then hacked off the flowering top and handed it to Kathleen.

"What do I do with it?"

"Suck on it," he said, trying not to think of anything except the cane.

Glory stepped closer to Deprived and nipped at the

gelding's neck. Kade placed his hand on the mare's withers between Kathleen's legs. "Sugarcane is the sweetest thing in the world, except for your lips, kitten," he said softly, leaning closer to touch his lips to hers.

Kathleen forgot everything except the feel of him near her. The kiss was soft, warm. And wonderful. Unable to deal with her feelings, she ducked her head and broke contact.

"Suck on it, you said," she said in a semisteady voice. With the cane between her lips, she slid her teeth down the slender stalk. Kade was watching her intently. His eyes glowed like fire, and Kathleen realized the implications of her actions. She knew she should stop, knew she should kick Glory into a gallop and flee the scene as quickly as possible. Something in Kade's expression stopped her from doing what she should. Instead she pulled the cane slowly out of her mouth and ran a wet tongue around the end, barely touching it.

"You were right, it is sweet," she murmured as her lips again closed over the stick of cane.

"Enough, witch," he said, his voice strained. He pulled his hand from between Kathleen's legs and rubbed it as though it were on fire.

She grinned at him and tossed the cane over her shoulder. Kade whirled Deprived and took off down the road, leaving her in a cloud of dust. She caught up to him just as the barn came into sight. Between the fields of cane and the sea was a wide stretch of pasture where a herd of cattle grazed. There were also sheep, goats and a few stubby ponies. Around the barn itself were turkeys, chickens, pigs and more goats. Draft horses milled in the corral, looking just like the ones used in Ireland for field work. Their heavy feet were fringed with long hair, their manes and tails braided to prevent tangles. Their gentle, patient eyes watched

Kade and Kathleen dip cool water from a bucket near the fence.

"The grazing animals used to drink directly from the river," Kade told Kathleen as he showed her a man-made lake behind the corral. "They stirred up so much mud that sometimes they became stuck, drowning before anyone could pull them free. Immediately after the village was rebuilt, I had the workers dig this lake."

"Why did you rebuild the village?"

"The houses were little more than hovels, incredibly filthy and barely able to withstand a light rain, much less a storm or hurricane. The previous owner, an Englishman named Winthrop, did not care anything about his slaves, even built the main house on the rainy side of the island to avoid being in contact with the plantation workers. Sugar had become the best money crop, only it was expensive to initiate. Winthrop refused to invest capital to start growing sugar and kept putting in tobacco even after the market had collapsed. I liked the location of the island, so I waited until Winthrop went broke and bought him out."

At the mouth of the river was a large area of mud flats. A flock of tall pink birds stood in the water, bending their long necks and dipping their black-tipped beaks in the mud.

"Those are flamingos," Kade said, "they are beautiful creatures. I think I like them better than parrots."

"What are those?"

"They live in the rain forest and look a bit like the parakeets we saw earlier, only much larger and louder. Depending on what island they are from, parrots can be blue, green, red, or yellow. Ours are almost all green with a few red tail feathers. Sometimes a blue tail is spotted. That is rare though."

They left the shore and rode back into the interior of the island. Kade dismounted and lifted Deprived's front right foot. He dug a stone out from beside the shoe and walked beside the horse for a while before mounting again. The road went past two empty warehouses, and Kade pointed out the fields on the right where Mistral's tobacco was grown.

"I thought tobacco was a bad crop," Kathleen said.

"Not bad, just not profitable. The colonies grow the best, especially Virginia. What used to be grown on the islands was not as good and the market collapsed. Our crop is a special strain, excellent quality but hard to maintain. All my cigars are made from my own tobacco, rolled special in the Carolinas for me."

The road branched off, and a trail continued up the rising slope, winding into a forest of banana trees. A wide stream wound its way through a heap of limestone boulders. The horses forded it, and then Kade and Kathleen dismounted to rest. Kade climbed one of the boulders to pick some bananas from a tree. He peeled back the skin on one and handed it to Kathleen, then peeled his own. He took a bite and rolled his eyes to heaven, as though he were tasting a piece of its glory.

Kathleen took a small bite. She did not chew, she did not swallow. She just sat there, her mouth filled with the horrible taste of banana.

"Excellent," Kade said and finished his off in another bite. Kathleen did not know what to do. Maybe it would taste better if I chewed it some more, she thought. The mushy thing became mushier. She stopped chewing and tried to gather her courage to swallow.

Kade was peeling another banana when he noticed Kathleen's cheeks bulged out. "What is it, Kate?" he asked. She did not answer. He looked at her banana and realized she had not eaten anything after the first bite.

"You should get along well with Sampson, he hates

them too. Spit it out," he told her.

She tried to smile at him and discovered it was an impossible task with a mouthful of disgusting banana. After she spit it out and covered it with some leaves, she took a long drink from the stream.

"That is the worst thing I have ever tasted," she said. "Sampson must be a very smart man."

Kade opened the sack he had tied behind his saddle and pulled out a package of brown paper that was wrapped around some of Mattie's gingerbread. Kathleen ate that while he finished the bananas.

Refreshed and ready to ride again, they mounted their horses. The trail left the bananas behind, winding into a stand of leafy bushes.

"Coffee," Kade told Kathleen. "When the beans turn red they are harvested, then shipped to Virginia. Coffee has been in great demand since the colonies declared their independence from England. This war they have been fighting is causing some problems for the English islands while the rest of us, the French, Dutch and independents, are making a fortune."

"You take advantage of their fight for freedom to make money?"

"If I do not trade with them, someone else will. They exchange lumber and provisions for sugar and coffee. I also sell them weapons and gunpowder at a fraction of what some profiteers are offering."

To the right of the trail the mountain sloped steeply down to the sea. There were two small islands just offshore. "Those are used by some birds for nesting, especially doves," Kade explained. "We send a boat over regularly to gather them and their eggs."

"I suppose they fetch a high price, therefore you take all the eggs and kill all the birds."

"I suppose we do, which is why I am meeting with Harry Timpson tomorrow so we can make some changes in our harvesting methods. I intend to continue performing good deeds such as you shamed me into with those turtles."

"It is to your own benefit."

"I hope so." Kade raked his black eyes down Kathleen's body, a devious smile playing across his handsome face.

To divert his eyes, and the conversation, Kathleen pointed at a patch of bright green on Mistral's shore. "What is that?"

"Mangroves," Kade answered. "The trees grow in mud that is completely covered by the sea at high tide. Those large birds you see flying over the trees, the black ones, are frigates, and that"—he indicated a bird flying with bent neck and long, trailing legs—"is a blue heron. The mangroves are a good place to gather oysters and crabs at low tide as long as you avoid the crocodiles."

"Crocodiles?"

"Big, mean, dangerous creatures. Long, pointed mouths with sharp teeth and a tail that can break a man's leg with a gentle tap. The leather is extremely tough, as is the meat. They float on the surface, looking like a partially submerged log. When they move, it is faster than a whip. Occasionally the beasts come up from the mangroves into the streams. Two years ago one was found in the pond near the mill, though how it got there is a mystery. It almost took off the leg of a boy cleaning the grate."

There were so many things Kathleen had to remember to avoid: crocodiles, spiders, beetles and snakes. As far as she could tell, anything that breathed was dangerous. She considered putting Kade on the list as she again felt the hot touch of his eyes on her.

"What are those silver plants over that way?" she asked, pointing to the left along the edge of the island near another area of mangrove trees.

213

"Pineapples. A fruit that tastes like a bite of heaven itself. I guarantee you will like them better than bananas."

"I had some the other night in a tart Mattie made. You are right, I do like them."

They rode past a large cave, forded another stream and followed the trail as it curved around the side of the mountain, moving away from the gentle slopes of the plantation. Now they were on the wet side of Mistral, in a region of cliffs and rain forests. A profusion of greenery spread from the top of the mountain to the edge of the sea. Wild figs, ginger and gum trees spanned the top of the jungle canopy. Near the sea, coconut palms thrust into the sky, bending before the ever-present wind.

The horses moved into the forest's shadowed darkness. Towering ferns, vine-covered chestnut trees and cinnamon trees lined the overgrown trail. The forest vibrated with noise. Water dripped; animals croaked, squeaked and chirped; trees rustled and creaked; the ground squished; insects hummed. The trail led them to the edge of a cliff, momentarily freeing the riders from the confines of the thick canopy above them and allowing an uninterrupted view of the world around them.

A ribbon of white sand edged the island like lace. The sea changed from blue to green as it approached that sand, curling onto the shore in a crash of foam and water that sounded like a distant roar to the riders. Down the coast to the right was the southeastern tip of Mistral. Offshore was a small semicircle of black rocks surrounded by water.

"That is the crater of a submerged volcano," Kade said. "It barely breaks the surface, and then only at low tide. There is a little sand washed up on one side; the rest is rock. There are some beautiful corals there.

Good place for pearls, too. We can sail over there one day if you like."

"In the *Black Eagle?*"

"No, one of the sloops." In the harbor by the plantation village had been several small boats Kade referred to as sloops. They were larger than the longboats on the *Eagle* and were equipped with a mast.

"I would love to, Kade," Kathleen said, smiling up at him.

He tugged on an ebony curl that lay across her shoulder. "You must be very eager to learn to sail to so readily agree to spend time alone with me."

"I am alone with you now."

"Aye, that is true, love. And it is a blow to my ego that you ventured forth with me today to satisfy your desire to ride that beast between your knees, not what I have between my legs."

Kathleen's eyes opened wide. "You are completely impossible!" she cried, her face burning.

"You are wrong, sweet Kate. I am not impossible at all. Come a little closer and I will show you how easily I can be had."

Kade's intimate smile and the devilish gleam in his eyes caused more than just Kathleen's face to burn. From deep inside her came a heated longing that was so strong it frightened her. She kicked Glory and leaned into the cooling wind as the mare raced down the trail. Kade urged Deprived after them and the jungle closed around them.

Kathleen pushed Glory faster as Kade began to gain on her. She could not erase from her mind's eye the memory of the appealing warmth in his smile. Nor could she erase from her body the trembling need to throw herself into her master's arms and explore the secret world he alone could show her.

The trail widened. The gelding was at her elbow now,

and Kathleen was enjoying the excitement of the race. Without warning, Glory came to an abrupt halt, almost flinging her rider over her head. Kathleen sat up and stared in disbelief at the clearing the little mare had entered. Clearing was not the right term, she decided instantly. Enchanted glen was a better description, for they had truly entered a most magical place.

Right in front of Kathleen a shower of water cascaded over the edge of a white cliff, falling silently into a shamrock-shaped pool of water that was as green as the hills of Ireland. White sand surrounded the pool, glistening in the sun like cut crystal. Beside Glory a palm tree dangled its fronds on the surface of the water. Across the clearing sunlight fell onto a thatched hut on the edge of the forest.

The emerald pool emptied into a series of small waterfalls that tumbled between, around and over moss-covered boulders until they disappeared back into the jungle, headed for the sea. Flowers that looked like red lobster claws grew beside the lower falls; a profusion of crimson hibiscus bloomed around the edge of the glen. White and yellow orchids clung to the branches of trees, and standing on a rock near the base of the falls was a large green bird with two red feathers in its long tail. The parrot held a fig in its yellow bill. It flew into the air with a swish of its wings, dropping the fig in the pool as it squawked in alarm.

The glen was a place of peace and serenity, causing reality to shimmer and fade. Kathleen fell into its magic embrace. It was as though she had turned a corner on Mistral and found herself on the mystical moors of Ireland. She slid off Glory's back and into Kade's waiting arms.

"Am I really so impossible, kitten?" he whispered, his lips only inches from hers.

"No more than I," she breathed. He leaned down to

216

capture her mouth with his. The last remnants of reality disappeared as she lost herself in his kiss. Kade carried her across the moss-covered boulders to the small hut. He lowered her onto the soft sand and stood towering over her, looking into her hazel eyes and waiting.

The black depths of his eyes held Kathleen captive. They looked into her very soul; she had no secrets from this man. Nor did she want any. All she wanted was to feel his arms around her, to taste his lips, to experience again the passion she knew he could awaken within her. She lifted her arms to him. Her husky voice called to him, saying the word she had whispered in the garden when dreaming of him.

"Kade."

He descended on her with the raging hunger of a starving man, devouring her in a scorching kiss. His tongue plunged into her mouth, exploring the taste of her, the feel of her. The blue blouse disappeared, and before Kathleen realized what was happening, her chemise was quickly untied and opened.

Kade traced the dappled play of sunlight on her breasts with his lips, circling an erect nipple with light nibbles that drove her to madness as she strained for more. He lifted her skirt and his fingers pushed between her legs, caressing the moistness, exciting her soul. His head lay dark against her bare breast as he pulled an aching nipple into his mouth, sucking and biting the budding rose expertly.

Kathleen moaned and arched her back, her hands searching for an anchor in this swirling, thrilling universe. They found one in Kade's shoulders. Her touch soothed him, pleased him. He longed to feel those tiny hands against his bare flesh. She responded to his unspoken wish by pulling aside his shirt, touching the bronzed flesh and allowing her secret fantasies to come alive.

Her mind was pulled along with her body into a world of pleasure and passion. The blood in her veins ran hot and fast as Kade's tongue excited her body. His fingers moved inside her, pushing and caressing. He was driving her insane. She wanted more, had to have more.

One of the horses nickered. It was a sound Kathleen associated with Ireland and home, and it helped her break free of the whirling vortex of passion that held her captive. She was horrified by her weakness, terrified by her need.

"No, stop, please stop," she pleaded, pushing her lover away even as her body arched closer to him.

Kade dragged her beneath him. "We have only just begun, my love," he said, his voice deep and rough, his breath hot. His lips fell on hers, and her tide of pleasure began rising again.

No, no, no, she cried to herself as her body responded to his touch. With a shudder of despair, she forced Kade away.

"What is wrong?" he asked.

Kathleen staggered to her feet and ran to the other side of the pool. How could I do that, how could I enjoy it? A tremor seized her legs as her body remembered Kade's touch, as her heart remembered her fantasy.

She unfastened her skirt, letting it and her chemise fall onto the sand before she dove into the quiet pool. She needed to cleanse her flesh of Kade's touch, cleanse her body of her need. Her body sliced between drifting leaves and the emerald water wrapped around her, enveloping her in warmth and wetness. Deeper she went, until her hands touched the sandy bottom. Then she broke for the surface. Her head emerged into the air and she shook the water from her face just as Kade dove in, still fully dressed except for his boots. He caught her foot.

"Why did you run?"

She kicked him between the legs. Although the water blunted the blow, a stab of pain cut into him. Kathleen swam out of his reach and climbed onto the beach, confused and unsure of the emotions raging within her. She had enjoyed the ride, enjoyed the day, enjoyed him. Then they came to this clearing, this unreal place, and she gave in to the primitive thing inside her, the thing that at night dreamed about Kade, the thing that made Kathleen aware of nothing except him whenever he was near. The primitive thing made her enjoy his touch, made her enjoy his kiss, the thing that had almost caused her to submit to his hot, demanding passion.

I cannot let it happen again, if it does I will be lost. She wrapped her arms around her shoulders. *Perhaps I am lost already.*

Kade recovered from his pain, straightened up and stepped out of the water. He was standing over Kathleen before she could move away, his hair dripping onto the ivory of her skin.

"Now tell me what that was all about," he demanded, catching her hair in his hands and pulling her up to face him. Fear flickered in her hazel eyes as she winced from his grasp on her hair. He cursed himself and drew her into the shelter of his arms.

"I did not mean to frighten you, Katie," he said, thinking that was the reason she had run from him.

Kathleen pulled free. "I am not frightened by you, it was what we were doing." She stopped and corrected herself. "What I was doing. There is no way for me to prevent you from taking me like you did on the *Eagle,* but I will not willingly give myself to you."

She grabbed her clothes and stalked around the pool to where her blouse lay. After she was dressed, the soft

219

cottons clung to her damp body.

The look on Kade's face made Kathleen think he was going to rip her clothes off, throw her down on the sand and take by violence what she had almost given him. Yet when he spoke, his voice was calm, controlled. And cruel.

"Aye, I could take you like I did before, when you cried out in pleasure and pulled me as close as flesh will allow. You enjoyed it that time, Kathleen. I know it and you know it. And you enjoyed what happened before I left for Nassau. It could be even better if only you will accept what is inevitable."

Kathleen's resolve wavered. Why should she not submit to him? Her body was begging for more of the pleasure she felt at the touch of his hands. He was standing there, waiting for her. All she had to do was walk around the emerald pool and into his arms.

Emerald, emerald pool, Emerald Hills. How could I forget about going home, home to Ireland and Taran? Home to Father?

She felt as though she had been hit in the face with a wet branch. How could she ever face her father again after giving herself to a man who did not love her? Would he forgive her for being weak or disown her for soiling the name of O'Connor? Jarrett O'Connor was a proud man, a strong man. He had taught his children to be strong, expected them to be proud.

Kathleen turned away from Kade, allowing her common sense to make the decision. She swung herself onto Glory's back and waited. Kade pulled on his boots, pushed his knife into the top of the right one and mounted his gelding. He led the way out of the enchanted clearing, down a path that eventually led to the open beach. The horses turned left, heading automatically back to the stable.

A fire burned inside Kade. She had come so close,

then pulled away. When she had stood before him with her damp clothes clinging to that beautiful body, he had almost taken her. It would have been easy. Once he was inside her, moving with the ancient rhythm of passion, she would have responded. Yet something had stopped him. He had taken her by force once and had sworn never to do it again. Still, it was going to be hard to live by that oath if she did not give in soon.

A scream sounded above the crashing surf. Thoughts of Kathleen were abandoned as Kade kicked the gelding into a gallop. Sand sprayed up behind Deprived's hooves as he raced down the beach. As they approached the shipping village, more screams were heard, coming from the pier where a group of men were gathered.

Kade reached the pier before Kathleen. He flung himself off the gelding and raced to where a man was writhing in pain beside a shattered cask. Kathleen ran up beside Kade. She grabbed his arm to steady herself when confronted with the sight of the man's mangled body, thinking involuntarily of her brother's bloodied chest. The man was screaming again, a froth of red bubbles streaming from between his lips. A shattered keg lay beside the man, the black powder it had contained spilling onto the pier.

"What happened?" Kade demanded. The group of men parted, allowing him to see that Jake was lying nearby, one leg twisted unnaturally beside him. "Jake!" he cried and ran to the side of the Scotsman. The other man began to scream again.

"I'm fine, lad, just a wee injury. See to Max." Jake waved Kade away. The screams stopped beneath the quieting touch of Kathleen's hand on the man's brow, and Max lay dead in the afternoon sun.

"What the hell did you do?" Kade jerked Kathleen to her feet.

She shook herself free. "He was dying. I touched him to let him know he was not alone. How is Jake?"

All signs of pain on Max's face were gone, replaced with a serene look of peace. Kade remembered the strange way Kathleen had quieted the black stallion. Her spells must work to soothe the dying as well.

"Jake's leg is broken," Kade said, turning away from Max. He motioned to Pete Johnson, who was standing to one side of the pier. "Get Dr. Williams from the village, tell him I want him here immediately."

Johnson pointedly looked from Kade to Kathleen, drawing attention to the fact they were both wet. His eyes lingered on where Kathleen's blouse clung to her shapely breasts. A grin creased his dirty face as he left to carry out Kade's orders.

Kade swore under his breath as he noticed where all the men were looking. He dragged a piece of sacking from a crate and dropped it over Kathleen's shoulders. She pulled the knife out of his boot to use in slicing open the leg of Jake's pants, exposing the mess that was the old man's leg. Using the hem of her skirt, she wiped most of the blood away.

"The bone is completely through the flesh," she told Jake as she probed at the torn skin.

Kade reached for his knife. "Better give that back to me before you hurt yourself."

"This?" she said, holding the blade so the sun glistened along the honed edge. One of the men near Max's body struck a flame to light a smoke. Kathleen flung the knife directly at the man. The point struck the rolled paper of tobacco, pinning it against a crate and extinguishing the flame.

"You are standing in a pile of gunpowder," she told the astonished sailor. "Not a good place for a smoke."

She turned back to Kade. "What were you saying?"

"Never mind," he muttered. "Where is that doctor?"

he bellowed at the crowd of men who were now regarding Kathleen with more respect.

Jake chuckled. "Calm yerself lad. 'e'll be along. The lass did some fancy work with yer knife, don't ye think?"

"What if she had missed? There have been enough injuries around here today without her causing another one."

Kathleen glared at him. "I *never* miss, Captain Morgan."

"Kade, rile the lass some other time. Right now I be in a bit of pain and don't want to 'ear ye fussin'." Lines of pain showed white on Jake's weathered face.

The men moved aside as Dr. Williams pushed through the crowd, carrying a leather bag and wiping his forehead with a gigantic handkerchief. He looked down at Max.

"Dead," he proclaimed, then approached Jake. "This one's still alive."

"I am constantly amazed by your immediate grasp of an obvious situation,. Dr. Williams," Kathleen said in a dry voice.

He looked confused for a moment, and then his eyes narrowed as he recognized her. "What are you doing here? I gave orders . . ."

"Miss O'Connor is not the reason you were summoned, Williams," Kade said. "In case you had not noticed, Jake's leg is broken."

Williams directed his attention to the sheen of white bone sticking out of the red wound on Jake's upper leg. "So it is. I need to get this back under the skin, then set the leg. Hold him tight, Captain, this will hurt."

Kade held Jake's shoulders and Kathleen steadied his good leg. Williams lifted the broken leg gently, turned it a little so that the bone slipped beneath the torn flesh, then gave a quick jerk that set the old man's leg with a loud snap.

"Bloody 'ell!" Jake screamed.

Dr. Williams sat back on his heels and smiled benignly at his patient. "That was quite easy."

"For ye maybe, ye daft bugger."

"Since you have enough strength to complain, you can tell me what happened here." Kade indicated Max's body.

"A line started to give on that keg of gunpowder. Crazy Max was workin' right below it. I tried to pull 'im out of the way. The rope snapped and caught us both."

Jake's face went completely white as Dr. Williams bound his leg in a temporary splint fashioned from staves on the broken keg. The doctor closed his bag with a snap, and Kade lifted the old man off the ground.

"Put me down, ye big ape!"

Kathleen pulled the knife from the crate and slipped it into the waist of her skirt as Kade headed for the house with Jake.

"I will take the horses back to the stables," she told him before vaulting onto Glory. When she leaned down to sweep up the gelding's trailing reins, the sacking slipped from her shoulders and exposed such a delightful display of breast that Kade tripped.

"The way she 'andled that knife was somethin'. Hell of a woman ye got there, lad," Jake said.

"She is a child."

"How did ye get wet? Were ye afraid to allow the wee child to play in the sea alone?"

"Shut up, Jake."

"Whate'er ye say, *master*."

Kade quickened his step. His arms were getting tired, and it was still a long way to the house. "I had scheduled a meeting with Harry Timpson tomorrow on

224

the other side of the island. I will have him come over here instead. I want you there while I discuss the changes to be made in the island's birding and fishing, among other things."

"Ye mean yer not sailin' off tonight, yer actually gonna spend two whole days in a row on this 'ere island? Mattie will faint."

"I intend on spending more than just two days here, maybe several weeks. There are some things on Mistral that require my attention."

"It be about time ye listened to Daniels' complaints about that foreman fella."

"What happens on Mistral is none of Bog Daniels' business. He should be tending to shipping, not sticking his nose into Harry Timpson's affairs." He pushed open the door of the house with his shoulder, moving through the main room toward the kitchen.

"Speakin' of affairs, lad, what do ye plan to do wi' the lass? I don't like seeing 'er kept 'ere like this, ye should be sendin' her 'ome."

Kathleen dashed into the house and ran up the steps. Kade's eyes followed her. He wanted her so much it hurt. She was a creature of passion, of needs and desires. When he finally broke through her barrier of fear, the result would be worth the painful wait. He would allow her time to get used to him before trying again to take her.

He glanced at the landing a final time, then hurried through the dining room and down the hall to the kitchen. Jake squirmed uncomfortably. "Me leg hurts, lad, slow down a bit."

"That is exactly what I have in mind."

Chapter 17

Kathleen rarely saw Kade during the next week except at dinner. Most of the time he was either in his office filtering through the stack of papers on his desk or attending to plantation and shipping business.

Kathleen spent every morning at the stables, training the black stallion to accept her on his back for longer periods and to respond to her orders without the calming techniques she had used the first time she mounted him. Then she had called upon the peaceful serenity of her memories of Ireland to cast what her mother had called spells.

The rest of the day she rode Glory over the island, exploring the trails and roads. She studied the shape of the island and compared it to those on the charts she had memorized. She was convinced that Mistral was one of the unmarked islands north of Martinique and wanted to check the charts again to be certain, only she was afraid Kade would catch her in the study and guess her intentions.

The change that had come over her master since their ride around the island was astounding. He was a complete gentleman, making no demands on Kathleen, no crude remarks or leering stares. The only time he ever touched her was to hand her into and out of her chair at the table.

His new attitude surprised Kathleen. It also drove her crazy. The longer he did nothing to fulfill his promise to make her his mistress, the more Kathleen found herself unable to keep her eyes off him. Her gaze lingered on his face, her hands trembled when he brushed against her arm at the table, her voice choked up when he spoke to her.

She remembered the feel of Kade's lips at strange times, such as when she spilled her wine at the table and Kade gave her one of his slow, devastating smiles. She had been rendered completely speechless, dropping her fork and sending a boiled potato shooting across the room, narrowly missing Bog Daniels' head.

She remembered the strength of Kade's embrace at strange times also. One day as she was coming down the staircase, he was walking up. She tripped on the top step and fell down the next two before she could steady herself by grasping the iron railing. Kade had reached for her when she started to fall, then pulled back when she regained her balance. All the rest of the day she had been haunted by the sight of his arms opening to her.

By the end of the week she was jumpy and nervous, lonely and confused. She was so out of place on the island. Everyone had a job except her. No one talked to her except old Sampson in the village. He told her all about how to grow sugar and mill it, explaining the process in such detail Kathleen was certain she knew more about Mistral's cane than Kade did.

She also knew more about Harry Timpson, the overseer and foreman. Until this last week, Kade had rarely spent two days in a row on Mistral. Timpson had taken advantage of his absence to bring a reign of terror onto the workers of Mistral. He deprived them of their provisions, overworked them, and worst of all, he beat them.

Punishment for major crimes on the island was

decided and handled by Kade. He weighed the evidence, and if the accused islander was found guilty, Kade had the person and his family transported off Mistral to Barbados. The only exceptions were murder and rape. Both were punishable by death.

Punishment for small crimes was handled by Timpson. There was a tiny prison behind the sugar mill where those breaking the island rules were to be imprisoned for short periods. What Kade did not know was that Timpson rarely used that prison. He used his whip.

Kathleen came across proof of Timpson's punishment at the six-bed hospital in the plantation village. She was there to deliver some herbal tea Mattie had made up for a woman who had just given birth to her first baby. There were only two people in the hospital, both being tended by the island nurse, not Dr. Williams. One was Millie, the new mother. The other was a young man, no more than twenty. He lay on his stomach, his face turned to the wall.

"What is his sickness?" Kathleen asked Millie.

"Him not sick." The woman cuddled her baby to her breast, the infant sucking at the dark nipple. Kathleen watched for a moment, then tried again.

"He must be here for a reason. If he is not sick, then why is he here?"

"Him not like sister being pregnant. Him talk to Massa Harry."

"Why would that put him in the hospital?" Kathleen reached a finger to the baby, who grabbed it tightly.

"Massa Harry not listen to Milo. Milo get mad, Massa Harry get mad."

"They fought?"

"No fight. Massa Harry whip Milo."

Kathleen looked at the still form across the room, at the sheet pulled over the back, at the bare shoulders.

"Why did Milo talk to Timpson about his sister's baby?"

"Massa Harry father."

"He is married to Milo's sister?"

"No married, that why Milo mad. Sister young, like you. She not like Massa Harry, Massa Harry like her. She get pregnant."

"Do you mean Timpson raped the girl?" Kathleen's stomach turned over, and she experienced a rush of nausea.

"I not say rape."

"Then he did not rape her."

Millie laid the sleeping infant beside her, then lifted round eyes to Kathleen. "I not say that either. I not say anything."

That night at dinner Kathleen was silent. She responded to Kade and Bog with one-word answers, refused a second helping of pineapple tart and went directly to her room instead of joining the men in the living room for coffee. She was sitting up in bed, thinking about what Millie had said, when Kade entered.

He came through the door that led to his room, having discarded his jacket and vest. The top buttons on his shirt had been opened, and Kathleen could see the black hair on his chest as he sat down beside her. She scooted away from him.

"You were quiet tonight, Kate. Something wrong?"

"Nothing you want to hear."

He put a hand on the pillow beside her. The candlelight played over his face. Outside it began to rain, water running off the roof as thunder shook the house.

"When you are ready to talk, I will be in the next

room." He sat there for a moment longer, then left her alone.

For the last week Kade had completely avoided her, yet just now Kathleen had seen in his eyes that he still wanted her. She thought of Milo's sister. Timpson had wanted her, had taken her against her will. How long before Kade took her that way? Would women ever have a choice in their lives, would they forever be subjected to the whims of men?

She leaned over and extinguished the candle. The rain was still falling, drowning out the normal sounds of the night, the squeal of bats and calls of birds, the songs of frogs and the wash of the surf on the shore. Kathleen fell asleep to the sound of the wind, the sound of the thunder. And the sound of her heart beating faster as she remembered the light in Kade's eyes.

The next day dawned clear and clean. The rain had washed away the dust of the dry season, bringing forth a burst of new growth in the garden as the native flowers strained to take advantage of the needed water. Even though the main house was on the wet side of the island, it still suffered near the end of the dry season when the rain fell only on the tops of the mountains.

During the rainy season the life-giving moisture fell everywhere, causing a rapid growth in the crops and an easing of island tensions. The only thing the islanders dreaded about the rainy season was that it was also the season for hurricanes. The monster storms could uproot trees, level houses, drown livestock. And worst of all, hurricanes killed people.

Kathleen was getting dressed when Kade came into her room carrying a tray. The smell of bacon, eggs and coffee filled the air. Effie came in behind him with a small table. She placed it in front of the rocking chair

230

and left. Kade set the tray on the table and motioned Kathleen into the chair.

"What is the occasion?" she asked as she sweetened her coffee with honey.

"I am taking the morning off and thought you might like to take that trip out to the sunken crater. About time you learned something about sailing, too. Dr. Williams informs me your ribs are completely healed."

Kathleen hesitated with the fork halfway between the plate and her mouth. Was he trying to tell her he would wait no longer for her to begin earning her living on Mistral? If so, then it was also time to escape.

"I would like to go sailing. After that rain last night, it will be too wet to ride."

Kade took a piece of bacon from her plate and sat on the bed to munch it and drink his coffee. "I am having a sloop brought around from the plantation. She is about twenty feet long, easy to handle. Perfect for your first lesson. I will see you downstairs in five minutes." He set his empty cup on the tray and closed the door to the hall behind him as he left.

Kathleen took her time finishing her breakfast, then dressed in a simple white dress, the material thin enough to keep her cool. It was a new dress, one that Effie's aunt Euline had made from the material Kade had brought back from Nassau. She searched under the bed, looking for the sandals Kade had insisted she wear when riding around the island to protect her from spiders when she dismounted to rest Glory. She finally found them under her dressing table and slipped them on.

Kade had ordered Sam, the old man who worked in the stable, to sew a cinch on the blanket Kathleen used for riding. Sam had also put some pockets on it for her so she could carry a container of fresh water, a knife and a large conch shell.

231

Though there was ample water on the slopes of the mountains, there was none along the shore. The heat could quickly reduce someone to a state of fever. Kade told Kathleen to drink some water every hour whether she was thirsty or not. If she became light-headed or dizzy, she was to blow into the pointed end of the shell to summon help, one long blow followed by a short one.

Kade threw open the door. "Are you coming or not?"

"Right now, just let me tie my hair back."

He caught her arm to stop her. His fingers slipped into the ebony curls. "Leave it loose."

"It will get tangled in the wind."

"I like it tangled. Would you deny your master that small pleasure?"

He was so tall. So handsome. With his hands in her hair and the light in his eyes so soft and kind, Kathleen could not have denied him anything.

"Aye, master," she whispered. "I will grant you that pleasure."

His fingers touched her chin, traced along the line of her jaw. "You surrendered very easily, kitten. We shall have to discuss the granting of other pleasures I desire."

It had been a week since he had touched her like that. As his thumb brushed the corner of her mouth, Kathleen felt as though it had been a lifetime. His hand moved to her throat, smoothing the skin in the hollow of her neck.

"Do you like pearls?" he asked.

"I have seen only a few, those taken from oysters by the kitchen maids. They were beautiful, like a pastel sunrise."

"Some are like that. Others are like an Irish mist, mysterious and haunting. Do you still long for Ireland?"

"I long for home."

"There used to not be a difference, is there one now?" His hand was on her shoulder, slipping beneath the white dress.

"You said I would love Mistral, you were right. It is so unbelievably beautiful. Still, it is not home."

His fingers moved along the neckline of her dress, just beneath the edge of the material. A warm touch, a soft touch. A disturbing touch. Kathleen laid her hand on his arm just below where his sleeve was rolled up to the elbow. She felt the corded muscles and faded scars. She felt his strength.

He was leaning closer, the dark head bending over her. His lips were parting. He smelled so very masculine. So very wonderful.

"The *Slipper* is here, Kade!" Bog Daniels called out from downstairs.

"Shall we?" Kade whispered, his lips almost against Kathleen's.

"Yes," she murmured, the word barely stirring the air between them.

He raised up. "Do you want a hat?"

Kathleen blinked. "A hat?"

"For the boat, Kate. It will be bright on the water."

"Oh yes, the boat. A hat might help."

He had not kissed her, had not pulled her into his embrace and forced her to submit to his caresses. She should have been happy, but she was not. Instead she felt empty, as though a part of her body were suddenly missing.

On one end of the privacy screen hung Kathleen's hat. It was made of dried grasses, woven for her by Sampson. The brim sloped out over her shoulders, shading her from the tropical sun. On one side Sampson had left a small hole, just large enough to insert the stem of a flower or a parrot feather. A hibiscus flower drooped in the hole.

233

"My flower died," Kathleen said as Kade removed the wilted red petals. He reached behind him and produced from his back pocket a white orchid like the one he had put in her hair the day they went riding.

"For you, my lady."

"Have you planned the entire day so carefully?" she asked as she pushed the orchid's stem into the hat.

"Aye, Katie, that I have. And since the *Slipper* awaits us in the harbor, we had best be on our way."

As they walked down to the harbor, Kade's eyes kept drifting to Kathleen's face. The hat cast entrancing shadows on her lips and eyes, the white dress flowed around her as she walked. She was so beautiful, so small and desirable. He ached to feel her in his arms.

Yesterday Kade had overheard Bog talking to Mattie about Kathleen working with the black stallion, and a murderous fury had gripped him. He had immediately set off for the stable, intending to wring her neck for disobeying his orders.

When he had reached the clearing, he had seen Kathleen jump into the corral, a leather harness in her hand. The stallion had whistled a greeting and trotted over to her. Kade had watched in disbelief as the horse he called a killer, the horse that had nearly sunk one of his ships, bent his proud head and nuzzled into Kathleen's embrace.

"Good morning, Demon," she had said. "Hold still while I try this on you. See, it does not go in your mouth so there is no bit to bother you."

She had slipped the harness on the stallion, thrown the reins over his neck, and with hardly any visible effort mounted the horse. Her small form had looked even smaller on the back of the large stallion. The horse had reared on his hind legs, the morning light gleaming

234

on his black hide. With his front legs still cutting through the air, the beast had gathered his muscles and plunged over the fence in a leap that had left Kade breathless. Kathleen and the stallion had torn into the jungle.

"She is something," Bog had said as he stepped from the jungle behind Kade.

"I gave her orders to stay away from that beast."

"He follows her around like a puppy. He would never hurt her."

"After what I just saw, I might. She went against my orders. I will not tolerate that from anyone." Kade had turned to leave.

"Why don't you stop pretending to be so hard-nosed? That is not just some little slave girl you brought home. Kathleen is a woman, a beautiful, desirable woman. Since you are neither blind nor deaf, you must be aware of that, even though you don't seem to know what to do about it. Could it be she is more than the great Kade Morgan can handle?"

"Mind your own business, Daniels."

"Why don't we make it my business? Sell her to me."

"What makes you think I want to sell her?"

"It is obvious you do not care one whit for her; if you did you would send her home. Sell her to me and be rid of her."

"And you would send her home? I have seen the same look in your eye as that stallion has."

A commotion in the brush behind the stable had drawn their attention. Kathleen and the stallion had exploded into the clearing. The horse had soared over the corral fence, landing with a bone-jarring thud in a cloud of dust. Kathleen had slid from his back, pulled the halter off and patted his neck. Sam had opened the gate for her and the stallion had trailed after her through the opening.

"No, Demon. That is all for today." She had handed the harness to Sam. "I will rub him down when I get back from my ride with Glory. He is too excited now."

Bog and Kade had walked back to the house. Both men had been quiet as they remembered the magnificent sight of Kathleen on the stallion.

"I will admit, Kade, that I would love to have Kathleen melt in my arms the way she did for you that first night. I will even tell you that I would give almost anything to have that happen, but not at the risk of her happiness, which is what you are sacrificing by holding her here."

"She looked happy just now."

Bog had shaken his head. "As happy as a slave can be. If she belonged to me, I would put her on the next ship to Ireland."

"And never feel her 'melt in your arms'?"

"I didn't say I would let her go alone."

Remembering that conversation now with Kathleen walking beside him, Kade started to worry. Was Daniels in love with her? Would he risk Kade's wrath to help her escape? If he did, there was not a place on earth Daniels could go to hide. Kade would find him and he would kill him.

"Kade, it is beautiful!" Kathleen cried as she sighted the sloop tied to the end of the pier. The *Slipper* was a graceful craft, her hull curving up from the water like the half-opened wings of a butterfly.

Kade stepped into the stern and lifted Kathleen down beside him. He cast off, ran the mainsail up the mast, tied it off and set the tiller to steer the *Slipper* out of the harbor. Kathleen held the ship on course while he hoisted the jib. After all the lines were secured, he came back to sit beside her, his arm stretched across the back of her seat.

"Think you could sail her?" he asked.

She caught her tongue between her teeth and carefully looked over the set of the sails and lines. "The only difficulty would be tacking."

"Easy. Watch me." Kade stood up and untied the line that secured the boom. "First you release the mainsail, bringing her around like this." He ducked as the boom snapped across to starboard. He tied it off, changed the tiller's direction, then loosened the jib. It collapsed against the mast, the edges whipped by the wind. Kade grabbed the starboard line and hauled the sail past the mast. It immediately filled with wind. He tightened the rope and tied it off.

"Let me try," Kathleen said.

She took off her hat and handed it to Kade before untying the line holding the mainsail. By letting it out slowly, she maneuvered the boom across the boat to the port side. She tied it off and changed the tiller position, her hand brushing against Kade's accidentally. Their eyes met for a moment. Kathleen looked away first. She fumbled a little while untying the jib line. When it was released, the canvas whipped across the boat to the port side without catching on the mast.

She drew the line in but was unable to pull it tight enough to prevent the jib from luffing in the wind. She tied it off, removed her sandals and untied it again. With her bare feet planted firmly on the wooden deck, she leaned backwards and hauled on the line. The jib tightened a little, but not enough.

A pair of strong arms surrounded her as Kade put his hands over hers and pulled the line tight. With Kathleen between his arms, he tied off the rope and gave it an extra hitch. They stood there afterwards, his arms around her, her hair blowing across his chest.

Kathleen did not want the moment to ever end. She wanted to stand in Kade's embrace and sail forever across the blue sea. A frigate bird soared overhead, his eight-foot wingspread wider than the *Slipper*. Beneath the water beside them, yellow parrot fish schooled among the staghorn coral, and a giant grouper moved into the shadow of an undersea cave.

Kathleen saw it all, saw Mistral green and beautiful off the starboard side of the sloop, saw the white beaches glisten in the sun. They passed the small cove where the water from Emerald Pool emptied. Kade reached down and moved the tiller so the sloop heeled over to the port side. The bow pushed through the sea as the *Slipper* moved around the southeastern tip of Mistral. The sunken crater was in sight now, breaking through the surface ahead of them.

"We are there, Kate."

"Aye, so we are." She sighed and stepped out of his arms. He untied the jib, letting the canvas fall limp onto the bow, then brought the boom to the center position and secured it. Kathleen untied the halyard from the mast and lowered the mainsail. Kade secured the tiller and went forward to drop the anchor off the bow.

Kathleen leaned over the stern and looked into the water. "It is so clear, like air," she told Kade as he came up beside her.

He brushed the hair from her face. "Want to go over to the island?" The narrow strip of black rock and small bit of sand was about fifty feet off their port beam.

"How do we get there?"

"Swim." He shrugged out of his shirt and sat down to pull off his boots. "There are no sharks around today, so we will be safe."

Kathleen caught her lower lip between her teeth. A swim sounded inviting since it was so hot. Surely Kade would not try anything here, not with two fishing boats from the other side of the island nearby.

She unbuttoned her bodice and the dress fell from

238

her, pooling at her feet. Kade stopped tugging at his boots to stare at the soft cotton. Ever so slowly his eyes moved up her legs, over the chemise and up to Kathleen's face. He swallowed and turned his attention back to his boots. Kathleen knelt before him.

"Let me help," she said, pushing his hands aside. He sat back and watched as she slipped the boot from his left foot. She set it beside the right one, which he had already removed.

The chemise, already short, had ridden up her legs when she knelt. Her breasts, her hips, her slender waist were scarcely concealed beneath the fine fabric. Kade's throat began to ache.

"Ready?" she asked. Unable to speak, he nodded. She stepped onto the seat beside him and dove over the stern. Kade sat still for a moment, trying to forget how close her legs had just been to his face.

Kathleen was already halfway to the island before Kade dove in. She went under the water and surfaced a moment later holding something in her hand. The gentle waves carried her up onto the beach, and Kade came out right behind her.

"Look!" she cried, showing him the shell she had picked up from the bottom. It was extremely small; Kade was surprised she had spotted it. It lay in Kathleen's outstretched hand, green and smooth as it caught the light.

"Beautiful," Kade said, looking just past her hand to her breasts. The chemise clung to her, almost transparent. It revealed more than it concealed.

"I want to take it back. Do you have a pocket?"

"Aye, Katie, that I have." He took the tiny shell and slipped it into his pocket. Within a few minutes she had added three more to her collection, all the same emerald color. Next came a bright pink scallop with dark lines running out from the hinge, and a white shell called a Caribbean Vase.

Along the edge of the crater were tide pools. Kade uncovered a small octopus among the loose rocks in one pool. Kathleen poked her finger at it, and the octopus wrapped a tentacle over her fingernail, then slithered out of sight in a hole. They found a purple shell with a hermit crab inside, its claws barely visible from where it had retreated deep inside the gentle whorl of shell.

"He reminds me of the soldier crabs on Jamaica."

"Soldier crabs?" Kathleen asked as she tickled the crab's claw.

"They live on land, up in the mountains, inside shells just like this fellow. Once a year they get together in huge armies to march down to the sea, where they exchange their shells for larger ones. Then they all troop back into the mountains."

"Are there any on Mistral?" She returned the crab to the tide pool.

"Not that I have seen, but that does not mean there are not any. I have not spent much time here."

Kathleen sat on the sand and leaned against a rock with her legs stretched out on the sand. "Why is that?"

"My business has always been on the sea." Kade sat beside her, enfolding her hand in his.

"I like the sea," Kathleen said.

"You like land more."

"Yes."

"What else do you like?" He ran his finger across her palm and drew her into his arms.

"Horses," she said as his lips nuzzled her earlobe.

Kade's tongue slipped into her ear. She shivered. "Do you like that?" he asked.

"It would be a lie if I said no," she said, "but liking something and wanting to do something are two different things."

240

"I want to do this." Kade kissed the hollow of her throat, the curve of her neck. Her halfhearted struggles to escape his embrace began to weaken. He kissed the corners of her mouth, then placed his lips over hers.

She opened herself to him, moving closer to him. He ran his hand over the curve of her hip, onto her bare leg. Her flesh was warm from the sun, hot from his touch. The coating of sand on her legs looked like a frosting of sugar crystals. Her hands were around his neck, her breasts pressed against his chest.

Kathleen was lost in their kiss. How easy it is to fall prey to Kade's magic, she thought. All he had to do was smile, or touch her gently, or whisper in her ear, and she forgot everything except how much she wanted him. And she did want him. Wanted him with every part of her body, every part of her soul.

Kade drew back and looked at the woman in his arms. Her face was flushed, as were her throat and chest. The hazel eyes opened and he watched the blue-green light in them shimmer.

"Do you want this also, Katie?"

She dropped her gaze from his face. "Why do you even bother to ask? I am your slave, I have no choice but to serve my master."

"I want you to say it, to say you want me."

She stiffened. "I have nothing left that is mine except my words. Would you take that from me also?"

"I would have you say what we both know."

"If we both know it, what purpose do words serve? Take what is rightfully yours, I cannot stop you." She lay back in his embrace, lifted her fingers to his lips. "Take what you have tasted before, but leave me the one thing no person has a right to take from another."

His eyes raked down her body, across the ivory breasts, down the wet chemise to where his hand lay on her leg. "I want more than just your body, kitten. I

241

want you to recognize me as your master."

She sat up. "I have done that, and everyone on the island knows my shame."

"I want you to admit that you want me, to look me in the eye and say you will submit to me."

"For that you will wait forever." She stood to brush the sand from her legs.

He grabbed her hand and pulled her back onto his lap. "I will make you say it, Kate."

"Never, Kade, not if you hang me by my thumbs in the center of the village and turn me over to that foreman of yours."

"Timpson? What has he got to do with this?"

"Did you know he raped a young girl, forced her to live with him? When she became pregnant he threw her out, told her to go back to work in the fields. She became ill. The girl's brother went to Timpson to get her released from work. Timpson had him whipped."

"Where did you hear this?"

"When I visited Millie in the hospital at the plantation I learned about it. Sampson told me the rest."

Kade pushed Kathleen away from him and stood up. "If the islanders have a valid complaint against Timpson, they should come to me. Not once in all the years he has been foreman on Mistral have I ever been able to substantiate even one complaint about the man."

"I saw the whip marks on Milo's back," Kathleen said.

"You saw them? Where was he?"

"In the hospital. The nurse had given him a bed and treated the cuts herself because Milo refused to see Dr. Williams. I talked to people who saw Timpson tie Milo to a tree and beat him. And he is not the first. Others have scars."

"Why have I heard nothing of this?"

Kathleen walked to the edge of the water. The *Slipper* bobbed offshore. "Because you have not listened. Mattie and Jake have both asked you to check into the punishments Timpson is handing out. Bog Daniels tried to talk to you about it, you would not listen to him. Sampson said he had told you of the cruelty and you did not believe him."

"I have heard rumors before, checked into them. I never found anything."

"Whip marks are more than rumors, Kade."

"Why did the islanders not come to me?"

"You are rarely on the island. When are the people supposed to complain? Timpson is here all year, every year. They have to live under his rule, not yours. Besides, you demand evidence, proof of his punishments. How can they bring proof of what happened last month, last year?"

"When did you see Milo?"

"Yesterday. Sampson told me that Milo would be forced to return to the fields today, even though the whipping was only two days ago."

Kade turned Kathleen to face him. He lifted her chin and looked into her eyes. "Is this what was upsetting you last night?"

She nodded.

"Why did you not talk to me then, when I could have done something this morning?"

"Would you have listened to me or would you have walked off?"

He looked out over the water. The fishing boats were hauling in their nets and preparing to change locations. A canoe was headed for the sunken crater to search for pearl oysters.

"I would have walked off before you could tell me you had seen the whip marks." He turned to face

Kathleen. "I promise that I will look into these problems. The whipping I believe, the girl being forced I will have to investigate. If Timpson did force her, he will suffer the same fate as anyone else on Mistral who rapes a woman. Death by hanging."

She could not help grinning at him. "Does that rule apply to you also, master?"

He chucked her under the chin. "I will not have to rape you, Kate. Before I am finished with you, love, it will be you who will be attacking me."

"Dream on," she said and ran into the water. Kade was right behind her. They dove through a wave, surfacing halfway between the crater and the *Slipper*.

"Kate, do you see those shells attached to the rocks below us, the yellow and brown ones with the uneven edges? Those are pearl oysters. Go down and see if you can break a few loose, I will do the same thing."

They both took a deep breath, then sank beneath the surface. The water was warm. It surged over them, lifting Kathleen's chemise and exposing a bare buttock. Her hair floated like a dark mist, and she looked like a mermaid with her eyes the same color as the sea.

Kathleen pried loose two oysters with her hands, and Kade knocked six off with a stone he picked up from the bottom. They gathered the oysters and surfaced. He shoved them in the waist of his pants, and they continued swimming to the *Slipper*.

The sides of the sloop were too high for Kathleen to climb unaided into the boat. Kade sank a little way beneath the surface, and she stepped on his shoulder, then climbed on board. He handed her the oysters, then surged out of the sea and onto the deck of the *Slipper* like a seal coming out of the water onto a rock.

They dried off on a towel Kade had packed on top of a basket in the stern of the boat. Kathleen slipped her dress on and watched Kade pull his shirt over his bronzed chest. He put her hat on her head before sorting through the basket. It contained a bottle of wine and two wineglasses, some slices of cold roast, cheese and a loaf of bread.

They ate beneath the bright sun, Kathleen showing Kade how her mother tried to catch rays of sunlight in her hand and on her tongue. When everything was gone except half the wine, Kade used his knife to pry open the oysters. Kathleen searched through the slimy contents of the shells, finding four pearls.

Kade leaned his head back and let an oyster slide down his throat. Kathleen watched him, then looked at the white thing floating in its own juice in the open shell she was holding. She had eaten an oyster on the *Black Eagle* once and had found it disgusting.

"Try one," Kade said before swallowing two more.

"I would rather eat bananas," she told him. He finished them off, then took the pearls from her. He held them up to judge quality.

"Two of these are perfect. See how they look like candlelight trapped in a milky bubble?"

Kathleen peered between his fingers, watching the light play on the pearls. "What about these two?" she asked.

"Not as good, uneven and the surface is not smooth. Good color, though."

"What are you going to do with them?" She fingered the shiny surface of the pearls.

"They are yours, Kate."

"Are they not worth a lot of money?"

"Aye, that they are."

She handed them to Kade. "Then they are not something a slave should own."

"Do not be foolish, keep them."

"Then I shall throw them overboard."

Kade scooped up the shells she had collected. "If you

do, these go back also. Pearls should always belong to beautiful women, slave or no."

Kathleen gripped the hard pearls in her hand. "Am I beautiful?" she asked without looking at Kade.

"Like a dream come true."

She looked at him then. "Your dream?"

He went forward and hauled up the anchor, then untied the halyard for the mainsail. He stood there with it in his hands, fingering the knot in the end. "It has been a long time since I had any dreams." He looked out over the water.

She went to him and took the rope from him. "You should never stop dreaming, Kade."

"And what do you dream about, little one, besides misty moors and Irish hills?" He touched the side of her face.

She looked down at the rope she held. "Sometimes I dream about you. I am in Ireland riding Taran. And there is a ship offshore, your ship. And you are walking up the slope toward me and we do not know each other."

"And do we get to know each other?"

"Yes," she whispered.

His throat contracted so he could hardly speak. He pulled her against him, stilled the tremble of her body with his own. "I am turning command of the *Slipper* over to you, Kathleen. Are you up to it?"

She leaned her head back and smiled at him. "Aye, aye, Captain Morgan."

As she raised the mainsail, Kathleen thought about what she had told Kade. She had dreamed about him, had seen him as clear as she saw him now. What she had not told Kade was that it was an old dream, one woven under the eaves of the little house in Ireland long before she had ever met him.

Chapter 18

It was afternoon that same day when Kathleen mounted Demon for their first long ride together. The stallion was eager, his head high and his tail streaming out behind him as he cantered down the road between the two mountains, headed for the plantation side of Mistral. Kathleen wanted to tell Sampson about Kade teaching her to sail the sloop that morning. As she approached the branch in the road where it wound into the village, she noticed a group of plantation workers hurrying away from the sugar mill. They looked frightened and angry.

She held Demon until the people passed, then turned him in the direction of the mill. They rode past the warehouses and the sugar mill without seeing anything unusual, then crossed over the millpond to where the building for processing rum was under construction. There was a stack of lumber near the edge of the jungle, and from behind it Kathleen heard voices.

Demon's nostrils flared and he tossed his head. Kathleen put her hand on his neck to quiet him. She knew what had frightened him: the scent of warm blood. She rode the stallion around the lumber and saw Harry Timpson standing there, recognizing him immediately as the man Sampson had pointed out to her.

247

Timpson was a stubby man, short legs and trunk with big, fleshy arms. His neck was almost nonexistent, his head resting directly on his shoulders, a square head covered with a sparse growth of dirty hair. He had yellow skin and a red nose with little blue lines running across the uneven surface. His lips were always wet, too wet. His fingers were constantly clutching at his belt, as though searching for something beside the pistol.

When Kathleen saw Timpson behind the lumber, she knew he was holding what that something was. A bullwhip. He held it lightly in his hand, the tasseled end dripping with blood. The reason Kathleen had not seen him with it before was because Timpson never carried it when Kade Morgan was on the island. Which meant he almost always carried the wicked length of braided leather.

With Timpson was James Scholes, the assistant foreman. Scholes was twice as big as Timpson and almost as mean. And tied to the pile of lumber beside the two men was Milo, the plantation worker whose sister Esther had suffered the bad fortune of attracting Harry Timpson's attention.

Milo's back was completely covered with oozing welts. Kathleen could see the white sheen of exposed bone in places where the flesh had been flayed off by Timpson's whip. Milo hung limp from the bindings on his wrists, either unconscious or dead.

"Look what we got here, Scholes," Timpson said when he saw Kathleen. "A slave interfering where she don't belong. Maybe she would like a taste of what we just gave Milo."

"Why did you beat him again?" Kathleen asked.

"The boy wouldn't work. He's done been off two days sick."

"He was sick because you beat him against Captain Morgan's orders."

Timpson stepped closer to Demon, and the stallion bared his teeth. The foreman stopped. "Cap'n Morgan ain't working this plantation every day. If he wants results, he shouldn't complain about the way I gets them."

"That does not change the fact that you have gone against his rules. You raped Esther and you beat Milo, probably to death. The captain will not like what I have seen."

"Then we shouldn't let you tell him about it."

Timpson signaled to Scholes, who dragged Kathleen from Demon's back. The stallion reared and screamed. Timpson's whip whistled through the air, landing on Demon's withers. The horse bolted into the jungle.

"Now I got you where I been wanting you, girl. I seen you riding around this island while I sweat in the hot sun trying to get some work out of these lazy creatures Morgan hires."

"Like he hired you," Kathleen said.

Timpson coiled the whip and tapped it against his leg. "I'll not stand for you talking about me that way, what with you being even lower than the other trash on this island. It's about time you was put to work. There's only one thing that you're fit for and that's laying under me."

Timpson's breath smelled of whiskey and rotten teeth, reminding Kathleen of Rat Anders. She could not stop the shudder that passed over her.

"Maybe we should see what she's hiding under that dress, Scholes."

"Yeah, let's see what we got us."

Timpson put his fingers in the neck of Kathleen's dress and ripped downward. The cotton tore easily, splitting from neck to hem. It fell from her, revealing the chemise she wore. It was edged in lace that barely covered her nipples.

249

Kathleen was so frightened that her breath came in short gasps. It was useless to shout for help; anyone who might hear her would be too frightened to interfere. Timpson reached out a hand to touch her, and she jerked away.

"Hold her still or you won't be getting any of this when I'm finished, if there's anything left." Timpson ran a finger over the chemise around Kathleen's rose-colored nipple, and then he roughly pinched the tip. She cried out from the pain and tried again to break free from the hands that were crushing her arms.

"That's right, yell a little and let me hear how much you like it. I know what a woman wants, even a lady like you." He tore open her chemise.

"God almighty," he whispered as he stared at her breasts glistening with sweat and heaving from her efforts to escape Scholes. They were heavy breasts, full and round, and he could not take his eyes from them.

"Ever since that day I seen you riding through the village with Morgan, I wanted to see you without your clothes, wanted to see you standing before me all naked like this, those big breasts ready for me to suck and bite. When I finish with them, you'll be all wet and slippery between the legs, just waiting for me to tear into you. Sure am glad Morgan took that sloop out today, because I'm gonna have me a time, yes I will."

"And me," Scholes said.

"Not you, just me."

"Ya said I could have her, too."

"What we got here ain't for the likes of you. You can watch, then take your pick of the village girls."

Scholes wanted Kathleen, not a village girl. He did not argue with Timpson, though; he knew better. The scars on his back had taught him to always obey Timpson, no matter what the order.

"Yes, we's gonna have us a time, little lady,"

Timpson said as he reached for her breasts. "Then I'll get rid of you and make Morgan think you ran away, that way won't be no way of him knowing what happened to his precious slave."

Kathleen recoiled from Timpson as far as Scholes' grasp would allow. The stubby fingers were coming closer, the nails dirty and split. There was blood on them, Milo's blood.

"Stop right there, Timpson!" someone behind Scholes roared. Kathleen almost fainted as she recognized Kade's voice. "Lay one hand on her and what you did to Milo will look like nothing compared to what I will do to you."

Scholes turned and Kathleen saw Kade. His shoulders were squared, his hands clenched as they lay against the top of his thighs. Kathleen felt the brute force of his presence, saw the anger that quivered along the edge of his jaw.

Timpson dropped his hand to his whip. "You wouldn't do that, not to a white man."

"Do not test me, Timpson. You will come out the loser."

Timpson grabbed Kathleen. "Kill him, Scholes," he ordered.

Scholes turned and lunged. Though he was not as tall as Kade, he was just as heavy. He looked like a charging bull as he lowered his head and barreled straight for Kade's chest. Kathleen watched in horror as Kade lowered his own head to meet the charge. The two men slammed together, staggered for a moment, then came up fighting.

Kade rammed his fist into Scholes' jaw. Kathleen heard bone crunching. Scholes swung at Kade, who sidestepped the blow and pivoted his fist into Scholes' stomach. He followed that with a left to the jaw, then a right. The last one had the weight of his entire body

251

behind it, lifting Scholes into the air. Kade stepped back. James Scholes wavered uncertainly on his feet, then went down like a collapsed building.

Timpson twisted Kathleen's arm behind her, dragging her backwards. Kade advanced on them, fists clenched and black eyes like hot daggers. "Promise me you won't kill me, Morgan, and I'll let the girl go."

Kade kept coming.

"I can hurt her bad with this knife before you even get close and she won't be so pretty no more." Kathleen slid her eyes to the side. Timpson did have a knife. It was right beside her face.

Kade kept coming.

Kathleen felt the touch of the blade against her face. She tried not to trip as Timpson continued to pull her with him.

"Stay back, Morgan, or I'll cut her."

Kade stopped, balancing on the balls of his feet. "Why did you do this, Timpson?" He waved a hand at Milo's body.

"That boy dared tell me I was responsible for that bastard Esther has in her belly."

"Are you?"

Timpson lowered the knife a bit. "She led me on, working in the fields with nothing on but a ragged dress that barely covered her knees."

"Sampson told me you forced Esther to wear that dress."

"So what? I'm a man, I got a right to look at a woman."

Kade moved one step closer, and the knife went back against Kathleen's face. "You do not have the right to force any woman into your bed, and Esther is just a young girl."

Timpson grinned. "No younger than this one you been sharing a bed with."

"My bed is none of your business."

"And mine is none of yours, Morgan."

Kade took another step. "When the girl is forced it is my business. And when you tie her brother to a stack of lumber and beat him to death, that is my business also."

"I'll leave Mistral, go someplace else," Timpson said, stepping backwards again. His foot struck a rock and he tripped, his grip on Kathleen loosening.

She twisted away from him, wrenching the knife from his grasp before he could regain his balance. She crouched in front of Timpson, tossing the knife from hand to hand. Timpson stared at her hands, stared at the silver sheen of the metal as it flashed in the sun, stared at her bare breasts just behind the knife.

"Back off, Kate. I will handle this," Kade said, moving up beside her.

"He is mine, it was my flesh he touched, my life he threatened." The knife moved faster between her hands. Her eyes never left Timpson's.

"Give me the knife, Kathleen," Kade ordered. She turned to face him. What he saw in her eyes made his hair on his neck crawl. He held her gaze until that look disappeared. Her hand dropped to her side and her shoulders slumped.

The moment Kathleen lowered her hand, she heard a noise behind her. She whirled around, seeing Timpson pull the pistol from his belt and aim it at Kade. His eyelids twitched as he pulled back the hammer. Before they could twitch again, Kathleen whipped her hand out. The knife flew from her fingers and stuck in the center of Timpson's throat. He staggered backwards, the gun pointing at the sky as it exploded with a roar. The stubby body fell slowly, landing at Milo's feet. The black whip lay beside him, limp in the mud.

Kathleen stood still for a moment. She had killed a

man. A stream of red gushed around the blade of the knife, down the dirty white shirt, onto the hand that still clutched the curved handle of the pistol. She turned away, sickened and alone with her sickness. Kade opened his arms to her.

I do not need him, I do not need anyone, she thought. Then she ran into his embrace. Tears streaked down the dirt on her face, wetting his chest as he held her against him. They stood like that until Bog Daniels burst around the corner of the warehouse astride Glory.

The mare danced to a stop as Bog jumped from her back. "What happened?" he asked, looking down at Timpson's body. "I saw Demon come back to the stable alone. I saddled Glory and headed out the way he had come, hearing a shot just as I reached the village."

"Timpson pulled a gun on me and Kate killed him," Kade said. Kathleen shuddered in his arms. "Bog, could you find me a blanket to put around her?"

Bog pulled the one from beneath his saddle and handed it to Kade. Kathleen never lifted her face from Kade's chest as he wrapped the blanket around her shoulders. Bog brought Deprived from where Kade had left the gelding, and Kathleen pulled the blanket over her torn dress while Kade mounted. He leaned down and lifted her into the saddle in front of him. She curled into his ams, burying her head on his shoulder.

"Cut Milo down and see if he is dead," Kade told Bog. "I will take Kathleen home and come back." He turned Deprived and rode through the gathering crowd of villagers. After they turned onto the road that led to the main house, he touched Kathleen's cheek. "Are you all right, kitten?"

"I never killed anyone before."

"You will never have to again. I promise you."

254

Something in his voice told Kathleen that, if she asked him at that moment, he would send her home. She did not ask. She did not want to do anything that would prevent Kade from holding her, protecting her. Loving her.

After dinner that night, Kathleen fell asleep on the sofa beside Kade. He carried her upstairs to her room, holding her close to him as he listened to her steady breathing. After Kathleen's accusations against Harry Timpson that morning, Kade had gone to the village to talk to the workers. He had been surprised by the absence of people when he arrived. There were no children playing, no women carrying baskets of fruit on their heads, no men fishing on the shore. Strangest of all, the fields being prepared for a fresh planting of cane were empty.

Kade had arrived at Sampson's house just as the old man came out the door. Sampson told Kade that if he did not do something about Timpson, the villagers would. He told him about Esther and Milo, told him about the beatings Timpson gave the workers, told him everything.

Kade had been disgusted with himself. Until this last week on Mistral he had not thought of the plantation as business. He had ignored that part of the island, ignored the workers, ignored Mattie, Jake and Bog when they told him about their suspicions of Harry Timpson's cruelty.

The people began to reappear in the village, anger on their faces as they stood in small groups, talking among themselves. Sampson asked a young boy what had happened. The boy glared at Kade as he told about Milo's beating. Kade had immediately mounted Deprived and raced to the mill. Though he had been too late to prevent Milo's death, he had saved Kathleen.

Kade reached the top of the stairs and carried Kathleen into her room. Rain fell against the windows in a soft patter. He laid her on the bed and unbuttoned her dress. After slipping it from her body, he tossed it aside while his eyes devoured the delicious sight before him.

A silk chemise covered the tips of her breasts, wrapping over their fullness in a delicate froth of lace. The garment was just long enough to cover the ebony curls that nestled between her legs, its ivory softness clinging to her hips and waist. Below the chemise was a lush expanse of bare thigh, then sheer stockings that glimmered in the pale light. She turned onto her side and the chemise slid up over her bare hip. Kade's stomach muscles tensed, his throat ached. He wanted this girl, needed her. If only she would give in to her desires, give in to her need for him.

He crouched beside the bed and traced the line of Kathleen's jaw. She shivered as he fingered her earlobe, shivered again as he blew into her ear. He kissed her eyelids, allowing his lips to lightly brush against her lashes.

He moved his hand down her neck, across the top of her right breast. The touch was light, like the stroke of a downy feather, stimulating and exciting her so that her skin flushed wherever he touched. She rolled her head to the side and moistened her lips with her tongue.

Kathleen stirred as the intoxicating caress of her dream lover kindled her passion. His hand slid into the hollow between her breasts, and his fingers traced a path onto the roundness of her left breast, pushing under the edge of the lacy chemise. He drew circles around her nipple, his touch so tender and tantalizing she thought she would die with the need for more.

Her breath came in short, shallow gasps. Her hands clutched the sheets. Leg muscles became tense. The area between her legs was moist with need, with longing. Her dream lover moved his hand back to her right breast, stroking her through the softness of the silk. Kathleen pushed closer to the haunting promise of that touch and felt her lover's breath on her face.

In her dream Kade was beside her, his face hidden by shadows. Kathleen wanted to touch him, wanted to feel him on her, in her. There was a touch on her leg and she tensed. Kade's hand slid along her bare thigh and her legs opened as he reached for her throbbing wetness.

The tip of his finger touched her. She moaned. The pleasure was so real, too real for a dream. Before Kathleen could focus on that thought, Kade pushed aside the silk that covered her breasts and took her nipple between his fingers. Her hands tore at the sheets, her body quivered as his head lowered between her legs.

"Kade!" she cried as his lips touched her. His tongue licked her, then pushed inside her. Kathleen knew then that her dream lover was real.

He lifted his head. "I want you, Kathleen."

"No, Kade, please stop." She pushed at him and he leaned closer to her, threatening to devour her very soul with his nearness.

"You were dreaming about me just now. That dream can become real."

"No," she whispered as he ran his hands over her body. "No," she said again as her arms went around his neck. Kade twisted his hands into her hair, pulling her to him. She shivered as his tongue touched hers.

Her soul was on fire. Kathleen could not fight this man, could not fight her need for him. He rolled onto his back, pulling her on top of him. His teeth caught and held her lower lip while he pushed her chemise above her waist. He ran his hands around her hips and onto the curve of her buttocks.

She dropped a leg between his, her flesh burning where it touched his erection. Kade ran a hand down her stomach, around her hip and onto the curve of her buttocks. His fingers moved between her legs, and Kathleen jerked her lips from his as her body pushed against those searching fingers. His mouth closed over her breast. He flicked the nipple with his tongue, grazed it with his teeth, sucked it with his lips. Kathleen's legs began to tremble as Kade's fingers slipped into her. Her head dropped forward, her hair falling across his face to bury him in its silken darkness.

He ran his wet fingers up her back, grasping her waist and turning to lay her beside him on the bed. Then he moved on top of her. His lips were on her breast, his teeth sending flashes of fire through her body. Kathleen could not deny the burning need that Kade's touch evoked in her, could not deny the passion that was consuming her. She pushed her hips up, trying to touch that which Kade withheld from her.

He bit the tender flesh of her neck, and Kathleen raked her hands across his back, ripping his shirt. She tore it from his body, eager to touch him, eager to feel his naked flesh against hers.

Kade tore open her chemise, then lowered his head to her chest. His tongue circled her breast. His hands trailed over her waist, down her stomach. His fingers moved through the crisp hairs between her legs as his teeth scraped across the underside of her breast. She strained against him, trying to position herself so his fingers would be close enough to slip inside her.

"Kade, please," she moaned as he blew on her nipple.

"Please what?" he asked and moved away from her, leaving her burning body alone and cold. "Please what, Kathleen?"

"Why did you stop?"

He leaned closer, his lips almost touching hers. She drew a quick breath, tasting the nearness of him.

"Say you want me, Kathleen."

"Never. I will never ask you for anything, least of all your touch!"

"Not only will you ask, you will beg for it." Kade pushed his knee between her legs and covered her mouth with his.

The fire he had ignited in her before was nothing compared to the heat that consumed her now. He plunged his tongue into her mouth, and she sucked on its hard thrusts. His fingers pushed into her wetness, and she moaned in ecstasy. Desperate for him to enter her, she tore at the front of his pants until she freed his swollen penis.

She was so hot she thought she would die. He wrapped his arm around her waist and pulled her hips off the bed. The head of his penis touched her, touched the wetness, touched the fire. She was frantic for him, clutching at his hips and trying to force him into her.

"Say it, Kate! Say it!"

"No," she said, dragging her head from side to side with frustration. "I will not, I cannot!"

"Say it, damn you!" he roared, his arm pulling her off the bed. "Say it!" He dragged his penis across her. She gasped at the wonderful sensations that flooded into her loins. "Say it *now!*"

Kathleen's head fell back onto the pillow, her body arching into the curve of Kade's. The hair on his chest touched her nipples, his penis jerked against her wetness. His breath was not on her face. She wanted him so desperately. Was it worth the price he demanded?

No.

"Let me go," she said. Her body stopped shaking, her

voice was steady. She could taste the bitter flavor of her hate, hate for what this man wanted her to say, hate because she wanted to say it.

Kade's eyes held hers. She could see his anger, she could feel it. Then he smiled.

"It is only a matter of time before you give me what I want, and I want only one thing. Surrender, complete and unconditional." He touched his lips to hers, moving them so gently that she began to tremble. He pulled her lips between his teeth, then slid his tongue against hers.

"Submit to me, Kathleen."

"Never," she whispered. She would never submit, never. Even though her body seethed with unfulfilled passion. Even though her heart was breaking into a thousand pieces.

His kiss deepened, ravaging her senses and her soul as he lifted her to him. She became like molten iron at the scorching touch of his raging fire, molding herself against his body with a frantic, fevered passion she could not control. Then he pulled away, looked into her eyes and laughed. He dropped her back onto the bed and walked out the room, leaving her alone with her misery. Alone with her hate.

Kade shut the door to Kathleen's room behind him and leaned against it. His knees were weak, his heart beating so hard it was difficult to breathe. He wanted to go back into the room, pull her into his arms and finish what he had started.

He stood there, his arms aching and empty, his body and soul on fire. He remembered the burning pride in her blue-green eyes as she told him she would never submit. There had been more than pride there, though.

There had been a raging need. Soon she would be his, always and forever. If only she would say the words he had to hear, the words he could not live without.

He wiped the back of his hand across his sweating forehead and moved across the room to sit on the edge of his bed. Through the wall he could hear Kathleen throwing things. Glass shattered, and then the door shook as it was struck by something heavy. When the words she was shouting became recognizable, Kade grinned. He could make out some of them, including bastard, thief and a few that made him wince. He had wanted to make an impression on his stubborn slave. Obviously he had been successful.

The racket slowed, then stopped. Silence claimed the night. There was no way he would get any sleep that night; the memory of Kathleen in his arms was too fresh in his mind. He left his room, intending to get a book to read. As he reached the bottom of the steps, he saw a light coming from the study. He walked quietly to the door.

Kathleen was there, sitting on the windowseat and watching the rain slide down the glass. A candle burned beside her, and she was surrounded by darkness. Her eyes were red and swollen, her hands clenched into fists. She was so beautiful, the candlelight etching tiny shadows on her face.

She lifted a finger to trace a raindrop down the window. Then she dropped her head into her hands. Kade could not bear it any longer. He started to go to her. Her head lifted and he froze. She turned to where he stood concealed in darkness. There was pain in her eyes and a terrible, lonely emptiness. Then her eyes closed and she turned away.

Kade made his way back up the steps to his room. He lay on his bed, staring at the ceiling. The pain he had seen in Kathleen's eyes was nothing compared to what he was feeling.

He had wanted to break Kathleen's pride, to show her that the shame of begging belonged only to the beggar. How wrong he had been. The shame was his, even more so since Kade now knew that he loved her.

Chapter 19

Sunrise the next morning was spectacular. It looked like all the red and orange color in the world had been piled on the eastern sky. There was no wind, and the waves in the harbor were so flat they washed onto the shore without a sound. Kathleen slipped quietly out of the house, pausing for a moment to listen to the silence of the morning before running to the stables. She planned to mount Demon and ride as far from Kade Morgan as possible.

The stable door creaked as she opened it. Demon's blanket and harness were hanging in the stall beside Glory. Kathleen gave the mare a lump of sugar from the sack near the door. Demon snorted and tossed his head as she eased between the rails of the corral fence. He was nervous, excited. It took her three tries before she could tighten the cinch on the special blanket Sam had made for her. She checked the pockets in the blanket. Her knife was there along with a length of rope she had been using to practice the knots Skinner had taught her on the *Black Eagle*.

Kathleen emptied the unused water from the flask and filled it with fresh from the well behind the stable. She placed it in the pocket, checked the cinch again and mounted the stallion. They raced out of the clearing into the dark jungle.

There were no bird calls, no whirring of insect wings as Demon followed the trail down to the beach. Although the sun had climbed higher into the sky, the horizon still glowed red. Clouds began to gather at the tops of Mistral's mountains, spreading out across the island and casting shadows on the sea.

Kathleen's heart was heavy as she looked across the water. Ireland seemed little more than a dream remembered from another life. The solitary rides through morning mists, the hours spent in front of a fire at night surrounded by family and home were memories that belonged to someone else.

Her body still burned from Kade's kisses and caresses, her heart still ached and her eyes were still moist with unshed tears. She wanted to feel his breath on her breasts, his sweat on her lips. How long could she deny him? How long could she deny herself?

Demon shied as a lizard scurried across the beach, closely followed by another. The stallion calmed beneath Kathleen's touch. The sand crunched as his hooves broke through the crusted surface. A lone gull soared over the ocean. Kathleen stopped Demon and watched the bird until it was out of sight.

She urged the stallion on, reining him back into the jungle and riding along the edge of a stream. Demon dipped his nose in the water and drank. The day had scarcely begun, and it was hot, so hot that Kathleen's white dress clung to her body and her hair felt as heavy as wet wool. The stallion moved on, climbing the steep slope. Soon the path widened and they entered the enchanted clearing of Emerald Pool.

Kathleen slid off Demon and removed his blanket. She kicked off her sandals and crossed to a tree that bent beneath the weight of its fruit. She reached up and picked one of the mangos.

It split easily beneath the pressure of her knife. She

bit into the fruit, savoring the sweet juice. Demon wandered along the edge of the clearing, nibbling at the red flowers of a hibiscus bush. Kathleen watched him, thinking of Kade's black eyes and remembering how she had almost lost herself in their depths last night as he demanded she surrender to her passion. The sun was hot, burning her even through the thin cotton of her dress. She took another bite of the mango and pushed a stray curl from her face.

The thatched hut offered the only respite from the heat. Kathleen sat on the cool sand, leaning against a support post. She ate a little more of the mango, then tossed the fruit into the underbrush behind the hut. The warm air made her sleepy. Thoughts of last night drifted in and out of her mind. The clearing blurred, the sand was soft beneath her head.

On the edge of the jungle a chestnut gelding appeared. Kade dismounted, his eyes on Kathleen. He was wearing the brown suede boots that had inflamed her on the *Black Eagle*. He walked toward her, boots crunching in the sand. He knelt before her, the sun on his face.

His fingers touched the sticky juice on her lips. Kathleen smelled his cologne, saw the shadow of his unshaven beard. She thought of those boots, thought of the feel of them against her flesh. The handsome face of her master leaned closer to her. Warm air blew across her face.

"Oh God, you are real!" she cried, sitting upright and staring around her.

She was alone. The wind had returned to the island, whipping violently through the trees. Rain danced on the surface of Emerald Pool. Demon stood beneath the shelter of the sloping palm, his back glistening suddenly as the sun broke through the clouds. A rainbow burst across the sky, flaming streaks of red, orange, yellow, green, blue, indigo, violet. It split, becoming two rainbows. They both faded as the sun disappeared. Lightning flashed, thunder roared, the clouds boiled in a cauldron of dark sky.

The trees around the clearing were bending over; they looked as though they would break in half. Demon's blanket had been blown against a tree. Kathleen crawled over to it, unable to stand in the wind. Though the blanket was wet and heavy, she dragged it back to the hut.

"I have never seen such a storm," she said as a branch of the mango tree ripped loose and flew across the clearing and into the pool. The surface of the water erupted like a wave against the bow of the *Black Eagle,* a fury of white and green water that writhed upward, then fell back.

The palm fronds that thatched the top of the hut began to pull loose. Kathleen covered herself with the blanket. The wind screamed, the trees groaned. The rain pelted the earth as though driven mad, coming down so hard it began to cover the ground, unable to soak into the sand and dirt. Soon it was so deep Kathleen had to stand up. The wind crushed her against a post of the hut. She held onto it with one arm, held onto the blanket with the other.

The post began to collapse. She fell to her knees, dragging herself into the edge of the forest. With her back against a young palm tree and the wind in her face, she searched through the pockets of the blanket. Her hand closed over the conch shell. If she blew it, no one would hear. The scream of the wind would drown the noise. She dropped the shell and continued searching for the rope. When she found it, she almost sobbed with relief. Because of the knots, it was too short to use. She struggled to untie the dozen or so knots in its length, a difficult task with the rain pelting against her. After what seemed like hours, she loosened the last one.

She looked at the clearing. It had changed from a place of enchantment and beauty into hell. The pool had disappeared beneath a solid river of water and mud that poured unchecked over the limestone cliff. The sloping palm tree had collapsed, its shallow roots jutting into the air.

Kathleen could not hold onto the blanket, it was too heavy. It fell onto the ground beneath the water that had risen to her knees. She was blinded by the storm. Something brushed against her arm, and she screamed. The creature moved in front of her, blocking some of the wind and rain. Kathleen put out her hand, touching Demon's steaming coat.

She tied her rope around the tree, wrapped it around her waist and knotted the ends together. At least she would not blow away, and since the tree was young it was less likely to collapse in the storm.

The temperature dropped, and she began to shake with the cold and wet. Demon moved in closer, and Kathleen lifted her arms to his neck, pressing her face against the stallion's warm flesh as the world around her went mad and the water rose almost to her waist.

Kade was in the kitchen when Bog Daniels burst into the room. "This morning the barometer went to the top of the scale; now it is starting to drop, fast and steady," he said, his hair blown into wild disarray.

"You sure?" Kade asked, setting his coffee cup down on the table and turning to look out the window.

"The sky was completely clear at dawn, except for a weird glow in the east. There was absolutely no wind, then clouds began to gather over everything and the sea went completely flat. One of the locals said that caterpillars are crawling around in swarms and an old, native woman threw dry ashes in a pot of water and declared the world was about to end. On top of all that, the clouds to the southeast have turned purple with veins of blue lightning flashing through them. Looks like hell is going to break loose and we will be right in the middle of it!"

Mattie stopped boning the fish she held. "Hurricane," she said, voicing what they were all thinking.

"Get the servants, Mattie, and head for the caves above the village," Kade said. "I will fire off the cannon behind the stable to alert the plantation. They know to go to the caves past the mill, Sampson will see they make it. Bog, you get Jake and take him to the caves."

"What about the *Black Eagle?*"

"See that everyone in the village is safe, then take her out to sea with a skeleton crew and ride it out. I will stay on the island." He looked at Mattie. "Where is Kathleen?"

"She didn't come down for breakfast, 'er room was empty when Effie went up."

Kade's face went completely white as his heart fell all the way down to his feet. "She must be out riding, I will have to go after her. How much time do you think we have?" he asked Bog.

"An hour or so. She could be anywhere by now, Kade."

"I have to find her."

The wind was already shrieking over the island, and thunder rolled down the mountains. It was a long run to the stable, one made almost impossible by the debris flying through the air. When he reached the clearing, he saw that the corral and barn were empty. Sam had released all the horses to fend for themselves during the storm except for Glory and Deprived. Sam turned out the little mare just as Kade grabbed his arm.

"Have you seen Kathleen?"

"No, boss. Dat stallion, he's done gone too. She musta took him dis morning."

"Saddle the gelding, Sam. I will be right back."

Kade fought his way around the stable, past the well and to the cannon mounted near the edge of the clearing. He loaded it, turned his back to the wind and put a light to the fuse. It exploded with a roar, sending its message to the village on the other side of the island.

He leaned into the wind as he forced his way back to Sam. The old black man was flattened against the wall of the stable, holding tightly to Deprived. Kade pulled the horse and Sam back into the barn. The rain had begun to fall in thick sheets, stripping the leaves from the trees and pounding against the roof of the stable.

Bog Daniels appeared out of the storm. "Heard the cannon. Came to get Sam," he screamed against the sound of the storm. "Where you going to look for Kathleen?"

"Emerald Pool, it is one of her favorite places!" Kade shouted back. He swung onto Deprived, and the gelding lowered his head and pushed into the wind. Kade leaned close to the horse's neck. What if he did not find her? What if she had gone around the other mountain, or over to the plantation or to the mangroves?

It took an eternity for Deprived to reach Emerald Pool. Kade could not believe the destruction in the clearing. The palm tree that had always leaned beside the pool had collapsed, and the pool itself was buried under a deluge of mud. The hut had been blown completely away.

Kade dismounted and led the gelding behind him as he made his way around the edge of the jungle. The water rose past his knees, making walking almost impossible. He struggled on, straining to see through the fury of rain and wind for something, anything, that would tell him if Kathleen was there. His eyes were burning, and he lifted his hands to rub them just as Deprived nickered. There was an answering nicker to Kade's left. He fought his way past an uprooted tree, around a tangle of broken mango trees.

Then he saw her. She was huddled behind Demon, clinging to the horse as the wind tried to crush the pair against a palm tree.

"Kathleen!" Kade shouted as he ran to her. She did not hear him. Her face was buried in the stallion's neck. Kade pulled her arms from the horse, lifted her face. The ivory skin was red and swollen, the hazel eyes bloodshot and fogged. Her lower lip had been cut, her dress was plastered to her body along with her matted, muddy hair. She was the most beautiful sight Kade had ever seen.

Her eyes grew wide and her hand lifted to his face. "Are you real?" she asked. He laughed, tried to pull her into his arms. She was tied to the tree. He laughed again.

"Aye, my love, I am real."

She threw her arms around him, laughing with him. He held her against him, his arms around her and the tree. She was shivering and crying, laughing and smiling. He grinned at her.

"Nice day for a ride," he shouted above the scream of the storm.

"And to think only last week I was complaining that it never rained much around here!" she shouted back.

They stopped talking then. Hours passed, how many Kade did not know. He only knew that he had found Kathleen, she was alive and in his arms.

The water had risen to his waist, which meant it was almost to Kathleen's chest. If it continued to rise, he

270

would have to move her onto something higher. Suddenly it was quiet. The wind stopped, the rain stopped, the hell stopped.

Kade turned his head, looking around him as his ears rang in the sudden silence. The sky above them was dark. Stars twinkled, and the moon slid into sight as a lone cloud chased westward. Kade released Kathleen and stepped back. Demon moved to the side, nickering softly as he nosed Kathleen's shoulder. Deprived was nowhere to be seen.

"It is over," Kathleen said. "We are still alive."

"That was just the first half, Katie. Hurricanes have what is called an eye. It is a lull in the middle. We have about an hour, maybe two as big as this storm is, before the second half hits. We have to find some shelter. There used to be a cave above this pool. It has probably been buried, though." He pointed at where the waterfall used to be. The hill was a solid sheet of mud. "There is another cave between here and the house. We will go there."

"I am tied to the tree," Kathleen reminded him, fumbling with the rope as she tried to free herself. Kade bent to undo the knot. She put her hands on his shoulders, and he was very aware of her touch.

"Skinner teach you this?" he asked.

"He said if I ever want to hold onto something, to use this knot and it will never come loose. He said it was his own secret creation."

"The only thing secret about it is how to untie the thing."

She pushed her hair back. "Demon's blanket is somewhere around here. It has my knife in it."

The flood of water had receded now that the rain had stopped. Kade dropped to his knees, searching with his hands through the mud. He found the blanket about a foot away from Kathleen. The knife was still in the

271

pocket, as was her flask of water. He pulled them both out and stood up.

"Take this." He handed her the flask, then hooked his hand in the rope and sliced it off her. The moment she was free, Kade pulled her into his arms, kissing her soundly. She molded herself to him, holding so tightly that he never wanted to let her go. Finally he released her, tucked the knife in the top of his boot and picked up Demon's reins.

"We'd better get moving."

Kathleen slipped her hand into his. Kade lifted it and kissed her fingers. He could not believe how glad he was to find her, and how lucky. He lifted Kathleen onto Demon's back and started off. The trail had disappeared. He would have to find his own way around the mountain.

It was hard going. The air burned like a furnace, scorching their lungs. They stopped several times to sip the water from the flask, giving the stallion a drink from Kade's cupped hands.

The storm roared all around them, making the stillness in its center eerie and frightening. Birds fell from the sky, exhausted from being caught by the storm. Shearwaters and terns flocked to settle on mangled branches. A lone hummingbird rushed by Demon's head.

Time wore on, and Kade draped his arm over Demon's back to support himself. Kathleen put her hand over his. Their eyes met for a moment, and then he looked back at the ground and kept walking.

The storm was closing in again. Wisps of wind strayed through the eye and the trees leaned over as the smooth gray edge of the storm came closer. This time there was no rain, even though blue lightning ripped across the sky. A clap of thunder shook the ground beneath them, and the temperature dropped.

"We are almost there," Kade said.

The storm struck again, a raging, screaming, violent beast that devoured everything in its path. A parrot was blown from a tree, striking a rock. Its body exploded into a red mass of blood and feathers. Kathleen clung to Demon, her face pressed against the stallion's neck to protect her face from the cutting wind that blinded her, exhausted her.

Kade shouted something, but she could not hear him because of the storm. She leaned closer to him, and his lips closed on hers. The kiss was desperate, savage. He pulled her off the horse and into his arms as he moved his mouth to her ear, shouting, "We made it, we reached the cave!" He carried her around a tumbled pile of boulders and into total darkness. Demon entered behind him, and Kade lowered Kathleen to her feet.

"Stay here."

He left her alone. The wind roared outside the cave, crashing and screaming. When her numbed senses realized it could not reach into the darkness after her, she leaned back against Demon's solid strength and longed for Kade's arms to be around her again. A flame flickered into existence, glowing ever brighter as Kade touched it to a candle. The light chased away the fear and uncertainty of the dark.

"I left some candles here years ago when we were running as pirates," Kade said as he lit another candle, placing one on either side of a pile of blankets. He picked up a blanket, using it to rub down the tired, steaming stallion.

Kathleen sank to her knees, too exhausted and cold to stand any longer. Kade pulled her up. "We have to get out of these wet clothes. There is a hot spring further back in the cave caused by the old volcano beneath the limestone. We can warm up there."

He unbuttoned her dress while she clung to his arm. When she was naked, he wrapped a blanket around her, then pulled off his own clothes. With a candle in each hand, he led her further into the cave along a narrow path.

Kathleen was awed by the beauty surrounding her. The limestone had softened in the constant influx of groundwater, pouring through minute cracks in the ceiling and walls, dripping into fantastic shapes. The candle painted its golden light over everything, shining around and through the fantasy shapes so it looked as though the entire cave was decorated with crystal icing.

"How beautiful," she whispered, her husky, low voice echoing off the walls.

"Crystal Cave," Kade said. "This is one of my favorite places on the island. It has been years since the last time I was here." He stopped to place the candles in a niche on the wall near a pool of dark water. The light reflected off his body, turning him golden like the walls and formations.

"This feels great," he said as he stepped down into the water. Steam rose around him, thin fingers of white that alternately hid and revealed his sculpted, virile body. He reached for Kathleen. She laid her blanket aside, and his fingers closed over hers as she stepped into the water. The clinging heat of it embraced her, feeling like thick oil that swirled slowly around her legs as she walked deeper into the pool. The hot, slick water soothed her tired muscles, warmed her frozen feet, eased her aches and relieved her fears.

From somewhere deep within the cave came the incongruous sound of a waterfall. Kade explained that a stream off the mountain entered an opening about a mile above the hot springs, the water disappearing into the depths of the mountain.

Near the pool where she and Kade sat was a creation of such delicate beauty Kathleen could not take her eyes from it. Water had dripped from a fissure in the ceiling, forming on the floor of the cave a structure that rose and spiraled into the shape of a delicate bowl. Candlelight filtered through the sides of the bowl and into its contents. The water's surface was so calm and placid, like a serene thought in an empty church. Water continued to drop into the pool, which seemed to open its surface to take into itself the droplets so not even the tiniest ripple marred its perfection.

"Fairy pool," Kade said, and Kathleen could easily imagine gossamer-winged creatures peering over the edge of the magical pool to see their translucent reflections in the glassy surface of the water.

After the raging fury of the storm, the cave was a peaceful retreat of echoing silence, broken only by the music of the waterfall far away. Kathleen felt so safe, so protected. Her terror during the storm had eased the moment Kade had appeared from the wind-ripped darkness to enclose her in his warm, solid embrace. She would have willingly stood in the wind and rain forever if it meant he would always hold her.

The night before, she had sworn never to submit to him, sworn never to give him what he wanted. That had all changed now. She knew she loved him, knew she had loved him since that first moment in Morocco when she stood in chains on the slave platform and he stood in the back of the crowd with eyes so black she could see herself in them even at that great distance. The fact that he did not care for her, only wanted her, made what she was about to do incredibly difficult. But it was no longer impossible.

Kade rose from the water and stepped from the pool, his back to Kathleen. His muscles were tight and controlled beneath the glowing gold of his skin. His broad shoulders reflected the candlelight down onto his lean torso, down his tapered waist, down his slender hips and hard, firm legs.

Kathleen swallowed her pride, swallowed her fear. She stood, feeling the heavy water run down her breasts and stomach. "Kade," she said softly, the sound of her voice repeating again and again as the cave walls held onto the word, then released it, held it, then released it.

He turned slowly, and she stepped out of the pool. His eyes trailed up her gilded body, up her legs, over her stomach and breasts, up to her face. She could see the need in his eyes, but she saw the hesitation there also.

She put her hands on his chest, on the drops of water that clung to the thick hair that spread down across his stomach, flaring out to surround the solid erection of his penis. Kathleen moistened her lips and started to speak the words he had demanded from her.

He put his finger against her lips. "Do not say it, kitten."

Then his arms were around her, surrounding her, holding her to him with desperate, tender need. She wound her hands into his hair, dragging his mouth to hers. Their kiss was soft, gentle, hard, demanding. If Kathleen had any doubts left about the wisdom of her decision, they were destroyed in that kiss. Her heart and her love took wing as his hands ran over her body, discovering and exciting. His fingers lightly circled the tip of a swollen breast, and Kathleen could not suppress the moan that rumbled in her throat.

She moved her arms over his back, experiencing the tightly contained power of him. His lips covered her face with kisses and she shivered. His tongue explored her sensitive ear and she trembled.

He wrapped his hands in her silken hair, pulling her

276

head back. Their eyes met. Kathleen's soul surrendered. She was a captive of her love, a slave to her passion.

His lips tasted her, touched her. Her breathing was ragged, uncertain and uncontrolled. Thick hair brushed against her throat as his head moved down to her breasts. When his lips closed over an erect, throbbing nipple, Kathleen cried out, the shock of sensations that coursed through her more than she could bear. His tongue swirled over the rigid peak, and her body arched against him. Kade bent her backwards over his arm, ravaging her breasts with his lips, teeth and tongue.

He lowered her to the floor. Steam rose from the water, swirling around him so he looked like a legendary god summoned from the depths of a sorcerer's black magic. Kathleen reached for him and he came down to her, his mouth moving onto the heavy curve of her breast. The shadowed roughness of his unshaven face raked against her smooth skin.

His hands moved up under her arms, his thumbs curving beneath her breasts as his hands gripped her sides. He lifted her slight form, holding her just above the floor while his teeth closed over a small section of golden flesh on the curve of her breast. The bite was not tender, nor was it hard. Kathleen pulled away from him, moaning and shuddering as her body responded to the pleasure-pain.

"Do it again," she pleaded.

Kade smiled against her moist flesh and again his teeth claimed their prize. Steam curled around their bodies as he pulled the tip of her breast into his mouth, sucking on it with hungry lips. He took her past the point of madness with the slow swirls of his tongue, the quick nips of his teeth.

Her body was on fire, burning, freezing, exploding

and sinking into a whirlpool of pleasure. Her skin ached, it trembled, it cried out for more. She was like the storm outside the cave, raging and moaning, shaking and writhing.

She held Kade close to her breast, watching his teeth and lips as they tasted her, excited her, tortured her. Her hands moved over the surface of his body, over his shoulders and back, down his arms and sides. The hard push of his desire was against her leg, and she rubbed against it. He growled under his breath, his mouth sucking harder on her nipple as her hand clasped his penis.

Her tongue slipped into his ear, hot and wet. He gasped, pulling away from her breast. Kathleen moved her head down until his nipple was against her lips and she took it into her mouth.

Fire poured over his chest, down his legs, into his mind as her teeth scraped across his skin. Moans filled the cave, his moans. She lifted her head, her lips curving into a taunting smile. He descended on her swollen mouth, plunging his tongue into the velvet sweetness that awaited him.

He moved on top of her, trapping her beneath his body. His hands wound into her hair, forcing her to lie still as he caressed each of her breasts with slow, lingering kisses. His lips moved down, across her waist, over her abdomen. Then lower.

She writhed under the onslaught of sensual explosions he created within her, on her, over her. Where would he touch next, what part of her body would he brand with his lips, explore with his tongue? Kathleen opened her legs, exposing to him the part of her that throbbed and pulsed with terrible, demanding need.

His tongue flicked between her legs. The world shook and soared beneath her, hot clouds of steam poured over her, golden light erupted inside her. Her lungs struggled for air, her throat closing as she drowned in the tormenting pleasure of his touch. Darkness, thick and heavy, moved within her, centering between her legs and spreading outward in surging currents like giant waves on the surface of a dark lake.

"Please, Kade, please. I need . . ." she cried, unable to say anything else as the darkness poured into her heart, into her mind.

His tongue slid across her, into her, over her. Her muscles tightened, stretching and straining. Her fingers tore at him, ripping his flesh, dragging at his hair.

Kade raised his head, his lips wet with the sweet nectar of her. He tentatively placed his mouth against hers. Kathleen shivered at the first taste of herself; then she kissed him, drinking deeply of herself and of him.

"My love, my woman!" he said in a deep, rough voice. He lifted himself up, and with one swift move of his hips, Kade thrust himself into her.

A flash of lightning erupted in Kathleen's head as his swollen hardness moved deep into her. With each thrust into her body he filled her, surrounded her, excited her, pleasured her. Kathleen met his every stroke eagerly, lifting her hips to take him fully into her. His corded, muscular arms were braced on each side of her head. Perspiration beaded his brow, dropping onto her face. She wet her lips with the salt of his sweat.

Her fingers gripped the sides of his body, feeling the powerful strength of him. The candlelight cast shadows on his face, accenting the hard lines, tracing the strain of his passion as it sketched lines around the corners of his eyes and the sides of his mouth.

She wrapped her legs around his, placing her hands on his firm buttocks and forcing him deeper into her, wanting the thrusting power of him to move up inside her chest, inside her heart.

"Now!" she screamed, her voice choked and ragged as it ripped from the part of her he was possessing and devouring.

"Yes, Kate, yes," he cried, his breath hot against her face as it pushed aside the chilling steam of the pool. With another powerful thrust, he carried them up and over the edge of the universe.

Waves of darkness crashed against Kathleen's fractured mind, her head convulsively jerking from side to side as her body twisted in spasms of pleasure, pulling Kade deeper into her. His head collapsed onto her shoulder and his breath washed over her damp skin, cool and comforting.

Kathleen held him close, savoring the weight of him as he lay on top of her. He shielded her against everything except that moment, protecting her and covering her with his body. Slowly the heavy darkness within her began to clear, leaving behind a peaceful, fulfilled serenity unlike anything she had ever known. The last spasm of pleasure shook her slender hips, and she began to breathe normally again, tasting the hot, steamy air, smelling the musky odor of their sex.

"Damn," Kade said softly, his hand cupping the side of her face as he looked into her eyes.

She wrinkled her forehead. "Was I not any good?" she asked. His lips descended on hers, devouring all that was left of her. Kathleen pressed her breasts to his chest, kneaded his buttocks with her fingers, slipped her tongue into his mouth. Finally Kade pulled back, desperately drawing air into his lungs.

"You were absolutely terrible," he said as he rolled to his side, pulling Kathleen with him so he could stay inside her as long as possible. She smiled against his neck, her tongue trailing through the edge of his hair and into his ear.

"We shall have to practice until I get it right."

He drew her mouth back to his. He did not want to let her go, did not want to stop kissing her, did not want the storm to ever end.

"This steam is burning me alive," he finally said as he laid her beside him.

He stood, pulling her up with him. She wrapped the discarded blanket around her, and he took down the candles from the niche in the wall, lifting them free from their puddles of melted wax. By the time they walked back down the narrow trail into the central cavern, the candles were almost gone. He lit two more and placed them on the wall. Then he sat down on the blankets.

A devilish gleam sparkled in Kathleen's eyes as they traveled down his body. An instant rush of desire went over Kade. She released her blanket. It made a soft, rustling sound as it slipped down over her shoulders, over her hips, falling in a heap at her feet. She stepped away from it, moving closer to Kade. She straddled his lap, facing him.

"Time for my second lesson," she said.

He lowered his head, taking into his mouth a rigid, rose-colored nipple. Kathleen's head fell back, her hair swirling over his hands, down his legs. He trailed his fingers around her perfect hips, across the pure white flesh of her upper thighs, between her legs and into the slippery, hot wetness of her excitement.

Though tremors spread over every inch of her body, Kathleen refused to move. She forced herself to hold still even while her body ached to react to Kade's touch. She bit down on her lip, trembling with anticipation and excitement.

He touched the tip of a finger to the bud of her pleasure. She cried aloud and was unable to stop the writhing quiver that shot through her. She moved her hands behind her back, grasping his legs behind her buttocks. She refused to look at him, refused to allow anything to interrupt the immense pleasure he was giving her.

She dug her fingers into his flesh as she struggled to relax the rest of her body. He moved one finger against her pulsing center of sensual pleasure and trailed his thumb across the lips of her swollen opening. Kathleen pulled great breaths of air into her burning lungs.

Kade released her nipple and lifted his head to watch her. She could not see him, yet knew his eyes were on her. She felt wanton, wild. She was aware of the arch of her neck, the lift of her breasts that invited his fingers to caress their curving fullness. Chills swept over her as he blew softly on her nipple, then touched the tip of his tongue to the quivering peak. His fingers continued to excite her, stroke her, explore her. He slipped his hand further between her legs, touching that other private place.

A new tide of sensations overcame her. Heat flashed up her abdomen, down her legs, through her soul. All reality faded as Kade manipulated her and used her, excited her and pleasured her.

She strained closer to his tormenting fingers, not wanting him to stop, ever. Darkness flooded into her soul; bolts of blue lightning shot through her as his teeth nipped, then bit her neck.

"Kade!" she cried. "Now, please now!"

His hands circled her waist, lifting her as he stood. He laid her down on the pile of blankets. The wool pressed against her back, rough and sensuous. Kathleen dug her shoulders deeper into that wonderful scratchiness as she lifted her legs and wrapped them around Kade's neck.

One driving thrust buried his penis in her hot, pulsing interior. At his first contact with her throbbing flesh, Kathleen gasped and lost herself completely to her passion. He entered her over and over again, taking her ever higher up the towering mountain of her ecstasy until he carried her with him over the peak of sanity. Her legs slid from his shoulders just before he collapsed on top of her, her breasts crushed beneath his heaving chest, his face buried in the glory of her hair.

He lay heavily atop her body, tasting the sweetness of her sweat as he kissed her brow. Every ragged breath she took was a part of him, controlled by him. Kade ran his hands over her upper arms, then down her quivering sides until he touched her slender hips. Her legs were pressed against his, and she quivered with a last, lingering spasm of their lovemaking.

Never had Kade experienced anything like this. He looked into Kathleen's face. Her incredible eyes were watching him, their colors swirling as though blown by the hurricane outside. Kade was lost in the blue-green depths of her inner sea, which crashed and stormed with passion and emotion.

Her hands released their grip on his hair, and she trailed one finger seductively across his lips. She pressed her lips against his face, letting the roughness of his beard excite her anew.

The thought of what they had just shared made Kade begin to burn with need again. He was still inside her, growing hot and hard, swelling and filling her.

A smile pulled at the corners of her lips, and she pushed Kade onto his back. She caught the tip of her tongue between her teeth and lowered her head. Kade held his breath as her lips brushed against his erect organ. Her eyes were on his face as she slipped it into her mouth.

"Sweet, wonderful, Kate," he moaned, feeling himself enclosed in the heaven of her sweet lips. Her swirling tongue sent pulses of pleasure racing through his body. Her pearly teeth nipped the length of him, and Kade began to writhe, his hands full of her silky hair. When Kade began to twist and jerk beneath her touch, she swung a leg over him. His hot shaft slid deeply into her, her eyes closing as she savored the wonderful sensation.

Her head bent over his chest, her hair brushing softly across his flesh. She drew a stiff nipple into her teeth, but before she could begin to torture him with pleasure, Kade growled with a low, animal-like sound and pulled her mouth to his, tasting the wetness of himself on her lips.

Kathleen rode Kade like she had once ridden Taran across the rolling hills of Ireland. Her knees pushed into his sides as she came down on him over and over, gasping with delight as his hands touched her breasts. He squeezed her nipples with exquisite sureness.

Her fingernails dug into his legs behind her; tears glistened like miniature diamonds on her black lashes. Darkness filled her soul and pulsed through her body. Kade lowered his hands to her curving bottom, helping her to ride him even faster. She cried aloud as they both came, his burning seed erupting within her. Kathleen collapsed onto his chest and into his arms that surrounded her so protectively.

The darkness passed. Kathleen ran her tongue over the sweat on Kade's chest, then raised herself up to look into his smiling eyes. She was overcome with the emotion that flooded into her heart. This man had filled her with desire, need, and his own body. And he had filled her with love.

When the storm raging outside the cave ended, she would leave Mistral. Leave this man holding her, leave the man she loved.

Chapter 20

Sarita Ridley smiled her best smile, purposely tucked a purposely stray curl into her coiffure, and wet her lips with the tip of a pointed pink tongue. Ivan Flesher, captain of the merchant vessel *Christabel,* noticed all those things. His face, darkened by exposure to the sun and sea, turned ever so slightly to where Quint Cathcart was finishing the last of the bottle of wine served with dinner. Ivan offered Quint a glass of French brandy.

"That would be a perfect ending for a perfect meal, at least as perfect as one can expect on a tub like this," Quint said. Ivan ground his teeth together and turned his back to pour the brandy. He tipped the contents of another bottle into the glass, a bottle normally kept in the ship's medical chest.

"The *Christabel* is making good time, Mr. Cathcart. We should be at Mistral in two weeks," Ivan said. He handed the brandy to Quint and poured Sarita some sherry. When she took it from him, her fingertips touched his. She allowed them to linger for a moment. Ivan smiled at her. The laudanum he had put into Cathcart's brandy would soon make him sleepy, and then Quint and Sarita would retire to their cabin. Soon afterwards Sarita would be back with Ivan, as she had been almost every night since the *Christabel* left Morocco.

"None too soon either," Quint said, his words slurred. "I hate the sea and ships almost as much as I hate Kade Morgan."

"Quint darling, you promised you would not go on so about poor Kade," Sarita said, her voice gently caressing the name of her former lover.

"I will talk about that bastard any way I want!" Quint yelled as he slammed his fist onto the table.

"Yes, whatever you say, darling. We should go to our cabin now and allow Captain Flesher to do whatever it is captains do."

Sarita rose from her chair, and the diamonds hanging from her ears caught the light, shattering it into shards of color. She bent over Quint, trying to urge him to stand. He leaned his head against her breasts, his wet mouth drooling on her flesh. Then he passed out, falling face down on the floor.

"Damn!" she screamed, turning on Ivan. "You gave him too much, we will never get him out of here now!"

Ivan stepped closer to her, grabbed her arm and jerked her against him. How dare she talk to him like that? "Leave him there. He won't know what's going on unless you keep screaming and wake him up."

He twisted her arm behind her and brought his mouth down on hers. She struggled to free herself, but Ivan refused to lessen his grip. After a few minutes she began to respond to him, pushing her breasts against him so he could feel her hard nipples even through her dress. He shoved her away from him and ripped open the bodice of her dress.

"This cost a fortune!" she cried, grabbing the torn edges.

"Let that fool at your feet think he did it. Then he'll buy you a dozen more."

Sarita stared at Ivan, fear glimmering in the depths

286

of her gray eyes. Until now he had treated her with respect, gently and tenderly. She was the first lady he had ever been with and he had treated her as such, only he was tired of her nagging, tired of her abusive language just because she thought him beneath her socially. It was time he took control of their affair, time Sarita treated him like a man, not a servant.

Ivan sat on the chair Quint had fallen from, kicked the inert body aside and spread his legs. "Come over here, bitch."

Sarita did not move. Ivan leaned forward, grabbed her wrist and dragged her between his legs. He forced her to her knees and tore open the front of his pants. His penis stood erect before her face. He forced her head down, forced her mouth onto him. Her resistance excited him. He lifted his hips, pushing himself deeper into her mouth. Sarita's nails slashed across his hands, and he laughed.

"Get down on your hands and knees and raise your dress up," he ordered her as he released his grip on her head. She fell backwards, and Ivan pushed her down further with his foot. She stared at him for a minute, her exposed breasts white and soft in the lamplight.

"Do as I say, bitch!"

She positioned herself as he ordered and began to lift her skirts, her shapely limbs appearing slowly from beneath the folds of pink silk. When her knees came into view, she stopped. Ivan waved his hand to indicate he wanted the dress higher. She complied, completely exposing her legs and bottom to his intense gaze.

Ivan sat back in his chair and laughed. Sarita did not look like a lady now, she looked like one of the whores in Quint Cathcart's brothel. He watched the light move across her round, firm buttocks as they appeared from beneath her chemise just above her lace-trimmed garters. Finally he lowered himself onto her, ramming his hardness into the center of her softness.

She pulled away from him, crying out in pain. He held her firmly and continued to thrust in and out. She squirmed and screamed until he brought the palm of his hand down hard onto her bottom. She stopped then, a quiver running over her as the sting of his blow burned her flesh. He did it again and she threw her head back, her pointed tongue touching the tips of her pearly teeth. Ivan continued to spank her as he drove himself into her. She suddenly became wet and slippery inside, moaning and straining back against him. He stopped abusing her, began to treat her gently as he leaned forward, reaching around her to touch her rigid nipples, caressing her full breasts and putting his hot, wet tongue in her ear.

"Kade, Kade," she screamed when she climaxed. Ivan continued to push into her until he came. Then he pulled free from her wetness and rolled to the side.

Sarita had always responded to Ivan, moaning softly and whispering his name. Even in ecstasy she had been a lady, controlled and correct in her actions. Until now. She had abandoned her ladylike response beneath his brutal assault, straining and screaming like an ordinary whore. Then, when he switched techniques and began to treat her with tenderness, she had not even realized it was Ivan loving her. She had called Kade Morgan's name.

Ivan had always disliked Morgan, had cheated him and stolen from him. Now that dislike turned to hate, a hate that festered and soured, a hate that burned like a brand on Ivan's soul. Morgan would pay for this, pay dearly, Ivan swore as he turned his head to look at the smile on Sarita's face and the imprint of his hands on her buttocks.

*   *   *

Jarrett O'Connor passed under the framed supports of the entrance to Pennington Mansion and closed the carved door behind him. He walked across the land, feeling the springy earth beneath his feet, smelling the rosemary in the air. Clouds scurried overhead, piling up on the horizon and turning gray and dark. It would rain soon. He would have to hurry if he was to visit his wife's grave before meeting Niall on the shore.

His boots crunched on the stones that surrounded the lone grave. Jarrett reached out a hand to touch the wooden cross engraved with his wife's name. "Remember that letter I told ye 'bout, Mary, the one I got that demanded all that money for Katie's release? I didn't have no money, didn't 'ave nothing left after the fire because what we 'ad saved went to pay back the folks whose 'orses we were trainin' that died in the fire. So I sold Emerald Hills, sold it to that Pennington fella, the one what was always comin' round wantin' to buy us out. And 'e 'elped me send the money off to the kidnappers so our baby can come 'ome, not that there be a 'ome for 'er to come to."

Jarrett looked across the sea. "I be goin' o'er to the islands to live with Niall and 'is bride. Aye, Mary me love, ye would like the girl our son picked for a wife. Right bonny, wi' fair hair and blue eyes. Alice be 'er name. Alice O'Connor, 'ow does that sound to ye? Sounds good to me, that it does. I gotta go now, Mary me love. There be a storm comin'. I'll be comin' back to see ye soon, girl, real soon. And soon Kathleen will be 'ere too, she'll come 'ome and we'll start over. We'll get Emerald Hills back and we'll start over. Ye'll be proud of us, Mary girl. Aye, I'll make ye proud of me."

Jarrett touched the cross again. The wood was cold and rough. Mary deserves better, she deserves more, he thought. She deserves to live.

He hitched up his sagging pants, pulled his worn coat

around hunched shoulders and walked down to the beach. Niall was waiting for him, holding a lantern beside the curragh.

"Is it done?" he asked as he set the light in the boat and helped his father on board.

"That it is, son, that it is. Pennington leaves for London on the morrow. He'll send the money from there. 'Twill not be long before the bastards what 'ave me baby get it, and then Katie will come 'ome again."

Niall guided the boat into the sea. When it passed beyond the breakers, he clambered in and took up the oars. "Look at that," he said and pointed to the shore behind his father.

The waves took on a shape, changing from water to flesh as the stallion Taran emerged from the sea. The great beast shook his head, flinging kelp and salt across the shore, then he turned to look at the men in the curragh.

"Kathleen is still alive," Niall said as the *each uisce* whirled and galloped up the bank to the ruins of the house that showed black against the darkening sky.

"Aye, lad," Jarrett said. "For a time I didn't think so, but that letter we were sent 'ad 'er gold locket wi' it so I believe it to be true. 'Twas good of Pennington to pay what I asked of 'im after all these years of tellin' 'im I'd never sell Emerald Hills. If he 'ad not, I couldn't 'ave paid what they be askin'. If only the 'orses had not been killed in the fire, or if only there 'ad been some gold left from the bog, or if only there 'ad been another way to save Kathleen wi'out sellin' the land."

The water stallion raced down the slope and into the waves, disappearing in a mighty crash of foam and sea. With him went the last of the light as the clouds closed over the moon.

"Aye, and if only the sky would turn green and the grass blue," Niall said. He dipped the oars in the water, sending the curragh skimming across the surface of the sea.

The rain began, and Jarrett looked up at the sky. Niall bent his head and leaned into the oars, not wanting to see the rain wash away the tears on his father's face.

Chapter 21

Kathleen lifted her head and listened to the silence. Beside her, Kade slept with one arm around her waist. She did not want to wake him, did not want this time with him to end. Yet now that the storm was over, they needed to go back to the world outside, needed to discover if indeed there was any world left.

"Wake up, Kade. The storm is over."

He pulled her closer to him, his legs wrapping over hers, his fingers tangling in her hair. He laid his face against hers, and tears burned in Kathleen's eyes.

"Wake up," she said again, this time shaking his shoulder lightly.

"I am awake, kitten." His rich voice moved over Kathleen's tingling flesh as his lips touched her neck.

"The storm is over."

"I know. After the hurricane we were hit by a thunderstorm. That ended about ten minutes ago."

"You were awake all that time?" she asked as he kissed the hollow in her throat.

"Aye, my love."

"You were so still, I thought you were asleep."

"I was listening to you breathe." Kade pressed her to him. "You feel good." He ran his hands down her back and over her round buttocks, then kissed the tip of her nose. He released her and stood up to stretch.

"Where is Demon?" Kathleen asked.

Kade pulled on his pants. "He went out right after the thunderstorm passed. We have to get moving." He helped her to her feet.

She picked up her dress and dropped it over her head. Kade watched her fasten the buttons on the bodice, then pulled her into his arms and lowered his lips to hers. She wound her hands around his neck and rose on the tips of her toes to return his kiss.

When he pulled back, she smiled at him. "What was that for?"

"I wanted to make certain what happened last night was not a dream." He traced the line of her jaw with his hand, then laid her head on his chest and hugged her tightly to him. "I never want you to pull away from me again, Kate. Especially not now, not after knowing what it is like for you to come to me willingly."

Kathleen closed her eyes and filled her senses with the smell of Kade, the feel of Kade, the sound of Kade's heart beating beneath her cheek. When she was back in Ireland, she would remember this moment, remember it forever.

"I will come to you when you reach for me, I will give you my arms when you ask for them," she whispered.

Kade wanted to ask if she would give her love also. He stayed silent and kissed the top of her head before setting her from him.

"Time to go," he said. She smiled at him, a bright smile that trembled, then faded. She ran into his arms, holding him tightly and burying her face in his chest.

"I am afraid, afraid of . . ."

"Of what, kitten?" He tilted her head back to see her swirling blue-green eyes.

She wanted to say of never seeing you again, of living without you, of going home. She squared her shoulders and stepped back from him.

"Of starving to death before we get back," she said.

"To prevent such a terrible catastrophe we will leave immediately."

Kade picked up Demon's harness and walked out of the cave. What was Kathleen afraid of? He wanted to know so he could protect her from whatever it was. If he pressed her, though, she would never tell him. He had to wait for her to want to tell him, until she trusted him enough to share her fears and to let him help her conquer them.

Kade stepped from the shadows of Crystal Cave into a blinding sun that had just passed its zenith. He looked around in disbelief. The rain forest was no longer a place of darkness and intimacy beneath a leafy canopy of green. Most of the trees had been uprooted or had had all their limbs stripped away, their bark peeled back by the force of the storm. There were dead birds, dead frogs, dead flowers. Stripped of the protection of the forest, the mountain had surrendered its soil to the storm. Great piles of mud and rock had slipped down the steep slope. It was a miracle the cave had not been buried beneath a slide.

"Kade, your island, your poor island! Mistral has been destroyed!" Kathleen cried. Her beautiful eyes brimmed with tears. They began to spill down her stricken face, and Kade caught one on his finger.

"You would shed a tear at the destruction of your prison?"

"Mistral is more than my prison. It is your home."

He caught her to him, wanting to feel every breath she drew, wanting to catch her tears and hold them forever. "The island will recover," he said, "and the forest will grow again. It is the people I fear for, Kate."

"Then we should get moving," she said, belying her words by holding Kade closer.

"Aye, love, that we should." Kade reluctantly

294

released her and gave her Demon's harness. "Mount up, it is not far back to the stable."

Kathleen swung up onto Demon's back, not bothering with the harness. The stallion snorted and tossed his head as she whispered in his ear; then he followed Kade as he worked his way up around the face of the cliff.

Eventually they crossed the trail coming up from the beach. When they reached the stable clearing, they discovered that although the building was still standing, its roof and doors were missing. Kathleen released Demon into the corral, noticing as she did that the fence had collapsed on the far side. The stallion did not try to run. He stood quietly while she rubbed him down with a piece of canvas sacking. Kade gave him a pail of oats and an armful of dry hay that had been beneath a tarp in one of the stalls.

"The rope is stuck," Kathleen called to Kade from beside the well.

He went to her assistance. The windlass creaked and groaned as he turned it, hauling the bucket up from the depths of the well. It was filled with mud.

"Demon will have to find his own water," he told her.

They left the stable and headed down the path to the house. Most of the trees in this section of the jungle were still standing. At the last bend in the path, Kade stopped. Kathleen came readily into his arms when he reached for her.

"One last kiss before we go back?" he asked. She smiled, and his mouth moved over hers, their hearts pounding as one as their tongues touched and caressed. When he lowered his lips to her throat, she lifted her arms around his neck and held him tightly.

"Why did you name the stallion Demon?"

Kathleen laughed. "I named him after you."

He nuzzled her ear, then pulled back and looked

down at her. "Thought about renaming him?"

She caught her lower lip between her teeth and gave him a quizzical look. "Why? The resemblance still exists."

"I saved your life!" he protested.

"Demon also saved my life by protecting me before you came, yet he could still crush me in a moment of anger."

"You think I would crush you?"

"I am your slave."

"You are more."

She ducked her head, afraid he would see the need in her eyes. "Aye, today I am your mistress. Tomorrow or the next day or next week or next month you will tire of me and again I will be no more than your slave."

Kade grasped her face with his hands and forced her to look at him. His eyes searched her face. Kathleen did not know what he was looking for or if he found it. She only knew she never wanted him to tire of her. Finally he hugged her to him and pressed his lips to the top of her head. Then he released her, took her hand in his and walked around the final bend in the path.

The garden was gone; the hurricane had wiped it clean of bushes, flowers and trees. Deep rivulets cut through the soil, ugly and disfiguring to the memory of what had once been a place of beauty. The house was on the other side of the clearing. As they approached it, they could see that paint had been peeled from the walls and the red-tile roof lay in a heap behind the kitchen. A palm tree had fallen through a window on the second floor above the dining room. A torn curtain from a guest bedroom fluttered in the breeze.

Kade squeezed Kathleen's hand as a round figure came out of the kitchen door and ran down the path to them. It was Mattie, waving her arms and crying. Kade went to meet her, pulling Kathleen with him.

"Mattie, you are all right! What about Jake?"

"He be down at the 'arbor, leanin' on that crutch Sampson made for 'im and givin' orders to people that don't need 'em." She wiped the wetness from her eyes. "I can't believe ye is alive, lad. The storm passed over hours ago, Bog was gettin' ready to go searchin' for ye."

"After I found Kathleen we made our way to Crystal Cave and waited there for it to blow over. There was so much mud and water pouring off the mountain we had to wait for the thunderstorm to pass also. How is the village?"

Mattie glanced at Kathleen. "Ye must be exhausted, child. Yer room is dry, go change and get some sleep."

"Kade asked about the village," Kathleen said, taking a step closer to him and laying her hand on his arm.

Mattie noted the gesture and her face clouded. She looked at Kade. "Ye should see for yerself. Words won't be tellin' ye 'alf."

"Have you heard from the plantation?"

"Ye'd best be talking to Bog or Jake 'bout that." Mattie looked directly at him, and Kade's stomach tightened at the pain on her face. He pulled Kathleen around in front of him.

"Change your clothes and help Mattie with whatever needs to be done in the house."

"I want to see the village." There was a stubborn tilt to her head.

Kade cupped her chin. "Do as I say, Kate. I will come for you later. Do not leave the house without me."

Kathleen wanted to argue, wanted to be with him. "I will wait," she said.

He kissed her on the forehead, touched Mattie's shoulder briefly and walked across the gutted yard to the harbor. Kathleen watched him go.

"Be ye ready, child?" Mattie asked.

"Aye, that I be," she replied and followed the old woman into the flooded kitchen.

Kathleen was in the guest bedroom that the palm tree had invaded. The carpet had been rolled up and was waiting to be taken to the storage room for drying. She had stripped the bed, taken down the curtains for repair and was extracting bits of broken glass from the casing of the shattered window when someone came into the room behind her.

She did not need to be told who it was. She always knew when Kade was near; his presence seemed to set the air vibrating around her. The last piece of glass wiggled free from the molding. Kathleen dropped it in the box beside her, pulled off her work gloves and turned around.

His face was drawn and tired, and there were dark circles under his eyes. It had been almost four hours since she last saw him. He leaned against the doorjamb and rubbed the back of his neck.

She went to him immediately. He opened his arms and pulled her against him. They stood that way for a time, not talking. Kathleen could feel the tension in his body, she could feel his pain.

"Tell me," she said.

"The plantation workers made it to the caves before the storm struck. They split up and took refuge in the two largest. When the hurricane reversed direction, blowing directly into one of the caves, the people went deeper into the mountain to escape the wind. Water began to come in the roof of the cave through a crack in the lava. By the time the people discovered what was happening, they had been cut off from the entrance. The water kept rising. We have pulled out forty-seven bodies so far."

"They were drowning while we made love," Kathleen whispered. Her stomach turned and her head began to spin.

"Not making love would not have saved them, Kate."

"I wish you had not found me, I wish I had died!"

She tore away from him and ran from the room. He let her go. Outside the window, a glorious sunset colored the western sky. As the violet and rose spread higher and higher over the island, peace spread over Kade's heart.

"God, I want to thank you for not granting the wishes of a grieving woman," he said softly, "and thank you for granting those of an undeserving demon."

After dinner Kade carried Kathleen to her room, where they made hurried, trembling love. Then, in the silence of the night, he held her in his arms and allowed his troubles to wait for him.

She lay quietly in his embrace, listening to him breathe, feeling his heart beating against her breast. She thought about her love for him, love she had to keep hidden for fear that he would laugh at her weakness as he had once laughed at her impudence.

She pretended to sleep, sighing gently against his chest until he laid her beside him on the bed and got up to dress. Before he left, he brushed a final kiss across her lips.

Kathleen waited before rising to be certain he did not return. Then she dressed warmly, threw a few pieces of clothing into an old seabag and went to the study for the two maps of the West Indies, the sextant and compass.

The moon was high in the sky when she slipped out of the house. In the harbor the *Black Eagle* swung around on her anchor as the tide changed. The ship's main mast had broken in her battle with the hurricane, and it sagged onto the deck. Beside the *Eagle* was the *Slipper*. Kathleen had overheard Bog Daniels tell Kade that he had stocked the sloop for a trip to Martinique the next day to retrieve his ship, the *Gypsy Lady,* which was in port to have her hull sheathed with new copper. Bog wanted to bring his crew back to Mistral so they could rebuild their homes.

"If he is going to Martinique, that means Mistral is exactly where I thought it was on the maps," Kathleen told the night breeze. She lowered her bundles into the longboat tied alongside the pier and stepped down beside them. She released the mooring lines and picked up the oars. The boat moved silently away from the shore where the village had been.

Mattie had told Kathleen that the first onslaught of the hurricane had flattened all the houses and leveled two of the warehouses. After the eye of the hurricane had passed and the wind reversed direction, the village debris had been blown into the harbor and washed out to sea. Kathleen could see the outline of the remaining warehouse. The people who had lost their homes were sleeping there tonight. Some had lost their families in the cave tragedy.

The longboat bumped alongside the *Slipper*. Kathleen transferred her gear to the sloop, climbed on board and gave the longboat a shove to send it back to the shore. She stowed her bundles in the covered section of the sloop beside the water keg and food stores.

Kathleen slid her hand into the pocket of the wool dress she was wearing, fingering the seashells she and Kade had collected at the sunken crater. She felt again the touch of his lips on hers, the warmth of his arms around her.

The halyard on the mast snapped in the wind as

300

Kathleen hoisted the main sail. She tied off the line, released the tiller, and dragged the anchor on board. As the sloop moved out of the harbor, a blast of cold air came around the edge of the island.

After she rigged the jib and set the *Slipper*'s bow to the southeast, Kathleen pulled a blanket around her shoulders. A gull settled on the bow of the sloop for a brief moment, then spread its wings and drifted into the darkness. Behind the sloop, the island was nothing more than a memory outlined against the starry sky.

Chapter 22

It was almost dark on the day after the hurricane when Kade mounted his horse beside the sugar mill and turned the old gray up the road that led to the stable. He was tired, bone tired. They had taken a total of fifty-three bodies from the flooded cave. Three other people had also died during the storm. A young mother and her baby had fallen over the side of a cliff and into the sea. The third had been an elderly woman who had lain in the cave during the storm, watching the raging heavens and drawing her last breath.

As the old mare plodded up the road, Kade looked over the destruction in the orchards. The fruit and leaves had been stripped from the branches, yet most of the trees had survived. Off to the right, the plantation gardens lay buried beneath mud and stagnant water.

There were some horses grazing in the drier parts of the pasture. Deprived was among them. It was the first time Kade had seen the gelding since he found Kathleen during the storm. There was a terrible gash on Deprived's right foreleg. Kade knew the aged horse would have to be put permanently out to pasture along with the horse he was riding.

The trail parted from the road, and the storm-ravaged jungle closed around Kade. Among the debris of trees and ferns he heard birds, frogs and insects. At least some creatures survived the storm. Above him, a lone orchid bloomed in its lofty perch on a gum tree.

The stable doors had been located and were propped against the west wall. Beneath them the dry hay and grain was being stored. Tack was stretched out along the remainder of the corral fence to dry. Two stableboys were rubbing oil into a saddle. Kade dismounted and handed them his reins.

Demon snorted at Kade before trotting around the fence and into the yard. Glory was tied near the stable, and Sam was treating a cut on her rump. Demon nudged the little mare's neck. She nipped his shoulder and he nickered.

Kade told Sam to check on Deprived before heading down the path to the house. He needed a hot meal, a hot bath and Kathleen. A light showed from the kitchen window. He pushed open the door and was surprised by all the work that had been done. The floor had been covered with water after the storm. Now it was clean and waxed. The big wooden table had been scrubbed so hard it looked smaller. The ceiling was marked with dark rings where the tile on the roof had been blown away.

There were at least twenty people in the room. Since this was the only kitchen remaining on this side of the island, all the cooking for the people staying in the warehouse was being done here. There were pots and kettles everywhere, filled with stew.

Kade poured himself some coffee. He wrapped his hands around the cup and leaned against the wall, too exhausted to move. Mattie found him there about five minutes later.

"Kade! How long ye been standin' there, lad? Sit down, let me get you a bowl of stew."

He did as she ordered, eating by instinct. "Any chance for some hot water?" he asked.

303

"Been boilin' water beside the well all day for cleaning. There be a kettle there now waitin' for ye and Kathleen. Where be the lass?"

"I thought she was here." He finished the stew and Mattie filled his bowl again.

"I 'aven't seen 'er all day, figured she went wi' ye last night o'er to the plantation."

Kade looked at Mattie with tired, bloodshot eyes. "I left here last night about eleven o'clock. She was asleep then, in her room."

"Where could she 'ave got to?" Mattie asked.

Kade ran out of the room and up the steps to Kathleen's room, flinging open the door. The room was empty. On the dressing table were four pearls, the ones he had given her at the sunken crater. Last night when Kade left he had seen them in a small crystal bowl beside the bed, along with her seashells. The bowl was empty now, the shells gone.

"Just as she is gone," he said as pain ripped through his heart. He turned away from the pearls and left the house.

Even before Kade reached the harbor, he knew the *Slipper* would not be there. Bog Daniels had planned to take it to Martinique that day. Apparently he had also taken Kathleen. Kade clenched his fists. He would kill them both. The warehouse door opened and Bog came out.

"You did not take the *Slipper?*" Kade asked, his fists unclenching slowly.

"It was gone when I awoke this morning. I thought you had taken it to check around the island."

"I was at the plantation all day, we lost fifty-six people. I got back to the house ten minutes ago and discovered we have lost someone else. Kathleen is missing."

"Escaped?"

"I thought you had taken her to Martinique and was ready to murder both of you." He rubbed the back of his neck. "I will have to go after her."

"When are you leaving?" Bog asked as they walked to the main house.

"Immediately. Ride over to the plantation for another sloop, bring the biggest one and stock her for a month. I have to take a bath and change clothes, these are starting to grow onto me. Tomorrow morning I want you to take the *Black Eagle* to Martinique and leave her there to get her mast fixed. Buy as many supplies as you can and bring them back on the *Gypsy Lady*.

"See if you can find some plantation workers and a foreman, hire anyone you like. Explain my rules for Mistral and what happened to Timpson. I will be directing all activities on the plantation with you and Jake assisting until we get the island back to normal. By then you should have enough experience to buy that plantation you want."

Bog stopped outside the house. "How long have you known?"

"Ever since you made your first inquiry. I may not have paid much attention to my own plantation, but I made it a point to know what every other owner was doing, who was selling and who was buying." He slapped Bog on the back. "Get moving. I have a wayward woman to find."

Bog headed for the stable, and Kade went into his study. The maps tied with a green ribbon were missing. He had noticed them right after his return from Nassau, and he remembered smiling when he had realized they were the only ones with Mistral on them. He had not really believed she would use them. The sextant and the compass that had been beside the old *Black Eagle* logs were also gone. He closed his eyes for a moment, then had to force them open.

The climb up the stairs took forever. When he entered his room, he found Jake there supervising the water being poured into the porcelain bathtub.

"Is the lass gone?" the Scotsman asked after the servant left.

Kade nodded. "She probably took off on the *Slipper* immediately after I left last night, and with that damned sextant that almost got us killed off China six years ago." Kade dropped his clothes and stepped into the hot water. Steam clouded around his head, and he tried not to think of Crystal Cave.

"Where are ye going to look for 'er?"

Kade picked up the soap and began to scrub his hair. "Martinique is where she will head. That sextant will make her think she overshot it and is halfway to Africa. She will turn back, heading into the middle of the Caribbean. I will set sail in that direction and start a systematic search.

"Bog is taking the *Eagle* for repairs and bringing back some new workers and a foreman, if he can find one. The two of you set to work on the gardens first, drain them and save what you can. Then do the same for the pineapple and banana fields. After that, search the entire island for coconuts. Catch all the fish you can, salt it down. Hunt for turtles and bring them in for storage. Establish some type of enclosure to keep them in that hidden cove over in the harbor opposite the plantation village."

Jake dumped a bucket of water over Kade's head to rinse off the soap. He stepped out of the tub and dried, then pulled on fresh clothes and packed his seabag. "Search all the uninhabited islands in this vicinity for whatever you can gather. I do not want any birds or eggs taken. They were hit pretty hard by the hurricane, Mistral is littered with their bodies."

He sank into the leather chair in the corner of the room and stared around him. "Have I forgotten anything?"

"What 'bout repairs?"

"I guess we should not wait too long to start with that. After the gardens are settled, keep half the people fishing; the rest can start repairs to the villages. Rebuild this side first, then the plantation houses that were damaged, the warehouses, the livestock barn, the stable and finally the main house. I will be back before you get that far."

"And if ye aren't?"

Kade ran his hand through his damp hair. "Replant the sugar and send Bog out to look for me. If Kathleen comes back before I do, tie her to something solid."

"Ye should 'ave sent 'er 'ome when I told ye, lad."

Bog came into the room. "I agree with Jake. She does not belong here, nor does she want to be here. Send her home if you find her."

"*When* I find her what I do with her is my business, not yours." He stalked out of the room, directly into Mattie.

"I brought ye some aloe for sunburn. The lass will be burnt to a crisp in the sloop."

"Mattie, who decorated this house?" Kade asked.

"Who? I guess it was me, ye weren't interested."

"I hate that red or maroon or whatever in my room. Where did you get that stuff?"

"From ye, and I'll 'ave ye know it was the only thing ye decided on in the whole 'ouse!"

"You should not have listened to me. Change it to blue, dark blue. Every time I go in there I think of bloody sacrifices." He went into Kathleen's room for a moment, then came back out.

"What 'bout the rest of the 'ouse?" Mattie asked him.

"You did a good job." He ran down the stairs and out

the door.

Jake leaned against the rail around the landing. "What in 'ell as got into 'im? That room has been red for the last ten years."

Mattie stuck her head into Kade's room. "He's right, looks like a bloody sacrifice to me, too. Wonder why 'e wants it blue?"

Bog held Jake's arm as the old man limped on his splinted leg down the steps. "Haven't you ever noticed how when Kathleen wears blue the invincible Kade Morgan moons around her like a schoolboy in love?"

Jake grinned. "Ye should 'ave seen 'im when the lass was sick on the *Eagle*. Damn near drove the crew crazy. Then he made 'er share his cabin, though he weren't touchin' 'er 'cause of 'er ribs. He spent most of every night on deck, stalkin' around and growlin' at the moon, the tide, even the sharks. Durin' the afternoons 'e let her come out on deck and 'e walked into the mizzenmast twice while pretendin' not to notice 'er."

Mattie brushed past the two men. "When ye stop flappin' yer gums 'bout things what are none of yer business, I got yer dinner ready in the kitchen." She bustled off, mumbling beneath her breath.

Jake watched her go. "Before Kade fetched Kathleen 'ome to Mistral, Mattie didn't think the lad would ever settle down and raise a family."

"Do you think Kathleen is the right woman for him?"

"Aye, that I do. She be the first 'e e'er noticed outside the bedroom, and that includes that Ridley woman. Kathleen's also the first not to cower in fear when 'e's ragin' mad. She either laughs at 'im, ignores 'im, or rages back. Mattie's eager for them to settle their differences. She wants to see if Kade's children will look like 'is mother."

"She still miss Annaliss?"

"Aye, always will. The moment Annaliss came to Scotland to marry Stewart Morgan, Mattie was devoted to the child, for a child Annaliss was, younger than Kathleen and as green to the ways of the world as a newborn babe. Mattie saw Annaliss wedded to Stewart, assisted 'er when Kade was born. When Annaliss died, Mattie laid 'er mistress to rest beneath Scottish soil and, since she was afraid of losing the boy forever, I followed Kade to sea. He never even visited 'is mother's grave when we went back to Scotland years later."

"That was a long time ago," Bog said.

Jake hesitated before going into the busy kitchen. "That it was. Don't make it any easier to take. Kade is like 'is father, afraid to love, afraid to trust anyone to love 'im. He is treating Kathleen like 'is father treated 'is mother, and if 'e don't stop soon, 'e'll lose the lass."

"Have you said anything to him?"

"Ye know 'im, 'e won't be listenin' to anyone 'cept 'imself."

"Maybe when he finds Kathleen he will realize he has to set her free."

Jake shook his head. "Kade will bring 'er back 'ere and she will run again. This is the first time 'e 'as ever 'ad anyone go against 'im. It will take a bit of time for it to sink into 'is thick 'ead that the lass is every bit as stubborn as 'e is. I think she may even be worse than 'e is. I fear we be in for a long siege before Mattie sees what color eyes Annaliss's grandchildren will 'ave, if she e'er gets to see at all."

Chapter 23

Kathleen took a sighting on the sun and calculated her position. It was the fourth time that day. When she finished, she leaned back against the mast and looked at the sextant in her hand. Either it was wrong or Martinique had disappeared. It had been nine days since she left Mistral, nine days since she fell asleep at the tiller and sailed right past the island she was trying to reach.

She had cursed herself for not taking a reading while still on Mistral to confirm her position, then she had cursed the wind for taking her too far to the east. After that, she had changed direction and set a course due west. Now, according to her calculations, the *Slipper* was becalmed in the exact position where Martinique should be.

"Why could I not steal a sextant that worked?"

She tossed the brass instrument overboard. The sapphire water swallowed it with hardly a ripple. Kathleen felt better. She was back in control of her own destiny. No more relying on anything for help except herself. Above her, the mainsail hung listlessly in the heat. Perhaps she should take it down and throw it overboard also.

She went to the stern of the *Slipper* and pulled in her fishing line. It was empty. She put on another piece of bait, dropped the line back in the water and sat down to wait. The water was so clear she could see the bait hanging ten feet below the surface. She had surprised a gull on deck the previous day and was using the oily meat for fishing. So far she had only caught one fish, a pretty blue one just a little larger than her hook. She had laid it on the seat beside her, right next to the edge of the boat. While she baited her line, the fish had flipped its tail violently and flopped back into the sea.

She fanned her face with her hat and pulled the clinging bodice of her dress away from her damp skin. The white cotton clung to her again the moment she released it. She glanced over the stern and was shocked to see an extremely large fish swim up to her bait. The fish circled the hook and sank into the depths. A few minutes later it came back, then disappeared again.

Kathleen's stomach rumbled with hunger, and her tongue was dry and stiff. She had eaten the last of Bog's supplies four days ago, and her water would not last the night, even if she cut her rations again. The wind had died right after the food was exhausted, leaving hardly enough breeze to notice, much less fill the sail.

She sat back and wiped the sweat from her face. It was so hot; the sun beat down on the sea relentlessly. The blanket she had rigged to shade the stern of the boat did nothing to stop the reflection of the sun off the water. The only break she got from the heat was at night. The darkness was cool and restful, or at least it had been restful until Kathleen remembered the terrible stories Skinner had told her about sea monsters. Now she was thinking about them during the day, unable to keep herself from watching for sharks with cavernous mouths that swallowed ships and spit out the anchors. She shivered and tried not to think of Kade and how safe and secure she felt in his arms.

Her skin hurt. It had been burned by the sun,

scoured by the salt water. Her eyes ached from squinting into the bright light. She could barely see past the bow of the *Slipper*. Not that not seeing really mattered; there was nothing out there except more water and more sun.

The fishing line moved in her hand, and her heart jumped. She leaned over the stern of the boat. Her line dangled beneath her, empty except for the waterlogged bait. Maybe she was imagining things. Or maybe it was that grisly monster that lurked in the sea waiting for becalmed sailors to pass his way. After a sailor went totally mad with hunger and heat, the monster would pretend to be a dead fish. When the poor sailor tried to scoop up his unexpected prize, the monster did the scooping instead, pulling the unwary sailor into the sea and into its stomach.

"Don't ye be actin' like such a fool," she told herself in a thick Irish brogue. "Besides, there be no monsters 'ceptin' those what be lurkin' in yer mind."

She started to count all the monsters lurking in her mind at that very moment. Before she could get past six, a gigantic object appeared beside the sloop. Kathleen jumped up. The sun was in her eyes. She blinked and tried to focus. A huge shape rose above the rail, coming straight for her.

Kathleen gave vent to a terrible scream, clambering backwards as the monster bumped alongside the *Slipper*. She flattened herself against the mast, terror making her legs weak and almost useless.

The monster crept on board, causing the sloop to pitch and sway beneath its ponderous weight. It had the form of a man and stood upright as it slithered toward Kathleen. She pushed her back tighter against the mast, praying as she had never prayed before. The monster was between her and the sun; all she could see was its hideous outline. Soon she would feel its foul breath on her face, feel its slimy hands on her body. It would be covered with dripping seaweed, reeking of decaying flesh. It would have a touch as cold as death. It would put its mouth against her and suck her life away as it drank her blood. Then it would tear her body to bits and feed her to the sharks before sinking back into the depths of the sea to stalk its next hapless victim.

Kathleen could not breathe, could not run, could not fight. All she could do was stand there while the creature came closer, closer, closer. Her heart was beating so fast she could not think, could not even scream as the monster lifted its massive arms and placed its clawed talons against the mast, one on each side of her so that she was trapped. The shaggy head leaned forward, smothering her with its nearness.

Then it kissed her.

Kathleen began to shake and cry, tremble and faint. Kade swept her into his arms, crushing her against him. She clung to him desperately, afraid he would disappear if she let go. I must be mad, she thought, yet did not care if madness meant Kade would never stop holding her.

"I thought I would never find you," he said.

He kissed her again and again, not believing he actually held her in his arms. Then he carried her under the shade of the blanket, sat her on his lap and looked at her. She stared at him, wide-eyed.

"Are you real?" she asked, touching his face. His week-old beard scratched her hand, and she pulled back. "Do monsters have beards?"

"This one does. Do you like it?"

"It makes you look dangerous."

"I am, which reminds me of something I have been swearing to do ever since I discovered you had run off." He dumped her off his lap and started to pull her face-down across his knees. She wrenched free from him.

"Would you beat a starving woman?" she asked, putting the tiller between them.

"Aye, that I would, depending on how long you have been starving."

"Four days."

"I will hold off until you are fed."

"You are a most kind and benevolent master, Captain Morgan," she said as she slipped back onto his lap and wound her arms around his neck.

"I still intend to take my pound of flesh, Kate." He lifted her in his arms and carried her over the rail of the *Slipper* to his boat, the *Mosquito*. He went back for her gear, then untied the line and let the *Slipper* drift away.

"Why did you do that?" she asked.

He adjusted the *Mosquito*'s sails and turned the bow to the north. "Not enough wind to tow her. As it is we will have trouble breaking free from the current unless the wind picks up." He gave her a cup of water and some cheese.

"I could not pick up any wind, how did you manage?" she said between bites.

"By wetting the sails. That traps any air moving, not that there is much here."

She handed the cup back for more water. "Later," he told her. "Too much will make you sick. Feeling better?"

"Yes. Where are we and how did you find me?"

Kade sat on the stern of the *Mosquito* and watched as Kathleen rubbed the extract of the aloe plant onto her burned face and arms.

"I knew that the sextant you had taken would place you at least two hundred miles further east than you actually were. Once you discovered you had gone astray, you would naturally turn the *Slipper* around and head due west. I lined up on Martinique and came

314

after you."

She yawned and rubbed her eyes. "Do you think you could delay beating me until I get some sleep?"

"Why are you so tired, fishing get the best of you?"

Kathleen curled up on the seat beside him. "When we get back to Mistral I shall tie Skinner to the keel of the *Black Eagle* with that secret knot of his. I have dreamed about monsters every night, even thought you were one when you came on board the *Slipper*."

"Was that why you screamed? I was hoping it was because you were terrified of what I would do to you."

She yawned again. "I am completely frightened to death of you. Can you not see how I am shaking?"

The hazel eyes closed, and Kade wrapped his arms around her. She slept with her head on his shoulder, one small hand caught in the front of his shirt. He laid his cheek against her hair.

"Thank you again, God," he whispered. Instantly the sails on the *Mosquito* filled with a fresh, lively breeze. Kade put a hand on the tiller to steady the sloop and watched the clouds move across the sky above him.

Kathleen woke with a smile on her face. There were no monsters stalking her, no horrible creatures lying in wait. Her mouth was not dry, her stomach was not empty. And best of all, a strong, protective, familiar arm was securely wrapped around her. She snuggled closer to Kade and heard him chuckle.

"Wake up, kitten," he said.

"No, I like being asleep better."

Kade pushed her off the seat and onto the floor, sorely bruising her behind. "You are the laziest person I ever met."

"Why, because I like sleeping with you?" she asked as she struggled to her feet.

315

"Hold your tongue, girl, or you shall do more than sleep with me."

Kathleen thrilled to the warm intimacy of his voice, the threatened promise of his words. Her body seemed to act on its own. She stepped away from him, her fingers loosening the buttons on her dress and letting it fall down her hips and onto the deck at her feet. With the warm breeze caressing her skin and Kade's eyes on her, the world did not seem such a bad place, even if she was not in Ireland.

"You said you wanted a pound of my flesh. Where would you like to take it from?" she asked as her hand slipped down her side and across the top of her thigh in a provocative move she had once seen a girl make in Shannon on the docks. It had made her brother Niall trip over his own feet and fall into the harbor.

Kade gave her one of those devastating smiles that made her stomach turn upside down. "I had a different form of punishment in mind, Kate. Your suggestion is much better, however."

He came to her, his hands spanning her waist and running up her back. The tips of her breasts brushed against his chest, and Kathleen reached up to kiss him. His tongue moved over her lips, exciting her, thrilling her. As his hands explored her skin, ripples of pleasure spread over her tingling body. He lifted her into his arms and started to go below to the bunk under the bow.

"No, stay here," Kathleen said. "I want to feel the breeze on my face and you in my arms."

He kissed her again, his beard scratching her face. Her body was melting, her soul a wisp of sunshine trapped in a darkness of need. She ached to be touched, ached to be possessed by Kade.

Her hands slipped over his broad, powerful shoulders. He made her feel so small, so feminine. He moved

316

his lips away, and she pulled him to her again. He kissed the tip of her nose and stood her on the seat beside the tiller.

"I will get a blanket, I do not want splinters in your lovely behind."

"Or yours," she called after him.

He spread the blanket on the deck. "Lay down, wench," he ordered, and Kathleen complied. He shed his clothes beneath her interested gaze. His body was handsome. The black hair that covered his chest and tapered down across his waist flared into a bold mat that surrounded his erect manhood. His skin was dark, his muscles finely sculpted, moving beneath his flesh like those of a wild animal, a hunter who stalked its prey with stealth and strength.

Kade lowered himself to Kathleen's side. She ran her hands along the tight muscles in his upper arms, then across his stomach and down to the rigid proof of his desire for her. She grasped it firmly, slipping her hand along its hard length.

Kathleen bent her head, brushing her lips across the head. It was hot, the turgid flesh burning her tongue as she tasted him. The sun was warm on the back of her head as she drew him into her mouth, allowing her teeth to lightly graze him.

Her hair fell across his legs. He gathered it in his hands so he could see her face. Her eyes closed as she almost pulled her lips away from him, then lowered them again to the base of his hard need. Tenderness and love flowed over him, and he moaned as she massaged his inner thighs, her head lowering onto him again and again. The heavy silk of her hair was warm in his hand, and her rigid nipples excited him as they trailed through the fine hairs on his legs.

Another second of her sweet mouth on him and Kade would lose control. He wanted to make love to

317

her, long, tortuous love that would bond her to him forever. His fingers released her hair, and he pulled her up beside him, kissing her lips and capturing her firm breasts in his hands.

Kathleen arched into his touch, his fingers causing her to moan. His head lowered to her nipples. The scratch of his beard drove her mad with pleasure.

"Kade, yes, yes," she cried as he laid a pattern of tender bites around her breast. His hand glided down her stomach, dipping into the moist warmth between her legs.

She clutched him closer to her, touching his nipple with exploring fingers. A low growl sounded deep in his throat, and Kathleen trembled. His firm buttocks excited her. She caressed them, her fingers moving between his legs to grasp him from behind.

Kade nipped her neck, and she cried out. He lifted himself over her, slipping into her wet sheath. He moved slowly, filling her with his presence, his heat. She rose to accept him, thrusting her hips upward until he was completely enclosed within her. She tightened the muscles of her abdomen, holding him tighter. He threw his head back, the light touching his closed eyelids. Kathleen lifted her hand to his face, tracing the line of his jaw, down his neck and chest, around his stomach and onto the curve of his hips.

His lips touched hers, feeding on her tender kiss until it became savage and demanding. He withdrew from inside her, then reentered. She held his hips, pulling him deeper. The head of his penis touched her womb and she called his name, lost to the wonder of the moment. He began to move faster, thrusting and withdrawing, thrusting and withdrawing.

The sail above them cracked in the wind, the boat rocked in the grasp of the swelling sea and Kathleen rocked in the rhythm of passion as Kade took her higher than the clouds, higher than the sun. Together they exploded in a turmoil of light and color, sprinkling their joy over the sea as a shower of falling stars sprinkles the night sky with magic.

Kathleen pulled her legs together, trapping Kade within her. He eased himself onto her heaving chest, mingling their sweat as he had mingled their seed in her womb. Time passed, and the sun dipped to the edge of the horizon. Violets and roses bloomed in the banked clouds, spreading across the sky and enveloping the lovers.

Kade rolled onto his back, pulling Kathleen with him so she lay atop his bronzed body. Her hair was a curtain of darkness. His heart was so full, so rich with the wonder of the woman he held. The world had always been a hostile place for Kade, something to conquer and ignore. Now it was a place of beauty and pleasure, peace and gentleness. And warm, wonderful love.

Her head lifted from his chest, her lips swollen with his kisses. Her eyes were swirling pools of blue and green, and Kade's breath caught in his throat as he lost himself in those glowing depths.

"Why did you come after me?"

He touched the side of her face. "I told you I would."

"There was so much destruction on Mistral. You should have stayed." She moved off him.

"You mean you thought I would stay. No, lass, I said I would not let you escape me." He reached for his breeches, pulling them to him. From his pockets he pulled the four pearls, dropping them in Kathleen's hand. The last light of day shone like a candle on them, and then it was night, as was common in the tropics where twilight lasted no longer than the twinkle of a star. She closed her fingers around them. He grasped her hand, prying her fingers apart and taking the pearls.

"I should return them to the sea." He made a move to toss them into the sea.

"No!" Kathleen cried, grabbing his hand and holding it against her chest. "They were a gift!"

"You did not want them, you left them behind."

Her lashes glistened with unshed tears as she dropped her head and released his hand. "I did not want you to think I would use your gift to buy my freedom."

"What did you plan to use for money to book passage to Ireland?"

"The *Slipper*. I was going to send you payment for the sloop, and for the fifty pounds I cost you, once I was home."

"You prefer to steal than sell something you owned?"

"I would never sell a gift." The pearls clinked softly as Kade rolled them in the palm of his hand. "Do you still want to throw them overboard?" she asked.

"Nay, love, they were a gift." He dropped them into her hand. She held them to her for a moment, then went below to put them in the little sack that held her seashells.

When Kathleen came back on deck, Kade wrapped the blanket around her, for the wind was chill. The moon gave silver light to the night, and Kade stood naked against the mast, taking a sighting with his sextant.

"I hope that works better than mine did," Kathleen told him after he finished his calculations and marked their position on a chart. He adjusted the set of the sails, and the *Mosquito* heeled over as she turned her bow to starboard.

"A wild guess would serve better than that one.

When did you discover it was off?" He pulled on his breeches and a sweater, then sat beside Kathleen and pulled her into his arms.

"This morning. According to my sightings, the *Slipper* was directly on top of Martinique. Since there was no sign of Frenchmen, sand or coconut palms, I threw it overboard."

"How did you know that you were not wrong with your calculations?"

She smiled up at him. "Because I had an excellent teacher, although he is a most dour man with his stern stares and harsh commands."

Kade raised an eyebrow. "Stern? Harsh? I am offended."

Kathleen snuggled closer to him. "Maybe I can ease your offense," she said as her lips touched his.

The stars twinkled overhead and a lone dolphin surfaced beside the sloop, blowing its breath into the silence of night as Kade gave himself to the arms that held him, the love that possessed him.

Chapter 24

Dawn stretched its color and light across the sky, turning the sea a brilliant blue over which the *Mosquito*'s wake spread like a white cloud. Kathleen lifted her hair from her neck, allowing the breeze to touch her bare back. Kade handed her a cup of coffee he had brewed in the small galley.

"I am hungry," she told him.

"There is oatmeal to be cooked and some bacon to be fried. Help yourself." Kade adjusted the tiller and checked the set of the sails.

Kathleen wiggled her toes on the deck and grimaced. "I do not know how to cook."

He swung around to face her. "What is this? An Irish lass who can tame raging demons yet knows not how to conquer the simple task of cooking breakfast?"

"If you want to list my other shortcomings, I do not know how to sew, stitch, simper or flirt. I have never scrubbed a floor nor kneaded a loaf of soda bread. My skills are limited to riding horses, training horses and showing horses at the fair."

Kade chucked her under the chin. "There be another skill ye possess that ye 'ave forgotten, sweet lass, an' that be yer skill at makin' me bones turn to water and me knees knock together like a skeleton at midnight."

Kathleen wrinkled her nose at him. "You sound like

322

Mattie and Jake."

"Aye, Katie, that I do, an' it be no surprise since it be they what taught me to walk and talk and cook." He went below and a few minutes later had a kettle on the fire.

"Is it hard?" she asked, descending the steps behind him and peering at the bubbling oatmeal.

"Nay, love, but if you would like it to be, then come here." Kade opened his arms to her, and she sidestepped him.

"I meant cooking," she explained. He looked grievously disappointed, and she rolled her eyes at him.

"Not too hard, Katie, only a boat is not the place to be learning. If you decide to burn something to a crisp, we could be among the ashes."

"What can you do besides cook and navigate?"

Kade looked gravely wounded. "I thought last night had convinced you of another skill I possess. If you think I should practice more, we must discuss the issue of getting hard again."

Kathleen ignored him completely. He spooned up the oatmeal and she went on deck to eat, where he joined her after extinguishing the fire.

"Tell me about your family," she said, and Kade immediately got up to make minute changes to the sails, retying all the knots and checking all the lines. She waited until he started checking everything a second time, then went to him.

She backed him up against the mast. "Tell me," she said, her arms slipping around his waist. He hesitated a moment, then wound his hands into her raven hair. They stood that way for a time, the sea spray in their faces and the jib luffing in the breeze.

"My mother was fifteen when her family arranged her marriage with my father. He had a small estate in Scotland. They were married two years when I was born."

"Are your parents still alive?"

Kade ran his hand under Kathleen's hair, caressing her neck as he stared at the sea. "My mother died when I was eighteen. I left Scotland the next day."

Kathleen bit her lower lip as she calculated. "That must have been about twenty years ago."

He squeezed her tightly. "Seventeen, wench. I am not quite as ancient as you think."

She smiled up at him, then put her head back on his chest. "I do not mind you being so old, my mother told me to always respect my elders."

"I think I should have carried through with my original plan to extract that pound of flesh from your behind."

"Old people are extremely single-minded," Kathleen complained.

"Aye, that we are." He lifted her so her face was even with his. "And right now there is only one thing on my mind."

Kathleen ran her fingers around his lips, across his beard and behind his neck. "We think alike, master," she whispered and leaned forward to kiss him.

It was four days before the *Mosquito* came within sight of Mistral on the plantation side of the island, moving along its southern side. The mangroves swarmed with frigates and terns, the twin mountains were capped by clouds, the aqua sea foamed against the white beaches. Most of the silt stirred up by the hurricane had settled, and in places dark patches of turtle grass showed beneath the clear water, a purple blush on the clear complexion of the sea. A flock of flamingos flew past the sloop, their legs dangling behind them and their pink feathers flashing brightly in the sun.

As Kade tacked the *Mosquito* around the sunken crater, a stream of white mist shot upward from the sea near the bow. Kathleen shaded her eyes against the glare of the sun, and another white puff of water erupted from the ocean beside them. It floated on the wind, creating a rainbow. The blow was followed by a huge black creature breaking the surface. It slid its long body forward, diving back under the water, where it hovered like a shadow in the sea.

"What is it?" she asked Kade, her eyes alive with excitement as she strained to see the creature better.

"A whale."

Several more white puffs of water erupted into the air, and a pod of the giant mammals surfaced. Then, with a loud explosion of sight and sound, one whale hurled itself from the water into the bright sunlight. It turned over onto its back, pulling its long white side fins in graceful arcs like the wings of a great bird. Water streamed off its body. When it splashed back into the sea, a tremendous amount of water and noise heralded its leap.

"How beautiful!" Kathleen breathed as the whale gave another blow before lifting its butterfly-shaped tail in a dive. "Do they come here often?" she asked Kade.

He looked down at her, black eyes burning with an intense light. Kathleen's knees started to give way. She gripped the rail of the sloop behind her. She forgot her question, forgot everything except the man standing so close to her. He put a finger under her chin, lifting her head slightly. Another whale surfaced to breathe, giving a whooshing blow that startled Kathleen.

"I asked you about the whale," she said, her voice little more than a whisper. Her body burned like a fire under a midday sun as Kade leaned closer to her.

"These are humpbacks, they winter in the Caribbean, usually a bit further north. We do not often see them around Mistral." His lips touched hers. Their tongues met, and Kathleen leaned into his embrace. The whales surfaced again in front of the sloop. Kathleen turned her head from Kade's kiss to watch them.

He tightened his arms around her almost painfully. "I told you not to pull away from me again."

"I did not pull away, I turned away. I have never seen a whale before."

"There are whales around Ireland. They should have been easy to spot from the shore."

Kathleen watched as the whales flung their tails into the air, their black bodies disappearing into the depths. Then she looked back at Kade.

"If they did not swim through the middle of our stable, I would not have seen them. I am afraid my knowledge of things other than horses is less than extensive." She lifted her hands to his face, caressing the strong line of his jaw. "When we were in Crystal Cave after the storm, I promised I would not pull away from you and, if you reach for me, I would come to you. I meant those words when I said them, I mean them now."

"We were alone then, Kathleen, as we are now. Promises are easy to make in those circumstances and hard to fulfill when others are near. Soon we will be back in Mistral. Will you remember your words then?"

"You are my master, my lover. Show me respect, and require others to show me the same, and I will never forget my words, never forsake my promise."

Kade looked into her eyes, searching for the truth of her claim. He saw there her pride, the same pride that had made him buy her, the same pride that had made him love her. Would that pride destroy their relationship when he reached for her in front of Mattie and Jake, would it destroy her when he held her in front of Bog Daniels?

He released her to steer the *Mosquito* into the harbor. There was a ship anchored there, the *Gypsy Lady.* She was larger than the *Black Eagle,* her lines heavier, her hull broader. The sloop skirted her anchor line, and the shore of the cove came into view.

There was emptiness where once the village had stood. It drew Kathleen's gaze, and she thought of the emptiness on the shore of Ireland where her home had been. Were her mother and brother buried there? Were there flowers on their graves, had there been tears shed on their graves to ease their loneliness? She had promised not to pull away from Kade; would she be strong enough to run away from him again?

She slipped her hand into his. "I am glad to be back."

"Only because you did not succeed in escaping," he said as he untied the jib sail and let the sail fall onto the deck.

"Aye, that is true, master. But also because your island is beautiful and I do love it, though not as much as Ireland."

Kade turned the stern of the *Mosquito* so it pushed against the pier. He dropped the mainsail and tied the sloop to the pier. Kathleen went below to gather their gear. He was out of the boat when she came back on deck. She reached for his hand, and he lifted her up beside him.

"I shall do all I can to sway your affections in Mistral's favor," he said. He took their gear, and together they walked to the house. As they moved across the expanse of ruined gardens, Bog Daniels came out of the house.

"Land's sake!" he cried, mimicking Mattie, who rushed out right behind him.

"Ye found the lass!" she said as she pushed past Bog.

Kade put his arm around Kathleen. "That I did, Mattie. Saved her from the slavering jaws of a sea monster and fetched her home safe and sound."

Kathleen stiffened. If that sextant had not been broken, she would be on her way home. Home. It hurt to think of it.

"Where did you find her?" Bog asked as they went inside the house.

"Almost to Panama and in the middle of the calmest sea I have ever seen. I thought the current would have taken her closer to Jamaica. She held true to her course, though, even with that damned sextant."

"You should not curse the sextant so, for if not for its folly I would be on my way home and you would look a fool for not finding me." Kathleen took the glass of milk Mattie brought her. She drained it in one swallow, and Kade laughed at the line of white over her upper lip. He raised a tankard of cold ale to his lips, tossing the contents down as Kathleen had done her milk. When he finished, she checked his beard for foam. It was spotless.

He winked at her before leaning close to her ear and whispering, "I prefer to wet my beard with you, not ale." She choked and he laughed.

Mattie took the empty glasses and headed for the kitchen. "I'll 'ave 'ot water for ye in no time at all."

"Maybe we should mount that sextant on the wall in honor of its providential error," Bog said.

"Not so providential from my point of view. It cost me my freedom." Kathleen ran up the steps to her room, slamming the door behind her.

"She does not seem pleased about her rescue," Bog said, his eyes lingering on the closed door.

Kade leaned against the staircase railing and crossed his arms over his chest. It was time he put a halt to

Daniels' fantasy dreams of Kathleen.

"Not a night has passed since I found Kate when she has not cried aloud her pleasure," he said.

Bog's face turned white, then flushed bright red. "That is not what I meant."

"I know, but it is exactly what I meant. She belongs to me, Daniels, now and forever. Put aside those romantic ideas you have about winning her affections by assisting her to escape my demonic clutches; they will only cause her disappointment and you death. Find yourself another female to moon over, this one is mine."

"You are in love with her," Bog said, a look of disbelief dawning on his face. "I'll be damned, Kade Morgan is in love. I had thought you were merely intrigued by her because she is the first female who did not bow down at your feet and beg for you to grant her eternal misery at your side. I underestimated Kathleen, she has caused the impossible to happen. Let me give you some advice, Kade. Set her free, send her home."

"If you were right, if I did love her, it would not make much sense to send her home and lose her. Much more practical to hold onto her."

"By keeping her prisoner? You may be able to force her body to respond but you will never force her heart. Chances are that she loves you; otherwise she would have plunged a knife into that black heart of yours weeks ago. Set her free before you destroy that love." Bog turned on his heel and left the room.

Kade scowled. "This island is full of people with nothing better to do than mind my business."

Jake limped out of the study. "Daniels be right, Kade. Send the girl 'ome before ye lose what it is yer wantin', whether ye admit it or not."

"My relationship with Kathleen is none of your business, Jake. I know what I am doing."

"So do I, lad. I seen yer father do it to yer mother, saw 'im 'old onto Annaliss so tight he choked 'er to death."

"Mother killed herself."

"Aye, she drank the poison, but it were Stewart Morgan what drove 'er to it. Even though he loved Annaliss, he never told 'er. He thought it weren't manly, thought it weak to love a woman as he loved 'er. It frightened 'im and that fear caused 'im to lose 'er."

"I am not my father."

"Nay, lad, ye be yer own man. Always were. Still, ye ain't told Kathleen 'ow ye feel. Ye be too busy tryin' to force her to say it first, tryin' to force 'er to love ye so much ye won't 'ave to ever say it. Ye can't force someone to love ye, Kade, ye can only force them to 'ate."

Chapter 25

Kathleen leaned close to Demon's sweat-flecked neck. They had just passed the small cove beneath Emerald Pool and were headed down the beach to the harbor. She had seen a ship approaching the island and wanted to reach the harbor before it anchored.

She settled the sack she carried across Demon's withers and urged the stallion faster. They ran along the edge of the pounding surf where the sand was firm. Her green dress flew around her like a rippling wave, her hair was caught by the wind and whipped into a frenzy, as were Demon's mane and tail. The stallion plunged through the foaming surf, scattering the sea beneath his pounding hooves into thousands of droplets. She urged the eager stallion faster, and together they flew along the beach.

Kade was working with Jake on the rebuilding of the shipping village when a cry went up that a ship had been sighted approaching Mistral from the southeast. He laid down his hammer, wiped the dripping sweat from his brow and pulled on his shirt. He and Jake walked down the beach to the pier, where Kade picked up his spyglass to focus on the approaching vessel.

"Damn!" Kade said and refocused the glass.

"Ain't that the *Christabel?* I thought ye were waitin' for her."

"Aye, but not her passengers. Standing on the deck are Quint Cathcart and Sarita Ridley. What are they doing here?"

The *Christabel* dropped anchor, and a longboat was put over the side. Quint and Sarita settled into it, along with Ivan Flesher. When the boat drew up alongside the pier, Kade made fast the mooring lines before offering his hand to Sarita.

"This is a surprise," he said as she slipped her soft fingers into his. She lifted her honey-colored lashes and touched him gently with her gaze while he assisted her up the ladder. He could smell the rich scent of her cologne. Her breasts lifted as she inhaled, straining against her blouse, the white material edged with fine lace that rested lightly against her neck.

The golden highlights of her hair caught and held the sunlight, and Kade felt a rush of desire. Her ivory complexion colored slightly as she responded to his intense scrutiny. He purposely turned from her, upset by his feelings. He loved Kathleen, or thought he did. If so, why this excitement at seeing those cool gray eyes again?

Kade realized Quint Cathcart was waiting for assistance, and he grabbed the foppish man's shoulder, dragging him up the ladder. Quint waved a scented handkerchief in front of his face.

"Damned hot here," he said.

"No worse than Africa. What brings you here, Quint, and you, Sarita?"

Quint delicately wiped his brow. "I had business in the West Indies and booked passage on Captain Flesher's ship. Sarita"—he put a proprietary hand around her waist—"is here because I thought she deserved a trip after all the loving attention she has shown me."

Sarita involuntarily flinched from Quint's touch, then immediately pretended to stumble. She clutched Quint's arm and smiled into his furious face. "Thank you, darling. I caught my heel in this rough wood and almost fell. How wonderful of you to catch me!" His anger faded beneath her flattering words. She placed her hand on his arm and lowered her head slightly, glancing at Kade out of the corner of her eye with an appraising, expectant look.

"You are welcome to stay on Mistral until the *Christabel* sails again," Kade said. "The island sustained considerable damage during a hurricane that struck Mistral three weeks ago. The main house withstood the storm fairly well so you should not be inconvenienced. You might find the menus a bit erratic, however."

Kade turned to Ivan Flesher. "We have some business to discuss, Flesher. If you have any cargo for Mistral, unload it first then report to my study."

Jake caught Kade's eye and nodded toward the stretch of beach where it curved north into the harbor. Demon had just come into sight, plunging through the surf as he raced along the shore in the direction of the pier. Kathleen was astride the stallion, leaning so low over his neck she seemed a part of the animal. The black horse ran effortlessly through the white-capped waves, slicing the water into an explosion of sparkling drops until both horse and rider were surrounded by a crystal shower.

The huge stallion, the tiny rider, the sparkling rainbow that enveloped them. It was like a dream. Kade's breath caught in his throat, and his entire being ached with more than just desire. No longer did he doubt his love for Kathleen. She was the most magnificent thing he had ever seen or could ever imagine. What he felt for Sarita was lust for a beautiful woman. What he felt for the hellion on the back of that stallion was deeper, richer. It filled him to overflowing, and he thrilled to know she belonged to him.

The stallion's muscles flowed like thick water beneath his glistening skin, and Kathleen's legs clung tightly to his sides. They approached the pier without slackening speed, disappearing behind a stack of lumber. Demon's hooves pounded on the wooden pier, and then everything went silent as the stallion soared over the top of a stack of crates, landing with a bone-jarring thud in the center of the pier. A scream ripped from his heaving chest as he reared, slashing the air with razor-sharp hooves.

Wild tangles of ebony curls fell across Kathleen's shoulders and swirled around her waist and hips. She laid a hand on the stallion's neck and Demon instantly settled down, lowering himself onto the pier. The whites of his eyes showed and he nervously tossed his head until Kathleen again touched him.

The sun caught every drop of water that covered horse and rider, making the pair appear to shimmer in the heat. The pier was deadly silent; even the ocean had quieted its steady roar. There was no sound save the stallion's heavy breathing and the pounding hearts of Kathleen and Kade as they looked at each other. Her eyes were like whirlwind pools of aqua in the center of a thousand sparkling diamond chips of seawater.

"I saw the ship," she said in explanation of her arrival. Her husky voice had the effect of a sudden clap of thunder on a cloudless sky. She was breathtakingly beautiful, and Kade forgot everything except his need to hold this wonderful woman in his arms. He stepped forward and reached for her.

She came readily to him, sliding slowly into his arms with her hands winding around his neck. Her breath was soft on his face, her lips moist, parted and ready for his kiss. Quint Cathcart cleared his throat, and Kade reluctantly lowered his small slave to the pier.

"Kathleen," he said, "I would like you to meet some unexpected guests who just arrived on the *Christabel* from Africa." He did not release his hold on her, his hands remaining around her waist even as he turned her to face the people behind him, holding her in front of him. "This is Sarita Ridley, Quint Cathcart and Captain Ivan Flesher." Kathleen placed her hands over Kade's and leaned back against his chest. His throat contracted, and he wanted desperately to kiss her. "This is Kathleen O'Connor," he said instead, inhaling the scent of the wind and sea that clung to her hair.

Kathleen looked Sarita over carefully. She wore a silly hat with a half veil, both of which looked perfect on her. She held a parasol that shaded her from the harsh sun, and from the crook of her arm hung a tiny bag, its beaded surface sparkling as it swung in the breeze. Her skirt and jacket were made of burgundy silk, the style accenting her figure so a man's eyes would be drawn to the swell of her breasts, her narrow waist and curving hips.

Sarita was elegant, refined and beautiful. She reeked of poise, confidence and expensive cologne. She was the woman whose clothes Kathleen had worn, whose lover Kathleen had made love with. The woman who had wanted to marry Kade.

Kathleen forced herself to look away from that cool beauty, suddenly aware of her own tousled, wet appearance. Her simple dress, bare feet and untamed hair were a marked contrast to Sarita's groomed appearance. A feeling of inadequacy claimed her, something she had never experienced before.

Quint Cathcart made a rather elaborate bow to Kathleen, sparking a memory she could not place.

335

Those almost feminine movements of his hands, that pointed beard, those empty eyes; all were familiar. Even his style of dress was familiar, a pale blue waistcoat and white breeches, white hosiery and slipperlike shoes. He looked like a dandy dressed for a ball, not a traveler to the Caribbean.

She turned to Captain Ivan Flesher. He was a handsome man in a dark, forbidding way. Though not as tall as Kade, he still towered over Kathleen. She did not like him and remembered Flesher was the man Bog Daniels thought might be cheating Morgan Shipping. There was a terrifying intensity to the way he was looking at her. He seemed to be undressing her with his eyes, his hands rubbing suggestively across his upper thigh. She unconsciously pulled Kade's arms tighter around her, seeking protection from that piercing gaze.

"A most magnificent beast," Quint said, reaching out a hand to stroke Demon. The stallion curled his lip back, baring sharp teeth. Quint jerked his hand back. "A bit untamed, though." He took in the deep chest and strong limbs of the stallion. "Are you interested in selling him, Morgan?"

"No. Besides you would never be able to get him back to Morocco. On the ship that brought him to Mistral he killed two men and crippled a third."

"Certainly he is not as dangerous as that."

"He is unless Kathleen is near. She is the only one he tolerates to touch him." Kade lifted a hand to Kathleen's neck as he spoke, pushing it under the curtain of her hair and stroking her flesh.

She rolled her head slightly beneath his caress. Her breath quickened, her eyes closing briefly as her body responded to the intimacy of his touch.

"She is a mere child," Sarita said as she lifted her skirts to step away from the excited horse. "Do you think it safe to allow her near such a creature, Kade?"

Her silken voice trailed over Kade's name even as her eyes trailed over him.

Kathleen's temper flared. "Much safer than allowing you near his London creditors, Mrs. Ridley." She abruptly turned to face Kade. "I have to take my crabs to the house. I will tell Mattie to prepare the guest rooms."

"Crabs?"

"I was at the mangroves gathering some for dinner. Should taste great with that pineapple tart Mattie was making this morning."

"You think everything tastes great with pineapple tart."

Kade touched her earlobe. There was no one else on the earth at that moment except the two of them as she saw herself reflected in the dark lakes of his eyes.

"Aye, that I do," she said so softly none save the two of them could hear, purposely dropping her gaze down the front of his body. "Some things better than others, master." His eyebrows lifted slightly, his smile wrapping all the way around her.

Sarita smoothed her skirt and tried not to notice the way Kade's eyes were devouring Kathleen, or the way his smile included only that impudent child. He had never once looked at her like that, had hardly ever smiled at her.

When Quint Cathcart reached to take her arm, Sarita felt suddenly nauseous. The man's clammy touch had always revolted her, but never as much as now, when she was standing so close to Kade Morgan. She had only taken up with Quint because of the depleted state of her finances. She had been broke, completely broke, and looking for a new provider when Quint had introduced himself as an associate of Kade Morgan's. Then, when Quint had suggested this trip to the West Indies to see Kade, Sarita had been certain she would be able to use the time on Mistral to get Kade back.

She would crawl on her knees to be the object of his desire again. When she first arrived on the pier, she had felt his hot reaction to her presence, felt the burning touch of his eyes on her breasts. Now, as she watched him with the girl, she knew she had lost even before she had begun.

Ivan was almost drooling as he openly stared past Sarita to that wet, tangled child in Kade's arms. What was it about the girl? Never before had anyone noticed another woman when Sarita was around.

"I thought it was you he loved, my dear Sarita," Quint said quietly, his voice mocking and cruel. "I know a way you can seek revenge against Miss O'Connor."

"How?"

"We shall discuss it before dinner. I have to talk to Captain Flesher now."

Kathleen stepped away from Kade and vaulted onto Demon's back. Quint held his breath as the stallion reared, then leaped back over that same pile of crates without even taking a single step. Though the beast was certainly magnificent, he was no match for Taran. Quint's blood raced as he thought of that incredible stallion.

"She's really something," Ivan Flesher said.

Kade turned on the man. "You have business on your ship, Flesher," he growled. "I suggest you see to it."

Quint smiled a secret smile at the jealous anger on Kade Morgan's face. This was going to be fun, he thought as he waved his handkerchief in front of his sweating face and hurried after Flesher's retreating form.

Chapter 26

Kathleen stopped at the house to give Mattie the crabs and to tell her about the visitors before taking Demon to the stables. Her mind refused to release the memory of Sarita Ridley. She was so beautiful, so much a lady. She was everything a man would want in a woman. Why had Kade rejected her?

She finished rubbing down Demon and went back to the house, arriving just in time to see a flash of burgundy on the top step beside the landing. Then it was gone, moving into Kathleen's bedroom.

She ran up the steps and into her room. Sarita was there, pushing her pointed fingers through the contents of the crystal bowl beside the bed.

"Did you want something, Mrs. Ridley?" Kathleen asked, barely restraining her anger.

Sarita lifted one of the pearls, rolling it between her fingers, turning it this way and that. The candlelight inside the pearl glowed brighter where it touched her smooth flesh.

"This is your room?"

"Aye. The guest rooms are at the other end of the hall."

Sarita dropped the pearl back into the bowl. "Yes, I know where they are. Of course, I have never been in them. When I was on Mistral, I spent most of my time in Kade's room."

"I wonder why. He was not on the island while you were here."

"You are a most annoying and impertinent child," Sarita snapped as she swept past Kathleen and down the hall to the guest rooms.

"What was that all about?" Jake asked as he came up the steps, followed by two men who took a load of trunks and valises into the guest rooms. A young girl and a middle-aged man trailed behind the luggage, personal servants of Sarita and Quint.

"Mrs. Ridley thought she could intimidate me with her past relationship to Kade. I do not intimidate easily."

"You love 'im, don't ye, lass?"

Kathleen stiffened. "You know my position in this house."

"Aye, that I do. That don't stop ye from lovin' 'im."

"Love has nothing to do with my relationship with Kade Morgan."

Jake put his hand on her shoulder. "Love 'as nothing to do wi' life, yet it exists and for that I thank God. Ye can't be lettin' Kade get ye down, lass. Has 'e told ye about 'is family?"

"Only that his mother is dead."

"His mother weren't like ye, Kathleen, she weren't strong enough to stand up to 'er man like ye do to Kade. He respects ye for that. Until 'e met ye, lass, he never 'ad more than one use for a female."

"Things have not changed, Jake. He has only one use for me."

"Ye be more than 'is lover, Kathleen, ye be 'is friend. And that alone is more than I e'er thought could 'appen. Yer different from other women 'e's known. Yer strong and determined to do things yer own way, despite what 'e wants. If ye 'ad acted like other women

340

do around 'im, 'e would've sent ye 'ome in a flash."

"So in my determination to go home, I prevented that very thing from happening? I will bow down and kiss his feet right now if that is all it takes."

"That would've worked at first, Kathleen. Now I wouldn't be knowin'. Kade 'as changed since 'e bought ye."

"What should I do, Jake?"

"If ye love 'im, ye will wait the lad out. It be my guess ye will get e'erthin' ye want, 'ome and Kade, if ye can wait 'im out. He 'as no respect for a woman that is willin' to cower behind 'im, but 'e is not ready for one to stand beside 'im. Not yet."

"I do not want to stand beside him, Jake. I just want to go home."

"I know that, lass, yet I think ye also want more."

"What more I might want does not matter."

From the other end of the landing they heard Sarita Ridley directing where her trunks were to be placed. Kathleen listened for a moment, then clenched her fists.

"Except for tonight, Jake. Tonight it matters a great deal."

Sarita sat on the small sofa under the window of her room, watching the clouds scurry across the sky. She rubbed her forehead, trying to wipe away the dull ache from behind her eyes. During the years when she had been Kade's mistress, he had never as much as touched her in public, had hardly even spoken to her. Yet he had held Kathleen as though she were a piece of precious china. Sarita could have dealt with straight rejection more easily than his blatant fondling of that child in front of her.

"Headache, my dear?" Quint asked as he came into

the room.

"Yes, so say whatever you have to say quickly, then leave me alone."

"I was most surprised by your reception on Mistral, Sarita."

"Is there a point to this discussion, Quint?"

"Of course there is, my dear. The point is one I briefly referred to on the pier, a way in which you can take revenge against the girl who has replaced you in Kade Morgan's heart, if indeed you were ever there."

"What do I have to do?" Sarita asked.

"I need your help in retrieving some property Morgan has that belongs to me."

"What property is that?"

"Kathleen O'Connor. She belongs to me, a fact she is not aware of and one that I intend not to tell her for the moment. And you can be certain that her fate will more than repay her for any problem she may have caused you."

Quint liked the way Sarita's breasts swelled beneath the silk of her blouse, liked the way her hair caught the light coming through the window. He remembered the night on the *Christabel* when Ivan Flesher and Sarita had thought him unconscious. Her submissive response to Ivan's demands and their animal-like sex had been terribly exciting until he had really passed out.

"Tell me what you want me to do, darling," Sarita said as she stood and moved across the room to Quint.

"Your task will be simple. Divert Morgan tonight so I can talk to Kathleen."

"You saw him today. Once that child showed up, Kade did not even notice me."

Quint smiled at her bitter tone and reached to caress her face. "You are a beautiful woman, Sarita, a beautiful, aging woman. It is time you learned to use something besides your face and body to get what you want. Tonight I will bring up the name of a horse I own, Black Merrow. I want the conversation to stay on that subject until I signal you, then I want you to draw Morgan's attention to something else. Whenever I nod to you, bring up the horse again."

Sarita shrugged. "Whatever you say, Quint."

"That's my girl." He touched the curve of her breast. "Now, before we must begin preparing for dinner, I want you to do something for me. And if you do it well, when I leave Mistral with the O'Connor girl, I will see that you stay here to ease Morgan's wounded pride. You would like that, wouldn't you?"

Sarita leaned into Quint's caress. "What do you want me to do, darling?"

Quint spread his legs. "On your knees, bitch," he snarled as he jerked at the front of Sarita's blouse, tearing it open to her waist. "I want the same thing you gave Ivan that night when I was lying on the floor beside you, only what he did will look like nothing compared to everything I shall do to you. You will pay for lying to me about Morgan's affections for you, pay very dearly."

Her eyes narrowed as she sank to the floor in front of him, anger sustaining her as she took Quint's penis in her mouth. Even when he turned her over his knee and started spanking her bare bottom with hard, punishing blows, she did not fight him. Soon he would be gone, taking that Irish bitch with him; then Kade would be hers again, and all the pain in the world was worth that.

Quint pushed Sarita onto her hands and knees, reaching beneath her to pinch and squeeze her breasts. She forgot about Kade, forgot about everything except the burning heat of her body as she begged Quint to

343

spank her again before thrusting himself into her.

Kathleen took a bath and brushed her hair until it crackled. She opened one of the cupid-decorated jars on the dressing table and rubbed scented cream on her arms and shoulders, her breasts and stomach. She slipped her legs into black stockings and put on a black chemise. She pulled her robe on and stood in front of the open armoire, staring at the kaleidoscopic colors of the dresses until her head began to hurt. All she could see were Sarita's cool gray eyes, elegant coiffure and ivory complexion.

The door opened and Kade stepped into the room, partially dressed for dinner. His shirt was only half buttoned, his vest and jacket missing. He carried an armful of black velvet that spilled across his leg and onto the floor. She trembled a little as he moved closer to her. When he bent his head to touch his lips to her, she trembled even harder.

"What is it, kitten?" he asked as he cupped her face with his hands.

"Nothing," she said, her voice quavering slightly. How could she say that she was afraid of Sarita's sophistication, afraid of losing him to those gray eyes and golden hair? She knew what his response would be: How can you lose what you do not have, kitten?

Kade gathered her into his arms, pressing her head against his chest as he kissed her hair. Kathleen shut her eyes and let the steady, strong rhythm of his heart soothe her. When her eyes stopped burning, she stepped away from him.

"Is this for me?" she asked, lifting the black gown from the chair. It was such a delicate creation, the soft velvet flowing like the illusive promise of a warm breeze at midnight. She laid it back on the chair, her finger tracing the pattern of the lace on the bodice.

"I thought you might like to wear something special tonight, so I rode over to the plantation and picked it up. Do you need help getting dressed?"

"Mattie is coming to do my hair, she will help me with the buttons. Thank you for the dress, Kade. It is beautiful. You have been so busy, you should not have gone to the trouble of riding across the island for it."

"It was no trouble, I wanted to see you in it. I have another gift for you, something for you to wear tonight." He reached into his pocket, and as he withdrew his hand a sinuous trailing of brilliant gold flowed from between his fingers. At the end of the chain was a flash of blue-and-green color that looked like the sea around Mistral.

"It is an opal. I got it when I was in Nassau."

"Selling the turtles?"

"Among other things. Turn around, Kate."

Kathleen did as he said, and he placed the necklace around her neck, fastening it beneath her hair. The thumbnail-sized opal was surrounded by diamonds that flared out along the chain like the wings of a bird. The gems lay just at the top of the cleft between her breasts, startlingly against her tan skin.

"It is the same color as my eyes," she said as she touched it. The diamonds picked up the blue and green of the opal, reflecting it a thousand times in the mirror.

"I know, that is why I bought it." He turned her to face him, then clipped small earrings on her earlobes that matched the necklace. They sparkled almost as brightly as her eyes, and Kade's throat ached.

Kathleen touched one of the earrings. The stones were warm from being in Kade's hand. The dress and jewelry were meant to make her feel special. He must have guessed her feeling of inadequacy, and she loved him all the more for his understanding of her feelings.

Still, she was a slave and could not accept a gift of such expensive jewelry.

"Kade, I cannot accept . . ."

He laid a finger on her lips. "Do not say it, Katie, I do not want to argue with you tonight. I want you to kiss me instead." There was a light in his eyes that made Kathleen's stomach knot up, made her heart turn over and made her willpower disappear instantly. His magical charm had never been so compelling as at that moment with his broad shoulders straining beneath his shirt and the lamplight accenting the rugged handsomeness of his face. He had been working so hard to rebuild the shipping village and looked tired.

Kathleen wanted to make him smile, wanted him to know how much she cared. She pushed aside the reality that she did not want to face and reached up to pull his lips to hers. She slipped her tongue into his mouth and her hands into his hair. He lifted her from the floor, holding her provocatively against him as he carried her to the bed.

He laid her on the fairy-wing spread and covered her with his body. His lips moved down her throat, touching lightly on her rapidly beating pulse as he opened the front of her robe. He kissed the tops of her breasts, then pushed his tongue between them, tasting the sweetness of the flesh that lay beneath the shining opal.

Kathleen thrilled to the touch of his lips, shivered beneath the hot moistness of his tongue. Her body smoldered with desire as he lit within her a fire she knew could never be completely quenched, for it was the fire of love. He kissed her nipples through the black chemise, then moved his lips to her neck, sampling the creamy softness of the hollow in her throat.

His hair was soft and thick between her fingers, his body hot and heavy as it pressed her into the mattress.

346

She ached with love and wanted him to never stop touching her, kissing her, possessing her.

There was a knock on the door and Mattie called out, "Be ye ready for me, lass?" The magic of the moment was broken as reality flooded back in with a Scottish accent.

"Kade," Kathleen said as she lifted his head from her chest. The black eyes glowed with a hungry light that made her feel weightless and wanting.

"I know, love," he whispered as his mouth claimed hers again. "It is getting late."

He moved off the bed, then bent to run his hand up her stocking onto her bare thigh. He parted her legs and dipped his finger into the hot wetness of her. She gasped and strained against his touch. He withdrew from her, the look in his eyes pouring over her like warm water.

"If you look even half as beautiful in that dress as you do at this moment, Kathleen, you will capture my heart anew. I will be waiting for you downstairs."

After he went into his room, it took several deep breaths before Kathleen could find her voice. "Come in, Mattie," she managed to say as she turned to sit on the edge of the bed. Had he meant what he said? Had she captured more than his fancy, did she really have a hold on his heart?

"I thought I 'eard voices in 'ere. Did I disturb something?"

Kathleen touched the opal. "Kade brought me that dress to wear."

Mattie lifted the black velvet. "This be the dress 'e designed 'imself for ye. Euline's been workin' on it e'er since Kade came back from Nassau. She told me it was to be worn without petticoats." She arranged the dress on the bed and smoothed the skirt. "Kade must want ye to look yer best tonight."

"Sarita is very beautiful, Mattie. I will need to look better than just my best, and even then I shall feel inadequate."

"Remember, lass, 'e sailed away from 'er."

Kathleen held onto that thought as she slipped the dress on and turned for Mattie to fasten the buttons on the back. She studied the carpet at her feet to avoid looking in the mirror. When she lifted her gaze to the mirror, she could not believe what she saw. The low-cut bodice dipped becomingly down over her bosom, the tracing of lace around the edge revealing even more of her swelling breasts. Tiny jet beads sewn onto the bodice glistened and sparkled as she breathed.

Her shoulders were bare, the sleeves beginning just at the top of her arm and clinging tightly to her, then tapering to a point over the backs of her hands. They, too, were edged with lace and beads. The top of the dress was cut so it tapered down past her waist in the front and back, the beads accenting her slender figure. The skirt was full, and since there were no petticoats, it clung to her, gracefully outlining her legs when she moved. The folds of velvet were so deep and dark the light appeared to be absorbed into the dress, catching on the beads and shimmering like black stars.

Kathleen stared in disbelief at herself while Mattie coaxed her thick hair into a waterfall of curls held in place by ebony combs. The curls dangled, as they had that first night on Mistral, over her left shoulder so they brushed the top of her breast. The necklace and earrings were the perfect accent to the black of her hair and dress, accenting her eyes so they looked like gems themselves.

There was more to the change in her than just the dress and jewelry, however. There was a glow coming from between the chips of swirling blue and green in her eyes, as though they knew something Kathleen herself did not know.

It be nonsense yer thinkin', Katie me girl, she heard her father say. She refused to listen to him, because she knew there was something more, something illusive and shining that made her look more of a woman than ever before.

Kathleen lifted her skirts and put on a pair of black velvet shoes, her feet fitting them perfectly. She touched the earrings and necklace, smiled at Mattie and swept from the room.

As she walked down the shadowed stairs and stepped into the golden light of the fire, she felt Kade's eyes trace over the lace that concealed her breasts, felt him circle her tiny waist with his gaze, felt the touch of his glance on the clinging folds of velvet that draped over her hips and legs.

He stepped closer to her, touching his finger to his lips. She smiled at him, smiled her gratitude, her friendship. Smiled her love.

That smile set Kade's blood to racing even faster than the dress had done. The black velvet gave Kathleen's skin a softness that was so appealing, so exciting. The necklace and earrings captured every bit of light in the world, throwing it back in reflections of loveliness eclipsed only by those incredible eyes.

Kade had wanted to see Kathleen dressed in black, had wanted to see her taking off that same black. In his room waited a candle, ready for its wick to be touched with flickering flame so it could cast romantic light on that radiant skin, that reflecting opal. It waited to caress that raven hair and shimmer in those wonderful eyes.

The evening stretched before him like a thousand years, time wasted until he could take Kathleen to his room, stand her in the soft light and touch her lips with his, until he could drink of her passion and drown in her arms. He forgot about Sarita and Quint, who had come downstairs just ahead of Kathleen. Kade forgot about everything except the rapid beat of his heart and and the burning need in his soul as he took Kathleen's offered hand, pressing her fingers and inhaling the heavenly scent of her.

"You look lovely tonight, Miss O'Connor," Quint said as he brushed past Kade to take her hand, "not at all like the girl I saw astride that stallion today."

Sarita rustled the satin skirt of her gown as she gingerly seated herself on one of the sofas. "Isn't that dress a bit much for the child, Kade?" She felt faded beside Kathleen's intense beauty. She wished that she had worn something other than gray and that her diamonds would sparkle more.

Kade extracted Kathleen's hand from Quint's and tucked it in his, running his finger lightly across the small palm. "She is no child, Sarita."

Kathleen's breasts swelled above the bodice of her gown as she fought the tremor his touch evoked. She moved closer to him, pressing her shoulder against his arm.

"Perhaps. Still, she looks out of place in that gown. She might be more comfortable in some of those old things I left here."

"How kind of you to be concerned for my comfort, Mrs. Ridley," Kathleen said quietly. Her husky voice was barely audible over the crackling of the fire, yet it drew the attention of everyone in the room, including the servant who was lighting the candles on the piano. "When I first arrived on Mistral, I tried to wear some of your clothes since I had none of my own. Unfortunately, they were much too large for me."

Sarita raked her with a cold stare. "I could corset my waist that small if I wanted."

"Corset? Is that some article of clothing I should be

350

wearing?" she asked innocently, lifting her eyes to Kade as though she had committed some grievous breach of etiquette.

Kade squeezed her fingers and stifled a laugh as he noticed the sparkle of mischief in her eyes. He led her to the sofa and seated her opposite Sarita. He went to the liquor cabinet to pour wine for everyone, then leaned against the mantel. It was a position that allowed him to watch the play of light on Kathleen's face. He loved the way she tilted her head back to look at him, the way her eyes smiled at the corners as she allowed her glance to travel down his body. It was going to be a long evening.

"That horse you rode today, Miss O'Connor, reminded me of a gray stallion I saw earlier this year while buying some hunters." Quint adjusted the lace on his shirt, straightened his gray vest and brushed some lint from his pale blue jacket. He was also feeling faded beside the black of Kathleen's dress and Kade's evening clothes. Quint sat on the sofa beside Sarita and fingered the diamond stickpin in his cravat. "That stallion was far superior to Morgan's black, however. I tried to purchase him, only the owner refused to sell. I was most upset. He would have been the perfect stud for my own stables."

"How terrible for you," Kathleen said absently. She trailed her finger down the stem of her wineglass and counted the diamonds on Sarita's necklace. Thirteen. Unlucky number, she thought with a smile.

"Yes, it was terrible. I am most pleased, however, with the three hunters I did buy from him. One won the field at a meet in England outside London, a gelding called Black Merrow."

Kathleen's heart stopped. She had trained Black Merrow. He was out of Black Margaret by Taran and had been sold in February of that year to a man from

Morocco, a man named Quint Cathcart. The room began to spin around her, and she almost spilled her wine. She closed her eyes and forced herself to breathe deeply.

"What a strange name," Sarita said.

"Merrow is the name of the fairy folk that live beneath the sea off the coast of Ireland," Kathleen said, her voice sounding surprisingly normal. She opened her eyes. The room had stopped spinning, the wine was steady in the glass.

"How interesting," Quint said. "I had wondered what the name meant."

Kathleen's mouth was dry as old moss, her tongue wooden. She was almost exhausted from trying not to react visibly to this miracle that had come along just when she had begun to believe there was no such thing. She allowed herself to look at Quint. He was smiling at her, his thin lips looking most unnatural in that pose.

Dinner was announced, and Kathleen automatically put her hand on Kade's arm, moving across the floor as though in a dream. She was extremely grateful for the times she had done this since coming to Mistral. She was no longer confused by the elaborate settings of silver and china on the table, no longer amazed by the great quantities of food and servants that appeared, even if only she and Kade were dining. He handed her into her chair, his hand lingering for a moment on her arm before going around the table to assist Sarita. The cool gray eyes swept over him in a blatant invitation that almost broke through the hazy edges of Kathleen's excitement.

After everyone was seated and the first course of turtle soup had been served, Sarita turned to Quint. "Tell me more about this Black Marlin of yours, darling."

Quint wiped the corner of his mouth with his napkin

352

and smiled indulgently at her. "Merrow, not Marlin."

Kathleen laid her spoon down, afraid if she did not it would clatter against the bowl and betray her. "I am very interested in horses, Mr. Cathcart, especially hunters. Do you recall the seller?"

"That I do, a bandy-legged fellow as stubborn as an Irish donkey."

"A breed I am familiar with," Kade said, and Kathleen glanced at him. His eyes held hers for a moment, as though warning her not to say anything that might betray her situation. Sarita asked him a question in a voice scarcely louder than a whisper, and he was forced to lean closer to her in order to hear what she said. Kathleen took advantage of the distraction to chance another question, one that would sound innocent if overheard.

"Have you purchased any other horses recently, Mr. Cathcart?"

"I have been in contact with the same man who sold me Black Merrow. Apparently, he had suffered some misfortune and had no horses to sell. He expressed hope that he would soon regain that which he lost and I volunteered to assist him in any way possible, an offer he accepted."

Kathleen could scarcely speak when a servant asked if she was finished with her soup. The main dinner was served, a young pig, roasted with an apple in its open mouth. There were also the crabs she had gathered in the mangroves and a platter of poached fish that was part of a giant grouper Kade had speared near the reef that morning. There were fresh-baked bread and fruit muffins, candied yams with flaked coconut, peas and tiny onions cooked in a rich butter sauce, cheesed potatoes and pickled bird eggs.

Though Kathleen ate everything Kade put on her plate, she tasted none of it, not even the pineapple tart served with thick cream and blueberries. She was far too excited as she tried to think of a way she could talk to Quint alone.

Her chance came after dinner. In response to Sarita's question, Kade launched into a lengthy explanation of Mistral's damage from the hurricane. To Kathleen, he seemed a bit too eager to answer the question, just as he had been a bit too eager to listen to Sarita's idle chatter at dinner.

Kade began to explain his plans to clean out the well behind the stable and rebuild the warehouses near the harbor, and Quint asked Kathleen to accompany him outside for some fresh air. Once they were well away from the house, she stopped and looked back at the light spilling through the glass doors into the darkness of the tropical night.

"How is my father?" she asked.

"Eager for you to come home. How closely are you watched?"

"Not at all. My time is my own, except at night. I took a sloop once and tried to escape; now all the boats are guarded during the day. What will you do about Kade? He will come after me."

"Do not worry about that, my dear. I will arrange everything. All you have to do is be ready to slip away in the morning. The sooner we leave, the better."

"I will be ready."

The stars looked so much brighter than usual. They were so close Kathleen imagined she could almost touch them. She was going home, home to Taran and to Father and to Ireland. It was unreal and it was wonderful.

Kade and Sarita came out of the house, her hand on his arm. She was looking at him with those cool gray eyes, talking to him in that honeyed voice. Kathleen's stomach knotted up and she tore her eyes from them, looking instead at the ground beside her where roses had once bloomed.

By this time tomorrow I will be on my way home and, with any luck at all, I will never see Kade Morgan again. What does it matter how much attention he is paying that woman?

But it did matter. It mattered greatly, just as she had confessed to Jake that afternoon. She knew she would never forget Kade, never forget his kisses or the way his touch created music in her heart. She would always remember the ecstasy she had discovered within the circle of his arms, within the warmth of his smile.

She had only one night left to love him, only one night left to taste the sweat of his brow as it fell onto her lips, only one night to feel him inside her body, possessing her as no other man ever would. Only one night that mattered in the whole rest of Kathleen's life.

With a lift of her chin and a firm resolve in her heart, she laid her hand on Quint's arm. "We should go back now," she told him.

When they passed Kade and Sarita, Kathleen purposely let her laughter ripple a little longer and a little louder. She kept her eyes on Quint's face, looking at him as though he were the most interesting person she had ever met.

When the burning touch of Kade's gaze fell on her, she tossed her head slightly, letting the waterfall of curls move across the top of her breast and tangle in the lace there. The heat of Kade's thoughts reached out to her, and she could taste his scorching desire on the cool ocean breeze. A quiver of excitement moved over her.

By the time Kade had steered Sarita back into the house, Kathleen had refilled her wineglass. She lifted the sparkling crystal to her lips and met Kade's eyes across the top of the glass. The wine wove marsh-fairy fire throughout her body as she watched the raging desire in her lover's eyes grow hotter. She wet her lips with the tip of her tongue and touched the opal between her breasts with a finger that had only moments before been suggestively toying with the stem of her glass.

She sat on the sofa, and when Quint sat beside her, she gave him her full attention, looking trustingly up into his pointed, pale face, smiling with wonder at the cleverness of his words as he expounded on subjects as boring as himself. She concentrated on flirting, laughing and blushing at the things he said, things that did not deserve any of those reactions. And always she felt the touch of Kade's eyes, felt the heat of his existence, felt the hot moistness between her legs as she anticipated the night ahead.

Kathleen finished her wine and offered her apology for the sudden sleepiness that had come over her, forcing her to retire early. She had purposely not looked at Kade for the last half hour. Now she met his intense gaze as she glided across the terra-cotta floor to slip her tiny hand in his big one.

"I will be waiting for you in your room, master," she whispered, her voice throaty and low. The black of his eyes grew darker, causing the place between her legs to become even wetter. She climbed the steps and slipped into the darkness of the royal blue bedroom.

Chapter 27

Kade held his breath as he pushed open the door to his bedroom. Cathcart had kept him talking for almost an hour, long after both Kathleen and Sarita retired. He had responded to the man's questions with one-word replies, plying him with enough brandy to sink a ship. Finally he had switched to whiskey. Quint had immediately passed out. Kade had carried him upstairs, leaving him to the ministrations of his manservant. And now the night was his. His and Kathleen's.

The bedroom was dark. He closed the door behind him, and a light burst into creation across the room. Kathleen touched the flame to the candle, then straightened and turned to Kade. She was still dressed, her hair confined by the ebony combs. Kade leaned against the wall and took in the sight before him. The candlelight flickered uncertainly, casting shadows across the smooth planes of her face, the silk of her hair.

He was mesmerized by her beauty, by her very presence. She lifted her hands to her shoulders, and with a slight movement of her fingers the bodice of her gown slipped down across her breasts. Kade realized she had unbuttoned it while waiting for him, somehow knowing what he wanted. His fantasy was about to come true. His throat ached, his body tensed.

The black velvet drifted down to her waist, then over her hips, falling to the floor like a piece of midnight sky. Her skin glowed beneath the soft caress of the candlelight, her breasts rose and fell beneath the whisper of chemise she wore. The light filtered through the sheer silk, outlining the lush curves of her supple body.

The chemise ended just above the lace of her garters, and never before had Kade felt such an appreciation of black stockings. Kathleen slowly lifted her arms, pulling the combs from her hair so its darkness tumbled across her shoulders and over her breasts. The ends curled around her hips, and a fist twisted in Kade's stomach, a fist of longing and need. He moved closer to her and she dropped her hands to her legs, lifting the bottom of the chemise as though to remove it. He stopped her with a gesture, and she let the silk fall back onto the tops of her thighs.

He was near enough to hear her breathing, to see the delicate shadows of her eyelashes, to smell the freshness of her skin and the musk of her desire. He reached out and picked up handfuls of her hair, the heavy silk of it twisting around his fingers as he pulled her closer to him. He released it slowly, letting it stream down the front of her body.

The ribbon on her chemise was smooth beneath his fingers. He untied it, pulling it gently so it slowly released its bondage on Kathleen's flesh. The silk moved like an unspoken thought as it fell from her breasts. Kade caught his breath as her nipples hardened beneath the touch of the soft fabric. Candlelight moved across the ivory of her throat, glistening on the opal and diamonds that rested between her breasts. Kade forced himself to stay within the bounds of the fantasy, moving slowly so the

358

pleasure would last forever, not just a moment.

The ribbon continued to give beneath the pressure of his fingers until the chemise was completely open. He stepped back from Kathleen and watched as the black silk slid from her. Her hands moved up her bare thighs, over her lovely hips and onto her stomach. Then they moved higher.

When her hands were just beneath her breasts, she hesitated. Kade could not breathe. She reached for him, sliding her hands beneath his jacket, pulling it from his shoulders. He shrugged out of it, tossing it aside. She opened his vest, and it soon joined the jacket on the floor. She unfastened his collar, then unbuttoned his shirt. Each button received intimate attention, her fingers trailing slowly down his shirt until she came to the next one.

Kade did not move as she slipped the shirt from his shoulders, trapping his arms in the confines of material. Her lips pressed against the center of his chest, sending chills over his body. Her tongue rippled through the hair surrounding his sensitive nipples, her teeth lightly touching his eager flesh. The tips of her breasts brushed against him, and a shiver of excitement raced up his spine. Kathleen smiled up at him and moved her hands to the front of his straining pants.

He closed his hands and forced himself to stand still as she kneeled and pushed her mouth against the front of his breeches, her warm breath blowing through the fabric to brand his swollen manhood with her presence. Her hands moved over his buttocks and down his legs, then onto the black boots he wore, which came up over his knee.

She looked up, up into the black of Kade's eyes and the raging heat of his desire. Her entire body was on fire. The excitement of undressing for Kade, the intoxicating effect of him untying her chemise, the seething promise of what was to come; she could not wait any longer, not even long enough to undress him.

"Take me now," she whispered.

He unfastened the front of his pants, then lifted her and carried her to his bed. He laid her on the blue spread, the candlelight picking out the blue from her eyes and opals. His lips covered hers in a searching, possessive kiss.

Kathleen was consumed by the white heat of their flaming passion. His body pressed her into his bed, and she thrilled to the sensual touch of the satin spread. She moaned in abandoned ecstasy as Kade's hands moved up the sides of her body, creating tremors of pleasure.

He trailed kisses and caresses around her nipples, his hair falling onto her breasts. She ran her hands beneath his shirt, holding him tightly as the world within her spun and tilted and soared. His teeth raked across her tender flesh, bringing new waves of intense pleasure. She writhed against the hard push of his desire, excited by the fabric of his pants, the leather of his boots, the metal buckle on his belt. She dragged at his shirt until the tight muscles in his arms were exposed.

Kade ran his tongue along the crease of flesh beneath Kathleen's breasts. His teeth explored her waist, his tongue slipped into her navel. She seized his shoulders, forcing him back to her breasts.

"More, please more," she moaned and felt him smile against her skin.

He flicked the tip of a nipple with his tongue, and she almost died as his teeth touched her breast. He tantalized her, tortured her, took her ever higher with his teeth and tongue. After a million years of waiting, he pulled the nipple into his mouth and sucked on it, causing her to writhe in pleasure.

His hand slid down the side of her body, down the length of her leg, then back up along her silk stocking.

His fingers moved to the inside of her thigh, and then they pressed against her intimately. Kade smothered her cries with his lips, kissing her with savage intensity. He moved his leg between hers, rubbing his boot-covered knee against her.

"Kade!" she screamed against his lips and he raised up to watch the emotion on her face.

She arched against him, her hands dragging at his shoulders, tearing at his shirt. His dark head lowered again, his lips on her throat. She grasped his nipples between her fingers, massaging them in time to the movement of his knee against the fiery core of her soul. When she maneuvered her head down to draw his nipple into her mouth, he moaned and his body went rigid. He pulled his knee from between her legs and rolled off her.

"No, come back!" she cried.

"I want to feel you against my flesh, to know everything I touch is you," he said, his voice deep and vibrating as he stripped off his shirt and pants, jerked off his boots. He stood over Kathleen, his eyes raking over her flesh, over the silk of her stockings, then back to the nest of damp curls that beckoned his touch.

She could not stop staring at him. The candlelight flooded across his body, showing the strength and power of him. Her hand touched his chest, traced down through the hair that tapered across his abdomen then flared into a dark mat surrounding his penis. His erection was full and hard, rising proudly in front of him. Kathleen wrapped her hand around it, her eyes on his face.

"Come to me," she whispered, "come to me, my love."

As his body lowered onto her waiting flesh, she remembered this was her last night with him. She bit her lip to stop the tears that sprang to her eyes.

"Are those tears I see?" he asked, touching her face tenderly.

"Love me, Kade, please love me," she breathed.

He penetrated into the hot depths of her body, filling her with his throbbing presence. His lips touched hers for a brief moment; then he straightened his arms and rose above her.

His sweat glistened golden in the candlelight, and his hair fell across his forehead as he moved within her. She brushed it back, ran her hand across his face, down his neck and chest, memorizing him with her touch.

He moved his knees outside her legs so the tops of her thighs pressed tightly against him and put delicious pressure on her with each movement of his hips. He increased the speed of his thrusts.

The darkness swept over Kathleen with the driving fury of a thunderstorm. "Kade!" she screamed as she climaxed, the pulsing pleasure flooding through her. She held him to her as the waves of darkness crashed over her. Kade rode the waves of her body's pleasure, shuddering as he came.

He rolled to the side, pulling her on top of him. She raised her head, her hair falling across his chest as she traced his lips with a hesitant finger. He captured it in his mouth, sucking on it gently. Her teeth tugged on his earlobe, her warm breath exciting him.

"Are you trying to seduce me again so soon?" he asked.

She slid down beside him and laid her head against his shoulder. "I can never get close enough to you. It is as though there is a barrier between us, even when we are together like now."

"We have the rest of the night to find a way to remove that barrier, the rest of the night to be close," he whispered into her ear, his tongue swirling into her.

"Aye, my love, that we do."

The satin spread was cool and exciting under their naked bodies. Kathleen ran her leg up the side of Kade's body, loving the feel of him beside her. When her knee reached his hip, he put his hand on her leg and caressed its silken length. His body ached to take her again, and his heart swelled as he remembered her calling him "my love." If only it were more than a whispered endearment between lovers, if only she really loved him.

"I like these stockings," he said and rolled her onto her back, lifting her legs and wrapping them around his neck. He slowly pushed himself into her, filling her inch by inch and watching the rapture on her face. When he was completely enclosed within the hot velvet of her, he ran his hands over her legs again, his head turning to press a kiss to the silken length of those shapely thighs.

He moved within her, and Kathleen's body responded. She touched the sides of his body, trailing light fingers across his straining muscles. He threw his head back and closed his eyes, lost in the pleasure of her touch. The candlelight played across his face, and she drew him down to her, her supple body bending double as their lips touched in a kiss so savage and demanding Kathleen thought she would die from wanting more.

With a final driving thrust, Kade exploded inside Kathleen, taking her with him up the towering heights of his climax. Her legs slipped from his shoulders. She buried her face against his neck, afraid he would see the tears that were again flooding into her eyes. She loved this man, she needed him. And tomorrow morning she would leave him. She cried in silence, her tears mingling with the salt of his sweat.

The next day dawned bright and beautiful, the sky was blue as blue could possibly be, the ocean stretching away from the shore in layered shades of green and aqua, blue and violet. The clouds were swans that sailed the sea of the sky, the island a sparkling jewel matched only by the beauty of the woman sleeping in Kade's bedroom.

Kade walked across the ravaged garden to the harbor, thinking about last night. He could not live without Kathleen, could not face the future knowing she might someday disappear from him again. He would marry her, bind her to him forever. Then he would always be able to look into those swirling blue-green eyes, taste those soft lips, hear that husky voice call his name as he rode her and her passion to the heights of ecstasy.

He heard footsteps behind him and stopped, hoping it was Kathleen. It was a man, someone Kade did not know. He was a big man, with muscular arms and brawny build. Since he was dressed like a field laborer, Kade assumed he was one of the new workers Bog had hired in Martinique.

"Cap'n Morgan!" the man gasped. "I came from the other side of the island, there be trouble in the fields."

"What kind of trouble?"

"Big trouble, some workers don't like the new foreman. You'd better come, Cap'n Daniels sent me for you."

"Where is he?"

"Near the warehouses where the tobacco is cured."

"We will cut through the banana groves, that will take us around behind the trouble." Kade ran to the stable, the big man laboring to keep up.

"What is your name?" Kade asked as he saddled Casson, a bay gelding he had been riding ever since the hurricane.

"Waters, Cap'n."

"Did you run all the way here from the fields, Waters?"

"Aye, that I done. Cap'n Daniels said to hurry."

"There will be a bonus in this for you, Waters." Kade swung onto Casson's back just as Sam led out a white mare for Waters. They galloped across the clearing and into the jungle. Waters jostled around in his saddle like a sack of feed.

"You ever been on a horse before?" Kade asked.

"Can't say that I have, Cap'n. Don't ever want to again, either."

As they neared the end of the banana groves, Kade began to wonder why Bog Daniels had workers in these fields. It had been agreed to start the new plantings behind the village first. They crossed over the stream and rode past the two tobacco warehouses. The fields were empty, leveled all the way to the sea. No sign of workers, no sign of trouble.

Waters was new; maybe he had given the wrong location. Intending to ask him for more details about the area of the trouble, Kade turned in time to see the handle of a pistol swing through the air toward him. It landed with a sickening crunch on the side of his head. Blood spurted across his face as his body went limp. He fell from the back of the bay gelding, hitting the ground with a sound that reminded him of bones breaking. My bones, he thought.

Waters climbed off his horse and landed a solid kick to Kade's rib cage. He was unable to defend himself, the pain in his head so intense he could not overcome it to fight back. He could only lie there in a daze as the boot crunched into his body repeatedly. Pain racked him, blood blinded him. His mind filled with emptiness and his body went limp as he passed out.

Chapter 28

Kade lifted his head and winced as the pain throbbed anew, like a cannon exploding inside his skull. He was on the edge of the mangroves beside the hurricane-ravaged tobacco fields, lying half in and half out of a stagnant pool of mud and water. And not ten feet from him was a submerged log whose unblinking eyes were fixed on Kade.

"Crocodile," he muttered aloud, and the cannon shot off another round. He struggled to his feet, and the log instantly turned into a fast-moving creature whose cavernous jaws opened to giant heights, closing on where Kade's foot had been only moments before. The snapping teeth encouraged Kade to move faster as he staggered out of the mud.

Because of the pain in Kade's head, the crocodile was moving faster than he was. By the time he reached a pile of limestone boulders on the edge of the fields, the crocodile was only inches from the back of his leg. He scrambled up the boulders at breakneck speed and was still there an hour later when the crocodile gave up the hunt, moving back to the mangroves to stalk other prey.

It had been early morning when Waters had lured Kade away from the main house. It was almost sunset now. His head throbbed beneath his exploratory

366

touch. The gash on his temple was caked with blood and mud. The skin was laid open, and he knew if he probed deep enough, he would feel the raw bone of his skull. His body was bruised from the kicking Waters had given him. There were several cracked ribs, and his left shoulder was broken.

The reason for the attack eluded him. No matter how hard he tried to place Waters' face, he was positive he had never seen the man before. Maybe he was somebody new from Flesher's crew; certainly Ivan had reason to want Morgan dead. He had ordered Flesher to clear his gear from the captain's quarters of the *Christabel* in preparation for the new master coming aboard. Kade had already decided to appoint the first mate of the *Gypsy Lady,* Simon Barry, as the new captain of the *Christabel.*

Kade touched his head gingerly. He had known Flesher was angry about his dismissal; now he knew just how angry. He went along the stream until the mud of the mangroves was out of sight, then knelt to wash his face and take a long drink. Then he started to walk, heading down the road to the livestock barn. It would be a shorter distance to cross back through the banana groves. That involved an uphill climb, though, a climb Kade was not capable of making. He trudged through the dust and heat, cursing Ivan Flesher, cursing the man Waters, and cursing his own stupidity for not noticing that Waters kept calling him Captain, not boss like the plantation workers.

The sunset was beautiful, rose and crimson light staining the entire sky and wrapping the island in a peaceful glow that did nothing to lessen the heat. Mosquitoes buzzed in Kade's ears, and his boots wore blisters on his heels. He was about to cross the stream above the mudflats when Bog Daniels rode up on Glory, leading Casson behind him.

"Looks like someone tried to kill you," Bog said as Kade dragged himself into the saddle.

"Almost made it, too. I got a report this morning there was trouble in the fields and you needed help. When I got there, the only trouble was what was riding with me, a man named Waters. I thought he was one of the new workers you had hired. He knocked me on the head with his pistol, must have thought shooting me would make too much noise. I came around within eating distance of a crocodile." He groaned as the bay gelding's stride ground his shoulder against his body. "Did Casson go back to the stable?"

"He wandered in about three hours ago. Sam sent for me immediately, said the last time he saw you was early this morning when you and another man rode off to the plantation. He saw the other man near the harbor just before the *Christabel* sailed."

"So I was right, Ivan was behind this."

"Quint Cathcart is also gone. And so is Kathleen."

Kade almost gave into the pain racking his body. He remembered the way Ivan Flesher had been looking at Kathleen, and his stomach turned over. "What about Sarita?" he asked finally.

"She is still here, smiling like a cat that just swallowed the pet bird. When Jake and I tried to question her, she refused to talk to anyone except you."

They rode the rest of the way in silence, Bog taking both horses to the stables while Kade went into the house. He brushed aside Mattie's frantic wailing about his injuries and made his way to Sarita's room. His head was swimming when he reached it. He pushed open the door without knocking, surprising Sarita just as she was about to slap her maid. The young girl's face was already red with the mark of Sarita's hand, and Kade jerked the girl out of the way before she could be struck again.

"What do you mean, striking this child like that?" The maid cowered at the end of Kade's arm, her nose and eyes running. He picked up a lace handkerchief from the dresser and thrust it into her hand. "Clean yourself up," he said and pushed her out the door, closing it behind her.

"Explain yourself, Sarita." He needed to sit down or lean against something. He stood straighter and glared at the woman before him.

"You are hurt, darling! What happened?"

"Someone tried to kill me. You would not know anything about that, would you?" He grabbed her arm, crushing her soft flesh beneath his mud-caked fingers.

"You are hurting me, Kade, let go!"

"After you tell me what I want to hear!" He shook her roughly and tightened his grip on her arm. "Tell me about Quint and Flesher leaving, and why you did not go with them."

"I didn't know they would try to kill you, only that you were to be distracted until they could get away from Mistral."

"What about Kathleen?"

"Forget her, darling! She is just a child, I can give you so much more, anything you want. You should have seen how eager she was to leave, she doesn't love you like I do."

"Kathleen went *willingly?*"

Kade released Sarita so suddenly she fell back onto the bed behind her. He wrenched open the door and went to Kathleen's room. The crystal bowl beside the bed was empty; her shells and the pearls were gone, proving what Sarita said.

Kade sank into the rocking chair. Kathleen had loved him with fire and fury the night before, then sailed away and left him for crocodile bait. And to think he had planned to marry her. Now all he wanted to do was murder her.

Sarita entered the room and sank to the floor in front of him. "Listen to me, darling," she said. "I did not know they were going to hurt you, Quint only said that you would not be able to follow them. He told me all about Kathleen belonging to him, how you had stolen her from him. Let her go, you don't need her. We don't need her." She laid her head on his knee.

"What did you mean, she belonged to Quint?" Kade said, grasping Sarita's shoulders and forcing her to look at him.

"That is what he told me, that she was his and he came here to get her back. He said if I helped divert you last night at dinner so he could talk to her, he would leave me here to comfort you. Let me do that, Kade, let me show you how much I need you, how much I love you."

"Did you really think I would come crawling to you? I want you on the next ship leaving Mistral. Until then, stay away from me!"

He shoved her toward the door, and she ran from the room, her face streaked with tears. Kade scarcely noticed. He began to pace, thinking about Rat Anders. Right after Kade realized what a precious jewel Kathleen was, he had wondered why Anders had not sold her into a harem, deciding the man was too stupid to know what he had. Why had he believed that Anders was smart enough to contact Kathleen's father for ransom, to take her locket and have her write a letter confirming she was alive?

Someone else must have been behind the whole thing, from arranging the pirate attack to holding Kathleen hostage. Everything fit except for her being sold, which must have been an act of rebellion on Rat's part against his employer, who had to have been someone in Morocco, someone who wanted something

370

he could not buy. Like the most magnificent stallion he had ever seen, the perfect stud for his stables.

Kade ran down the steps to the living room. Just as Kade went into the study, Bog came in the house.

"Get anything out of Sarita?" he asked.

"Quint claims that Kathleen belongs to him and he came here to get her back. I think he was responsible for Kathleen's capture and Rat Anders was merely her keeper. For some reason, Anders decided to sell her behind Quint's back, which prevented Quint from collecting the ransom he wanted."

"Why would a man as rich as Quint want to hold someone for ransom?"

"It was not money he asked for, it was a stallion belonging to Kathleen named Taran. She once told me that although Demon was a magnificent horse, he would pale beside Taran. And last night Quint talked about seeing a stallion superior to Demon that he wanted to buy, only the owner would not sell. He said that the stallion would have been the perfect stud for his stables, and you know how obsessed Quint is with making his stables unbeatable. I can imagine how angry he was when he could not purchase the stallion he wanted. Then Quint said he had been back in contact with the owner, who had lost everything due to misfortune. Quint mentioned helping the man regain that which he had lost."

"Quint Cathcart volunteer to help someone, much less someone who refused him something he wanted? Doesn't sound like our Quint," Bog said.

Kade was piling charts on the desk, the ones of Ireland that Kathleen had tied with a red ribbon. "I think he demanded that Kathleen be exchanged for the stallion and her father agreed. If so, Quint is taking her to Ireland now on the *Christabel.*"

"And you are going after her?"

"Damn right I am going after her!" Kade whirled around so fast he almost fell as his head objected to the sudden movement. He grasped the edge of his desk and collapsed into his chair.

"Ye are not goin' anywhere 'til Dr. Williams gets a look at ye," Jake said as he came into the study, carrying a bowl of water and towels. "That gash on yer 'ead can't be ignored."

"I do not need a doctor, I need a ship. Is the *Gypsy Lady* ready to sail?"

"It will be some time before ye can go off on 'er, lad."

Kade shot up from his chair. "That is my ship—"

"Don't start listin' reasons wi' me," Jake said, interrupting Kade. "The *Gypsy Lady* suffered some damage last night. The rope runnin' from the wheel to the rudder was cut. All the fishin' sloops had mischief done to 'em, too. Some be sunk, others stove in. Looks like Flesher's men 'ad a busy night." He pushed Kade back into the chair.

"Watch it, Jake!" Kade cried, holding his shoulder and scowling at the Scotsman. "The steering rope is not the only thing broken around here."

Bog sagged against the wall and shook his head in despair. "Steering ropes take time to fix. It will be several days before you can follow Kathleen."

"By that time the *Gypsy Lady* will never be able to catch the *Christabel*. I need the *Black Eagle* and I need her now." Kade winced as Jake cleaned the mud and blood from his head wound. "The mast should have been replaced by now and her hull scraped clean."

"And 'ow do ye plan on gettin' 'er? Martinique be a long swim from 'ere."

"I will go by canoe. The natives use them to travel between islands, I can do the same."

"Think this through, Kade," Bog said. "Even if you manage to make it to Martinique alive, you will need a crew for the *Eagle,* men who know the ship and her

372

master. Wait until the *Gypsy Lady* is fixed; then you can take her and your regular crew to Martinique."

"I cannot wait that long, they have Kathleen."

"They don't want Kathleen dead, Kade, Quint needs her alive to exchange for the stallion."

"There is a lot they can do to her without killing her, Bog. She could not bear that being done to her."

"She could not bear it, or you could not bear it?"

Kade slumped in the chair. "Both."

"I will get to work on replacing that steering rope. You get your head stitched up." Bog greeted Dr. Williams as he came into the study, then left for the harbor.

"What else be wrong wi' ye, lad?" Jake asked, a concerned frown on his face as he took in Kade's blanched appearance. "I never seen ye slump like that before."

Williams dumped his medical bag in the center of Kade's maps. "It looks like he has been severely beaten."

"Kathleen was right," Kade said. "Your ability to immediately grasp an obvious situation is amazing. What was it that gave it away, the gash in my skull? Or maybe the cracked ribs and smashed shoulder?"

"No need to be sarcastic with me, Captain Morgan," Williams said as he probed the depths of the wound on Kade's head. "Save your anger for whoever it was that tried to kill you. I overheard your plans to chase after the Irish girl. You will have to delay them by at least two weeks because of your injuries."

"I will delay them by two hours, not two weeks. After you sew up my head, I am going across the island to get that steering rope replaced. By this time tomorrow I want to be on my way to Martinique."

It was two days before the repairs on the steering

ropes were completed. The damage had been extensive, and the entire length had to be rethreaded through the rudder. Sunset on the third day saw the *Gypsy Lady* ready. Kade paced the stern deck while Jake talked to Mattie on the shore. Finally the Scotsman boarded the longboat and rowed out to the ship.

"About time," Kade growled. He whirled on Bog Daniels. "Are you planning on taking this brig out or do I have to assume command?"

"We are leaving now. All hands up anchor! Ready there forward? Heave away!"

The first mate of the *Gypsy Lady* and intended captain of the *Christabel,* Simon Barry, was on the bow of the *Gypsy Lady.* He raised his arm and signaled to Bog. "Anchor's apeak, sir!"

"See to your mainsail, Mr. Barry," Bog called out. The men were ready along the topsail yards, standing upright in the breeze that rocked the *Gypsy Lady.*

"Let fall!" the first mate cried out, and the sail dropped, filling instantly with wind and sounding like the discharge of a cannon. Simon moved along the rail, checking lines and directing men. As he reached the stern of the vessel, the mainsail bellied out like a pregnant peasant and began pushing the *Gypsy Lady* through the dark sea.

"Sheet home, Captain Daniels," he told Bog.

"Excellent, Mr. Barry. I shall miss your efficiency as my first mate, but wish you luck on your command of the *Christabel.* Take the helm, please."

Bog stepped away from the wheel and Simon grasped it confidently, his eyes on the crew as they continued lowering sails at the command of the second mate.

Kade stood at the port railing. Bog joined him as the ship heeled over in the breeze, her empty hold making her light and responsive. Stars appeared among the rigging, and the moon was a crescent in the sky.

"Have you decided which route you will take, Kade?" Bog asked.

"I will follow the shipping lanes past Bermuda."

"And when you find her?"

"The *Christabel* mounts fewer guns than the *Eagle*. Flesher would be a fool to fight and I want to avoid provoking him into a skirmish. I plan to take her at night, using the black sails and flag."

"Yer gonna 'oist the Morgan Promise?" Jake asked, referring to the pirate flag the *Black Eagle* had sailed under. It was a black flag emblazoned with a sword thrust through the eye socket of a silver skull, the tip of the sword dripping with crimson blood.

"Aye, Jake."

"And what then?"

"I will reclaim that which is mine."

"Will ye take 'er 'ome?"

"Mistral is her home now."

"Me and Mattie, we'll be goin' back to Scotland after this trip, Kade. We'll not be party to yer plans for enslavin' the lass any longer."

Kade showed no reaction to Jake's remark. "I will not stand in your way, nor will I submit to blackmail. Kathleen belongs to me. Her place is on Mistral, not Ireland."

"I. 'ad thought Stewart Morgan was the most stubborn, 'ard'eaded man I'd e'er be meetin', but I be wrong. 'Tis 'is son that claims that title. Ye want to stifle that lassie's love, choke it to death like yer father choked Annaliss."

"Mother killed herself," Kade said, the words grinding out past his clenched teeth. His hands were gripping the railing, his knuckles white, the muscles in his arms taut and rigid.

"A woman can't be livin' on naught 'cept morsels of

love tossed to 'er like crumbs to a beggar, and that was all Stewart gave yer mother. While ye was away at school, 'e accused Annaliss of cheatin' on 'im. He treated her bad, Kade. When she recovered, she tried to leave 'im. He caught her and brought 'er back, lockin' 'er in 'er room wi' no 'uman contact, not even Mattie. A year later when ye were due 'ome from that school in England, Stewart let Annaliss out the day ye arrived, only he didn't tell 'er ye were comin' and she went direct to the kitchen and drank the poison."

"You are lying, Jake, just like you lied when you told me that same story seventeen years ago."

"Nay, lad, it be the truth, and ye knew it were or else ye would not 'ave run from yer father like ye done. Ye knew what 'appened was not yer mother's fault, ye knew it was yer father's 'ard'eaded ways what drove 'er to kill 'erself, not bein' able to tell the woman 'e loved 'ow 'e felt, thinkin' it made 'im less of a man. He thought 'e couldn't 'old onto Annaliss unless 'e kept 'er behind a locked door, just like ye are 'olding onto Kathleen by lockin' 'er away on Mistral. Ye expect 'er to love ye yet don't give 'er anything of yerself in return."

"I gave her more than I have ever given any woman."

"Did ye tell 'er ye love 'er?"

"I showed her in every way I could and she left me twice."

"Showed 'er? By keepin' 'er a slave, by not lettin' 'er go 'ome? Yer a fool, boy, a damn fool. Tell the girl ye love 'er, it'll no' make ye less of a man. It'll make ye more of one." Jake reached into his pocket and pulled out a folded sheet of paper. "Kathleen left this when she went wi' Cathcart. Read it, Kade, read it and know that it was ye what drove the lass away, just like Stewart drove Annaliss to drink that poison. It's time ye let the past rest, Kade, time to let all the old pain die before ye lose that girl."

Kade clutched the letter in his hand, his knuckles white as he stared at the creamy paper. Why had Jake not told him earlier that Kathleen left a letter for him? When he opened it, he knew why. It was addressed to Jake, not to him.

Jake,

By the time you read this I will be gone, Quint Cathcart is taking me home.

You were right, I am in love with Kade. But I also love my father and could never abandon him, not even if there was a chance that someday Kade might love me just a little.

Please know that it hurts terribly to leave, almost as much as it would hurt to stay.

Kathleen

Kade leaned back against the rail and let the wind stream unchecked onto his burning face. She loved him. The only thing he had ever wanted in life was her love, and he had been too blind to see it was already his.

"Too blind and too stupid," he said. "Please God, help me find her. I love her so much, please let her be all right."

Three weeks later, Kade stood on the deck of the *Black Eagle,* his shirt open to the waist, the wind blowing it tight against his chest. On the top of the mizzenmast the flag known in every ocean and every sea as Morgan's Promise curled in the breeze. The crimson blood on the sword caught the moonlight for a moment, drawing Kade's attention as he checked the set of the sails.

"You have the helm, Mr. McBradden," Kade told

Jake as he went to his cabin. He strapped on his sword, pushed two loaded pistols into his belt, and thrust the jewel-handled dagger into the top of his right boot and a smaller knife in the left one. His boots extended up past his knees, allowing him easy access to the weapons they carried.

On his desk lay the letter in which Kathleen had confessed her love for him. Kade opened it, his heart beating faster as her words swam across the page. He put the letter down and adjusted his sword so it hung low on his left hip before going back on deck.

The night air was cold, sending a chill across his skin. Good fighting weather, he thought, makes the sweat dry quickly, keeps the muscles tight and ready. The crew was gathered near the mainmast. They were dressed in black, as was Kade. He tied a scarf around his upper right arm that echoed the colors of the Morgan Promise, then stepped forward to address the crew.

"Gentlemen. Our adversary is less than an hour ahead of us. Try to avoid bloodshed where possible but understand this: I will not accept less than total surrender from every man on board. Remember that Kathleen O'Connor is on the *Christabel* and our first concern is her safety. Protect her with your own life if necessary."

Some of the men clutched their cutlasses tighter, those who had befriended Kathleen during her stay on the *Black Eagle*. Kade turned to Skinner, his chief gunner.

"Take your gunnery crew and charge your cannon. If Flesher fires on the *Eagle,* wait for Jake's orders and then hit the *Christabel* below the waterline. Place your shots so we will have time to transfer her crew to the *Eagle.*"

"Aye, Cap'n, I'll stand ready." Skinner gave orders

to his men, and they headed below deck to prepare the cannons.

"Michael, you go with Skinner," Kade said, laying a hand on the boy's shoulder and pulling him away from the rest of the crew.

"I wanna fight," Michael said, brandishing a cutlass almost as long as he was tall.

"Are you questioning my orders, Mr. Lennox?"

Michael straightened, his face glowing with importance at Kade's use of his surname. "No sir, Cap'n Morgan."

"Then I suggest you go below. You have been promoted to gunnery mate, a craft you will learn while attending to your normal duties. Your training is to begin immediately."

"Aye, aye, sir!" Michael cried, tripping over his own feet in his effort to join Skinner as quickly as possible.

"That should keep the boy out of trouble," Jake said.

"Exactly," Kade replied. He turned to Simon Barry. "Mr. Barry, if we are able to approach the *Christabel* without an alarm being raised, I want you and Mr. Grimstead to take out the watch. After that you will see that the helm is protected from sabotage and stand ready to assume command once I have secured the vessel. Dr. Williams, pick an assistant from the crew and establish your station on the stern of the *Black Eagle*. Any man who feigns an injury to avoid fighting is to be shot."

"I am a doctor, Captain Morgan, not an executioner."

Kade narrowed his eyes and clutched the hilt of his sword. "If you allow even one capable man to stand away from the fight, I will hang you from the yardarm and personally stripe your back with my whip! For every man that runs from a fight, three die because they did not have the benefit of their companion's presence beside them."

"I will not shoot a man seeking asylum from death."

"Mr. Barry!" Kade said. "Throw the doctor overboard, we no longer have need of his services."

"Aye, Captain." Simon grabbed Williams and dragged him to the rail."

"Stop, stop I say!" Williams cried.

"Shut him up," Kade ordered.

Simon pressed a knife against Williams' neck. "Another word and I will open your throat, Doctor. Since your job is to save lives, you should start with your own."

"I will not be a party to murder."

"By saving one, you might kill three. Would you rather be a party to that?"

Williams stood stiff in Simon's grasp; then his shoulders slumped in defeat. "I will do as ordered."

Simon released him and pressed a pistol into Williams' hand. "Take your station, doctor." Williams mopped at his brow with a handkerchief before scurrying away like a frightened rabbit.

"He ain't cut out for this type of business," Jake said.

Kade nodded. "Now he knows that no matter how panicked he might become during the fight, he has more to fear from me than from anyone else." He turned to Simon Barry. "You will make a good captain, Mr. Barry. Once we have control of the *Christabel*, I will leave the punishment of the men supporting Flesher in your hands."

"I appreciate your faith in me, Captain Morgan, and I want you to know that I have prayed every night that we find Miss O'Connor safe and well."

Kade looked down at Simon's earnest young face and smiled. "Then I have no doubt we will do so, Captain Barry."

Chapter 29

Kathleen slipped off her nightgown and quickly dressed. Why did Quint Cathcart need to talk to her so urgently? It was almost midnight. She had been asleep when he awakened her by knocking on her cabin door, insisting she come immediately to Captain Flesher's quarters. Her stomach protested waking up, just as it had been doing every morning since she left Mistral.

As she fastened the last button on her lilac dress, she tried not to think about the first time she had worn that same dress. It had been on a walk with Kade beneath the starry expanse of night sky on Mistral. He had wrapped his arms around her, leaning her back against him so they could count the stars.

I must stop thinking about Kade, he is a piece of my past, not my future, she told herself. He did not even care enough to come after me this time, even though I did not want him to.

Sarita Ridley had stayed behind on Mistral when the *Christabel* sailed, and Kathleen could only guess why Kade had not come. Their last night together she had almost convinced herself that he truly cared for her. Now she knew better, for now he was with Sarita, riding the crystal sands of Mistral, swimming the aqua waters, making love on the blue satin bedspread.

A knock on the cabin door pulled Kathleen away

from the painful memories of Kade. She adjusted the bodice of her dress and opened the door. It was Ivan Flesher, the dim light in the passageway accenting his hawklike features. Kathleen took an involuntary step backwards.

"Miss O'Connor, I came to escort you to my cabin. Are you ready?" Ivan's groin began to ache. His wait for this luscious morsel was almost over.

"Yes, I am ready," she said, her lashes lowering slightly over her eyes as she bent to pick up a warm shawl to drape over her shoulders.

Ivan held out his arm, and Kathleen placed her fingertips on his sleeve. Her touch sent shocks throughout his entire system. He took a deep breath to steady his nerves. He had been waiting three weeks for this moment. Now that Ireland was a little more than a week away, he had told Quint that he refused to wait any longer to collect his payment for stealing the *Christabel*. Ivan glanced down at the shining hair of the girl on his arm. How lovely she was, how small and dainty. He was going to enjoy extracting his payment from Morgan's little whore.

After they entered his cabin, Ivan handed Kathleen into her chair. She looked up at him questioningly. "Where is Mr. Cathcart?"

"Here, my dear," the now familiar voice said as the door opened to admit Quint. He was resplendent in crimson evening dress, looking like a bird with his pointed beard and beady eyes.

"You must wonder why I insisted you join us this late, Kathleen," Quint said as he seated himself across from her.

She arranged her skirts and avoided looking at Ivan. "Yes. You said it was some urgent matter."

"First, let me explain something I am sure you have been wondering about, which is why your intrepid lover has not followed us as you feared he might. The morning we left Mistral, Captain Flesher dispatched one of his crew to eliminate any possibility of Morgan coming after you."

Kathleen felt suddenly sick. "Eliminate? Do you mean you killed him?"

Quint smiled. "Yes, my dear, I mean exactly that."

It was as though the world had dropped away from beneath Kathleen's feet, leaving her alone in a whirling mist of shock and grief.

"You look upset, Kathleen, let me get you some wine," Ivan Flesher said.

"I do not feel well, I must return to my cabin."

"I am afraid I cannot allow that, my dear," Quint said as Ivan pressed her back into her chair. "We have not yet had our discussion."

Kathleen looked at him through hollow eyes. Quint wet his thin lips with a pointed tongue. He reminded her of a snake.

"You can blame Captain Flesher for the lateness of the hour," Quint said, "but he refuses to wait another moment to receive payment for our use of the *Christabel.*"

"I do not understand."

"Then let me explain. Captain Flesher was relieved of his command of this vessel by your former lover, but when Flesher learned of my need to take you to Ireland, he agreed to ignore Morgan's dismissal and take us there immediately in exchange for a special payment."

"There was no need for him to steal the *Christabel.* We could have waited for another ship from Mistral."

"I did not want to wait, I wanted to leave immediately."

"You hardly know my father, why are you so eager to return me to him?"

"I am only eager because of the reward for that service, a reward I have been anticipating since the first time I saw you astride that great stallion."

"Taran?"

"Yes, Taran. If your father had sold me the horse when he had the chance, so much unpleasantness would have been avoided. Soon the beast will be mine, though, and all this will be over."

Kathleen felt as though her bones had disappeared, leaving her an empty bag of skin and grief. Her mother and brother had died, her home and the Emerald Hills stables destroyed. And now Kade's death. All because she had called forth the water stallion from his home with the Merrow fairy folk.

"If what you say is true, why did Rat sell me?"

"That was a most unfortunate decision on his part, one that I assure you he paid for with his life. His reason was a lame one, not surprising from a man of Rat's lame intelligence. He claimed you were a witch, said you drove him to it with those 'witch eyes' of yours."

Kathleen's disregard for Rat's abuse had led him to what he considered the ultimate abuse, selling her into slavery. She shuddered to think how right he would have been if anyone other than Kade had bought her. Better that she had been sold into prostitution; at least then Kade would still be alive.

Quint took a sip of wine. "Enough of that. Now it is time for you to pay Captain Flesher for use of the *Christabel*."

"I have no money."

"It is not money that he desires, my dear. It is you. So, until we arrive in Dublin and I can exchange you for Taran, I am placing you at his disposal."

Kathleen felt a hand on her neck. Before she could react, she was pulled roughly into Ivan Flesher's embrace. He forced his mouth onto hers before she could even scream.

"No!" she said through clenched teeth as his lips ground into hers. "Stop, let me go!" she screamed when he wrenched his mouth away to drool on her neck. He had clasped her wrists tightly in his fist. Kathleen had no way to fight him. Her dress was tangled around her feet and when she tried to kick him, she fell to the floor with Ivan on top of her. She heard Quint laughing, heard herself sobbing.

"Don't fight me, Kathleen," Ivan said, his voice thick, "I'll make it good for both of us."

A shudder passed over Kathleen as he again descended on her lips. He ravaged her mouth with painful thrusts of his slimy tongue. Kathleen fought a rising flood of nausea that threatened to overcome her. When she tried to push him away, Ivan slapped her, an ugly snarl on his face.

"I know you laid willingly for Kade Morgan. I want a little of what you gave that bastard right now or I'll throw you to my crew!"

His eyes narrowed dangerously, and Kathleen knew he was serious. Another hard slap across her face brought her to a quick decision. She forced her body to relax under Flesher's crushing weight. The bodice of her dress gave way beneath the pressure of Flesher's groping hands, exposing her breasts to the crazed man's hungry stare.

He pinched her nipples painfully. Fear rose in Kathleen's throat, threatening to choke her. She bit her tongue until blood filled her mouth as his lips followed his fingers onto her nipple. She struggled against the weight of Ivan's body. The movement excited him and he dug his fingers into her other breast.

Oh God, please help me to bear this, Kathleen prayed silently. She forced herself to become limp and closed her eyes to the sight of Ivan Flesher sucking her nipple. The moment she stopped struggling, he slapped her again.

"I want to hear you moan, bitch. I want you to squirm under me like you did for Morgan!" His hand grasped her breast so hard Kathleen was forced to cry out from the pain. "That's it, again," he said. Kathleen whipped her body sideways to avoid his touch. Ivan slammed his knee between her parted thighs.

"That's it, sweet bitch. You know you want it as much as I do." His words became slurred as his wet lips slid over Kathleen's sweat-slicked skin. Then suddenly she was free, his body was off hers and she saw Quint hand Ivan a length of rope to tie her with.

Never, she thought and threw herself against Ivan's legs, causing him to crash backwards into the table. Grabbing her skirts to keep from tripping again, Kathleen struggled to her feet. Quint was in front of her. He backed her against the wall and slapped her, once on each cheek, brutal blows that took her breath away. Ivan handed Quint a knife, which he used to slit her dress from torn bodice to the floor.

"Take it off," Quint ordered. Kathleen let the dress fall from her shoulders. She was aware of Ivan's muttered exclamation, aware of Quint's lusting stare. She kept her gaze on the knife.

"Now go over to the bed," Quint said, and Kathleen edged along the wall. "Tie her up, Flesher."

Ivan was knotting the rope to the post at the top of his bed, his eyes glinting in the lamplight. Kathleen tensed. The lamp was fastened to the wall to the left of her head. When she lifted her hand to it, Quint pressed the knife against her chest.

"Don't move," he ordered. She forced herself to smile beguilingly at Quint.

"There is no need to tie me. Like Captain Flesher

said, I laid willingly for Kade, I can do the same for you. I will even show you one of his favorite games."

Quint's eyes narrowed and he pulled the knife back a few inches. "Is this a trick?"

"How could I trick two big men like you and Captain Flesher? I am only a weak, helpless female."

Ivan moved closer, standing directly in front of the lamp. "Show us this game."

"First, Kade likes me to dance for him, like this." She began to sway slightly, her hands running up her naked flesh. With no music and with the lamp shining golden on her body, her movements took on an entrancing, magical aura. Quint stepped back to give her more room, the knife still poised in front of him.

Kathleen continued to move slowly, her hair rippling across her shoulders and around her breasts as her arms lifted over her head. She arched her back and her breasts stood out invitingly from her body, drawing the attention of both men. With a sudden sweep sideways of her left hand she grasped the lamp, scorching her fingers on the hot glass. She ignored the pain, ripping the lamp from the wall and throwing the flaming whale oil onto Ivan. He screamed and stumbled backwards, beating at his burning clothes with his hands.

Quint was frozen with surprise. Kathleen lunged at him, tearing the knife from his limp fingers. He threw himself at her, forcing her to the floor. Instinctively she sliced at him, feeling the press of the knife as it cut through cloth and flesh. The blade bucked in her hand as it glanced off bone. Quint released her to clutch his left arm. Kathleen rolled to the side and threw her back against the wall just as the door to the cabin burst open.

Two burly members of the crew stood there, staring in disbelief at the scene in the cabin: Kathleen's naked body, the knife in her hands covered with blood, Quint cowering on the floor and holding his arm as blood spurted from between his fingers. Ivan was on fire, and one of the men ran to his aid, pulling the blanket from the bed to smother the smoking flames. Ivan collapsed unconscious into his arms.

Quint pointed at Kathleen. "Take her to the hold and lock her up, then fetch the ship's surgeon." The man still standing in the doorway approached Kathleen cautiously. She was waving the knife in front of her, crouched and ready to spring.

"Stay back," she warned. A heavy form attacked from her other side, flattening her beneath it on the floor. It was the crewman who had gone to Flesher's aid. He wrenched the knife from her fingers and dragged her to her feet.

"This be right nice," he said as he jerked Kathleen against him.

Quint staggered to his feet. "Lock her up, nothing else. I have some unfinished business with her. Whatever is left will be thrown to you and the crew."

The man sneered down at Kathleen, his fetid breath making her retch. He threw her across his shoulder and followed his friends out the door, down a passageway and several ladders to a cell in the hold.

"This ought to keep ya. Too bad we gotta wait." He ran his hand over Kathleen's buttocks, then tossed her on the floor, knocking the breath out of her.

"I don't fancy waitin' to sample this," one of the other men said. "Maybe we should take our share now."

"Yeah, Cathcart ain't got no right givin' us orders. You hold her." He fell on Kathleen, his hands bruising her flesh.

"Stop!" she screamed. The men appeared not to notice her struggles. One held her, the other groped her breasts and pushed his gnarled fingers between her legs.

"Dear God, please help me!" Kathleen whispered in horror as the man reached to open his pants. At that moment, the ship lurched sideways with a grunting of wood that sounded like the entire hull was going to collapse inward.

The man stopped, the front of his breeches halfway open. "What the bloody hell was that?"

"We better go see, this'll wait." They released her and ran out of the room, slamming the door and throwing the bolt. A key scraped in the lock, and then everything was silent.

Kathleen lay in a huddle of hair and tears, her body twitching with revulsion. If only I had not called forth the water stallion, she thought. So much horror, so much death. All of it my fault. She crept to the corner of the room farthest from the door and wrapped her arms around her shivering shoulders.

It was almost midnight. The moon came out from behind a bank of clouds, pouring its cold light onto the silent deck of the *Black Eagle* as the ship closed in on the *Christabel,* whose sails looked like disembodied ghosts floating above the dark sea.

"Feast your eyes on that, Jake," Kade said softly.

"Aye, makes me old blood move a little faster. Though I don't miss the danger of piratin', I do miss the thrill of the hunt."

"Flesher made this hunt easy."

"He thought ye dead."

Kade laid his hand on a rope, checking the tension of the hemp as a crewman tightened it to prevent the silk sails from luffing. He nodded to the sailor, who tied off the rope and climbed the ratlines to check another sail.

"About you and Mattie going back to Scotland after this run," Kade said, "it will not be necessary. I am taking Kathleen back to Ireland, something I should have done as soon as I bought her."

"Ye sure ye want to do that, Kade? She loves ye."

Kade listened to the mast creaking in the wind. "I would rather her love me in Ireland than hate me on Mistral." He raised his spyglass and studied the *Christabel*. There were only two men on deck, the watch and the helmsman. They were passing a bottle between them. It angered Kade that Flesher allowed such negligence. Still, that negligence would allow the *Black Eagle* to approach without being spotted, lessening the chance of anyone being killed.

The *Eagle's* crew was gathered on the starboard rail, grappling hooks in hand. The ship moved alongside the *Christabel* like a shadow. When there was less than ten feet separating the ships, Kade signaled to Simon Barry. He and Martin Grimstead grasped ropes and swung across to the *Christabel*. They landed on the deck in their stocking feet, scarcely making a sound. They approached their quarry from behind and had them bound and gagged within minutes.

Kade signaled for the hooks to be thrown. The air quivered with movement as a dozen arms stretched out, the ropes singing as they sailed across the dark water, the metal hooks groaning as they caught on the *Christabel's* rail. The ropes were quickly hauled in, the crew manually closing the gap between the two ships. The sails on the *Eagle* were quickly reefed so the ship would not hinder the movement of the *Christabel* and alert her captain to danger.

When the hulls touched, the *Christabel* lurched sideways, her wooden hull groaning. The ships were made fast to each other, and the *Black Eagle* crew swarmed across the boarding planks. The *Christabel's* hatches opened, and her crew stumbled onto deck. Their faces registered shock, then rage. Hands grappled for weapons, pulling belaying pins from the rails, dragging knives from boots.

Cries and grunts were heard, the thud of wooden clubs against soft bodies, the collapse of bodies onto the deck. *Eagle* crewmen climbed into the rigging to cut loose the billowing white sails. The canvas collapsed against the masts, as limp as old petticoats. The two ships slowed, swinging into the current.

Kade grasped a rope, checked to see that it was secure, then swung into the thick of the melee, most of his weight on his right arm to protect his broken left shoulder. The sound of ringing steel filled the air as he pulled his sword. He parried the thrust of a sailor's cutlass, jumped over a body and hurled himself against a man raising an ax behind Simon Barry's back.

Kade slashed through the soft flesh of the man's upper arm, then whirled to avoid the downswing of a belaying pin wielded by the man who had attacked him on Mistral, Waters. Kade snaked out his left arm, slammed his fist into Waters' face and winced from the pain the blow caused in his shoulder. Waters stumbled backwards, then pulled a pistol from his belt. Kade's hand clutched the jewel-handled dagger. With a flip of his wrist, he sent the knife soaring across the *Christabel*'s deck to land in Waters' chest. The pistol fell from the sailor's limp fingers, and his body crashed to the deck.

Kade turned in time to meet the sword thrust of one of the *Christabel*'s officers, a man named Ian Dermot. They fought across the deck, moving toward the bow. Dermot let his guard down, and Kade plunged his sword into Dermot's chest. He wrenched it free and watched the man collapse, than ran up the steps to the forecastle.

He pulled his pistol, moonlight glinting darkly off the barrel as he took aim at the ship's bell. He squeezed the trigger, then sidestepped the wicked crack of a whip that came whistling through the air in his direction. His bullet struck the bronze bell, causing it to scream in protest, and he loosed another shot from his other pistol. The second loud clang of the bell caused the fighting to slow as the crew of the *Christabel* glanced at the tall man standing on the bow of their ship. Those who recognized Kade immediately threw down their weapons in surrender, realizing that they were fighting their employer. Only small pockets of fighting remained, and Kade assumed those were the men loyal to Ivan Flesher.

Kade glanced at the *Black Eagle,* confirming that Jake had heard the bell above the skirmish. The Scotsman threw up his hand in a salute, then gave the order for the bow anchor on the *Eagle* to be released. The sea swallowed it in silence. By the time the ships had settled slightly in the water, all resistance from the *Christabel's* crew had been overcome. Smoke from discharged pistols drifted upwards past the idle sails.

Kade lifted his sword and summoned his officers. "Mr. Thorpe, select some men and secure the crews' quarters, the galley and the hold. Mr. Peters, marshal a guard for the powder magazine and see that the cannon are not loaded. Mr. Barry, gather the *Christabel's* crew amidships. After I talk with them, see that the wounded are taken across to Dr. Williams for treatment."

The crew of the *Christabel* moved to the center of the ship. Simon Barry had their weapons gathered and stacked on the stern; he assigned guards both there and around the prisoners. Then he climbed to the forecastle and stood beside Kade.

Kade sheathed his sword, and with his hands resting on the wooden rail, addressed the assembled men. "For those of you that have not yet realized what is happening, I am Captain Kade Morgan of the *Black Eagle,* owner of Morgan Shipping. I am here to regain possession of the *Christabel,* which was stolen from me by Ivan Flesher, former captain of this vessel who was relieved of his command while the ship was anchored at Mistral."

Murmurs of surprise drifted through the captured men. Kade silenced them by lifting his hand. "Any further resistance from the *Christabel's* crew will be dealt with as mutiny. Your new master is Captain Simon Barry. Captain Barry, the command is yours. I am going below deck to confront Flesher. Find the man who has my dagger in his chest and retrieve it for me."

Kade ducked his head as he went down the steps to the captain's quarters. He reloaded his pistols, thrust them into his belt and unsheathed his sword. He listened at the cabin door, then lifted the handle and let the heavy door swing open. The smell of burned flesh permeated the room, and the floor was stained with fresh blood. Quint Cathcart was standing beside the bed, his hand on Ivan Flesher's blanched forehead.

"I heard the fight," Quint said. "Flesher is already dead, there is no need for your sword, Morgan." His left arm was wrapped in a towel; blood had turned the white cloth red. He went to the desk and picked up another towel to press over his wound.

"Where is Kathleen?" Kade asked as he stepped forward to press the point of his sword against Quint's neck.

The feeble light in the cabin gleamed dull blue as it ran along the blade. Quint tore his eyes from the weapon and lifted his gaze to Kade's face. The same dull blue glowed deep inside those black eyes.

"Aren't you interested in how Flesher died?"

"Not particularly. I was going to kill him anyway."

Quint's lips twitched. "You are a cold bastard, Morgan."

A hint of a smile curled around Kade's curving lips.

"Not as cold as your man Waters wanted me."

"Flesher's man, not mine. He was afraid if you were not dead you would come after him. Too bad Waters did not succeed, although I thought we should only maim you. I wanted you to suffer when you learned that Kathleen was gone."

"Why?"

"Hate, Morgan. Pure, simple, unblemished hate."

"The same reason you had Emerald Hills attacked."

Quint's eyes widened. "Very good, Morgan; you figured it out by yourself except for one thing. That was not hate, it was greed. I wanted Taran."

"Is one horse worth so much?"

"That one is."

Kade pressed the sword tighter to the pale skin and watched Quint's pointed beard quiver. "Is he worth your life?"

Quint licked his dry lips with an equally dry tongue. "There is no need to kill me. Kathleen has not been harmed."

"Her home was destroyed, her mother and brother killed, her own life almost forfeited because of your lust for a horse. At what point do you consider harm to have taken place?" Kade pulled the sword back from Quint's neck, sickened by his own anger. If he killed the man in cold blood, it would place him in Cathcart's category.

He glanced around the cabin, noting the rope tied to the bedpost above Flesher's body. Then he saw Kathleen's lilac dress lying in a discarded heap beside the bed. He touched the soft fabric with the tip of his sword. The bodice was ripped, the skirt sliced from waist to hem.

"Where is she, Quint?" Kade asked, his voice cold as iced steel.

Quint slipped his hand beneath the top towel on his

arm. "After she threw the burning lamp on Flesher, she attacked me with a knife. I had two of the crew take her away."

Footsteps sounded in the hall, and Kade turned to the door just as Simon Barry entered the cabin. "Ship is secure, sir," Barry said, "and Mr. Thorpe reports a locked cell in the hold. Maybe Miss O'Connor is being held there." He handed Kade the jewel-handled dagger and looked at Quint, his eyes widening in surprise.

Kade reacted instantly, whirling in time to see a flash of light as Quint discharged a small ivory-handled pistol he had hidden beneath the towel pressed to his arm. The bullet slammed into Kade's already broken left shoulder. Anger deadened the fiery pain. With a sweeping swirl of his right hand, his sword slashed through the air. The point sliced through the pale skin beneath Quint's beard, opening the thin flesh like the belly of a fish.

Quint's fingers tightened on the trigger of his pistol; then he realized he had already discharged the weapon. He stared at Kade, delighting in the spreading stain on Morgan's black shirt. Quint was so excited by Morgan's wound that he did not pay attention to the pain in his own throat, nor the blood that poured freely from his neck.

He did notice a funny gurgling sound every time he took a breath, and looked around to see what it was. All Quint could see was the ceiling of the cabin, the wood glowing with a dull sheen. Quint turned his head to the side and realized he was lying on the floor. He tried to get up, but his body would not move. The bubbling, gurgling sound grew louder; then everything was quiet. Deadly quiet.

Kathleen heard the footsteps approaching the door

to her cell. She had no weapon, nowhere to run. She pushed her back closer against the wall, burrowing into the corner as a chill of fear swept over her. The footsteps stopped. She lifted her chin and stilled the tremble of her lips as she summoned her pride. She would not allow whoever was outside that door to see her fear, only her anger.

A key scraped in the lock, the latch squeaked as it was lifted, the door creaked as it opened. A shaft of light cut into the room, outlining the form of the man standing in the passageway.

"You dirty, low-life, slimy excuse for a person!" Kathleen shouted, her voice rising until its husky timbre vibrated in the corners of the damp room. "If you come one step further into this room I will slice your scurvy neck into ribbons, I will scratch your runny eyes out of your ugly face, I will make you regret the day you were born!"

The man did not move. Because he stood with his back to the light, his face was hidden in darkness. He looked like a specter from the grave. Fear clutched at Kathleen's throat. She felt as if she were choking and drew in a desperate breath.

Her heart froze. The air was filled with a familiar scent. A rich cologne that never failed to make her knees weak, her body melt.

"Kade?" she whispered, afraid to trust her senses.

"Come here, kitten," he said, his voice rich and deep, soft and wonderful.

Kathleen threw herself across the room, landing in his arms and burrowing as close as she could to him. He crushed her against him and she could scarcely breathe. Kathleen did not care. She was safe in the arms of Kade Morgan, that was all that mattered.

Kade hardly noticed the searing pain in his shoulder through the joy of again holding the woman he loved.

He pulled her even closer to him, his hands tangling in her hair as he pulled her face up to his.

"Are you all right?" he asked.

She nodded and gave him a weak, tremulous smile. Kade saw the bruises on her face and bent his head to touch his lips gently to hers. She opened her mouth, drawing his tongue into her and kissing him with a ravenous, desperate hunger that he answered willingly.

"I want you," she murmured against his lips, looking up into the black eyes she loved more than life itself. She kissed him again, her tongue darting against his, her teeth tasting his lips.

"Here, Kate?"

"Here, now," she breathed.

Kade placed her back against the wall. He loosened his pants to release his hard, throbbing manhood. With his hands on Kathleen's waist, he lifted her and lowered her onto him. Her legs wrapped around his waist and her head fell back as he repeatedly pushed himself into her.

It was over in a matter of minutes. Kathleen exploded into a thousand pieces as Kade shuddered with the force of his own release. She collapsed against him, her breathing ragged and strained.

He traced the path of tears down her cheek. "Think you can stand, kitten?" he asked. She nodded, a smile pulling at the corners of her mouth as she unwrapped her legs from his waist. He leaned her against the wall and fastened his breeches. The light from a lamp in the hold glowed golden on the sheen of her sweat. He lifted his hand to wipe away the blood smeared on her breasts.

"Blood?" Kathleen asked when she saw what he was doing. Then she noticed the stain on Kade's shirt. "You are hurt!" she cried, touching him gently as she pulled the shirt from his wound. "You were shot!"

"It is nothing," he said. "The shoulder was already broken."

"You could have been killed," she whispered in horror, then remembered that she had thought he was dead.

"Put this on," Kade said as he untied the scarf on his right arm and pulled his shirt off. He slipped it over Kathleen's head, and the black silk slipped down over her body, falling at her feet.

"It appears to be a little large," she commented wryly.

Kade pulled the shirt back up and fastened the top button. Her body was completely lost in the folds of silk. She looked so small and vulnerable. He gathered her into his arms, lifting her and holding her tightly against him.

"You cannot carry me, your arm . . ."

He silenced her with his lips. "Nothing could stop me from carrying you."

She dropped her head onto his right shoulder, and her breath touched his bare flesh in a moist, warm softness. "Everything that happened was my fault, Kade. Quint had Emerald Hills attacked to get Taran, and he had Rat hold me hostage for the same reason, only Rat got mad and sold me to you. Quint came to Mistral after me and told me he killed you. When I heard that, I wanted to die, too."

Kade's heart swelled, his eyes burned. "It was not your fault, kitten, none of it.

A sob tore from inside her and she clutched his neck tightly. "But it was! I called forth the *each uisce,* the great water stallion. That is who Taran is, the *each uisce.* If I had not summoned him, none of this would have happened."

He pressed his lips against her forehead. "The story of the *each uisce* is a fairy tale, kitten, there is no such beast."

"So my father said until Taran came out of the waves."

"I would like to see that. Would you call him forth for me?"

"The water stallion belongs to the Merrow folk of Ireland, the fairies that live under the sea. He can only be summoned from there."

"Then you will be able to show me, for I am taking you home," he said as he carried her down the passageway outside Simon Barry's new quarters.

She stiffened, looking up at Kade in disbelief. "To Ireland?"

"Aye, home to bonny Ireland, sweet Kate."

He ducked his head as he climbed the steps onto the deck of the *Christabel.* Kathleen snuggled close to Kade, very aware of his strong arms and the shaggy hair that fell across her hands circling his neck.

When Kade crossed the boarding platform to the *Black Eagle,* a cheer rose from the men there. "I think they missed you almost as much as I did," he said. Kathleen smiled, and then her attention was drawn to the silk sails on the *Eagle* and the flag on the top of the mizzenmast.

"Have you turned pirate again?"

"Only for tonight."

"I have always had a fantasy about a handsome pirate captain stealing me away and making passionate love to me until I drop from exhaustion."

Kade grinned. "Maybe I will remain a pirate for a little longer then, my love."

He carried Kathleen to his cabin and lowered her to the bed, kneeling beside her when she refused to release him. "I have to go, Kate," he said, gently disentangling himself from her arms.

He pulled a clean shirt from the armoire and put it on without taking his eyes from Kathleen. He walked back to the bed and placed his hand on the side of her face.

"It was not your fault," he said. "Cathcart was mad, insane. You cannot blame yourself for what he did."

Kathleen laid her hand on his. "Come back soon and convince me of that," she whispered. His smile wrapped around her, his fingers touched her lips. Then he was gone.

Kade was standing on deck, watching the *Christabel*'s sails fill with wind as Simon Barry turned his ship toward England. There he would discharge the men loyal to Flesher and take on a load of cargo before returning to Mistral.

The *Black Eagle* heeled to starboard as Jake McBradden turned her bow in the direction of Ireland. The black sails were still aloft, and the light from the moon slid along their edges like oil. Kade rubbed the stiffness from his left shoulder, feeling the bulk of his bandages. Dr. Williams had removed the bullet, cleaned the wound and bound the entire shoulder with heavy wrappings.

Kathleen came out on deck, wrapped in his satin evening cape. On him the cape came to just below his knees, on her it swept the deck around her feet.

Kathleen lifted her face to the chill breeze and hugged the cape closer around her as the edges lifted in the wind. A flash of the red lining caught her eye as the billowing folds tangled around her legs. She leaned back over the port railing, letting the wind catch in her hair. The ocean was dark except where the moon painted a silver path across the rolling surface. Stars twinkled overhead, the ship cut quietly through the waves, the silk sails sighed as they yielded to the embrace of the wind.

The peace and serenity of the ocean seeped into Kathleen. The air smelled fresh and clean, and she inhaled it deeply. She longed to feel the warmth of Kade's body pressed against her, to lean her head on his firm chest and to feel his arms around her.

A tall, dark figure stepped from the shadows, as though summoned by her thoughts. His profile was strong and hard under the silver moonlight, his shaggy mane of hair ruffled by the wind. There was an air of isolation around his giant figure as he stood there beside her. Kathleen pulled the cape tighter around her body as chills threatened to make her tremble. She could feel the heat of his body as he moved closer. Her eyes locked on his lips, so full and sensuous. So close.

"Come here," Kade said as he pulled her into his arms, his body sheltering her from the wind as his lips descended on hers. When he raised up, she smiled into the darkness as her hand traced the line of his jaw.

"I read your letter to Jake."

"You did?" she asked weakly, suddenly feeling twice as small as before.

"Aye, that I did." He ran his hands up her back and wrapped his fingers in her silken hair. "And I have something to say to you. You are a beautiful, brave, determined, soft, desirable woman, Kathleen O'Connor." He lowered his lips onto hers. "And I love you."

The last words were whispered against her mouth, and Kathleen drew them into her as she pressed tightly against the hard length of Kade's body. He lifted his hand to the side of her face as he drew her tongue into him, drinking deeply of her kiss.

Kathleen could not believe what he had said. He loved her. This man holding her, this man she loved, loved her. She clung to him, afraid she would collapse without his support. Her arms slid over his shoulders and around his neck, pulling him closer to her. When she began to gasp for air, Kade released her lips.

"I have wanted you, Kathleen, since the first moment

I saw you standing on that slave platform. And when you spit at me I started loving you and have not stopped since, though for a long time I spent every moment denying it. You have turned my world upside down and sent it spinning out of control and I hope it never returns to normal again."

Kathleen felt as though the air around her had shifted, as though the world had altered form and shape, trapping her in a dream that she never wanted to awaken from.

"Kade, oh Kade!" she cried, the words almost a sob. "I love you so much, so very much. I thought I would die when I left Mistral, thinking I would never see you again. Quint had said he would see to it you did not follow, then when he said you were dead . . ." Her voice broke as she started to cry.

"Katie, my sweet Katie," Kade said as he held her, feeling the glory of her love flowing through his veins like hot wine, melting the coldness he had tried to hold onto even in the heat of his love for her.

"Kiss me, my love," she whispered, and his lips came down on hers, sending her already soaring emotions higher than the highest cloud.

He pulled one hand free from her hair, slipping it beneath the satin cape so he could cup her breast, his fingers lightly touching her rigid nipple. She moaned against his lips, and Kade swept her into his arms.

"I shall make love to you until you faint," he told her as he carried her across the deck and down the steps to his cabin.

"That might take days."

"We can only hope," Kade replied, and Kathleen was lost in the warmth of his voice and the wonder of his love.

Chapter 30

The *Black Eagle* cut through the emerald waters, the glaring masthead drenched by rain that sheeted out of the sky. Kathleen leaned over the railing, tasting the rain and salt spray on her face until Kade pulled her away from the bow, insisting that she put on the oilskin coat he had brought up from the cabin.

"But I grew up in rain," she protested as he bundled her in the stiff cloth.

"Be quiet or I will kiss you," Kade said, and she began to talk nonstop of senseless subjects until he was forced to make good his threat. Kathleen melted against his solid form the moment their lips touched. The world swirled away beneath the pressure of his mouth and the heated touch of his body against hers, which she could feel even through the confining oilskin and dense rain.

She pulled away from him suddenly and screamed "No!" just as Michael, the cabin boy, started to dump a bucket of slop water over the side of the ship. Kathleen dashed across the wet deck and grabbed his arm.

"You must warn the Merrow folk or they will send a storm to sink the ship," she told him. The foremast creaked loudly, as though it were already bending beneath the weight of a storm. The canvas sails cracked sharply, and several sailors scurried into the rigging to adjust the lead lines.

"What is a Merrow folk?" Michael asked.

Kade laid his hand on Michael's shoulder. "An imaginary folk the Irish believe live beneath the sea. According to Kathleen, they have tempers, trap the souls of drowned fishermen in lobster pots to keep them warm, and have an unbelievably magnificent stallion that they loan to her on occasion."

She grinned, remembering Kade's uncontrollable laughter when she told him about the Merrow folk and how he had tickled her unmercifully while accusing her of telling him lies.

"When we reach shore, I shall take great pleasure in proving your skepticism wrong," she told him curtly.

A wicked gleam flashed in Kade's eyes. "Then, Katie me lass, 'tis a moment I'll be lookin' forward to wi' great delight, for I do enjoy yer pleasure so very much. And now I'd be right beholdin' to ye if ye'd show this fine gunnery mate the proper way to be dumpin' 'is slop."

Kathleen rolled her eyes at his affected Irish accent. "'Tis right glad I'd be to do that, Cap'n, for I'll not be wantin' to anger the Merrow and 'ave me soul trapped in a lobster pot at the bottom of this 'ere bonny green sea."

She leaned over the rail, cupped one hand to her mouth and shouted, *"Chughaibh an t-uiscei!* That means watch out for the water," she told Michael. "You can dump your bucket now."

He did, and the sea spread open to take into itself the bucket's contents. "Did ya see that, Cap'n?" he asked Kade. "It opened right up and there weren't even a splash."

"The rain has your brains addled, boy," Kade grumbled uncomfortably as he stared at the smooth surface of the sea. Not even the rain was making a mark on the slick surface where the slop had disappeared.

Kathleen laughed. "That is nothing, wait until you see Taran."

"I shall not have long to wait, kitten, for yonder rises the jewel of Ireland."

Kade pointed at the horizon, and Kathleen grasped the rail tightly as a sliver of land rose above the rain-swept sea. Kade wrapped his arms around her, and together they watched as the *Black Eagle* closed in on that beloved coastline. The ship began to roll with the swells as the waves curved into the nearing shoreline. Kathleen's heart was in her throat, and excitement made her tremble. Kade pressed his lips to the top of her wet hair, and she snuggled further into his comforting embrace.

The ship curved around the southwestern tip of Ireland, where deep bays cut into the island. The helmsman steered the *Eagle* in close to the shoreline, passing a group of seals sunning themselves on an outcrop of rock. And then—miraculously, it seemed to Kathleen—they had arrived at the rocky shores and kelp-littered beaches of Emerald Hills.

The rain stopped, and the sun, already halfway to the western horizon, burst from behind a cloud, igniting an emerald fire that blazed across the land that rose beyond the beaches. The sea around the *Black Eagle* was translucent, and the wind caught the top of the cresting waves, sending a crystal shower flying backwards over the green water.

Kade released Kathleen so he could take the helm, and she immediately threw off her oilskin, opening her arms to the sunlight that fell on her like a favored child. It enveloped her, wrapping around her like a shimmering cloak, flaming like black fire along the length of her ebony hair while it caressed her upturned face with the soft touch of a lover.

405

Kade wanted to hold her, to feel her energy and taste the life force that enveloped her. He could not bring himself to interfere with her communion with this land that had spawned her. He gave orders for the anchors to be cut free, the sails to be reefed and a longboat dropped onto the gleaming surface of the sea.

Storm clouds moved uneasily across the sky, shying away from the sun and casting shadows on the sea that had turned lime green beneath the golden caress of the sun. Black-headed gulls soared above the rigging of the *Eagle,* and from somewhere came the bubbling song of a curlew, symbolic of the wild place to which Kade had brought this woman he loved.

Kathleen was halfway down the side of the hull before Kade even realized the boat had been lowered. "Come on, old man!" she shouted up at him. "I have a horse to call forth and a father to find."

Kade joined her in the bobbing longboat, chucking her under the chin for calling him an old man. Happiness radiated from her like ripples spreading in a pond. Alan Hatch and Frank Anderson, the two men stationed in the longboat to row it to shore, were caught in her mood. Anderson playfully punched Hatch on the shoulder, causing the boat to rock. Kade almost fell overboard, which brought a shout of laughter from Jake as he scrambled down the side of the ship into the boat.

Kade grabbed the side of the *Eagle,* regaining his balance and some of his dignity. Hatch shoved his oar against the painted hull of the *Black Eagle,* pushing the longboat away from the ship. Then he and Anderson dipped their oars in the clear water, sending the longboat speeding across the waves to the shore.

The smell of the land permeated Kathleen's senses; she tasted the rich flavor of peat on the clean wind and heard the bleating call of sheep on the bogs. The islands on the horizon glowed in the golden sunlight, and she saw a *glaucog,* an Irish fishing boat, put out from one of them, its sail pristine white against the cloudy sky.

The longboat scraped against the pebbled bottom, and the crewmen jumped out to drag it onto the shore. Before Kade could help Kathleen from the boat, she placed her hand on Alan Hatch's shoulder and jumped onto the foam-flecked beach.

"Watch this," she cried as Kade stepped out of the boat. She was wearing the clothes Michael had scrounged from Skinner during her first stay aboard the *Black Eagle,* the gray pants and shirt. She kicked off her boots and lifted the legs of the pants to step into the edge of the surf, the cool water licking at her bare toes as she wrinkled her nose with delight. Then she closed her eyes and called upon the *each uisce* to come forth from its home beneath the sea.

Nothing happened. Kade was embarrassed to witness this proof of his skepticism about the fairy folk. Then, out past where the *Black Eagle* swung on its anchor, a monstrous wave began to form. It rushed into the shore so fast it overcame the waves before it, smothering them with its size and speed, its crest streaming behind it like the tail of a mighty steed.

The giant wave broke as it reached Kathleen, swirling all around her yet not touching her. She dropped her hold on her breeches and lifted her arms. Directly in front of her, the foaming surface of the wave began to change. The head of a stallion appeared, its mane heavy with salt water and seaweed. As the wave continued to curl in upon itself, the front legs and barrel chest of the horse appeared.

With a screaming cry that drowned the final roar of the dying wave, the *each uisce* tore loose of the clinging sea and thundered onto the shore. It was huge, well over eighteen hands, and as it reared and screamed again, Kade looked up into the turbulent green of the beast's eyes. Spreading across those liquid surfaces was a pattern like sunlight moving through clear water.

He knew he was looking at something not mortal, and a chill of fear crawled over him. He took an involuntary step backwards as the stallion crashed its hooves onto the wet sand. The ground actually shook beneath that impact. The stallion shook its head to free itself of the clinging seaweed before whirling on its hind legs. Its flowing tail dragged along the sand as it sped back into the edge of the water and into Kathleen's waiting embrace.

She seemed to float up onto the stallion's towering back, her hands clutching the wet mane as the stallion pawed the sand impatiently. She tossed her head, her hair swinging freely around her as she laughed down at Kade's incredulous expression.

"Do you believe now?" she asked, and then she was gone as the stallion tore up the side of the rising slope in great, ground-eating strides, moving across the rolling fields of green like a ship under full sail on a smooth sea.

"I can almost understand Cathcart's fanatical desire for that stallion," Kade told Jake as the Scotsman began to light his pipe.

"Aye, 'tis a fine specimen of 'orse considerin' it should not exist. If that be a sample of the type of magic the Irish wield, 'tis glad I am that the lass insisted Michael alert those fairy folk about the slop water. I would 'ate to be seein' a storm they called down."

The fishing sloop that had put out from the outer islands landed on the beach, and two men came ashore. Kade knew immediately who the older one was, knew from the stubborn tilt of his head, the proud set of his shoulders; even the determination in his walk was familiar. This had to be Jarrett O'Connor, the man Kade had once accused of abandoning his daughter to her fate in Morocco.

If he had still harbored such beliefs, they would have

408

disappeared the moment he saw the love and pride on the old man's face as Jarrett watched Kathleen ride along the top of a hill, her hair flying out behind her and tangling with the water stallion's mane.

Kade was surprised by how old Kathleen's father looked; his green eyes were faded like the leaves of flowers pressed between the pages of a forgotten book. Ghost eyes, Kade thought and felt a chill of death on the wind.

"Ye brought me Katie 'ome," Jarrett said, his gaze climbing up Kade until he reached the top. "Who be ye, sir?"

"Captain Kade Morgan of the vessel *Black Eagle* anchored offshore. You must be Kathleen's father."

"Right ye are, Jarrett O'Connor. And this be me son, Niall."

Surprised by that introduction, Kade turned to Niall. He looked nothing like Kathleen. He was just under six feet tall, with reddish brown hair that bushed out in the wind and eyes the color of his father's: a young, fresh green that took in Kade's size, recognizing his strength and power, noticing the pistol in Kade's belt and the dagger in the top of the right boot.

Though faced with an obvious disadvantage, Niall advanced on Kade with a steady step and threatening fists. "Are you the man that stole my sister and killed my mother?"

"Are you the brother she thinks was killed?"

"I am asking the questions here!" Niall yelled, taking another step closer and brandishing his clenched fists.

Kathleen rode slowly around the ruins of her home, taking in the crumpled limestone and burned interior of the house. There was rubble and filth everywhere, and she saw that a family of pigs had been living there.

Anguish clutched at her, making her stomach turn

409

over and her heart beat irregularly. "All the lye in the world would not make this place fit even for Mother's memory," she told Taran, and the stallion swiveled his ears back to listen to her. He blew out his breath, and the drooping petals of a flower beside the front stoop brushed against the smooth stone.

There was a dark stain there, a stain made by greed and obsession, a stain made by Mary O'Connor's blood. Kathleen tilted her head back and looked at the patchwork sky where gray clouds hurried across the pale blue that stretched to the horizon.

Taran took a step backwards, and Kathleen touched the corded muscles in his neck to calm him. "Kade says it was not my fault, yet when I close my eyes and see again Mother's blood being spilled and hear the voices of the pirates and smell the burning flesh of the horses, I know I caused it, Taran."

Across the overgrown yard was the heap of burned timber and wet ash that had once been the center of Kathleen's dreams. She had thought she would spend the rest of her life in there raising horses, training horses, loving horses. So much had happened since she last stood in that warm barn, pitching hay to the broodmares and currying Taran's salt-encrusted tail. And so much had changed.

Since there was no sign of her father near the ruined house, Kathleen turned Taran back to the beach. She needed the warm reassurance of Kade's presence to fill the emptiness in her heart. As she topped the rise, Taran slowed. Kathleen saw below her the beached *glaucog* and a familiar, bandy-legged figure.

"Father!" she cried, and Taran responded to her urgent request for speed, flying down the grassy slope, leaping effortlessly over the scattered boulders.

Kade scarcely noticed Niall's threatening stance. His

attention was on Kathleen as he admired the fluid grace of her supple body atop the magnificent stallion. He felt the immediate tightening of his loins that just the thought of her always caused. As she raced down to the beach, he looked at Niall.

"The man you seek vengeance against is dead. Turn and greet your sister, Niall O'Connor," Kade said, grasping Niall's shoulders and forcing him to turn around.

Taran came to an abrupt halt on the beach, his head thrown up and his hooves sending a spray of sand into the air. Kathleen threw herself off the stallion's back and was running before the sand had settled. She stopped dead as she recognized the young man beside Jarrett.

"Niall," she breathed, not believing it was true and remembering suddenly her dream that when she came home everything would be as it was before. The stain on the stoop proved that dream to be a lie. Kathleen tightened her fists and pushed aside the wave of pain that came with the bitter, bloody memory of the disaster she had brought down upon her family.

"Welcome 'ome, daughter," Jarrett said. When he did not open his arms to her, Kathleen felt the stiff reserve that had hampered her relationship with her family settle back onto her. She almost sank beneath its ponderous, unwanted weight.

Kade watched the awkwardness of Kathleen's homecoming and ached for her. She was such a passionate, giving woman. It hurt him to see her restrained this way by a father she loved so deeply. He recognized in both Jarrett and Niall's attitude their belief Kathleen was so strong that she did not need, nor would she welcome, their embrace.

How she must have hated me that first day on the Black Eagle when I forced her to stand in my arms while she cried, he thought, realizing now how

411

restrained her relationship with her family had been. Then he remembered her running into his arms after she killed Harry Timpson.

Strange, he thought, I was the one who was cold and uncaring, yet I taught this warm, trusting woman what love should be, what it can be when friendship and understanding form its base. At that moment Kade loved Kathleen so much his heart felt as though it were dying with the intensity of his feelings.

"I thought you were dead," Kathleen said to Niall.

"Almost was. The fishermen out on the islands came to the mainland when they saw the fire from the stable. They took me back with them and sewed me up."

"Mother?" Kathleen asked, the strength of her voice shadowed by the pain Kade saw in her eyes.

"Buried o'er yon 'ill, daughter."

Kathleen lifted her chin, and Kade saw the sparkle of unshed tears on her lashes. "Where did you come from in the boat, Father?" she asked. "Are you not living on the mainland?"

Niall answered her. "Father lives with me on the islands now, me and my wife Alice."

"Wife?"

"Aye," Jarrett said, "and me first grandchild be on the way already."

Kathleen felt as though she had been gone a hundred years. "What made you come to the mainland just now?"

"I was getting ready to go out fishing when I saw that ship dropping anchor. Father and I set out immediately, hoping it was news about you, Kathleen. We had no idea you might actually be here. We have not heard from the kidnappers since the ransom was paid two months past. Captain Morgan said the man responsible for attacking Emerald Hills is dead."

The mention of ransom caused Kathleen to cast a

look at Taran, who was cropping grass beside the beach. Then she turned to Kade. A quick thrill went over her as his lips curved slightly beneath her gaze.

"Captain Morgan is right, he killed the man himself."

"I'm be'olden to ye, Cap'n Morgan, for bringin' me daughter 'ome," Jarrett said.

"You will have to be more than just beholden, Father," Kathleen said as she moved to stand in front of Kade. He lifted a hand to her face, touching the soft lips that smiled beneath his light caress. He pushed her hair behind her shoulders, and she turned back to face her father and Niall, noting the surprise on their faces as she leaned into Kade's embrace. Kathleen saw how old her father looked. The brilliant green of his eyes was faded, and his weathered face was lined with deep wrinkles.

"You owe him fifty pounds," she told her father and felt Kade's chest rumble with laughter. "He bought me at a slave auction in Morocco."

"Slave?" Niall said, looking as though he were about to pound Kade into fish bait as he clenched his fists anew and took a threatening step forward.

"An extremely misbehaved slave who caused me a great deal of trouble," Kade said menacingly. Kathleen cast him a sideways glance, and he winked at her.

"I'll no be 'avin' ye talk about me Katie that way," Jarrett said, bristling like a rooster.

"He only said that to irritate me, Father, but it did not work. I want to see Mother's grave. Come with us, Kade."

"You go, Kate. I have to send some orders back to the *Eagle.*"

Kathleen walked briskly up the slope beside her father. Taran trotted behind them, dropping his head over Kathleen's shoulder like a great dog, not a

413

legendary stallion. She stroked his nose and he blew against her ear.

"Be yer story about slavery true, lass?" Jarrett asked.

"Very true." She wished she had put her boots back on; the grass was cold against her ankles, and mud oozed between her toes.

"I paid the ransom, why would they sell ye?"

"I was sold before you agreed to the terms set for my release. The man holding me became angry and sold me out of spite."

"I've not much money, but what I 'ave I'll give Cap'n Morgan to release ye."

"There is no need for that, Father. Kade would not take your money."

They were beside the grave now, its wooden cross dewed with rain that glistened in the slanting sunlight as the day drew to a close. Jarrett put his hand on Kathleen's arm. "Ye call the cap'n by 'is Christian name?"

She looked into the faded green eyes. "I love him, Father."

"Did 'e force ye to bed 'im?" Jarrett asked, anger straining his voice as he gripped her arm tightly, his fingers bruising her flesh.

Kathleen lifted her chin defiantly. "I was his slave, Father, he had the right. That has changed, though; Kade loves me as I love him."

Jarrett scowled at her. "Ye think it be love, do ye? 'Tis not love ye find in the tangled remains of a violated bed, Kathleen. Love can only be found in friendship and in respect. Love is a noble, generous emotion, not one reekin' of rape and slavery."

"It was not rape, Father, not even the first time when I had been on his ship less than a day," she said quietly. "You have to understand that if not for him I would have gone to a brothel, a horrible place the like of which you cannot imagine. I would not have lived a week there."

"Then 'tis gratitude ye feel, lass, not love."

"Aye, it is gratitude. It is also friendship and respect, caring and understanding. He has saved my life more than once at the risk of his own. He has fought for me, he has killed for me. I have given him my love, I owe him my life."

Jarrett stomped off, his boots dragging through the clumped grass. Kathleen knelt to touch the base of the cross where it rose from the mounded dirt of the grave. "Mother, hear my prayer and feel my tears as they moisten the earth above you. I am sorry for the pain I have caused, sorry for the horror and heartache. Please forgive me and know that what I told Father was the truth. Kade made me more than a slave, he made me a woman and I love him."

Kade came upon Kathleen and Jarrett while they were talking. When he heard Kathleen confess her love for him, he smiled. No matter how often he heard her say it, it would never be enough. When Jarrett stalked off, he went after him.

"I want to talk to you about Kathleen," he said as he stopped the Irishman.

"Do ye truly love me Katie?"

"Aye, I love her, Mr. O'Connor, but it is not the daughter that you lost that I love, it is the woman she became during her ordeal. Most women, and most men, would have crumbled beneath the horror of what Kathleen endured. Yet, even when things were at their worst and she was about to be auctioned to the highest bidder as a slave, she defied anyone to defeat her. She faced her fate with more courage than you can imagine, courage that made me love her in spite of myself."

*　　　*　　　*

Kathleen touched her fingertip to a drop of water about to fall from the cross. Pain and grief clutched at her heart, and she ran away from her mother's grave, away from the memories. She ran to the top of the highest hill overlooking what had once been her home. Her sorrow then broke free, and tears ran unchecked down her face.

Kade saw her run from the grave. When sobs began to shake her slight form, he started after her. Jarrett stopped him.

"Let her be, lad. She'll not take to anyone when she's like that. Never would."

"She will for me."

Jarrett shook his head. "Even if it be love she feels for ye and even though she lets ye call her Kate as ye done on the beach, she'll not 'old with ye seein' 'er cry. Kathleen never cried much. When she did it was always alone."

"Maybe that was because you allowed her to, Mr. O'Connor. It does not mean she prefers it." Kade went quickly up the hill after Kathleen, stopping a short distance from her.

"Katie," he said softly.

Through the veil of her tears, Kathleen saw the familiar, strong arms waiting for her. She ran into Kade's embrace and buried her head on his chest.

"It hurts so much," she said as she wrapped her arms around him. "Mother was so happy and free, so light and winsome, like a sparkle on clear water. Now she is dead and I killed her."

Kade tightened his hold on her and laid his head on top of hers. "Nay, love, not you. Greed killed your mother."

The next morning Kathleen left the *Black Eagle* and

416

rowed to shore, where she and Taran went for a long ride over the mist-shrouded bogs. She had once missed her solitary rides; now she did not like being alone. She wanted to be with Kade. After her ride, she visited her mother's grave.

"I thought I would be findin' ye 'ere, daughter," Jarrett said as he came up from the beach. "Alice, that be Niall's wife, wants ye to come o'er to the island to meet ye. She be too big wi' child to make it o'er 'ere."

"I would like that, Father. I want to meet the woman that finally captured poor Niall."

"If ye 'ad come 'ome last night where ye belonged, ye would've."

Kathleen sat on the ground and pulled her knees up, wrapping her arms around them. "I *was* where I belonged, and that is with Kade. That house you live in is not my home, nor do I think it is yours."

"Ye be right, lass. Still, 'tis the only place I 'ave left, just as Cap'n Morgan was the only way ye 'ad out of the 'ell ye were in. I won't be approvin' of what ye done, Kathleen. Neither will I condemn ye for it. If ye truly love that man, then 'old onto 'im, for I believe 'tis love 'e feels for ye."

"I know it is, Father." Taran charged down the slope above them, nickered a greeting to Kathleen and raced away. "It is hard to believe all this happened because of him," she said, watching the stallion send up a shower of sand behind his pounding hooves as he ran into the waves.

"What do ye mean?"

Kathleen looked surprised, then remembered that although her father had agreed to the impossible task of trading Taran for her, he did not know the story behind the kidnapping.

"Let me tell you everything that has happened," she said and launched into a description of the pirate

417

attack after Niall was wounded. She described the attempt to trap Taran by driving him into the sea and told her father about her own capture. she only briefly mentioned her time on the pirate ship and with Rat Anders, not wanting her father to know all the horrors she had experienced. She did tell him about the slave auction, about her attempted escape from the *Black Eagle* and how she broke her ribs and almost died.

When she told him about Mistral, she closed her eyes and saw again that tropical paradise. She tried to paint it with words so her father could see it as she had, so he could smell the flowers and feel the trade winds, so he could taste the pineapple tarts that Mattie McBradden baked and experience the awesome power of the hurricane that had caused such destruction to the island.

Just as she started to tell him about stealing the sloop and trying another escape, Kade joined them. He sat beside her, leaning back against a boulder. He played with the ends of her hair while he told Jarrett about rescuing Kathleen from an imaginary sea monster, which brought tears of laughter to the old man's eyes and a burning blush of embarrassment to Kathleen's face. Then Kade explained how he had been tricked into leaving the house the day Kathleen left Mistral with Quint Cathcart.

"Do you remember the man who bought Black Merrow and two other hunters from us last February, Father?" Kathleen asked when she saw Jarrett's questioning look at the mention of Cathcart.

"Aye, that I do. He wanted Taran, too, wouldn't take no for an answer."

"How right you are," Kathleen said. "It was he who hired the pirates to attack Emerald Hills. I saw only Rat Anders during my captivity, so when Cathcart came to Mistral I thought him a friend and left with him, having no idea he had caused the whole terrible thing to begin with."

"Cathcart? What for?"

"For Taran, of course. I did not know until I was already on the *Christabel* and three weeks out of Mistral. He said he had received a letter from you agreeing to the exchange of Taran for me. That was when he discovered Rat had sold me to Kade and he came to Mistral after me."

"Me letter," Jarrett said softly. There had been no letter from him to Cathcart, nor had the ransom request mentioned Taran. It was money the letter had demanded, lots of money, every shilling he had received for selling Emerald Hills.

"Yes, your letter agreeing to the exchange," Kathleen said. "Why did it take so long for you to answer, Father?"

"It took some time for it to come to me, which reminds me, Katie. Here be yer necklace what come back." Jarrett reached into his pocket and pulled out the gold locket. Kathleen took it reverently. She opened the engraved heart and showed Kade the miniature portrait of her father and mother.

"She was beautiful," Kade said.

Jarrett glanced up and smiled. "Aye, that she was." Then the smile disappeared. "I got things to do 'ere, Kathleen. Maybe Cap'n Morgan will take ye out to the island. Alice be waitin' for ye."

Jarrett went to the ruins of the house and sifted through the debris behind the remaining wall until he found an iron poker. Gripping it in his fist, he set off across the fields, the fields that had once made up the bulk of Emerald Hills but were now a small piece of Pennington Estates.

Chapter 31

Kathleen and Kade rowed out to the islands that hovered on the horizon. They were rugged islands, battered constantly by the sea as it flung itself against their rocky cliffs in a crescendo of anger and foam. Kathleen spotted Niall mending his fishing nets. He waved to them and waded out beyond the fury of the surf to guide their boat around the boulders hidden beneath the surface. He helped Kathleen out, and then he and Kade secured the longboat above the reach of the surf.

"You go out of here often?" Kade asked, indicating the fierce waves pounding against the rocky beach.

"Every day," Niall said. "I have to make a living and the best fishing is in the deep water."

"What about Emerald Hills? I would think raising horses would be easier than negotiating that turmoil," Kade said. Kathleen slipped on the wet rocks, and he caught her before she fell.

"Niall does not like horses, nor do they like him," she said, clinging to Kade's arm so she would not fall. Niall pointed out the path leading to his home, and Kade steered Kathleen up it ahead of him.

"I always wanted to be a fisherman," Niall said from behind them. "After I recovered from the wounds I received in the pirate attack, I married Alice O'Shea, bought an old *glaucog* and a few nets. No horse will ever pin me against a stable wall again."

"What about Father? He is a horseman, not a fisherman."

Niall laughed. "You should see him trying to cast a net. He looks like he is throwing hay to a corral of yearlings." The laughter disappeared, and a pained expression clouded his face. "Father would be happier back on the mainland, but there is no life for him there anymore."

The house appeared from behind a pile of rocks, a two-story cottage that looked ready to fall off the face of the island into the teeming sea below. Kathleen knew without entering what she would find inside, for the house on Emerald Hills had been similar to this. There would be a tiny kitchen and pantry on the back of the first floor, the main room taking up most of the space with its big fireplace where most of the cooking and socializing was done.

On the second story would be two bedrooms, one slightly larger than the other. Since the island had little space for animals, there would be a small shed somewhere nearby where one cow and a few pigs were kept. Behind the shed, the family chickens would be scratching through the sparse layer of soil, searching for whatever worms and bugs they could find. There would also be a cat to keep the mice under control.

Niall threw open the front door and stamped his feet before entering. A pretty blond-haired girl, as pregnant as could possibly be imagined, greeted him with a kiss on the cheek.

"Ye must be Kathleen, me husband's long-lost sister," Alice O'Connor cried, her voice full of bubbling laughter that reflected in her blue eyes and crinkled her upturned nose.

"God bless all in this house," Kathleen said as she

entered the cozy room, giving the traditional Irish greeting. "And you must be Alice," she added before finding herself enclosed in a smothering hug.

"Who might this giant be?" Alice asked as Kade ducked his head to enter the house. When he raised it back up, his head bumped the ceiling, forcing him to remain in a stoop.

"Captain Kade Morgan," Kathleen introduced him. "My rescuer from kidnappers, sea monsters and other various terrors. Is that soda bread I smell?" She sniffed appreciatively, and Alice laughed again.

"That it be, and almost done, too. Come in, Cap'n Morgan, we 'aven't never 'ad a sea cap'n in the 'ouse afore, we be 'onored. Niall," Alice cried suddenly, "get yerself out of this 'ouse and take those boots off! They be smellin' like fish!"

She shook a towel at her husband and shooed him back out the door, then took Kade's arm and pulled him into the center of the room. He hit his head again, bringing another gale of laughter from her.

"Be careful," she cried, "I'll not be wantin' any 'oles in me ceiling nor in yer 'ead."

"Captain," Niall called from the open door. "I have some warming-up whiskey out back, come have a sip."

"My name is Kade, not Captain. And now that you mention it, I do feel a bit chilled." He hunched over as he left the house, yet still managed to bang his head a third time. Kathleen winced, and Alice gave a gale of laughter.

"'Tis a fine man ye 'ave caught, sister-in-law," she said as she sank into the rocking chair and fanned her face. "A right 'andsome example of masculinity. A big one, too," she added.

"You have caught a fine one, also," Kathleen said, "one I thought was dead. I cannot believe Niall lived with that horrible wound he got during the pirate attack."

Alice stopping laughing for the first time since Kathleen had entered the house. "Aye, 'orrible it was. When me pa fetched 'im out to the island, I thought 'e was a goner for sure. 'Twas weeks before we were sure 'e would live. When I knew 'e weren't gonna die, I decided 'e was the man for me and started courtin' 'im even afore 'e could get out of bed. It weren't long before me and Niall were married, and I been luggin' this around e'er since." She patted her bulging stomach, and Kathleen saw the baby kick, a slight push outward against the wool of Alice's dress.

"When are you due?"

"Two more months, though I be as big as a 'orse now. Niall said if me stomach gets any larger 'e will 'ave to build a stable to keep me in, the bedroom be gettin' too small." Alice peered at Kathleen from beneath the profusion of blond wisps that had escaped her braid. "And when be ye due, sister-in-law?"

"When am I due for what?"

Alice laughed, a merry sound that Kathleen was quickly growing to like. "No need to play coy wi' me, sister-in-law. Ye may not be married to that big stud of yers, but the way those black eyes of 'is linger on ye tells me ye share more than just looks, and that glow on yer face tells me that ye be bearin' that man's child."

Kathleen's hand flew to her stomach as she realized the truth of what Alice was saying. She had not had a monthly cycle since trying to escape on the *Slipper*. And there were her constant stomach problems on the *Christabel* and that strange light she had seen in her own eyes, as though her body knew something she did not know.

"I must be about two months along," she said, her

423

voice so low the fire in the pit almost drowned her words. She could feel a smile starting at the tips of her toes and spreading upwards until it reached the top of her head. Her entire body was singing as the word "baby" kept repeating over and over in her head. Not once in her entire life had she thought about having children; now the idea consumed her, and she longed to shout her news to the world.

Alice turned her attention to the covered kettle sitting in the fireplace. "The bread smells done, could ye do the 'onors and swing the kettle around?"

Kathleen picked up a towel and lifted the baking kettle away from the fire. Using a poker, she speared the blocks of burning peat on the lid and dropped them on the hearth. When she removed the kettle lid, the aroma of the soda bread rushed out in a wave of delicious promise that made her eyes water. She wrapped the bread in the towel and was just lifting it out of the baking kettle when Niall and Kade came in the door. Kathleen stopped dead. She gave Kade a smile so bright that he forgot to watch his head and banged the ceiling a good blow.

"We'll be needin' to build a new 'ouse if ye keep doin' that, Cap'n. Sit down before ye knock yerself sense-less," Alice said as she waved Kade into Kathleen's abandoned chair. "I'll be gettin' us something to drink. Come, 'usband," she ordered Niall.

Kathleen set the hot bread on the table behind the open door, then turned back to Kade. His long legs were stretched into the middle of the room, his body filling the small chair to overflowing. He smiled at her. She dropped the towel she was holding and almost fell over a stool.

"You seem nervous," he said and pulled her down on his lap. She sat stiffly, not knowing how to tell him about the baby. He pushed a strand of hair back from

424

her face and she moistened her suddenly dry lips.

"I have something to tell you," she said. Before she could continue, Alice and Niall came back into the room. Kathleen jumped up, blushing furiously at having been caught sitting on his lap.

"We ain't got enough chairs for the lot of us, so sit back down," Alice said as she poured cold milk for her and Kathleen. Kade and Niall had dark, bitter stout.

Alice settled herself in the rocking chair, and Niall pulled a chair away from the table, dragging it over beside his wife. Kathleen sat on the floor at Kade's feet, very aware of his hand on her shoulder. She glanced up at him, and he touched her upper lip.

"Milk moustache," he said, and she licked it away beneath the warm caress of his eyes.

"Tell us what happened to you since the attack," Niall said, and Kathleen launched into the story, aided now and then by Kade and interrupted occasionally by questions from Alice. A large gray cat wandered into the room and curled itself into Kathleen's lap, kneading her legs with its paws. She scratched its head, and its purr rumbled forth just as Kathleen was coming to the end of her story.

"Quint Cathcart told me he had a letter agreeing to exchange Taran for me, then said that Ivan Flesher had demanded I was to be his payment for the trip to Ireland. I knocked the lamp onto Flesher, grabbed Quint's knife and cut his arm. Two sailors burst into the room and they locked me in the hold, where Kade found me."

Niall set his empty glass on the table. "I saw the letter Father got about the ransom, Kathleen, and it said nothing about Taran, just money."

"Quint said . . ."

"Doesn't matter what he said, we received the letter five months after the attack. It had your locket in it and a demand for money. Since all the horses were gone, either burned in the fire or killed by the pirates, all we had left was the deed to the land. Father sold it to Lord Pennington."

"Pennington, is that the old lecher you said wanted to marry you?" Kade asked Kathleen.

"The very same. Why would he want to help Father? He has been trying to buy Emerald Hills for years and Father turned him down each time, just like I turned down his proposals. And what about that letter Quint received? He said he was taking me to Dublin, as it requested, and the exchange for Taran would be made there."

Kade's hand was in Kathleen's hair, winding through the silken threads. Suddenly it tightened, his fist clenching as a thought occurred to him.

"How did you receive the ransom note?" he asked Niall.

"It was posted to us here."

Kade released his hold on Kathleen. "How would Cathcart know you were here? He would have sent it to Emerald Hills. And you said it arrived five months after Kathleen was captured, yet she said her locket was taken from her immediately after she was transferred off the pirate ship, about a month after her capture. And five months after the attack Quint was headed for Mistral. He could not have sent the demand, and besides, he did not want money, he wanted Taran."

"Lord Silas Pennington," Kathleen said, the titled name sounding like an obscenity the way she said it. "Niall, if you and Father were out here when the original posting from Cathcart arrived, his is the closest house to ours. It might have gone there."

"Pennington was in England until three months after the attack."

"He must have come home, discovered the ransom

426

demand had been delivered to him by mistake and realized he had Father right where he wanted him." Kathleen felt as though a knife had been driven under her ribs. Would the pain she had caused by calling forth the *each uisce* ever end?

"Then why did he wait two more months to send the false ransom letter demanding money?" Niall asked.

Kade answered him. "To make certain all hope was lost for Kathleen's return. By the time your father received Pennington's false demand for money, he would be so excited to discover Kathleen was still alive that he would not hesitate to sign over his own soul to the devil to get her back."

"That be the way it was," Alice said. "He sold the next day. Lord Pennington paid 'im just barely enough money to meet the ransom."

"What happened to the money?" Kathleen asked as she moved the cat off her lap. It immediately began to smooth its ruffled fur with its pointed pink tongue, its tail whipping from side to side.

Niall clenched his fists. "Pennington told Father he would handle sending it to the kidnappers via his London solicitors. Not only did he get the land, he kept the money!"

"Why did he send Cathcart a letter saying he agreed to the exchange?" Kade asked. "He had what he wanted, Emerald Hills. He even had the ransom money."

Kathleen turned to face him, her face tense and pale and a lump in her throat so big she could hardly speak. "We talked to Father this morning, Kade, telling him about Cathcart receiving the letter agreeing to exchange Taran for me. Right after that he said he had something to do and he headed off across the fields, walking inland."

"He went after Pennington," Niall said and was

halfway out the door before he finished talking Kathleen was hard on his heels with Kade right behind her.

"Be careful," Alice called after them as they made their way down the winding path to the beach, "and God be wi' ye."

Jarrett O'Connor did not ring the bell at the entrance to Pennington Mansion. He threw open the massive carved doors and walked in his wet boots across the spotless marble floors, looking into every room he passed until he reached the study. There he found Lord Silas Pennington, his gray head bent over an open account ledger.

"Ye thought ye were clever, didn't ye? Buyin' me land and takin' me money," he said as he entered the room so angry he could scarcely draw a breath.

Silas closed his ledger and dropped his hands onto his lap beneath his desk. He took in the agitated appearance of his visitor, the flushed face and glinting eyes, the labored breathing and firm grip on the iron poker.

"I did not hear my butler announce you, Mr O'Connor," he said. "Whatever you want will have to wait until I return from Dublin. I have an appointment there day after tomorrow and must finish these accounts before I leave."

"There be no need to be announced, and I won't be waitin'. I came to get back that which ye stole from me, and I be wantin' it now!"

Jarrett rapidly closed the distance between himself and Pennington, his heavy boots clomping on the wooden floor. He drew a rasping breath and fought the pain that seized at his chest. It had taken him such a long time to cross the hills he had once owned, longer than ever before with his asthma forcing him to stop frequently to wait for his breathing to slow and the clutching pain in his chest to subside. I be gettin' old, he thought, and his fist closed tighter around the poker.

"Stole? As I remember, it was you that came to me offering to sell Emerald Hills."

"After ye sent me a false ransom demand for Kathleen. The letter from the real kidnapper didn't ask for money, 'e wanted that great stallion of 'ers, Taran." Pennington shifted in his chair, leaning slightly to the right. Jarrett lifted his poker a little in response.

"This tale of yours is quite fascinating, tell me more," Silas said. "Let me summon the butler to bring us something to drink."

"I'll not be needin' a drink, nor will ye. I came 'ere to get back the deed to me land."

"Even if I were so inclined to give it to you, Mr. O'Connor, it is not here. I have forwarded it to my lawyers in London for safekeeping." Silas smiled a little, thinking of how easily the Irish believed English lies.

"Then ye knew I'd be comin' for it."

"There was a chance that once Kathleen was returned to Ireland, she might reveal what the original demand had been." Pennington shifted in his chair again, moving even farther to the right.

"Ye were right, for me daughter is back and she does know what that thievin' scum, Quint Cathcart, wanted. Cathcart be dead now, killed by the man that brought Kathleen 'ome. And before 'e died 'e said 'e received a letter agreein' to exchange the stallion for 'er."

Silas lifted his right hand to finger the scar on his neck. "Is there a point you are trying to make?"

"Aye, there be a sharp point," Jarrett said as he waved the poker at Pennington, his anger almost blinding him. "Ye somehow got the ransom demand from Cathcart and sent 'im word agreein' to what 'e was wantin'. Ye wanted Kathleen returned to ye, though what ye were gonna give Cathcart I've no idea. What did ye 'ave planned for 'er, Pennington? Tell me!"

Silas dropped his hand to the top of his desk, his fingers resting lightly on the edge of the carved oak. "I planned to marry her."

"Usin' what force?"

"Perhaps none. I planned on making her delivery from the kidnappers look like an elaborate rescue, me risking my life to save hers. I would capture whoever was with her, force them to reveal the perpetrator of this sordid affair, then have the thief sought out and killed. Unfortunately, the money paid for her ransom would not be recovered." Silas let his fingers slip off the desk, lowering them so they were out of Jarrett's sight. He laid them on the handle of the top drawer of his desk.

"If your daughter failed to offer her hand in marriage as a reward for my brave rescue, I planned to allow you to continue raising horses on Emerald Hills, even going as far as to finance the rebuilding of the stables and the purchase of new mares. And if that were still not enough incentive to convince her to become my wife, I would threaten to have you and your son killed."

Jarrett's heart was pounding so fast he could no longer stand. He sank into one of the stiff chairs positioned in front of Pennington's desk. He rested the poker across his lap and rubbed his left shoulder. Pain was shooting down his arm, all the way to his hand. Because of one man's greedy desire to own Taran, so much death and destruction had occurred, so much treachery and deceit. Jarrett stopped rubbing his shoulder and picked up the poker again.

"Ye may 'ave me land, but ye'll never get me daughter," Jarrett said. He forced himself to stand, fighting the weakness of his legs and the choking pain in his chest.

"I still have a chance." Silas closed his hand around the small, pearl-handled pistol in the drawer and lifted it out. He pointed the pistol across the desk at Jarrett. "Though I did not build a traditional dungeon beneath this house, there are some rooms near the cellar that should do nicely for what I have in mind. You will be locked in one and held until your daughter agrees to become Lady Pennington."

Kathleen was the first one out of the longboat when it reached shore. She gave a sharp, clear whistle, and Taran came charging across the bog, his mane flying and his tail lifted into the wind.

Kade grabbed her arm before she could throw herself onto the stallion's back. "I will not allow you to go after him alone."

"Then you ride with me." She wrapped her hand in Taran's mane, pulling herself onto the stallion. "Coming or not?"

Taran's eyes, so strange and eerie in their abnormal color, were on Kade, and the stallion's lip curled back to expose his teeth. "Will he let me ride?"

"If I tell him. We do not have time to argue, Kade," she said impatiently, and Taran stomped his huge feet as he caught her mood.

"Who is arguing?" Kade vaulted onto Taran's back, causing the stallion to immediately scream a protest.

"Whoa, whoa," Kathleen said as she calmed the horse. She leaned close to his ears and whispered something. Kade felt a tingling sensation on his skin, was aware of the sudden hush of the surf, the low whisper of the wind as Kathleen wove a magic spell over the stallion like the one she had cast on Mistral

431

when she charmed Demon into accepting her on his back the first time.

Taran tossed his head a final time, bending his neck back to fix his eye on Kade for a moment as though in warning. Then he gave a snorting nicker and pawed the sand.

"How about you, Niall?" Kathleen asked as she ran her hand over Taran's neck. "He can hold all three of us."

"You know I do not like horses, then ask if I want to ride that creature? Nay, sister, I would rather crawl to Pennington's."

"Crawl fast," Kathleen said as she signaled Taran into action. The stallion gathered himself, and his powerful hind legs dug into the sand as he threw himself forward, the instant speed almost causing Kade to lose his seat.

"Hang on!" Kathleen cried and urged the stallion faster. Kade wrapped his arms around her waist, his hands holding fast to Taran's mane. Though terrified for her father's life, she wanted the ride to go on and on. The thrusting strength of Taran's ground-eating strides, the hard strength of Kade's arms, the wind in her face and Ireland's gentle beauty surrounding her; Kathleen loved them all and she wished the moment would never end.

They came to the stone fence that marked the boundary of Emerald Hills. Taran jumped the obstacle effortlessly, his stride never breaking rhythm. He seemed not to even be aware of his riders as he ran across the spongy fields.

Kade leaned his head down to Kathleen's ear. "I love you," he said, and she turned her head to offer him her lips. The kiss reassured her and made her remember the precious life sheltered within her body. She snuggled back into Kade's embrace, warmed by his presence and his love.

Pennington Mansion came into view as Taran topped a hill. There were several sprawling buildings to the east of the house, servant quarters, barns and storage sheds. The house itself was massive, an ugly mass of granite and limestone that squatted like an unwelcome guest in the midst of the muted colors of the countryside.

Taran skidded to a stop at the foot of the steps rising to the entry, and Kathleen dismounted instantly. Kade stopped her before she entered the house. Her face was lined with anxiety, her blue-green eyes wide with fear.

"We cannot go charging in there without a plan," he said and thought of all the times he had done exactly that in his life, charging headfirst into a situation with nothing except his wits and sword to protect him. Now everything had changed. He had something to live for now.

"Pennington will kill Father, Kade, I know he will!"

Kade pulled her against him. "Listen to me, Kate," he said, tilting her head back so he could see her face. "You are to stay behind me no matter what happens." The swirling colors of her eyes slowed a little, and he laughed.

"I have seen that look before. If you do not do as I say, if for one moment you move out from behind my back without my express permission, I will collect that pound of flesh you owe me."

Kathleen could not stop the smile that forced its way onto her face. "You are the most exasperating person I have ever met."

"Only because I am the only one who ever looked past that angelic face and saw the devil hidden inside those eyes," Kade said. He released her, and she obediently walked behind him as he entered the arched doorway to Pennington Mansion.

The marble floor was marred with a trail of wet, muddy footprints that Kade followed, moving so his boots made a minimum of noise. Behind him he heard only silence. He glanced over his shoulder to check on Kathleen. She had slipped her own boots off and was walking barefoot across the cold marble.

His large frame cast larger shadows on the paneled walls of the hall, Kathleen's shadow a small echo of his. Voices could be heard coming through the closed door at the end of the trail of footsteps. Kade halted outside and motioned Kathleen to stay where she was while he looked for a weapon. The room they had just passed was a library, and Kade went into it. Several dueling pistols were on display in a glass case that was locked. On the wall above the case was a set of crossed sabers and matching daggers. He weighed the advantages of a sword, decided it would be clumsy in tight quarters, and took down the two daggers.

He slipped one into the top of his boot and held the other concealed in his hand with the blade turned up and pushed against the sleeve of his shirt. When he came out of the library, Kathleen was standing with her ear pressed to the door, listening to the conversation inside. Although the voices were muffled, Kathleen could hear Jarrett O'Connor's Irish brogue. There was a sharp edge to his voice, as though he was in pain.

Kathleen put a trembling hand on Kade's chest. "I heard everything," she whispered. "We were right, Pennington sent the false ransom demand hoping to force Father to sell Emerald Hills. He sent Cathcart a letter agreeing to exchange Taran for me; he planned to force me to marry him to regain Emerald Hills for Father. He said he was going to hold Father prisoner until I agreed."

Kade's fingers tightened on the dagger. His jaw was set firmly, and a muscle twitched over his temple.

Kathleen lifted her hand to his face. "I love you," she whispered. He put his arm around her for a moment, holding her close. Then he moved her behind him.

Kade checked the door. It was locked. He took a step back, judged the size and weight of the door, then slammed his foot against it, tearing it off the hinges. It exploded inward, splinters of wood flying across the room as the door crashed against a table. The sharp sound of glass breaking and the dull sound of books falling were heard.

Kade stepped through the opening, his shoulders as wide as the door had been, his head almost touching the top of the empty frame. To his left an extremely old man was standing behind a desk, a pistol clutched in his extended hand. The lamp on the desk flickered its yellow light onto the pearl handle, spreading up to the scarred, gaunt face of Lord Silas Pennington. Jarrett O'Connor was also standing, his right arm swinging upwards with the poker as he rushed at Pennington.

All action in the room stopped when Kade kicked the door in. He took in the scene quickly, noting with a wave of revulsion the man who wanted to force Kathleen to be his wife. Pennington's skin was marked with brown liver spots, his body almost a skeleton with decaying flesh stretched tight over the pointed bones. His lips were purple, his straggling gray hair like strands of white slime that crept over his forehead and fell below his starched collar. There was evil in the sunken eyes, evil and anger. Kade seared Pennington with his stare as he advanced a few steps into the silent room.

"Drop the gun," he said, his voice rich and resonant, like a low note on a viola. It was the voice of a man in command, a man to be obeyed without question, without pause.

The moment that Pennington obeyed Kade, Jarrett

O'Connor brought the hooked point of his poker down on the old man's head. At first there was no blood, only a bewildered exclamation of surprise from Pennington as he pitched forward, his face smashing against the desk. Then the blood came, rushing in a crimson flood over the torn flesh, through the sparse hair, across the ledger book. Pennington's body fell to the floor, the hand holding the pistol clinging to the edge of the desk for a moment, then falling.

Sickened by her father's violent act, Kathleen covered her mouth with her hand and clutched at Kade for support. Her father was a man of principles, a man of strength and wisdom. And he had struck down another man in cold blood.

"I 'ad to do it, Katie," Jarrett said, "I lost Niall to the sea. All I 'ad left was ye, and 'e wanted that."

Kathleen almost staggered as she moved around in front of Kade. Even after she killed Harry Timpson she had not felt so uncontrollably ill. That had been in self-defense; even her attack on Ivan Flesher had been to save herself. This was different. This was murder. The reassuring touch of Kade's hand on her shoulder kept her from breaking down completely.

"I survived captivity under the pirates, I withstood the cruelty of Rat Anders, I overcame Kade's attempt to crush my pride. Why did you think I would be so weak as to give in to Silas Pennington?"

"Ye be me daughter, me baby. I 'ad to protect ye."

Kathleen lifted her chin and fought the rush of tears his words caused. "You never treated me like a baby, never. The first thing I remember is you teaching me to take care of myself, to be strong."

Jarrett's shoulders suddenly slumped. "Ye never needed me to teach ye that, ye were already strong. Ye were always so sure of yerself, grabbin' hold of life and not lettin' go, not needin' anyone to 'elp ye wi' anything."

Kathleen felt as though a fist had slammed into her stomach, knocking the breath out of her. He had thought she did not need him, yet every day of her life she had relied on his strength, his wisdom. She had believed in herself only because he had taught her she could believe in him and because he loved her.

"I love you, Papa!" she cried. "And I need you, I have always needed you. It was you that gave me the strength to grab life, to hold on without compromise. It was you . . ."

Her voice was so choked by sobs she could not continue; then her scream rent the air as Jarrett's face turned white as death. He dropped the poker and clutched spasmodically at his chest. His knees gave way beneath him, and his body fell slowly, crumbling into a heap on the polished surface of the wooden floor, the light from the desk casting a golden ring around his fallen head.

Kathleen ran to him, hearing as she did Niall's voice as he entered the room and saw Jarrett on the floor. Kathleen tried to lift her father. Kade was there beside her, helping her. His arms went around her as he told Niall what to do.

Niall took Kade's dagger, cutting away Jarrett's jacket and shirt to allow easier breathing. It was too late. There was no rise and fall of the chest, no rasping breath passing through the white lips. There was no heartbeat, no pulse. There was no life.

"His heart gave out," Kade said as he cradled Kathleen in his arms. Niall sat back on his heels, and his hand touched the side of Jarrett's face.

"He began having spells after he learned that Mother had died. I knew it was a matter of time."

"I killed him," Kathleen whispered as she stared at her father's face, "like I killed Mother." She began to wail hysterically, her mind caving in beneath the pressure of her guilt.

Niall leaned across Jarrett and grabbed Kathleen's shoulders. "Stop that! It was not your fault!" He slapped her, and she stared glassy-eyed at him; then her head fell forward and she was quiet.

"You can hit me until I am as dead as Father," she said softly, "but it will not change my guilt, it will not wipe away the debt I owe."

The house servants came running at the sound of Kathleen's screams. They gathered in the hall outside the open door, none daring to enter except the butler, his manner as stiff and formal as his clothes.

"The master is dead," he announced after checking Pennington. "I will summon the constable."

"Bring me some brandy," Kade ordered as he lifted Kathleen and carried her out of the room, taking her into the library and sitting her on the sofa there. He covered her with a blanket a maid brought, and when the brandy arrived, he forced her to drink a large draught.

She swallowed obediently, then lifted her eyes to his. The thick lashes were wet, her tears glistening like diamonds in the soft light. "Everything I love dies. I cannot love you, I do not love you."

The words fell like dark rain in the room. "Stay with her," Kade told Niall and left the room.

It was sometime later when he came back to the library, having explained everything to the constable summoned by the butler. A search had been made of Pennington's study, uncovering a hidden safe that contained Quint Cathcart's ransom demand, a copy of Pennington's letter to Cathcart agreeing to the exchange of the stallion for Kathleen, and a copy of his letter to Jarrett demanding a money ransom. It also held the deed to Emerald Hills that he had said was in London, along with the ransom money he had extorted from Jarrett.

Kade handed Niall the deed. "This is yours; the constable will arrange with the local magistrate to have the ownership of Emerald Hills transferred back to you. I have arranged for your father's body to be taken to the nearest church. He will be buried beside your mother day after tomorrow."

Kade sat beside Kathleen and cupped her face with his hands. She looked through him, aware of neither her surroundings nor Kade. "I have sent for Dr. Williams on the *Black Eagle*," he said. "It might be best if Kathleen stays here tonight. The butler has agreed and is preparing a room now."

Niall fingered the parchment of the deed he held. "Thank you for your help. I don't know what I would have done without you."

Kade clasped the younger man's shoulder and stood up, pulling Niall with him into the hallway. "Now I need your help. After the funeral I will . . ."

His voice faded as the two men moved away from the library, walking together down the passageway. Niall nodded occasionally as he listened to Kade. Their footsteps faded, then fell silent.

Kathleen wrapped her fingers around the edge of the blanket and squeezed her eyes tight. "I do not love him, I do not love him," she said over and over, as though the words could change the lie to truth. Unless she truly believed she did not love Kade, she would never be able to let him go.

Chapter 32

It rained the morning of the funeral, stopping before the casket was delivered to the grave. Kathleen stood beside her brother, listening to the words being read over their father and to the water dripping from the leaves of the hazelnut trees nearby.

The surf crashed onto the beach beyond the rise, and gulls cried as they soared overhead. Clods of dirt were tossed onto the top of the casket as it was lowered into the ground. Kathleen heard Kade talking to the minister, talking to Jake McBradden, talking to her brother Niall. Then she did not hear him anymore; he was gone just as her love for him was gone.

Niall pushed a wooden cross into the soft earth above the new grave, and Kathleen saw that her tears had made little dark blotches on the freshly turned soil. She moved away, walking up the hill behind her so she could feel the wind on her face. The ground was spongy with the morning rain, and it smelled of memories best forgotten, memories of laughter shared in front of a fire, memories of love shared in a house where now only pigs lived. The smell of the earth reminded Kathleen of everything she had ever loved, everything she had caused to be destroyed.

Below her the *Black Eagle* was anchored in the cove, the masthead dipping its carved beak almost to the surface of the water. The stern swung around, and Kathleen watched the tide go out, exposing a little more of the shoreline after each wave receded. Soon the barnacle-covered rocks could be seen, tide pools filled with crabs and eels were created and the beach was alive with birds searching the kelp-littered sand for food.

There was activity on the *Black Eagle,* men climbing the rigging and standing erect along the yardarms. More men were dragging the anchor up from the seabed, lifting it ever higher until it was level with the railing on the starboard bow. The pennant of Morgan Shipping, a black flag with the letters M and S emblazoned in silver and red, was hoisted aloft on the mizzenmast, and the men standing on the yardarms began to untie their leashlines, preparing to lower the sails and put the ship under way.

Kathleen heard footsteps behind her. She did not turn, knowing it was Niall. He stood beside her, watching the activity on the *Eagle.*

"You are not going with him?" he asked.

"My place is here, seeing that Father's dream is kept alive by rebuilding Emerald Hills." She fingered the folds in the skirt of her black dress and watched the mainsail drop, men clinging to the bottom to force it to run out smoothly.

"What about your dreams?"

"I have no right to dream."

The *Eagle*'s mainsail hung limp though a stiff breeze was causing the ship's pennant to snap and curl. A tear stretched from the top of the sail to the bottom. It will have to be replaced, Kathleen thought.

"And what about the baby you carry?" Niall asked.

"That is my concern, not yours."

The crew began to cut away the damaged canvas so they could raise a new sail.

441

"What will you do when the child asks about its father? Will you explain that you sacrificed a life of love and happiness to hold onto someone else's dream?"

Kathleen closed her mind and heart to the pounding truth of his words. "If I had not called forth the *each uisce . . .*"

"Then Cathcart would have found something else to covet," Niall said, "something else to give him a reason to destroy Emerald Hills. It was not so much that he wanted Taran as it was the fact that some Irish peasant dared say no to him."

"It is my fault!" Kathleen turned to run away. Niall caught her and held her.

"You have spent your entire life running away from the people who love you because you were afraid to love them, to need them. It is time to stop."

"No! It is not true!" She covered her ears with her hands, but Niall's voice came through anyway.

"Yes it is! The only person you have not been able to run from is Kade Morgan, and that is because he would not let you. He held onto you until you realized that he was more than just a man whose kisses you desired. He held onto you until you recognized him as a friend, until you opened your heart and let him inside. Now he needs you to overcome your little-girl fears and prove that you are the woman he has been waiting for his entire life, a woman who needs him, a woman that will let him need her."

Niall released Kathleen, and she dropped her hands. He was right. She was running from Kade, just as she had run from her own family because she was afraid if they knew she needed them they would think her weak.

The *Black Eagle*'s crew was still working on the mainsail. It would take time to finish replacing it. Enough time for Niall to take her out to the ship.

nough time for her to go to Kade and tell him that she
ad not stopped loving him, to tell him she carried their
hild.

She turned to Niall. "I love you, brother!" she cried.
And I need you, desperately and immediately!"

"To take you out to that ship about to get under
vay?"

"The very same."

She lifted her skirts and raced down the hill. Taran
vas grazing near the copse of hazelnut trees beside the
raves. He threw up his head, and his hooves ripped
hunks of sod from the ground as he charged after
Kathleen.

"Faster, you great beast!" she cried, and together
hey went up the final rise, then down onto the beach
vhere the feeding birds flocked skyward in alarm.
Kathleen put her arms around Taran's neck, feeling his
varm breath on her shoulder.

"Go home," she told him, "back to the Merrow folk,
ack to the legends from which you came. Go home,"
he whispered and ran her hand along the dappled gray
lanks that looked like morning light on a storm-tossed
ea. With a shake of his flowing mane, Taran ran across
he kelp-littered sands, across the pebbled bottom of
xposed seabed, into the teeming wake of a dying wave.
Ie lowered his head, and the next wave poured over
im. Then he was gone.

Niall ran to the beach, his face flushed, his hair bushy
nd wild. Kathleen helped him drag the *glaucog* into
he water; then she climbed in and lifted the sail while
e steered the rudder.

"Tell Alice I missed her at the funeral, and tell her
hat her baby will be a girl," Kathleen said.

Niall grinned. "How do you know that?"

"I saw it in her eyes. And I shall have a boy, a big one
hat looks like his father." The *Black Eagle* loomed

above them now, and Kathleen reached out to grab the rope ladder Jake McBradden dropped over the side.

"Kathleen," Niall said as he steadied the *glaucog*, "want you to know that although I will not be living on Emerald Hills, it will always be there if any of my children are horse-people like their grandfather and their aunt."

"I will come back and see those children, Niall O'Connor," Kathleen said. She threw her skirts over her arm and began climbing up the side of the *Eagle.*

"And maybe I will come to the West Indies and see yours!" Niall called after her as he steered his boat for home.

Kathleen swung herself over the top of the railing and glanced at the mainsail. The men had just finished tying the lines and were ready to drop the new canvas into the breeze.

"I am just in time," she told Jake.

"That ye be, lass. I 'ad the men raise 'er slow, for knew ye would be comin'."

"Then you knew more than I did, Jake. Where is Kade?"

"In 'is cabin."

Kathleen took a deep breath and headed down the steps to the captain's quarters. The door was partially open. She stepped inside. Kade was in the leather chair, his legs stretched into the center of the room, a cigar between the fingers of his left hand and a brandy snifter in his right. His eyes were closed, his hair falling onto his forehead. Kathleen shivered as she looked at him, remembering all the times she had lain in his arms while his hands moved over her bare flesh.

The light from the window fell across his rugged handsome face. The smoke from his cigar swirled around his head; the brandy glowed like warm chestnuts in the crystal snifter. Kathleen knelt before him, her eyes on his face.

Kade could smell the fresh scent of the wind and sea as she came to him. Through his lashes he saw the angle of hair that cascaded across her shoulders, falling in lush waves and curls to her waist. Her face was flushed, her eyes sparkling like a waterfall beneath a tropical sun. He wanted to sweep her into his arms, to show her in a thousand different ways how much he loved her, how much he wanted and needed her. He did not, though. He waited.

She took the cigar and brandy, setting them on the desk beside the chair. Then she ran her hands up over Kade's legs, across his chest and onto the wide expanse of his shoulders. His eyes opened, the light in them pouring over her like dark honey.

"Master," she whispered.

"'Tis I who was the slave," he said and watched the smile on her face shy away for a moment, then come back as her lips curved slowly upwards.

"I almost let you go."

"I would not have gone. I would have waited forever."

"But the sails were being lowered, the anchor lifted," he said.

"Niall told me that you might change your mind faster if you thought I was leaving you. Last night we ripped the sail to give you time to decide."

Kathleen pushed away from him and jumped to her feet. "It was a trick, the two of you planned the whole thing!"

"Aye, that we did. And we did a fine job of it, for here you are and here you shall stay."

He stood up, towering over her so that she felt very small. He gathered her to him, his hands moving up her back, into her hair, and along her face until his fingers touched her lips.

445

She took one of his hands and placed it on the curve of her stomach. "I carry your son inside me," she said and felt the tremble in his muscles. His eyes narrowed and his fingers pressed tighter against her. Beneath their feet, the *Black Eagle* sprang to life as the ship caught the wind in her sails.

"I love you," Kathleen said. Kade pulled her into his arms, holding her so close she thought she would die and still she wanted to be closer.

"My son," he breathed against her lips. "I love you Kathleen, I love you so much that it hurts."

She leaned back and gazed into his face. "Then take me home to Mistral and I will heal those wounds, as you have healed mine."

"Home," he said, his voice rough with emotion. "There is a grave in Scotland near a place I once called home, a grave that has been waiting seventeen years to be watered by tears I never shed."

Kathleen circled his neck with her arms. "We shall shed them together."

"As man and wife," he said and smiled, causing her breath to catch in her throat. His lips came down on hers and Kathleen's heart overflowed with the warm wonderful, magical thing this man had created within her. Love.

Now you can get more of HEARTFIRE right at home and $ave.

Preview
Four Brand New
ZEBRA
Heartfire
Romance Novels...

FREE for 10 days.

No Obligation and No Strings Attached!

❤

Enjoy all of the passion and fiery romance as you soar back through history, right in the comfort of your own home.

Now that you have read a Zebra HEARTFIRE Romance novel, we're sure you'll agree that HEARTFIRE sets new standards of excellence for historical romantic fiction. Each Zebra HEARTFIRE novel is the ultimate blend of intimate romance and grand adventure and each takes place in the kinds of historical settings you want most...the American Revolution, the Old West, Civil War and more.

__FREE__ Preview Each Month
and $ave

Zebra has made arrangements for you to preview 4 brand new HEARTFIRE novels each month...FREE for 10 days. You'll get them as soon as they are published. If you are not delighted with any of them, just return them with no questions asked. But if you decide these are everything we said they are, you'll pay just $3.25 each—a total of $13.00 (a $15.00 value). **That's a $2.00 saving each month off the regular price.** Plus there is NO shipping or handling charge. These are delivered right to your door absolutely free! There is no obligation and there is no minimum number of books to buy.

TO GET YOUR
FIRST MONTH'S PREVIEW...
Mail the Coupon Below!

Mail to:

HEARTFIRE Home Subscription Service, Inc.
120 Brighton Road
P.O. Box 5214
Clifton, NJ 07015-5214

YES! I want to subscribe to Zebra's HEARTFIRE Home Subscription Service. Please send me my first month's books to preview free for ten days. I understand that if I am not pleased I may return them and owe nothing, but if I keep them I will pay just $3.25 each; a total of $13.00. That is a savings of $2.00 each month off the cover price. There are no shipping, handling or other hidden charges and there is no minimum number of books I must buy. I can cancel this subscription at any time with no questions asked.

NAME _____

ADDRESS _____ APT. NO. _____

CITY _____ STATE _____ ZIP _____

SIGNATURE   (if under 18, parent or guardian must sign)   2220
Terms and prices are subject to change.